To:

Lorraine

I hope you
enjoy it.

Mike

KNIGHTLIGHT

PRELUDE TO THE DARK MESSIAH
BOOK ONE

A novel by

M. D. Rossi

BALBOA
PRESS

A DIVISION OF HAY HOUSE

Balboa Press books may be ordered through booksellers or by contacting:

Balboa Press
A Division of Hay House
1663 Liberty Drive
Bloomington, IN 47403
www.balboapress.com
1-(877) 407-4847

Because of the dynamic nature of the Internet, any web addresses or
links contained in this book may have changed since publication and
may no longer be valid. The views expressed in this work are solely those
of the author and do not necessarily reflect the views of the publisher,
and the publisher hereby disclaims any responsibility for them.

The author of this book does not dispense medical advice or prescribe the use
of any technique as a form of treatment for physical, emotional, or medical
problems without the advice of a physician, either directly or indirectly. The
intent of the author is only to offer information of a general nature to help
you in your quest for emotional and spiritual well-being. In the event you use
any of the information in this book for yourself, which is your constitutional
right, the author and the publisher assume no responsibility for your actions.

Any people depicted in stock imagery provided by Thinkstock are models,
and such images are being used for illustrative purposes only.
Certain stock imagery © Thinkstock.

Printed in the United States of America.

ISBN: 978-1-4525-7220-8 (sc)
ISBN: 978-1-4525-7222-2 (hc)
ISBN: 978-1-4525-7221-5 (e)

Library of Congress Control Number: 2013906633

Balboa Press rev. date: 04/26/2013

To the Righteous Iconoclast

And to The Resistance—James 4:7

TABLE OF CONTENTS

ACKNOWLEDGEMENTS

I wish to thank many for inspiration that helped me continue the crafting of this novel. This was to be a "Man's Story for *Manly Men*," and it still is, but it was my wife, Leda, told me there *must* be a "love interest," and so there is. Thanks to The Big Cheese—Joey Repasky—my close friend who assisted me in editing my drafts, and for sharing support for the State of Indiana, and in our mutual enjoyment of firearms. I owe him a book. The Tlck—Jeffrey Clark—inspired me in forging his character and has been a great friend, I am in his debt. Thanks to Cheri Clark—my *Final Editor* on this novel. And with spiritual guidance in mind, I must acknowledge and thank my Pastor and friend Dave Keesee of Calvary Chapel Crawfordsville, my brothers and sisters at Calvary Chapel and WSRC—The Source—88.1 FM—Crawfordsville and Maranatha Christian School. Also thanks to the late George Markey and his family whom I love, Chuck Smith, Gayle Erwin, Chuck Missler, Mike Macintosh, and Damien Kyle, the late Dr. Walter Martin, Ken Ham and Dr. Kent Hovind.

Since the day I put my faith in Jesus Christ, and in the Word of God, back on January 2nd, 1980, I've been a Christian, a Conservative, a Creationist, an Apologist, and a confronter of cults and the occult. The men above have been a source of encouragement and growth for me. I still have much room to grow, and the day will never come when I will be able to say anything different. Above and beyond all, I thank the Lord Jesus Christ. He thinks of me and therefore I am.

Now there were many encouragers . . . some knew they were encouraging me, some did not—My late Grandmother—Nonie wanted me to write, and so I did. I just wish she'd been able to read it. I also thank my wife Leda, again, my mother Donna Rossi, Cindy Ellingwood, Susan Rummey, Dennis Beach, Greg Sabens (Dennis and Greg gave me encouragement on another project, that spilled over to this,) Sheriff Gary McHenry, Adam Current, Rob Johnson—Author—KYOA, Dave Brindle, Andrew Borden, Joe and Amy Repasky, Gloria Stevens, the Shane Hudson family, my family (The Woodalls and Yunds) and friends participating at the Vanity Theatre in Crawfordsville IN, with whom we are the Sugar Creek Pla yers. Thanks to Mackenzie Hepburn for my "Sting" photo on the back of this novel! And thanks to my father Ted Rossi, The entire Sanderlin Family in Denver, and William and Christine Rossi for putting up with their Dad while he wrote his novel. But I warn them that I've already begun the sequel.

I wish to thank The Town of Waveland IN, the residents of Waveland, The Waveland Police Department, The Town of Crawfordsville IN, all of my amigos from INDOT—Indiana Department of Transportation, IOT—Indiana Office of Technology, ISP—Indiana State Police, and DNR—Department of Natural Resources, DHS—Department of Homeland Security, ATC—Alcohol Tobacco, The Montgomery County's Police Department, Governor Mitch Daniels and Governor Mike Pence, because without personal experience with the above and my many friendships, I would have had far less context for the story. Also, I wish to thank Larry Blamire and his wonderful, faithful troupe of actors and the entire cast of actors and writers of Mystery Science Theater 3000 and Riff Trax for making me laugh, and enabling me to pass the laughter on to others. I thank the creators and cast of Dr. Horrible's Sing-along Blog, including Joss Whedon and special appreciation to Ben Edlund. I also wish to thank Bill Carmichael and Deep River Books for their salutation to my work with "Honorable Mention" in the Deep River Books 2011/2012 Writer's Contest, and Bill's personal encouragement afterwards.

Thanks to all,
M.D. Rossi

1

THE FIRST SIGN

(From the notes of First Agent Christopher Griffin)

Life on this planet is a cliché. What has happened before is happening, and will happen again, with very few exceptions. Mankind has little choice, even in those exceptions. Repeating history is the fate of the mortal who has not studied the fate of his predecessors, and still that is no guarantee, for that has also been done before, and here we are.

There is nothing new under the sun, so says the inspired Wisdom of Solomon. Here is another truism, if you will: "We exist in the once-and-future present." The human condition was death-prone yesterday, is death-prone today, and will be tomorrow. As with the Anakim, the Emim, the Nephilim, the Gibbor, the Zuzims, the Rephaim, and the Gadarenos, they were of old, they are, and they will be tomorrow. However, and paradoxically so, it has not always been that way, and it won't be that way sometime in the future . . . . But that is exactly why Knightlight exists.

Rural Montgomery County, Indiana—
Present Day, June 15th

Darkness followed on the heels of the fading sunset like a predator stalking its own mortal enemy. Silently, fireflies danced above the farmland surrounding a dense forest. Night was beginning its reign. The air was thick and humid, and a mist was beginning to rise and coalesce, shrouding the landscape. It was summer in Indiana, and with it, cicadas sang in varying flourishes of intensity like the surge and ebb of a tide. Crickets chirped fearlessly, tree frogs croaked their salutations to one another, and coyotes prepared to howl mournfully, as the night sky filled itself with familiar stars. To the east, the lights of the small town of Waveland could be distantly seen glowing above the tree line, and to the northeast, the brighter hue of Crawfordsville lit the horizon.

Most of the rich farmland near the forest was owned by the Amish. Big barns, silos, and large houses stood soundly on huge tracts of farmland. The Amish are simple but adamant in the practice of their way of life. They keep to themselves on the whole, unless they need to travel to Waveland to work, or even farther to Rockville for supplies and the sale of goods to the outlanders.

The Amish are skilled and extremely self-sufficient, knowing the ways of the land using Biblical principles and they put in an honest day's work for an honest day's wages. They are strangers to technology on balance, having turned their back on the ever-changing customs and progress of the outlander's world. But like any colony of people that choose to escape society, there are ample ills that cannot be simply abandoned. Seclusion is no defense or cure for the darkness in the hearts of man, and it can often be beacon to another darkness that sees easy prey. Though Amish proficiency, unity and determination had prepared their people to face almost anything nature could throw at them, none of them expected the need to prepare for slaughter.

Daniel Beiler had just pulled off "SR-47" in his black mule-drawn carriage after passing Lake Waveland and the Turkey Run Golf Course, wound around two bends, and then turned onto his long drive. His buggy was clean but the black leather interior had become dingy from constant use, and the aged suspension would creak loudly whenever it hit a bump. The drive ahead, nearly half a mile long, led up to his massive barn and his home beyond, on the expansive property that he owned outright. He was a peaceful and reasonably content man who had lines etched in his leathery face from years of good humor. Pride was perhaps his only outward failing.

The broad-brimmed hat that covered his head had absorbed much sweat in the heat of the day and was finally drying in the slight night breeze of the still very warm evening. Daniel realized early on that day that he should have worn the straw hat, but he made his choice when the day was cool. His beard was a respectable length for his age, and gray hairs were creeping into it, giving it a salt-and-pepper kind of look which signified that a new elder might be in the making.

Daniel was glad to be home after spending the evening at the Hostetler farm. He had delivered a natural gas tank to Amos

Hostetler for his stove, and loaned him some tools that Amos had requested to borrow. While he was there, the two spent a little too much time discussing Amos's son, John, and his potential marital intentions with Daniel's daughter Katie. There would be no official announcement of the pairing of the children until November, assuming that they continued to be a couple at the Sunday night sing-alongs. Manipulation of the children's lives was customary, and when successful; it demonstrated authority to the Elders who watched for those traits. Daniel wanted those traits noticed.

Nearing the barn, Daniel noticed that the gaslights of his home beyond were unlit, which was not usual when darkness fell. Still, the sight made him slightly uneasy. He sensed that something was wrong. He guided his mule down the lane between white wooden-railed fences that paralleled the drive. It was dark enough that he had to use the fence itself to keep square in the lane, and the single front lamplight allowed him to be seen but did little to reveal the path ahead. He looked to the east and saw that a slice of moon was beginning to rise, but he'd be inside by the time it gave him useful light. The carriage was almost to the corner of the left fence where he'd turn to reach the barn and park his carriage for the night.

Belle, the mule pulling Daniel's carriage, pricked up her ears and began to shake her head. Daniel noticed that his hands were trembling while holding the reins. He then realized that he no longer heard the cicadas, the tree frogs, or even crickets. He heard nothing over the hoof-clipping sounds of Belle's steps, and the carriage wheels crushing the gravel of the path beneath. All was dark and far too quiet as he approached his barn. An irrational dread overcame him. Then a shape moving suddenly caught his eye to the left, and in a blur, Belle was struck by something hairy and massive, knocking her sideways, overturning the carriage, which skidded behind Belle's limp and fallen body and too came to rest on its side.

Daniel was stunned, confused, and quite shaken as he tried to right himself within the tight enclosed carriage now lying on the ground. Dust had been kicked up because of the spill, and outside the badly cracked front window, Daniel could see the body of Belle, unmoving, on the ground just outside. He could not see much farther than that because of the dust and the dark. He tasted blood in his mouth and could feel the thick liquid running down his forehead. He sat up, tossed his hat to the side, and reached up to open the side door that was now above him. He struggled to open it, but it would not budge. Wondering whether his mule was struck by a loose bull running at full tilt, he still was completely unsure of what on earth had just happened, and he began to fear the darkness.

Suddenly the door with which he was struggling was ripped from his grasp and pulled clean off the carriage, to Daniel's further amazement. Daniel shrank back inside the buggy and listened as the door landed somewhere off in the distance. He heard a deep growl very near him. His pulse was raging, making the sound of river rapids in his ears for fear's sake. His breath was coming in short, tight heaves, as he struggled to listen beyond himself for anything that would tell him what was just outside the carriage. He heard heavy footsteps in close proximity. He craned his neck upward while bracing himself, because the carriage was none too stable, and he peered out the opening above him. Then a massive arm reached down from above and grabbed his entire head in a rough palm, with fingers locking around his skull. In an instant he was lifted and tossed thirty feet from the carriage, tumbling toward his house and into the lower wooden fence rail that ran the length of his drive.

Lying there for a moment, dazed, Daniel realized that he'd landed well enough and nothing seemed to be broken; but it wasn't a gentle landing, and danger was very near. He heard weighty footsteps on the gravel coming in his direction. Then his nostrils made him aware of a thick smell that reminded him of a dead deer on a hot summer's day, like a festering carcass that he would have avoided . . . and he smelled something like sulfur within the stench.

He looked up to see what had tossed him so effortlessly, but the black silhouette was almost upon him. Terror struck him as he saw the dark and giant "thing" before him. He gained his footing and dashed toward his home as fast as he could.

Darkness was still between him and his house, but he knew the way to his home, and hopefully to safety. Unfortunately, he did not see what was before him on the ground and he tripped, making contact with something soft but unyielding in the yard. He landed on his stomach and gravel bit into his palms. Getting up and looking behind him, he saw the mammoth shape getting nearer, taking long yet strangely casual strides. It was the stride of complete dominance before a helpless victim. Daniel looked down at what had tripped him, and in the naked light of the rising moon, he recognized the head and torso of his brother. A stifled scream escaped his lips. He looked up again and realized that he was almost within the giant thing's grasp. Daniel pushed himself backward, regaining his footing. He turned to the house and sprinted to the porch steps, where he then saw his wife and children, lifeless by the porch steps. Horror gripped Daniel, panic encompassed him, and then something even more powerful both gripped and encompassed him. He was lifted high into the air; a single hairy hand grasped both of Daniel's legs in an astonishingly large hand, and the other wrapped itself tightly around his head. He was pulled in two different directions . . . and then Daniel knew no more in this world.

✦

The heavy rains began an hour later and lasted for three soaking days. When Amos Hostetler finally dropped by, he found the Beiler homestead vacant. He assumed that the household had gone to town, so he left the tools he had borrowed in the unlocked barn, and went back home expecting to hear from Daniel soon, within a day or two at most. Nothing looked abnormal. Well, other than the fact that a couple of the fence rails on the drive had been repaired recently, and the workmanship seemed . . . hasty. It wasn't until six days after Amos's visit that a missing person's report was filed and the small Waveland Police department got involved.

Sheriff Braxton, 59 years old last May, sporting silver hair, was following the eye doctor's orders; he was wearing glasses now, and not just to drive. Braxton drove out to the Hostetler farm and interviewed Amos, noting the date when Daniel was last seen. Then he visited the Beiler residence, where found nothing denoting violence in the disappearances, just a little dust indicating that it had been at least a week since the Beilers had last been home. Braxton checked the cooler and found spoiled milk. He looked in the closets to see whether any clothing seemed to have been packed for an unannounced trip, but he could not tell whether anything was missing. He checked the root cellar and found canning jars both full and empty, but little else. He checked the barn, seeing that the equipment looked in order, and noting that all the livestock slips were empty and the coach was gone, which might indicate that the Beilers were traveling. He admitted to himself that he knew too little about the Amish, but as far as Braxton could determine, the Beilers could have simply taken a trip to any other Amish farm in any other state, and there was no clue as to where that might be. The simple life that the Amish lived made it difficult to obtain information about them, or know their whereabouts, when you weren't actually speaking to them.

Braxton filed his report and kept tabs on the Beiler farm when in the neighborhood, and on Amos as well, but there was not much else he could do. The report sat idle for many days, until other bodies were found, and the sightings began.

2

The Interview of Years Past

Arapaho County Jail, Centennial, Colorado—October 17, 1994

Dominic Moreau, "Nick" to his friends, age 28, sat at a metal table in the empty room and waited for the FBI agent to come in and begin to interview him. He still had residual ink stains from being fingerprinted two days before. He was mainly of Italian descent, despite his last name being French, but he referred himself only as an American. He had black hair that was becoming longer than he liked, almost reaching his shoulders. It was swept back and tousled because he'd not been allowed so much as a comb. His eyes were a striking dark brown, and he sported a tight beard and mustache—black as well—which were usually well trimmed, but jail time gave everyone that disheveled look. Though smallish in stature, only 5'8" tall, he had a fight in him that would never surrender when family or friend needed defense, but he found that there were things in this world that did not yield or retreat until they destroyed all he loved, regardless of the fight in him. He'd recently discovered that he was not strong enough to save his family. Now he felt alone, hopeless and helpless. He felt that even God had abandoned him.

8

Dominic was handcuffed to the table that was bolted to the floor, and he sat in an immovable chair, also fixed to the ground. He was facing the two-way mirror across from him. It was a chilly room because someone in control of the room's temperature had intended it to be so. The room smelled of stale cigarettes and coffee grounds. The walls were painted a dreary gray and were unadorned with the exception of a single motivational poster on the wall. In bold letters it read, "Simplicate . . . Don't Complify!" Obviously, it was somebody's idea of a joke. Nick sat alone, silent, forlorn, and helpless in an uncaring room.

Every time Dominic thought about the events that landed him there, tears would well up in his eyes, followed closely by anger. What happened was simply horrible and no one believed him. Just two days ago, Dominic was taken into custody with the blood of his wife covering much of him, his lifeless child in his arms, and his home ablaze. He was in shock and the appearances weren't just suspicious, but incriminating. Now he mourned for his family and wanted justice for them, but he was a captive. He wanted the police, the FBI, even the military to help him find and kill that "thing" that destroyed his family, yet it was he who was seen as the murderer, perhaps even insane, and his pleas for help went ignored because of his impossible story. He had waived his Fifth Amendment rights and told the police on the scene what had happened while there was still time to pursue the thing and kill it. He nearly grabbed an officer's weapon so that he could demonstrate the urgency to hunt it down, but the police were all over him and subdued him quickly. Before he knew it, he was processed and locked in jail.

Dominic was to be in front of a judge in the afternoon, but now the FBI wanted to "interview" him, which he believed was just politically correct speak for "interrogate," so he sat there, with emotions raw and deep, and waited. Intermittently, he prayed that God would intervene, but he admitted to himself that part of him was angry at God for letting this happen to his family. He knew,

9

for example, that Job had suffered greater than he, but he also knew that suffering sometimes becomes so painful that it makes a man lash out at the very ones he loves, and he loved God. He also knew that God was in control of this universe, and nothing happened without God's permission . . . so God was allowing the hurt he felt . . . allowing his confusion, his grief . . . . Pain was now the core of his heart, and a bitter helplessness was the root of his spirit.

With a click, the windowless door to the room unlocked, and then swung open, admitting an officer that Dominic had seen before, and apparently the FBI agent. The agent wore a dark suit jacket and pants and a light gray shirt with a red tie, and though he seemed quite fit for his apparent age, he looked as if he was ready for retirement. The agent signaled to the officer that he wanted to speak to Dominic alone, so the officer nodded and exited the room, locking it behind him.

Dominic looked at the agent as he took the seat across from him and clenched his jaws, knowing he would have to relive the event yet again for this stranger. He took a deep breath, looked down at his cuffed hands, and resigned himself to the circumstances for the moment, feeling quite defenseless. He knew despair more intimately than he'd ever known it.

"Put your wrists on the table, please," the federal agent said almost politely, but with a strong and authoritative voice. Dominic complied while the agent reached over and unshackled him, letting the cuffs drop onto the table. Dominic picked up the cuffs and handed them to the agent.

"Just leave them there, Mr. Moreau. I trust you aren't going to use them as a weapon," the agent said with a raised eyebrow, a knowing eyebrow. He cleared his throat while he gazed at the prisoner before him, sizing him up, and choosing his introduction carefully. He had many introductions in his repertoire. "My name is Griffin . . . Agent Christopher Griffin. My information tells me that you have waived your Fifth Amendment rights and agreed that I could come and interview you without having any council representing you, is that correct?"

"I agreed," said Dominic.

"Why did you agree, Mr. Moreau?" Agent Griffin asked.

"Because I figured that since I am only guilty of trying to protect my family, there must be something bigger going on if the FBI wanted to question me about it, and I need all the help I can get. I figured that there was something about my case that matched other cases."

"Sound reasoning, Mr. Moreau. I *am* here because I *might* be able to help you."

"You might?" Dominic asked. "Mr. Griffin, so far I've been treated like a murdering nut-job, instead of a victim. The police act as if I was the one who hurt my family, and they locked me up when I should be out there hunting my wife and daughter's killer, and burying my family." Tears welled up in his eyes. He bit back at them.

Griffin remained silent and observed Dominic's body language for details that might confirm earnestness, dishonesty, or insanity.

Dominic knew that he was being studied and that he was being observed beyond the mirror behind Agent Griffin. He really couldn't care less. "How are you going to help me?"

"Mr. Moreau, I am very sorry for your loss," Agent Griffin said with sincerity. "We are going to have a little talk. I'll ask you some questions; I'll listen to your answers. I'll ask more questions, and by the end of our brief discussion, I will know whether I can help you or not."

"May I see your ID and badge?" Dominic asked.

Agent Griffin smiled slightly at that, as if there were something funny about the question. He pulled his jacket open and on his belt was his FBI badge. Then he reached into his jacket pocket and pulled out several plastic cards, looked through them for a second, and then placed all but one back in his jacket pocket. He placed the ID faceup on the table and slid it across to Dominic. It looked official, but the fact that he had several cards in his pocket aroused Dominic's curiosity, perhaps even his suspicion. Dominic slid it back, and the agent placed it back with the others.

"So, you're FBI?" Dominic asked, still unsure of the man who seemed to be holding all the cards, literally.

"I am today, Mr. Moreau, and I've been so, off and on, for many years," Agent Griffin politely replied. "Now, I became aware of your case within minutes of your 911 call, Mr. Moreau, and since I was already in the area, I did a background check on you, and I diverted my attention to your case because it was obvious to me that it intersected my own. At this time, I believe you to be a casualty, perhaps a combatant, but not the aggressor. So let's get to it then, and we'll see if I'm right."

Dominic was astonished that his 911 call had attracted the attention of the FBI so quickly, but was encouraged by it nonetheless. "So the FBI is aware of that thing?" he asked. Then another thought came to him and he became angry. "Is it part of some government experiment and you're here to clean up the mess? Are you responsible for my family's murder?" he demanded, his eyes turning to flame as if the embers in his heart had been stirred.

Agent Griffin showed no sign of any emotional reaction, and he answered gently, "No, Mr. Moreau. If we could have prevented it, I promise you that we would have."

Dominic discerned a genuine sincerity in Griffin and it shamed him.

"But the FBI is aware of that thing?" Dominic asked, calming down, regretting his instant anger.

Agent Griffin took out a notepad and pen from his jacket pocket, flipped it open, and made a few notations, seemingly ignoring Dominic's query. Dominic tried to be patient as he waited for Agent Griffin to finish his notations and reply.

Griffin wrote, "*Moreau is cautious, and seems to be able to rapidly put events together in logical succession, drawing possible conclusions under stressful situations. He is naturally distraught because of the tragedy, but his mind is still reasoned. Even his agreement to be interviewed was based on such logic.*" He made a few other notations regarding Dominic's body language and demeanor, and then he looked up at Dominic.

"Aware of that *thing* . . . ?" Griffin paused and lowered his voice. "Yes, Mr. Moreau. But I believe you may be inferring a connection and conclusion that I did not intend to imply. I said I was FBI today, which does not presuppose that I was acting in the interests of the FBI two days ago."

Dominic did not know what to say to that. A statement like that was nothing less than confusing. He didn't know whether Griffin was playing games with him, or was just "semantically anal"; but his gut told him that this man may be the only way out of jail, so he held his peace for the moment.

Agent Griffin observed Dominic for a moment and then wrote, "*Moreau seems to intuitively know when not to argue about semantics, and to not let his frustration show. I respect that.*"

"You served in the Army Reserve after the draft had ended, Mr. Moreau. You volunteered. Why?"

At that moment, Dominic began wondering whether indeed this was more of an interview, rather than an interrogation. Preferring the former to the latter, he responded calmly and tried to stay focused on the discussion, reining in his emotions until it was over.

"I was recruited in 1984. I didn't have any real plan for my life, being just out of high school, so I thought I'd serve and be fed three square meals a day while I worked out what I wanted to do for the future. It paid for my college as well. Though I've grown to be more of a patriot in the years following, I don't claim that it was necessarily a patriotic choice . . . initially."

Agent Griffin noted, "*Moreau is well spoken and refreshingly honest,*" and then said, "You attend Christ Fellowship, a local nondenominational church. Why?"

Dominic's eyebrows rose and furrowed, and his eyes made obvious his puzzlement at the question. "I'm a Christian. I have faith in Jesus Christ and we are raising our family . . . I mean . . . ," he choked, "we *were* raising our family in a Christian home." Burning tears flowed from his eyes and Agent Griffin gave him time to regain his composure, observing him, trying to discern whether the expression of his feelings was honest. Dominic could sense himself being studied, but his emotional state did not allow him to care whether or not he was. Only when Dominic's composure was attained did Agent Griffin continue.

"Your record shows you to be a law-abiding citizen and that you are active within your church and your community. Up until this incident, your neighbors have had a high opinion of you. Unfortunately, the news media immediately became interested in your case, and has altered the public's perception of you, of late. I'm afraid that you have already been tried in the court of public opinion due to media hacks. Sorry. You are a gun owner, and have a concealed carry permit. Your weapon, a 1911 .45-caliber semiautomatic handgun was found at the scene of the crime with only your prints on it, and it had been discharged until the magazine was empty. No gunshot wounds were found on your family and State Police ballistics reported that they have not found any of your discharged rounds, only brass casings. Mr. Moreau, where did the bullets go?"

Dominic gritted his teeth and steeled himself against his emotions. Now he would have to say the insane. It made him angry. Teeth together, he spoke.

"I discharged ***every single round*** into that monster," Dominic said.

"All right." Griffin accepted the answer. "Next, how did the fire start?" he asked while he continued to make notations.

"That *thing* ripped up our gas stove and threw it at us. It hit Sandra, my wife, and nearly cut her in half." His eyes began to water and his throat was strained, torn between anger and sorrow. He made the effort to speak through the pain that hit him head-on, again.

"It backed Lisa, my daughter, and me into the living room and I grabbed my gun off the fireplace mantle, and then moved my daughter and myself even farther back from it. I started shooting at it from the back of the living room, and that just made it angry. It howled and shrieked at us and threw furniture, and hit the walls around it, breaking through them. It wouldn't back off and I had to keep my daughter from getting hit by the objects it tossed. By then, I could smell the gas from the kitchen, and I knew I had to get us out of the house. It came closer and I shot it again, and again, and we just barely got around it. I backed into the dining room, next to the kitchen, with my gun pointed at it, and we slowly backed toward the front door." Dominic sniffed and let more tears run down his cheek.

"Then that monster grabbed a burning log out of the fireplace and tossed it between us and the kitchen. I got two more shots in, the last two I had, and then the kitchen exploded. It tossed my daughter and me through the plate glass window, cutting her throat and face, and arms, and stomach. I landed . . . right on top of her," he sobbed. "It was as if that monster knew what would happen, and was actually trying to kill us in the explosion," Dominic cried.

Agent Griffin waited patiently, still making notes of observation about the man, but feeling empathy and great sorrow for what this man had been through.

"Take your time, Mr. Moreau," Griffin said and silently waited.

"Then, when I knew that I couldn't stop the bleeding, I just held my daughter, and I knew Lisa was . . . gone. I laid her down and went back in for my wife's body. The thing was gone by then and the house was on fire. I found Sandra and pulled her body outside, knowing she was dead, too."

"Then you called 911 on your wife's cell phone, and the police and ambulance came and you were taken into custody," Griffin finished for him, so he would not have to voice it.

"If you know so much about me, then you've read my report and know what I've told the police. My story isn't changing because it's the truth, and that thing is still out there."

"You are quite correct about my knowledge of you, Mr. Moreau. However, I have one other question for you that has *not* been asked by Arapaho County's finest, nor the Colorado State Police . . . ." Agent Griffin let the sentence hang there for a moment.

Dominic, looking puzzled, wiped his eyes with his sleeve and finally asked, "What's the question then?"

Agent Griffin looked straight into Dominic's eyes, and his gaze had gravity in them. He then leaned in closer, across the table, beckoning Dominic to do the same. Dominic complied, and gave Agent Griffin his right ear. Quietly yet distinctly, Agent Griffin whispered only two words: "Which monster?"

Dominic pulled back in astonishment. He could not be certain whether the agent was mocking him or whether the question was legitimate. By the intonation, Dominic was of the belief that the question was not only legitimate, but deadly serious. The agent looked at him, waiting for a response and looking as if he expected a seriously considered answer. Dominic thought for a moment. Yes, he had told the police that it was a huge, hairy, monstrous creature, which was a general but accurate description, though it had not occurred to him to categorize it in terms of "type of monster." He looked up for a moment and then back to Agent Griffin. He leaned toward the agent and whispered, "Did you ever see the movie called *The Howling*? I . . . I think it was something like a werewolf, a *big* werewolf."

Agent Griffin nodded slightly, slowly, seriously, and backed away from Dominic. He rose and signaled to the two-way mirror, indicating that he was ready for the guard to open the door. Aloud

Griffin said, "I'll be taking Mr. Moreau with me. Please process his release. He will be remanded to my custody."

Dominic relaxed and exhaled, as if he'd been holding his breath throughout the interview. The door opened and was held by a very suspicious officer who eyed the agent incredulously. Agent Griffin grabbed the knob and waited for Dominic.

Dominic rose slowly. "Where are we going?"

Agent Griffin held the door for him and said, "Unfortunately, Mr. Moreau, our first stop is, of necessity, the scene of the crime."

"I thought you'd already been there. Why don't we start higher up the canyon than that? Surely you've been able to track that monster beyond my home."

"I have been to your home more than once, and I know all that I need to know. But we are going there because what remains of your clothing and your important belongings are still there, Mr. Moreau. You will need them where you are going," Agent Griffin replied.

· · ·

It took roughly half an hour to process Dominic's release to Agent Griffin. The Post's master sergeant, being slightly suspicious, questioned Agent Griffin's authority to take a prisoner from their custody, but only until his superiors verified his authority to do so, and the release was expedited. Dominic gathered his belongings, which were returned to him by the quartermaster, and then the two exited the station with suspect eyes upon them from every officer. Agent Griffin did not seem to notice the wariness of the police, and walked with Dominic confidently, as if he owned the place.

The two men walked out into a rain-filled sky that was turning to sleet, and Agent Griffin increased their pace to his rental SUV. It was a Jeep Grand Cherokee with dark window tinting, and it looked as if Agent Griffin had been four-wheeling it because the side panels and undercarriage were caked in clay. Agent Griffin unlocked the vehicle remotely. It was a time when vehicle remote controls were not ubiquitous, and it impressed Dominic. Griffin pointed to the front passenger seat as silent instruction for Dominic, and both climbed inside, out of the cold and wet October air.

Both fastened their seat belts. Griffin started the engine and Dominic looked in the back seat and saw what looked like a military case for a satellite phone, ammo boxes, and an AR-15 that was strapped in the rear, behind the driver's seat. All the way in the back were more cases that looked military, which he could not identify.

"OK, who are you, Griffin? You have enough equipment in here to start your own war."

"I am just as I said, Mr. Moreau . . . and we are **both** in a war. Unfortunately, you were not prepared for it, and it cost you dearly," Griffin said with a frown of empathy. "I will explain all you wish to know, but first we need to make you ready to understand." He backed out of the parking slip, changed the gear to drive, and pulled out of the station's parking lot, then onto the parkway, turning right on South Chambers Road, following its curves toward the new highway C470, ultimately to take them west, in the general direction of Dominic's home. Griffin turned on the heater and the wipers, as the precipitation began to obscure the view ahead.

Agent Griffin seemed to know the way to Dominic's home, so Dominic relaxed a bit and watched the traffic ahead, not knowing whether he should talk further with Griffin. The wiper blades went back and forth, and at the sides of the front window, ice began to collect. Then, as if someone flipped a switch, the freezing rain turned to snow, and thick, wet, heavy flakes fell from the dark clouds above. Griffin pulled right, toward the on-ramp of C470, taking them toward the mountains, and the snow was now making slush on the pavement, and coating everything else in white. Poor visibility slowed their trip. Directions were never a problem in Denver if you could see far enough west, because the mountains were always to the west.

Dominic sat silent, watching the snow become thicker, the traffic slower, and seeing the mountains grow under a canopy of dark, water-laden clouds. His mind drifted to their destination. He could still see his house in his mind, looking very much like the last time he gazed upon it, burning as the police arrived that night, followed soon by the paramedics and the fire department. He replayed the events of that evening just two days ago, knowing that he would be haunted by them forever . . . and then he remembered something he had not noticed before.

"You were there!" he said, turning toward Griffin, breaking the silence. "I saw **this** jeep behind the second fire engine . . . . And you, *you were there!*"

Griffin nodded. "I was there, Mr. Moreau."

"What is going on here, Griffin? I want to know."

"There are more things in heaven and earth, Mr. Moreau, than are dreamt of in the philosophies of men . . . ," he paraphrased Shakespeare's Hamlet, in all seriousness, keeping his eyes on the road.

"That's not an answer. What were you doing there?"

"Are you sure you are ready to know, Mr. Moreau? Before you answer, I want to tell you this: If you know, then you will never be able to . . . **un**-know. If I show you what's behind the curtain, so to speak, you will have a dangerous knowledge that will make you responsible for possessing it. It made me responsible for it, but I was up to the task. Are you sure that you are up to it, Mr. Moreau?"

Dominic was puzzled by that. "I don't really know what you are talking about, Agent Griffin, but I *do* want to know why you were there, what you were doing, what you know about that monster, and everything else you know that you are not telling me."

"So be it," he said and continued to drive.

Dominic waited a couple of impatient moments and then erupted, "Well then, **tell me.**"

19

"I said I'd *show you*, Mr. Moreau. You will have to be patient for a little while. After my interview with you, it was clear to me that you are ready to know. I'll tell you a little, then show you more than you may wish to see, and then I'll explain it all to you. Can you be patient for the next half-hour, Mr. Moreau?"

"I can, if you tell me a little now."

"Very well." Agent Griffin turned off C470 at the Wadsworth exit and headed south, where it changed to South Platte Canyon Road, but their rate of travel had greatly decreased. Dominic knew the way, and it appeared that Agent Griffin knew it just as well. "In my pocket I have several IDs. One, as you know, is my ID for the FBI, but I have one for the CIA as well. I have one for the DOD, one for the Secret Service, one is for FEMA, one is for the NSA, one is for CDC, one is for the DIA, and so on . . . . I have one for each branch of the military, and I also have various credentials that give me access to MI5, the Mossad, and most NATO nations' intelligence agencies. I also have badges and uniforms where needed. Are you getting the picture, Mr. Moreau?"

"Are you telling me that you're a spy?"

"Good guess, Mr. Moreau," Griffin said with a slight chuckle, "but incorrect."

They turned on Deer Creek Canyon Road and headed west. It was only a few more miles until Dominic would be pulling up into his driveway, but they were down to 10 miles per hour. "I am a field agent for a private organization that often does government contracted work, largely for *our* government, but sometimes for foreign governments . . . legally, I assure you. Field agents of this organization have been afforded security status, and access to virtually every security organization with which our nation is allied—and, by special permission, sometimes to nations who are not our allies."

"A private contractor to the Government with security access, you mean like Halliburton, or contractors for national defense like Northrop Grumman?"

"There are similarities, I suppose, but our organization is unique in that it requires us not just to have civilian security clearance and access, but to actually be credentialed by these government agencies so we may interact unhindered, and with due authority."

"Authority to do what, exactly, and who on earth could secure those kinds of credentials?" Dominic was intrigued, and not just a little awed by the agent's obvious authority. It made him almost wish that he ended each sentence with "Sir."

"I'll answer the second question first, Mr. Moreau."

"It's Dominic. I mean, you can feel free to call me Dominic . . . or Nick for short."

"President Harry S. Truman, after consulting with then Secretary of Defense James Forrestal, wrote the first executive order to give our organization the credentials that would assist us in performing our job with the most efficiency and effectiveness. Even though Forrestal was initially against the idea, he acquiesced when he saw what he was up against. That was in 1947. Truman's Ex-O was to be known only to key members of Congress at the time, and the subsequent Presidents of the United States. I was there at the meeting where we convinced President Truman of the necessity, and the second meeting shortly afterward, where he met and conferred with our Director, Bensington Redwood. Truman also penned a personal letter to be passed to each president in succession, stressing the importance of our organization, and the need to continue supporting it. Fortunately, each president since either has been in agreement with President Truman's request—I can specifically name Presidents Carter and Reagan—or has been ambivalent and has never voided Truman's Ex-O, thus actively or passively supporting the accreditation of our organization, since each Ex-O endures only with the consent of each successive president, or the lack of it being rescinded."

"I understand how executive orders work, but those are supposed to be public knowledge. Under the Freedom of Information Act, we are supposed to know what laws, treaties, and contracts the Presidents have signed."

"I'm impressed, Mr. Moreau," said Griffin, and Dominic noticed that he did not use "Dominic" or "Nick' in addressing him, as he'd offered. "But the Freedom of Information Act was not signed until 1966 by L.B.J., and does not pertain to *certain* nationally secure information that is ongoing. Unlike Operation Paperclip, MK Ultra, and other *dubious* secret US initiatives, we protect and defend the people. And remember exactly *what* I said: Since nobody past Harry Truman issued any subsequent Ex-O, no President after had to sign *anything.* The first Ex-O was pertaining to nationally secure information, and beyond that, you cannot document something that never happened; i.e., no other executive orders were created or denied pertaining to my organization, and so it stands. On the chance that, in the future, the Ex-O is ever released to the public, it would be so completely *redacted* that nobody would be able to make heads or tails of it. I honestly would rather that it becomes public knowledge . . . . That way we would never have to act covertly . . . at least as far as Americans are concerned."

"And the answer to my first question?"

"Ah, there is your tenacity. Very good," he added with a nod. "To correctly answer your first question, I suggest that you should have asked, '*What is our organization?*' and then, '*Authority to do what, exactly?*' But that is how I would have asked it."

"All right, Agent Griffin, what is your organization, and what exactly do you do?"

"Please open the glove compartment. I have my business card in it."

Dominic opened the glove compartment and on top of the rental insurance receipt was a single, simple business card paper-clipped to it. Dominic pulled it out and examined it.

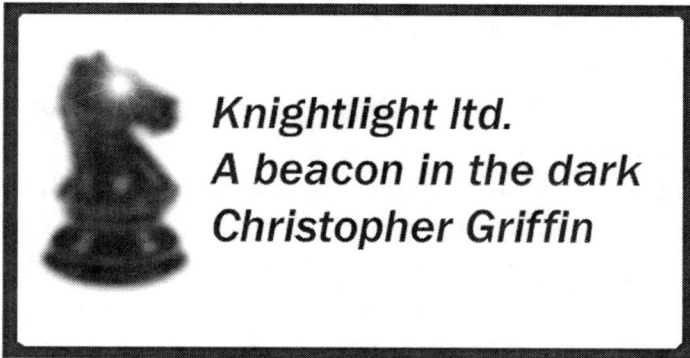

Knightlight ltd.
A beacon in the dark
Christopher Griffin

"Knightlight ltd . . . a beacon in the dark . . . ," he read aloud. "What's Knightlight?"

"We are an organization that is privately funded, but as contractors, we do recoup some of our expenses with American taxpayers' money, when our services are specifically leased, for a specific task, in accordance with appropriate secrecy and interdepartmental accountability. Otherwise, we act in the best interest of humanity on our own, but with very limited accountability."

Dominic placed the card back and closed the glove compartment. "And what does Knightlight do?" he asked.

"This world is a very dark place, Mr. Moreau. It is dangerously dark," he said as he made a right turn up toward Deer Creek Canyon.

"It is . . . ," Dominic agreed and reliving the recent horror once again. It smote him deeply.

"Ignorance compounds the darkness," Agent Griffin continued. He looked at the man seated next to him and sympathized with Dominic's wound, so he attempted to move on with the conversation to bring him back from his obvious despair.

"Can you tell me what was happening in 1947, Mr. Moreau?"

"Um . . . give me a minute. World War II was over. Russia became our adversary . . . ."

"Politically accurate, Mr. Moreau. You are partly on the right track . . . continue."

"OK . . . ." Dominic thought again. "Oh, wait . . . Roswell. It's got to be Roswell!"

Agent Griffin began to chuckle. "Interesting, but no, Mr. Moreau. Right year, but no, not Roswell."

"Perhaps then I'll let you tell me," Dominic said.

"At the end of World War II, something very significant happened. The concentration camps were discovered and the Nazi-initiated Holocaust was verified to be more than true. The systematic extermination of the Jews was documented fact, quite similar to Stalin's multiple "purges" of his own population. What we saw, however, was only a glimpse of the darkness then. Many thought it ended with the war, but they could not have been further from the truth. If you know your history, you should know that long ago, during the Babylonian invasion, and even before that, Israel was a people that this *world system* always wanted to destroy, because they were, and are, the children of the Promise. This world system hates whomever God loves and whomever loves God. Total eradication was ever tried against the Jewish people, ever attempted, but never achieved. Recent events of the 1900s depict only the continuation of the story, not the end, not by a long shot."

Dominic nodded and began to understand the line of thinking, for he knew its significance, if not its destination. "And at the end of the war, no country wanted to repatriate the Jews en masse, including America, though since the early part of this century, there was a movement to give the Holy Land back to the Jews," Dominic said.

"In 1897, actually," Agent Griffin corrected him. "That was the year of the first Zionist Council concerning the subject, though Biblical prophecy had declared it many times as something that would occur, and to be accurate, declared it all along. From that date, Jews began purchasing land in that area from Jordan. Technically, they owned much more real estate than what was given to them in 1947."

"Ah . . . ," Dominic said, completely allowing the correction.

"The Nazis' *attempted* extermination of the Jews was merely the catalyst of the event to which I allude, but even that was not nearly the beginning of it. Assuming you know your Bible, you also know that Abraham was promised what we call the Holy Land by the Lord Almighty Himself as an inheritance. It was a God-given property for Abraham and his posterity. King David eventually bought the bulk of the land, and all of it was still Israel's property when Israel came back to their land after their captivity by the Babylonian and then the Medo-Persian Empires. Though they owned the land, it soon came under Grecian control, until the Romans seized it completely from the Jews. The Jews were scattered throughout the globe, yet unlike any other nation in the history of this planet, they still retained their culture, and are ever God's chosen people. Later, of course, the Muslims took the land from the Romans, then the Crusaders took it from the Muslims, then the Mamelukes took it from the Crusaders, the Ottoman Empire took it from the Mamelukes, Great Britain took it from the Ottomans after World War I, giving much of it to Jordan as a reward for assisting Britain in the war, and the land by then had been given the name of Palestine. Prior to and after the Second World War, it was wasteland of largely vacant and useless property . . . but it was still a property concerning God's Promise to the Jews. Now do you understand the significance of 1947?"

"Well, it was the year *before* the United Nations gave the region of Palestine back to the Jews. And, as you say, it really was a desolate area at the time, filled with sand, swamps, and scorpions, with nomads and feudal Arab tribes."

"Yes, but what is the significance of that day, March 14, 1948, beyond the Nation of Israel being born in one day, Mr. Moreau?"

"The clock started ticking," Dominic answered confidently.

"Excellent! You are on the right page, now. So why then is 1947 significant?"

"Most of the political work for that event took place in 1947 . . . the drafting of the UN bill, and I suppose it included the planning for the inception date, so . . . ." He thought for a moment, and then he understood. "You *knew* it would take place, you *knew* the clock would start ticking, and somehow you could prove it to President Truman," Dominic said as if by epiphany, which it was.

"Bravo, Mr. Moreau, bravo! Well, certainly not *me* alone, and certainly we weren't the *only ones* who knew. Remember, once the clock started ticking, many other events were about to be set in motion, some predictable, some dire, and some remarkable."

It was all coming together in Dominic's mind, but what Knightlight ltd was, and how it was connected to Israel, he was still uncertain. He chose to work it over in his mind with the information he had before he asked further. Better to be thought a fool than prove it by speaking too quickly.

Griffin was very satisfied with the man sitting next to him. He knew he was making a good choice in him. Ahead, he saw Dominic's driveway, and noted that the Salvage Team was still at work. He slowed the SUV down and pulled in next to the truck that was being loaded while the snow fell heavily. Technically, Dominic's home was still a crime scene, so salvage was being carefully executed, documented, and cataloged. Griffin rolled down his window and spoke to the man in camouflage fatigues, who seemed to be in charge of the operation. To Dominic, the man looked as though he could wrestle an elephant to the ground while drinking a mug of beer, without spilling it.

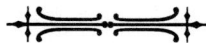

⊹═══⟩⊹

Dominic looked at the ruin of his house. The once two-story residence was reduced to blackened bones and scorched earth, and the steam that continued to rise from it made it appear as if its spirit were leaving it. It was no longer anyone's home save Death's. Tears bit at his eyes and he could feel his sinuses trying to fill. Just fifty hours ago this was the best place in his life. It was the place he worked all day to see. It was his life because it was his family's home. Now it was gone. Dominic fought against the tears, and now the shakes, as waves of emotions were beating down upon him.

"How much longer, Agent Keefer?" Griffin asked the man outside the Jeep.

"We're almost done here. Half an hour tops and we will be gone," the man responded.

Griffin turned to Dominic and said, "This is Agent Keefer, my partner."

"Hello, Agent Keefer." Dominic managed.

"Pleased to make your acquaintance, Mr. Moreau," said Agent Keefer.

"Put his bags in the back. We're headed to the site," Griffin ordered.

"Copy that," the man replied, and he grabbed the already packed luggage pieces and placed them in the back seat of the SUV.

"The site?" inquired Dominic.

"Ten more minutes, Mr. Moreau. Patience," Griffin replied. He backed onto the road and turned the way they had come, retracing the way back down to South Platte Canyon Road, and turned south.

"You might want to go north if you want to head back to Littleton, or Denver," Dominic suggested. "This heads to Martin."

"I know, Mr. Moreau," he said as he opened the console between the two of them, where he pulled out a Lockheed Martin visitor's badge. "Please clip this to your shirt."

Dominic looked at it for a moment and then complied, clipping it to his shirt pocket.

"So . . . 1947, Knightlight's inception date, and Roswell's date are just a coincidence?" asked Nick.

"Do you believe in coincidences?" asked Griffin.

"No," replied Nick.

"I am glad to hear that," said Griffin.

"That also is not an answer," said Nick.

Agent Griffin smiled at that and said, "Knightlight's mission is unfortunately covert, to a great degree, Mr. Moreau, and I am constrained to conceal and *contain* certain happenings. But the UFO phenomenon is not containable . . . therefore our government and others have allowed certain distractions to sate the curious who might otherwise learn the truth about the phenomena, and spread panic. Roswell was one such distraction the CIA allowed to spread in order to conceal certain defense initiatives; Area 51 is another. I, of course, was and continue to be against governmental misdirection of the public, as it also gives validity to conspiracy allegations that amount to lies. I hate lies. They could have at least said the Roswell and Groom Lake happenings were National Defense testing, *not alien conspiracies*, and left it at that. To you, I'll say that aliens are not what they *appear* to be, and perhaps I'll be able to enlighten you further, and explain their role in Knightlight's mission. But that is not what is at hand."

They drove in silence for a few more minutes, as Nick pondered what had been discussed. Then, as they neared a large gated industrial complex, Agent Griffin pulled into the Lockheed Martin complex at the security gate, and came to a stop at the security post. He rolled down his window.

"Welcome back, Mr. Griffin," the guard said, and handed a sign-in sheet to the agent.

"This is the visitor I mentioned," Griffin said as he passed the sign-in sheet to Dominic, who took it upon himself to print his name, the time, and his signature, and then paused.

"What do I put here where it asks for 'purpose of visit'?" Moreau asked.

"Leave it blank," said Griffin, taking the clipboard and passing it back to the guard.

"Thanks, and have a safe visit," the guard said.

Agent Griffin waited for the guard to open the gate and then he pulled into the complex, driving around several buildings and then heading straight for a garage that had two armed security guards standing at attention outside. He parked, turned off the wipers and the headlights, shut off the engine, unbuckled his seat belt, and announced, "We're here."

They both exited the vehicle, and Dominic followed Griffin, who went straight to the guards. They too had visitors badges, but they wore the generic blue jumpsuits of security guards. Griffin pulled his FBI credentials and showed them to the guards. It was clear that they recognized him without the identification, but Griffin seemed to be a man who went by the book.

"Have you had to chase anyone off?" Griffin asked.

"No, sir," replied the closest guard.

"Is Agent Wells inside?" Griffin asked.

"Yes, Agent Griffin. Agent Wells has been here for nearly an hour, and there are two FBI M.E.s with him," the guard said.

"Very good. This is Dominic Moreau," Griffin informed the guards. "He gets the credit for the trophy. Treat him as you would me."

"Yes, sir. Welcome, Mr. Moreau," the guard said to Dominic, who nodded and extended his hand, which was grasped firmly by the guard.

Then Dominic asked Griffin, "Trophy?"

"Let's go in, Mr. Moreau," Griffin said, without a hint of explanation.

The guard unlocked the door next to the big garage door and allowed them entry. Their footfalls echoed in the large garage bay, and in the center of the garage, three men stood quietly conversing over a large table with something big lying on it, under a black plastic tarp. Behind and around the table were many and various portable medical supplies, forensic devices, and equipment on portable tables. Air handlers blew a heated wind across the bay to keep the place warm, but it felt to Nick as if they pushed him toward the three men, and toward an undesirable destiny. Whatever was under the tarp, Nick already knew that he'd have to look at it. Nick wanted to turn and run, but his body kept pace with Griffin as if it could do nothing else.

As Moreau and Griffin approached, the three men ended their conversation with the only word that was clearly heard by Dominic: "thermite." Agent Wells, a tall, dark-skinned man, and two medical examiners observed the newcomers and patiently waited for the two to join them. Griffin made introductions, identifying Agent Wells as his *other* partner, and now all stood next to the shrouded table.

"Have all samples been obtained and cataloged?" Griffin queried.

"Yes, First Agent. Forensics gathered all required evidence and data, and we're just waiting for you and Mr. Moreau to visit before I gave the go-ahead for sanitization," Agent Wells said in a deep, very masculine voice.

Nick noted by Wells's comment that he'd been *expected* to be there, meaning the "interview" must have been a formality, his presence there never in question. Nick looked at the large covered table with foreboding. He hoped against seeing what he thought might be beneath the tarp. A shudder ran through his spine at that thought.

"Very good," Griffin said to Wells, and then turned to Dominic. "This, Mr. Moreau, is the trophy," Griffin announced without further ado, and he motioned for the M.E.s to remove the tarpaulin. Both men grasped one end each, and uncovered the table. Griffin had prepared Moreau a little on the way to the facility, but there was really nothing anyone could do to prepare another for such a sight.

Dominic's eyes grew wide as the tarp was removed. A monster upon the table was revealed, as a magician might reveal his feat of prestidigitation, not knowing that the trick had gone awry until the audience reacted in horror. He reflexively pushed himself away from the creature, letting out a shocked gasp. His body remembered and reacted to the danger that his mind had yet to comprehend. Agent Griffin put his hand on Dominic's shoulder to help steady him, knowing exactly what a shock to the system it is to see a nightmare while awake.

It was horrible to see, awful to smell, but there on the table was the massive and clearly dead body of the monster that had murdered Dominic's family.

Dominic gazed upon the carcass of the beast that was over eight feet long, maybe nine. The beast was completely hirsute, its lifeless black eyes stared skyward, and it had the teeth of a lion. Its massive hands had black fingernails, thick and strong. Everything about this beast was a horror, and the smell it produced was not from decay, but a musky stench that it seemed to naturally exude. And there were the bullet holes that Nick had inflicted upon it two days ago. *Ghastly* has become a seldom-used term, but a ghastly sight it was, and somehow the creature still had the power to make men quake. Its prowess had not diminished much even in death.

After taking in the beast, looking up and down its carcass, Dominic noticed something odd. It appeared that the creature's head had been severed from the body and was pushed against its neck to make it a complete corpse. Dominic, overwhelmed by the encounter, staggered back from the table, at which point Agent Griffin planted both his hands on Dominic's shoulders. Griffin nodded to the M.E.s that they could reshroud the creature. Once again the black tarpaulin was placed over the corpse.

31

"Dominic, are you going to be all right?" Griffin asked, using Moreau's first name for the first time.

"That—that's the monster," Dominic stammered. "It killed my family," was all he could speak.

"Yes," Griffin said grimly. "I know."

Dominic went down on one knee, then both, finally leaning forward on his hands, and great sobbing tears spilled from him and he cried in heaves. He made his hands into fists and clenched them tightly.

Griffin gave Dominic a while to come to himself. The room was silent for his sake. Soon, Dominic brought himself under control, wiped his tears with his coat sleeve, and stood himself up again slowly, but it was a struggle to stand, even with Agent Griffin's assistance. He took several deep breaths and brushed Griffin's arm gently away from him, nodding, showing that he was going to be OK now.

"What *is* that?" Dominic managed to speak.

"That is what the Old Testament, in the original Hebrew language, calls a Rephaim, Mr. Moreau," Griffin said. "But *monster* is just as accurate. They are deadly, fearsome, and powerful creatures."

Griffin took Dominic by the arm and led him to the table once again. He uncovered only the left arm of the beast and moved Dominic's hand toward it.

"Feel his arm, Mr. Moreau. This is no costume . . . it is no trick. This is a real creature . . . as real as things *can* be, in this universe."

Dominic touched the hairy arm, relenting from his hesitancy, and could feel the powerful muscles beneath. He looked at the massive hand and knew that this was no beast of fantasy, but genuine and completely substantial. A chill ran through the core of his being as full realization came to him that this creature had recently walked this earth with murderous rage against his family. Part of him thought, even hoped, that the monster that attacked his family was all in his mind, because it was truly unimaginable that this monster could be real, but he *had* seen it, he *had* fought it, and there it was on the slab. His confirmation of sanity was of little comfort.

"How did you kill it?" Dominic asked as he felt the dead thing's arm.

"I said it was *your* trophy, and I meant it, Mr. Moreau. You put the contents of your entire magazine into the beast. The round that struck him in the head is what did him in, though. These creatures are very tough, to say the least. We followed the creature you had mortally wounded until we were upon it, and then we expedited its demise. You were the one who stopped this thing before it killed more. You are now one of a very few who can say that."

"Where did this thing come from?" Dominic asked, still reeling mentally and trying to sort it out within the context of what he perceived to be **reality**.

"You already know the answer to that question, Mr. Moreau," Agent Griffin stated.

"The pit of *Hell*," Dominic replied.

"Exactly," said Griffin.

"Why?" Dominic asked.

"Because our adversary, the devil, knows his time is short, and that places humanity in grave danger," Agent Griffin said. "The storm is building, and there are more fantastic events that will soon come upon mankind . . . because the clock *is* ticking. The countdown has begun on this planet. But this is reality, Mr. Moreau. This is no longer the secret war. It is no longer something you read in the Bible as a historical footnote. And you above all should know that this is no longer a spectator's war."

"So . . . Knightlight's mission is something on the lines of "hastening the second coming of Christ" or "impeding the rise of the Antichrist"?

"Nothing so grandiose, Mr. Moreau. Those events are not even close to being in mankind's control. We are much more practical. We are simply protectors and defenders of the unarmed and ignorant, until such a time as we are unable to assist any further. We have goals, and an agenda, but they too are relatively simple. We are occupiers of spiritual territories and the resisters of the gates of Hell. Some of the weapons of our warfare *are* carnal, but we are also armed with the Sword of the Spirit, until the Spirit of God is placed back upon Israel once again."

"I want to know more," Dominic said matter-of-factly.

"Most people don't, Mr. Moreau," Griffin said and paused. "You should be *absolutely* sure."

"I want to know more, Agent Griffin," Nick said with conviction.

"Then I *want* you to know more as well, Nick," Griffin agreed. "I want to show you all that is behind the curtain, hidden from you, and most of mankind. Come with me and I will show you all you wish to see."

Dominic locked his eyes with Griffin's and nodded his answer.

THE CRYPTO-ZOOLOGISTS CONVENTION

(From the notes of First Agent Christopher Griffin)

Scientific knowledge is no substitute for knowledge of the Creator. Though scientific study has great value, all forms are limited in scope, temporal, and ignorant of the spiritual. Science is possible only within an environment of order and can be conducted only by an orderly being endowed with the ability to understand it. Conducted properly, science is methodical, determined, thoughtful, disciplined—even creative and imaginative—but it can be conducted only because this universe is ordered, allowing such scrutiny. Order never comes from chaos. Order is never an accident. Man, a created being, was designed to be able to scrutinize and comprehend. Science provides important tools, but it is essential to keep them in perspective as merely the tools that reveal the ordered workings of the creation. Science provides natural facts, never Truth, as facts may change but Truth endures. Therefore, measure Truth by the Word of God. There is no other faithful standard.

Statistics and simulations do not qualify as science, and are far lesser in value because within each method or formula is the intent to produce hopeful results which are neither fact nor Truth. They are often a means to validate an agenda.

When rightly applied, science can reveal the majesty of creation, and can point one to Truth, thus exalting the Creator. Applied improperly, it blinds one to majesty, exalts the scientist and the created, and stupefies the one who wields its power without acknowledging the Creator. It can illuminate and reveal the handiwork of the Creator, or boastfully and foolishly reveal the darkness within one's own self.

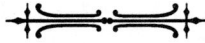

Washington State University, Beasley Coliseum—Present Day, June 19th

In the large auditorium, only one-quarter full, a lone figure stood in the spotlight on the stage. He wore the clothes of an adventurer: an Australian "bush" hat, a brown leather belt, mountaineer boots, and khaki shirt and pants, all fitted to his somewhat chunky frame.

The moderately rotund man at the podium, roughly 45 years of age, looked out upon his audience and smiled. He had been invited to attend the conference as the keynote speaker. The conference would be over soon after his address, but the man wanted to bask in the adoration of his audience as long as possible before he revealed his surprise to them. After all, he believed he'd earned his place at the center stage. This was proven to him by the fact that he had achieved his status by hard work in the field, and had often been published, as well as the fact that he had been a prominent and recurring guest on a major satellite network's channel for the show *Monster Hunters*. But more to the point, it was he who was chosen to be the bearer of the "surprise." The man: none other than Malcolm Carson, "crypto-zoologist at large," who had received generous applause as he entered the stage and now was ready to speak.

"My friends and colleagues," his voice echoed across the excessively expansive room, "thank you for having me. I welcome you all to the final day of the fifteenth annual convention of the S.I.U.—Scientific Investigations into the Unknown. Thanks also to Washington State for hosting this event!"

Of course, hearty applause followed. Malcolm raised his hands, and slowly lowered them to quell the noise so that he might begin his speech. The first day of the convention had seen the largest crowd, but that was the day for enthusiasts to get autographs and souvenirs, and to dress in weird costumes and view displays. It was more of a circus on day one, rather than a conference. The second day had a smaller crowd and was filled with lectures and workshops. The final day offered assurances that only the "serious and engaged" would be in attendance since most of the hoopla had passed. The crowd was calming down, so Malcolm began.

*"**Vindication!**"* Malcolm shouted passionately. The crowd went silent, and he left them so for a few moments before he began anew. "Vindication is coming! Today, with all of our cell-phone cameras, video recorders, our growing populations, satellite imaging, and the World Wide Web-cams, I expect it is soon that we shall have the evidence we need for vindication of what others consider to be a pseudoscience," the man spoke confidently.

"Yes, vindication is important, but not for selfish reasons." Though that statement was in reality a lie, it was not a conscious one. "It is so that the scientific community can accept us as the true scientists we have always been, and rather, that they may join our ranks, to which we would graciously welcome them." More applause at that, and he paused again to allow it.

"My doctorate and years of experience are not enough to bring the mainstream into our fold, nor are all of our degrees and experiences combined." He stretched his hand out to the audience, palm up, and panned it across the crowd. He was a competent speaker, but concerning gesticulation, he was somewhat stiff; perhaps he was just naturally ungraceful.

"The preponderance of physical evidence is just around the corner, and immutable evidence will follow, but it will take all of our efforts to bring the *truth* to light!" The audience gave their approval and voiced their agreement with him, while some simply clapped their hands; the few jaded media representatives present took a note or two and looked on, wishing for something newsworthy.

"My friends, *science* is the key to unlocking the unknown. It has always been so. It is no secret that we, the investigators of scientific truth, search for what is hidden, though it may presently be evident only through witnesses, influences, and indirect proof. After all, DNA was believed to exist before the double-helix structure was discovered. The quark was hidden from man for many years, but was known to exist by its influences and indirect evidences, and the same can be said for the Higgs boson—the 'God Particle,' that was all but obtained at CERN."

He paused again, receiving many nods and positive feedback from the audience, though he knew he was "preaching to the choir." During that pause, and on cue, a silver screen was lowered behind Malcolm and it stopped just above and behind his head. As soon as it stopped, the lights were slightly dimmed, and high-resolution images of monsters were projected on the screen for all to see.

"Let's examine what we know about Bigfoot . . . Sasquatch . . . the Yeti . . . the Wendigo . . . the Skunk Ape, the Grey Man, the Yowie, the Boggy Creek Monster, and all that fall in that category based on hominid taxonomy. For clarity's sake, and just for the moment, please allow me to call the genus 'Agnostopithecus,' since we should all be able to agree that we still lack knowledge about these creatures." No contrary voices erupted, though many knew that their silence was acceding to his egotistical takeover of the other terms, but now was not the time to point it out.

"What do we know about the Agnostopitheci? Physically, we know that these hominids are larger than man. They are stronger than man. They have no fear of man . . . on the contrary, they usually inspire great fear in man. They are certainly hirsute. They are witnessed to have piercing eyes. They are usually solitary, but there are many exceptions to that. They have long arms and legs. They are clearly physical because they leave footprints, throw objects, mark their territory, they leave carcasses of their kills, and strike cars, dwellings, and people as well. They've been known to utilize tools. They are omnivorous. And generally, they smell awful." There were many snickers at the last statement, as Malcolm intended there to be.

"We know little about their evolutionary progenitors. Presumably or possibly they stem from the gigantopithecus branch of the familial tree, but we lack conclusive information. Are they our ancestors the Neanderthals? We clearly don't know. Socially, their behavior is sometimes gentle, sometimes hostile. They *seem* to raise or rear their young, and are nurturing protectors of them, but that *is* based upon deduction and deconstruction of the facts. They have been known to vocalize by loud and terrible shouts, screams, grunts, growls, and many and other varied vocalizations and forms of communication. They have been known to knock on trees or rock as a communicative expression. Thus far, they seem to leave none of their dead behind. They are capable of making war . . . ." Murmurs erupted at that.

"Seriously, my fellow crypto-zoologists, their ability to war is demonstrated by existing reported attacks, and they seemed to be coordinated, and this has even become more common. And why not? Bees war with wasps. Ants war. Apes war. In fact, there are many examples in nature excluding man. Yes . . . all of the above examples are evident, and more is known about them . . . but we must always remember that they are *animals* nonetheless! That is the salient and most important fact, as I'll explain." Malcolm knew that some of his comrades held the opinion that these creatures were ghostly manifestations. They believed that they could be supernatural beings. To Malcolm, that was foolish and outside the bounds of pure science.

"Ladies and gentlemen, animals can be captured, whereas 'spirits' cannot. They *can* be captured alive if you are completely prepared for the capture and containment of the beasts. And of equal import, capture is possible only *if* you happen to *be there* to make the capture, when *they are there* to be captured. Most of our study and individual excursions are to *witness* the animal; however, I say that a live *capture* of an Agnostopithecus *must* be attempted, and *must* be our collective goal. Even the acquisition of a dead specimen would be nearly as valuable. Obviously, I'm not suggesting shooting one unless it is in self-defense, but I believe that we can all agree that a specimen must be acquired as evidence.

"I know some of you have other foci. I too acknowledge that I've spent my time divided by the search for other crypto-animalia. Perhaps you've seen me on the show *Monster Hunters*?" He plugged his TV show shamelessly. "But I believe it is of the utmost import that we *unite* for a single cause. I believe that for vindication's sake, of the science we hold dear, and for the furtherance of the study, we must narrow our focus, for a period of time anyway, and that focus must be squarely upon the Agnostopithecus." The last statement evoked a new flurry of murmurs . . . some agreeing and some clearly dissenting. Malcolm raised his hands to quell the noise.

"I know there are many here invested in other proofs and scientific studies at this time. I do not diminish their value. I know there are literally hundreds of ongoing crypto-zoological studies all over the world. But not only do I suggest a unity of study with you, my esteemed colleagues, for a time anyway, but I suggest something greater. I have a proposal for you that I wish you to consider seriously . . . ." Malcolm allowed a pregnant pause. "I want to hire most, if not all, of you for a two-year excursion, and I presently have the means to offer complete funding for such an extended proposal." Silence and rapt attention were what Malcolm expected from his last statement, and he was not disappointed.

"I'm getting ahead of myself," he said, and the crowd returned from "at attention" to more of an "at ease" as they relaxed. But they clearly gave him indications of desiring to hear more from him. "I have been approached by a well-known petroleum concern, with an offer that I believe is our best chance, in the near future, to locate and capture a living specimen of Agnostopithecus. This benefactor wants to beef up its public image, and a large part of that will be having its own unique mascot—the Sasquatch!"

There was uproar in the audience. First, the notion of "full funding" was of universal encouragement, but the capture of a live Agnostopithecus as a mascot! Well, the notion of it was initially insulting. Commercializing and literally capitalizing on a captured specimen would be nothing short of a circus, not a scientific endeavor. The reporters, on the other hand, finally had something interesting to make note of, and they did so with fervor. Malcolm raised his hands and visually tamped down the audience until it was again silent.

"Let me explain our thinking, please. I know that the first impression is an affront to you, as it was initially to me. I understand, and was of the same opinion as you . . . initially anyway. But this makes perfect sense if you will allow me to lead you to the conclusion I've arrived at." He waited for them to listen, not just hear him.

"My experience, and I think I can get your agreement on this, is that our searches have been conducted only on a small scale—some might even categorize them as 'weekend excursions.' The duration and scope of any of our individual searches has been extremely limited, highly disparate, and uniquely uncoordinated. I'm at Pike's Peak, Colorado, searching for an Agnostopithecus, while Stuart Granger there is on the moors in England searching for the Beast of Bodmin, while Jason Sheffield's team is in Point Pleasant, West Virginia, examining the evidence of the Mothman, while John Cosworth and his team are in Canada on Lake Okanagan studying the legend of the Ogopogo. That is the fact, well sometimes anyway, because another fact is that we spend too much time out of the field, waiting for sightings, planning an investigation, and arriving too late. Too late! There are many divergent studies, many divergent teams, limited time, limited resources, too long after the fact of a sighting due to logistics, lack of manpower and funding. And let's face it, we come home with very, very few success stories. This is the reality, my friends." He waited to see whether they could face the truth. It appeared that reluctantly, dejectedly, they did.

"Why is this? You know as well as I do. It is because of, first and foremost, funding . . . and more, a lack of singleness of purpose with no unity between us because of another reality we must face . . . we are competing against each other. Sure, we publish and share our findings, and I'm not saying that competition is necessarily a bad thing, but between the sum total of our efforts, we are not advancing the cause." The truth was undeniable, but hard to admit.

"However, I am of the belief that there is a way for success in the totality of 'us.' Have each of you ever asked yourself, '*What would I do if I actually had the opportunity to capture a live Bigfoot?*' We go out on each excursion without the thought of capture as we only want to capture it on film, or find a carcass of a dead Agnostopithecus. *But we fail each time!* We must be geared for something greater than what our individual efforts can achieve. Where is our commitment to bringing home the proof, instead of ancillary evidence? Where is our resolve to finally put our expertise and ambition toward undeniable substantiation of what we've invested our lives in?

"I suggest that to properly find what has, until now, been *unfindable*, we must have the funding, the manpower, the equipment, and the sheer and unified *will* to find it. Science itself is an act of the will, from inception to conclusion. With a unified will, in a well-funded, extended-duration, single-focused mission of discovery, capture, and study, we can achieve what has heretofore been impossible. Now what university or zoo is going to be able to fund such an initiative? There are none with the will, and none with the resources . . . absolutely none. What about the entertainment industry . . . they would surely be interested and could provide substantial support, but only if we already had possession of a Sasquatch. I can tell you that *Monster Hunters* has an annual budget of only fifteen million dollars when they have abundant advertisers. That would not fund this type of venture for a single month, let alone two years.

"There are few industries and private concerns that could fund this scope of a venture with money to spare, and a vested commercial interest in it. Ford, GM, BMW, Infiniti—none of these has a vehicle named Sasquatch, nor indeed wants one. Microsoft, Google, Apple . . . no interest. But one industry has literally hundreds of millions invested in advertising alone, quarterly, and has money to spare. The petroleum industry! I know it sounds like we are prostituting science with such an arrangement as I've been offered, and we are not speaking of De Laurentiis's *King Kong* here . . . . But think, my friends, think. Who or what organization could come close to this type of excursion? Only a G-7 government or Russia or China could come close to the type of funding that would guarantee success."

It was true. Never had there been an expedition on the scale of what Malcolm was proposing, and never had there been financial backing for an undertaking of this magnitude.

"Now ask yourself, what single taxonomical crypto-zoological animal has been seen on six out of seven continents? We know that there is not a single creature that is more prevalent than the Agnostopithecus, and that makes it the clear choice for the hunt! This deal I've struck provides everything we need, even things we don't need, and guarantees us exclusive study rights, in a facility that they are building at this moment, and care rights that will also be funded beyond the two-year period, and as long as the creature lives. All they want is to have trademark ownership of a living specimen and freedom to film it in safe captivity, under strict humane rules, using it as their mascot. All other rights are ours!"

Silence.

"Ponder it, my friends . . . ***ponder it***!" He gave a final pause, knowing that the conclusion would be embraced in the light of logic, and sound reason, even if some might consent only by consideration of the financial "bottom line."

"***Vindication is on the table!***" he proclaimed. "And that is what we require for the future of our field!" And with that, there were cheers and applause, lasting for a full minute.

"To conclude, I will open the floor for a question-and-answer period. I have handouts for all of you to scrutinize. I *am* blatantly soliciting your support, offering guaranteed employment with benefits, and I encourage you to join the team. Again, this is not to disparage any of your favorite or personal studies or sponsors. That is to say that all the studies are of import, but with one single complete and undeniable success, we can find all the funding we need afterwards from many other sources, and perhaps focus on every other crypto-zoological subject as a unit, a discovery *'force'* to be reckoned with, if you will. Let me also add that this team will make history, and its fame will endure beyond our lifetime! Thank you for having me, and now I open the floor to discussion."

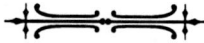

⊹≕⊱⊰≕⊹

Before any questions there was another round of applause and Malcolm absorbed it radiantly, triumphantly. Malcolm fielded many questions before the evening died down, and in the end he was extremely satisfied at the resounding responses he received. As the crowd was thinning out, and as he had left the stage to be on the floor among his peers, he was approached by a man wearing a brown suit. The man was tall and lean and looked studious and very serious. He caught Malcolm's attention, and Malcolm excused himself from the waning discussion he was involved in and walked over to the man.

Malcolm extended his hand. "Malcolm Carson."

The man shook his hand and replied, "Jim Tenor, State Department." He showed Malcolm his ID, which was quite official.

Malcolm raised an eyebrow and said, "State Department, um . . . to what do I owe the pleasure?"

"I'm here unofficially to ask you a few questions. Questions that may have official implications, depending upon the information you have. Can we speak in private?" Tenor asked.

"I have a few people to talk to before I leave, but I'm going to eat dinner at the Bob Evans down the road from here. Why don't you follow me there and we can talk. Is that private enough?" Malcolm asked.

"That will do. I'll wait for you outside by your car and will follow you there."

"I'll be about half an hour," Malcolm said, and he rejoined his peers, somewhat perplexed.

Time passed rapidly for Malcolm as conversation moved from topic to topic and each was given due discussion, and question upon question was answered. It quickly came time to bid his peers adieu. Malcolm gathered his notes, sign-up sheets, handouts, and other possessions, put them in order, filled his briefcase, and made his exit as cleanly as possible. He wished his daughter would have been available to assist him at this event. He was busy enough just as the speaker, and all the more having to take names and sign books. Fortunately, he was able to have a table with a college-loaned computer available for anyone who wanted to order his books. The PC afforded online sales from his website, thus not eliminating the need to lug his laptop around, hope for a Wi-Fi connection, or carry his own supply of books.

Thank God for the World Wide Web and PayPal, he thought. Of course, on his way out of the auditorium, others wanted to start conversations with him, but he made it clear that although he would like to discuss more, it was time for him to go.

Malcolm exited the building and found his car with an apparently patient Jim Tenor, from the State Department. "Bob Evans," Malcolm reminded the man, and both entered their vehicles and pulled onto the sparsely trafficked street that would take them to their destination. Upon reaching the restaurant, they parked side by side, both exiting their vehicles, with Tenor now carrying a briefcase as they entered the establishment. They were seated by a young lady with a "Hi, I'm Becky" name tag. She led them to their table and passed them menus, which they glanced at briefly, at which point Malcolm ordered the Southern-fried chicken dinner with a Dr. Pepper, and Tenor ordered coffee, black. Becky was off to the next table, and Malcolm looked at Tenor, now prepared to discuss what seemed so important to the "unofficial" visitor from the State Department.

"What would you like to know, Mr. Tenor?" Malcolm inquired.

Tenor set his briefcase on the table and opened it. He pulled out a file folder, opening it but keeping the contents from Malcolm's view.

"What can you tell me about the organization called Knightlight?" he asked.

"What?" replied Malcolm, "Night light? Like the child's room night light?"

"No, Knightlight beginning with a *K*, not an *N*, Mr. Carson. It is an organization that is funded, at least in part, by taxpayer dollars, and credentialed with official State Department authority. It is an organization that I am trying to nail down to determine whether Federal monies are being misappropriated."

"Well, I suppose that is your business, but I assure you that I've never heard of the organization, and will be glad not to take up any more of your time," Malcolm said, ready to send the man packing.

"Can you tell me anything about the man in this picture?" Tenor pulled an 8-by-10 photo from the folder and handed it to Malcolm.

"Why, it's me, of course," Malcolm said, since it was a still of one of his expeditions.

"Look behind you, over your left shoulder, Mr. Carson . . . the man standing behind you."

Malcolm turned in his seat and looked over his left shoulder, and then back at Tenor. "Just kidding," he said, and then he looked at the picture and studied the face of the man behind his image.

"Well, I remember his face. In fact, I've definitely seen him before, but I can't tell you who he is."

"I already know *who* he is. I want to know what his relationship is to you. The photo you're holding was taken at fourteen-thousand feet, in the Himalayas in 2009, Mr. Carson. Do you remember that expedition?"

"Yes, Tenor, the Yeti expedition; I remember it well. I suppose he was one of our set techs. The studio sends a team for cameras, lighting, makeup, and so on, sometimes up to ten men as crew when we travel. Why? Is he in some kind of trouble? Smuggling, perhaps?"

"I have no comment to share with you apart from saying that the man in the photo is a Knightlight employee and that the organization is being looked at for possible financial malfeasance, unless, of course, you can level any charges of your own. So . . . can you?"

"I don't know anything about the organization of which you speak, nor anything about the man in the photo. Have you contacted the organization directly? That's where I would have started," offered Malcolm.

"Investigations tend to announce themselves, Mr. Carson, providing ample time for the hiding and revising of information pertinent to the investigation. Sometimes it is best that they begin unobtrusively, silently. I am canvassing the background of the staff at this time as a pre-investigation, a '*potential*,' if you will. Again, I remind you that this is not a *formal* investigation . . . yet." Tenor reached for the photo in Malcolm's hand, placed it back in the file, pulled out another photo, and handed it to Malcolm.

"Do you recognize this photo, Mr. Carson?" Tenor asked.

"I do. It is a photo from my book, *Monsters Alive*, published three years ago. I was trying to portray my adventurous side in this photo, but I think the camera added about twenty pounds to my face here. I've never liked this photo. I was on location in Wyoming at Grand Teton National Park, with my crew and other biologists in the background setting up camp . . . . Oh . . . I see . . . that man is back there in this one too. Funny, I've never really noticed him before . . . but I have literally thousands of photos in my publications, whether published in book or magazine form."

"I find it hard to believe that you have *never noticed him before*, Mr. Carson. These are photos from *your expeditions*. Are you trying to tell me that you don't know the men around you in a group of no more than twenty? I'll ask you once more, while this is still an unofficial inquiry: What do you know about this man, and what do you know about the organization known as Knightlight?"

"First, I don't appreciate your tone, Mr. Tenor. Second, I am *very* engaged and occupied during my excursions. I have a singular focus toward scientific discovery, and I devote my full attention to it. I have data to analyze, scripts to read and edit, camera shots to set up, trails to traverse, tracks to study, information to gather, hides to set up, and a very tight time-window to work within. To be blunt, I don't have the time or inclination to fraternize with the hired help, so once again, I'll reiterate that I do not know that man, or anything regarding this . . . Knightlight. So I bid you good day."

"Very well, Mr. Carson. Good day to you." Tenor gathered his photo, placed it in the folder, and placed that in his briefcase, closing it and locking it. He rose, and saw Becky coming with his coffee. He tossed three dollars on the table and turned to leave.

"Just one question I have for you, Mr. Tenor." Malcolm prevented Tenor's clean exit.

"What?" Tenor asked impatiently as he turned around.

"What is that man's name?"

"Dominic Moreau," he said, and left, as Malcolm pondered the name.

4

THE WITCH QUEEN

(From the notes of First Agent Christopher Griffin)

There were two trees in the Garden of Eden, and everything God made was good. One tree was the tree of life, while the other was the tree of the knowledge of good and evil. They were real, substantial, but both represented choices and consequences, though neither was anything but good. This was the pre-test for mankind, but the fact that man failed this test was no surprise to God, as He knew that one of His angels was going to cheat. God wanted both angel and man to fellowship with Him forever, but also had something to show the angels regarding faith:

First, that there is always a choice to obey God, or not. Second, that obedience is an act of faith. Third, that sin isn't found in the severity of a crime, it is simply in the fact of a crime, or rather, to break any law is to break <u>The Law</u>. Fourth, that although faith can prevent one from choosing sin, Love can overcome sin after the fact. Fifth, that redemption comes at a price, and someone must pay it. Sixth, that redemption can be received only by faith. Seventh, that a people, blind to

God, separate from Him, could have faith in Him and trust Him, while one-third of His angels, ever before His Loving Presence, could dare to have no faith in Him.

Sin is the nature of man, as a result of the Fall, and Evil is ever attractive to him. If the tree of the knowledge of good and evil were not beautiful, desirable, it would have been easy to avoid, regardless of how one was enticed. Sin is pleasurable for a season, until the consequences come. Sin hates righteousness, because righteousness causes sin to see itself for what it is. Sin hates the mirror of truth.

Rural Montgomery County, Indiana—
Present Day, June 21st

Montgomery County has varied and multilayered "underground subcultures," one of which Darlene Campbell belonged to. Darlene was a witch, plain and simple. She called herself a child of nature, a daughter of Ishtar, Astarte, Ostera, and Eostre, but she was no less a witch. She communicated with the ethereal elements of this world and believed that she had the power to command the forces of nature. She believed that she was a conduit to Semiramis, and even Lilith. She was the Queen of her Wiccan order, and her secret name was Ba'ala Semir.

Darlene, at the age of 46 now, had long rusty-brown-colored hair, or as she called it "cinnamon"-colored hair, but some of it was artificially colored so the grey could not be seen. She kept her hair neatly behind her in a ponytail, unless she was clothed in her witching robes, and then she'd let it flow over her shoulders and down her back. She was reasonably attractive and graceful but she definitely had a dominating personality. On normal days, she dressed in long tie-dyed skirts that hid many mystical tattoos on her legs and thighs, and she always wore sandals except in the winter. She often wore earth-tone halter tops, revealing a few other, more *mainstream* tattoos and lots of cleavage, and on her left hand, she sported a black daisy wedding ring that was tattooed on her ring finger. Only a very select few knew to whom she was married.

To the outside world, Darlene seemed just a small-business woman who dabbled in New Age products and must have forgotten that Woodstock was nearly 50 years behind her. She made and sold homeopathic remedies, ointments, oils, candles, potions, and *herbs*, though not necessarily completely legal herbs, from her home. Unbeknownst to the general populace, her home doubled weekly as a temple for the coven over which she presided. There were forty-seven solid members of her coven, with many others who were yet to be committed members, but hers was the largest coven in Montgomery County, and recently she noted how it was growing in popularity.

Darlene knew that there is a fundamental desire within people: They want to believe in, and belong to, something greater than themselves. They want to commune with something that transcends their mortal beings, that confirms and affirms their existence in this world, giving meaning to their soul. Christians call this a "God-shaped *hole* in one's heart" that desperately needs God to fill the void, but usually the godless will try to fill it with anything and everything *but* God in the pursuit of fleeting happiness. Men settle for far less than God's unending joy.

Darlene knew that people wished for comforting knowledge of what lay beyond their mortality, *apart* from Biblical truths, so they would not feel the guilt of *sin*. Truth sheds light on sin, and that is always uncomfortable. When sin is exposed, a choice becomes evident: to continue in it or repent from it. Nobody needs to be instructed in *how* to sin, because it comes naturally in this fallen world. It is, sadly, the new *norm*, and it abides with *all*. And when sin is exposed, it is easier to run to the comfort of darkness than to face the light . . . ask any cockroach. Darlene knew that men want to hide their sin. She also knew that men want to find purpose in this life, and above all, they desire to be in control of it. Men want to seize destiny with both hands and shape it to serve themselves, and she was glad to be their guide. Darlene pointed the *way* for those seekers of easy answers, while lifting herself to a higher plane than the lesser mortals whom she would keep ignorant of her deeper wisdom and designs.

Darlene communed with the spirits, and they spoke to her increasingly. They whispered secrets to her, and promised more secrets to come. She now knew things about people, their deep and dark secrets . . . exploitable secrets. She knew what people did in private, when they thought they were alone, when they thought the dark solitude hid them. Her knowledge gave her power over men and women alike. When the need arose, she exercised her power with skill and authority. In all she did, whether it was manipulating the lives of others, casting spells and enchantments, blackmailing some, or murdering others, she convinced herself that it was all for the greater good. But she was a blind guide, not seeing the true ends to her means. In complete ignorance, she did not acknowledge those facts, or let them stop her as she exercised her free will. After all, she was the self-proclaimed "Prophetess of Balance," bringing harmony to this county, perhaps farther, and she believed that the future would take care of itself. Time would reveal to her which course her life would take, but she could not see the road to Hell upon which she traveled. She knew of others all over the planet who had similar desires, aspirations, and abilities as she, but she believed that these elitists could be surpassed, conquered, and subjugated with her singleness of devotion to her art and practice. She felt sure she had the edge above all others on those terms.

Like most people in this world, Darlene was her own champion in the narrative of her life. Few in their own narrative ever perceive themselves to be evil, even if they are. Darlene would never entertain the notion that what she practiced was Satanic, per se. She saw herself as a master of elemental forces, which were inherently neither evil nor good, but simply energies to be tapped, trapped, or sapped, and conformed to her will. She believed and lived by the Aleister Crowleyism: "Do what thou wilt." But more, she saw herself as the leader of a new harmonious blend of many religions, compatible even with the philosophy of evolution because only the truly evolved could master the elements. Her faith, she was convinced, was harmonious with all religions on some level at least, with the single exception of Biblical Christianity. She knew her enemy, and though she thought herself to be an illuminated being, she lacked understanding that she was at war with the Light.

Like most people, Darlene justified herself in ignorance of what true justification is, and in complete ignorance of Truth. She saw herself as a spirit of love, not knowing that True Love hates what is evil, and defends His children from it. On the other hand, but never on equal terms, evil hates the children of Love in complete defiance of Truth, though not always in ignorance of it. God is Love. Yes; but He is also

Truth and Justice, and so much more. Yet one thing more that Darlene did not know is that Truth is a sword against the hardened lies of evil, and though evil has an end, Truth will outlast it eternally.

Today, Darlene was preparing for the Summer Solstice ritual, a "high" day on her list of Wiccan "holidays." She would have full attendance at the site of the ritual, and as a bonus, the moon would be full. The best part, in her thinking anyway, was that the spirits had spoken a promise to her. They said this very night she would summon a visitor who would teach her in the ancient ways of power and deep magic. She knew that the blood of the moon was best, and tonight, there would be blood. She began to hum to herself as she prepared her ritual "spices." Her humming was an incantation in itself. She was a devoted practitioner of the occult, and all aspects of her life took the form of some incantation, or worship, or communion with the spirits of the world around her, whether eating, cooking, casting, sleeping, or bathing—even her sensual expression was part of worship. Her worship helped in the renewal of her spiritual energies. She was a true believer, which made her one of the most dangerous persons on the planet: a self-consumed and focused weapon ready to be unleashed.

Darlene's phone rang as the aroma of her preparation wafted up to her nostrils. She inhaled deeply, and smiled. The phone rang again. She knew who was calling, so she refocused her thoughts and put on the mask of joyous harmony. She had many masks and they all served her well.

"Light, Herbs, and Spices! Darlene speaking," she answered.

"This is Taylor, Darlene. Can you speak coven?"

"Yes, Bradley, Only the spirits are with me," Darlene said, giving the go-ahead that she was free to discuss all matters Wiccan. She inhaled the fragrance of her making, again.

"The gatherings tonight will be at moonrise, as you requested, the Thirteen know that you want to meet them in the Shades Glen, and I have told everyone else that the sensual worship will be on your property in the field. But I don't have an offering. Are you sure one will be provided?"

"Bradley, you insignificant moron," is what she wanted to say. However, she answered with an extrasweet, "Bradley, my cherished disciple, tonight is not your responsibility, it is mine. We will have all that we need. You've just confirmed all that you needed to, so be there in your sacred robes, and we will partake in the beautiful power of the earth-spirits this night."

"Yes, my Priestess, we will have full and formal attendance tonight. I look forward to it, my Queen," Bradley said.

"As do I, my cherished disciple. May the high goddess enlighten and protect you. Goodbye," she said, and pressed the "end call" button without waiting for his benediction.

Bradley Taylor was a midlevel wizard, but not progressing in demonstrable illumination, influence, and power, as Darlene demanded of her higher-level councilors, priests, and enchanters. He was a high-level sycophant and toady though, which disgusted her in many ways, and though he was not short on physical attraction, *that* can only get you so far. Still, he was loyal to Darlene, and reasonably served his purpose. But Darlene had intentions of eliminating all her followers who were not spirit-filled and those who demonstrated weakness in the summoning of power. All that would be at some point in the future. She had several disposable worshipers. She wanted her coven to wield power and shake the very heavens; weaklings need not apply.

Darlene stopped herself from dwelling on Bradley, as those thoughts were negative energy. She closed her eyes and mentally washed herself of him, to focus on the task at hand. She took a few cleansing breaths, and mentally reined in her spirit. When she opened her eyes, she smiled, returned to her brewing spices, and continued the musical enchantment over them. She let her mind drift forward to tonight. Tonight would be a turning point for her coven, and she relished the thought.

5

GENESIS 6:4

(Excerpt 1 from *History of the Conflict*, by Knightlight Director Bensington Redwood)

In the beginning of this universe, God, the Creator of All Things, created space-time and stretched it forth, and He created particles within the framework of space-time. And the elements were unshaped, and darkness covered the bottomless pit created for and reserved for the devil and his angels. And the Holy Spirit of God hovered over the surface of the transitory things which He created. And God, by His Holy Word, spoke, "Let there be Light," and the universe was energized and illuminated in every desired way. And God saw what He had created so far, and declared that it was good, perfect . . . flawless. And God established limits to light and the lack thereof. And God gave names to the light and the darkness that we may know their meaning—Day and Night. And God established a reference for time, and all this was done to set the framework for life in this universe. All this was done on the first day.

The above is paraphrased by me, but my objective is to demonstrate the Author's brilliance within the phenomenological language of the text of the first five verses in the Holy Word of God. There is such depth in so few words. It can be fully appreciated by a genius and a child at the same time, and with the same understanding of the Author's intent. The Author truly knows about that which he speaks. After the six-day event we call "Creation," all that God created was good and perfect . . . until a freewill decision was made to reject faith in God's Word, at which point the perfect creation fell. It has never been "good and perfect" since. Today is most certainly not the key to the past, as the evolutionists' maxim states, for today is evil, and the past was clearly not. The earth was cursed after God's Word was rejected, and death and separation from God prevailed, yet for roughly fourteen-hundred years God extended mercy toward mankind until man's ubiquitous sin forced God into judgment. During that time, the sons of God saw that the daughters of men were beautiful, so they contaminated the genetic line of mankind with their spawn. The sons of God were demonic beings, formerly angelic beings, who once stood before the very face of God, and still had no faith in Him. Faith and trust in God's Word, with thanksgiving, humility, and mercy to others, are the keys to the Kingdom of God. God exalts His Word even above His own name. These beings had deposed God's created master of the earth, man, and began their plan to usurp the world that man inhabited. Thus arose the "mighty men" of old, men of renown, the giants, the terrors, the monsters . . . both then . . . and afterward.

Pine Hills Nature Preserve, 17 miles SW of Crawfordsville, Indiana—Present Day, June 21st

In the summer, Pine Hills is green, lush, and secluded. On sunny days, light streams down from the canopy of leaves high above onto the wood-chip paths and abundant undergrowth. It is one of Indiana's secret treasures. Few people walk the quiet, tranquil trails compared to its adjoining sister-park, Shades. Still, hikers, hippies, conservationists, families, and youth have visited it enough to warrant the installation of wooden stairs over the shale paths that had become worn by erosion and the treading of man. On any given day, Pine Hills averages about thirty visitors. It could actually be more than that, but many ignore penning their name in the logbook at the park's entrance.

Pine Hill was the *first* nature preserve in Indiana, and is best known to this day for its unique landmark, the Devil's Backbone—the natural and narrow one-hundred-foot-high rock ridge with a carving of the devil's face on the shale path.

Pine Hills is overshadowed, literally, by Shades State Park and close neighbor Turkey Run State Park, concerning notoriety and popularity. It's the most primitive and least visited of the three parks, and all three are connected by Sugar Creek and by dense forest. It is there that Bill Donovan, web-designer and amateur nature photographer, chose to take his girlfriend, Cindy Stroud, for an outing on a warm late-evening hike. It was approaching Independence Day and Bill wanted to get some snapshots of the woodland before crowds of hikers overtook the parks. The time indicated that it was a half an hour before sunset, but that actually *is* sunset in the forest. The nature preserve closed at dusk. This quiet evening, Bill and Cindy walked the wooded trails alone, as far as they could tell.

"Bill, can't we rest for a bit?" requested Cindy softly. The hike was not something this city girl was used to. Oh, she could shop for hours, but the floors in the Tippecanoe Mall in Lafayette were even, and nothing like the trail they were on now.

"Sure," Bill replied, just as gently. Fauna are skittish at noise and Bill was hoping to get some high-resolution photos if possible, and if the light held out. "I can take a few shots before it gets too dark. Go ahead and get your second wind."

"I wish I'd worn my tennis shoes, instead of these new hiking boots. I should have broken these in before today. My feet are killing me," Cindy said.

"Take them off and rub your feet. You might want to check for any rocks that have snuck in." Bill moved about twenty-five feet away from Cindy to get to the edge of the trees where a glen was visible. Perhaps he might capture a deer grazing on the other side.

"Sneaked in," Cindy corrected.

"Sneak, snank, snuck." replied Bill, to demonstrate that he'd use whatever word he wished, even if it didn't exist.

"This place is pretty, Bill," Cindy said as she began to unlace her left boot. "We should have brought a blanket and a bottle of wine," she called quietly to him so as not to scare anything.

"That's strange," said Bill, looking around.

"What, the wine or the blanket idea?" Cindy asked.

"No . . . listen . . . ," Bill said, and she did.

"I don't hear anything," she said, but then she did hear something. She heard a low, deep growl, almost imperceptible. "You mean your stomach?"

"No . . . ," he called back to her quietly, "I mean I don't hear any birds, or squirrels, no woodpeckers . . . nothing but the slight breeze."

"And your stomach," Cindy added. "Maybe we scared them?" Then the breeze shifted and Cindy added, "Did you just fart?"

"What?"

"I said your stomach is growling, and I think you just polluted the planet."

"Um . . . ." Bill listened to himself for a second. "No it isn't, and no I didn't. But if I ever do, it is only to add an *air of suspense*," he said with a smile.

"I heard it, and just smelt it. That doesn't mean I dealt it." She listened, and the growl was a little louder, a little clearer . . . and then she realized that it was coming from behind her, not from Bill. Cindy froze. "*Bill . . . ,*" she said quietly, but desperately, and he turned toward her.

As Bill looked above and behind Cindy, his face registered awe, then sudden horror. Behind her, in the shadow of the tree next to her, was a nine-and-a-half-foot nightmare. Fear gripped his entire being. What Bill saw was covered in shaggy brownish-black hair, and though it was in shadow, it was clear that this thing had bright yellow eyes, and its lips were parted in a . . . a *smile*? No, Bill noted somewhere in his mind that there was nothing friendly-looking about that grin, and monsters don't smile; it had to be a snarl. The snarl widened to reveal deadly looking teeth.

"Run!" Bill yelled, and he threw his camera as hard as he could at the monster's face, but faster than Bill could blink, the monster raised his right arm and easily deflected the camera.

Cindy got up with her left boot untied, but she lunged away from the tree near where she had been sitting, and made a mad dash on the trail away from whatever was behind her. Mentally she was trying not to lose her boot or trip on her laces. She had not seen what was behind her, but she did not need to know because if Bill had such a reaction to what he had seen, then she didn't *want* to see it.

The monster moved *fast* toward Bill. Seeing Cindy take off, Bill started to run in the opposite direction so the creature would chase him instead, but he had taken only perhaps five steps when he was yanked backward and tossed even faster in the opposite direction. He was panicked and dazed, and as he saw the creature standing over him in the fading light, he kicked, rolled, and tried to get up, but was suddenly grasped and lifted by his neck, by a huge and rough hand. A strong and massive arm pulled Bill close to its owner's face. Struggle as he might, the grip of the hand was unbreakable.

The monster *was* smiling. Its breath was rancid; its teeth were aged, but menacingly sharp. To Bill's astonishment, the terrible beast spoke. It was the last voice he would ever hear on this earth.

"ἄχρηστος," spoke the deep and coarse voice, and the sound of it was "*anaxios*" in Bill's ears. The meaning was simply the word "useless."

Bill did not know what "*anaxios*" meant, or what language it might be; all he knew was that he was helpless and mute before the beast. He felt the pressure on his neck increase and the hot, rotten breath of the creature against his face. His eyes bulged and his tongue swelled, and then he felt and heard his neck snap, at which point his limp body was released and allowed to drop to the ground, face to the side, his body completely paralyzed below the neck. His throat and the rocks against his face were the only things he could now feel, and it was excruciating. He saw huge feet moving away from him, back toward the path, in the direction of Cindy. He started to see stars, but he could not feel that his lungs were crying out for air. The sound of the creature's heavy footfalls faded as it pursued Cindy, and then was replaced by the sound of his fading pulse within his ears. Bill started to cry, but his vision was now dimming. He hoped someone would find him in time to save him, but he knew he was finished. He hoped Cindy had time to get to the car, but he doubted it. His mouth moved to speak, but he uttered nothing. His conscious thought changed to images only. He saw the face of his mother, the time she opened her birthday gift when Bill was 6 years old; then he saw his childhood friend Kenny, when they had a sleepover in his treehouse. Then images came to him so fast he could not spend a thought on any. The images became faster, but fainter, and then faded away. Increasing darkness engulfed Bill's sight until it completely went black. His heart slowed, and then stopped.

Cindy had run in sheer panic, covering at least 150 yards before the creature began its pursuit. She had just reached the long wooden stairway that would take her up out of the valley, and onto the path toward the park's still-distant entrance. The stairs were placed so people could more easily traverse the rock face without eroding it further, and prevented hikers from sliding down. They were an obstacle to Cindy, not a comfort. She chose to climb the hill on all fours, which was faster than taking the stairs. Regrettably, it took only a few moments for the monster to close the distance, and as she clambered up the hill, halfway up now, she looked down, and at its base was the giant black, overwhelming presence of the monster. She screamed. The sight nearly caused her legs to buckle, but she would not let go of the hill, or let herself slip. The "thing" just stood there staring at her, motionless. Fear and despair tightened in her breast, as she knew Bill was not going to come to her rescue. Instantly, instinctively, she put her every effort into getting up the hill as fast as she could scramble.

Cindy neared the top and was dismayed when she saw the monster almost at the top itself, taking a different route. She stopped her ascent, turned around, and slid down the hill, trying not to tumble . . . she was only *mostly* successful. As she gained speed toward the bottom, a tree root snagged her left foot, sending her forward and rolling to a stop at the bottom. She was dusty and bruised, but capable of fleeing, or so she thought. The beast ran down the hill at an angle with great speed and agility. Power and ferocity could be seen with every stride it took closer to her. Cindy tried to run, but her legs would not move. The monster snatched her up in his right arm as he overtook her, and it continued to run with Cindy in tow, her feet in the air kicking helplessly. She was absolutely its captive.

"Let go," Cindy screamed, and the monster seemed to chuckle at the command, not slowing its pace. Terror and hopelessness gripped her and held her as tightly as the monster did. Cindy Stroud began crying as she was carried over the hills, through the forest, disappearing from the world she knew.

6

KNIGHTLIGHT

Present Day, June 21st

Dominic Moreau was now older, stronger, and wiser than he'd been when he first interviewed with Agent Griffin. The loss of his wife and daughter years ago haunted him only in his dreams. He knew he would see them in the future when this transitory world no longer held him down. His life had transformed from sorrow, which he believed would dominate him forever, to contentment and purpose, as his heart healed from the deep wounds of the past, and calloused over. In that time he'd recovered his sense of humor, and opened himself up to close friendships. He learned that the Joy of the Lord can be with a man even when the happenings of "happiness" were absent.

Nick had been with Knightlight nearly twenty years now. He had trained hard for many of those, but training never really ended. He had learned much about Knightlight, and the nature of the world around him, and he grew in wisdom and knowledge. He'd also learned combat tactics, stealth tactics, and killing tactics—and what's more, he knew when to use them and when to restrain them. He learned much about politics, and rules and regulations of every aspect of the agency, and more than ever, he trained himself daily in the study of the Word of God. Of equal import, he learned the discipline of prayer and fasting. He was schooled in cults, and the occult, and could spot them and counter them on many terms. He became familiar with his enemy, the principalities and powers of the air, the rulers of darkness in high places. And he was trained in the tearing down of their strongholds, both spiritually and physically. All were preparatory requirements for Knightlight's specialized combat role. He became the exceptional agent that Christopher Griffin expected him to become.

Dominic was not a replacement for Griffin, as Griffin never intended to retire, but he became an experienced "Trinity Agent" and, later, a Trinity Team Leader. In fact, he was now the leader of Strike-Team Bravo, second only to Strike-Team Alpha. Team designation was based on the number of successful and conclusive missions accomplished by the teams. Bravo had almost caught up with Alpha, perhaps supplanting them soon.

Knightlight is an agency that is impossible to simply join. A candidate must be recruited and have an appropriate background that is compatible with Knightlight's mission. The requirements include a complete faith and trust in the Bible with an astute understanding of the authority of sacred Scripture, adding nothing to the Word of God, and never subtracting anything from it. The candidate must know history within a Biblical context, and have an ongoing, growing, and personal relationship with Jesus Christ, as Savior and Lord, that is a way of life, as opposed to a religion. To become an actual full-blown "field agent," prior military training, police training, or Federal Agency law enforcement is mandatory. An agent candidate must also have a personal reason, some direct experience in engagement of the enemy sufficient enough to draw Knightlight's attention.

Nick met all necessary qualifications on that fateful October day in 1994. His probationary period demonstrated to Griffin other important qualities such as wisdom, faithfulness, courage, and even grace, mercy, forgiveness, and love. When Nick was found to be in error, even in sin, as all men are capable of and all susceptible to, he repented, sought forgiveness, and demonstrated the desire to let the Word of God change him and transform him.

Dominic had thrown himself into his work from the start. Getting beyond the loss of his family, he found a renewed faith in the Lord. Now he understood his purpose in this world. He was committed daily to take the fight to the enemy, or at least hold the line. He knew the enemy, and the various faces the enemy wore. He knew what evil lurked in the hearts of men, because he was aware of the evil in his own heart that would continually surface, and was continually in need of cleansing by the Grace of God. He also knew why the police, the military, the FBI, CIA, or any government agency could not effectively engage their enemy on their own. The war Knightlight was engaged in could not be fought by strength alone. The battle could not be won with any combination of firepower, intelligence gathering, or espionage. It had to begin in prayer, and be led by the Spirit. Sure, there were other secret US initiatives that dealt with other types of *paranormal threats*, but those had nothing to do directly with Jesus Christ. Unfortunately, a few of the secret initiatives were completely antithetical to Christ, because governments, even his, like to cover all bases just in case, and different governing administrations brought their various "virtues and sins" as agendas and policies. Eventually there would have to be a decision that determines what side the United States will be on when it comes down to the final conflict. It does not look good for America, as a Nation, thus far.

The battle must first be engaged on one's knees, before the Lord our God, and the United States Government cannot, will not make *that* a priority. In God We Trust, for far too many, has become just a quaint slogan. Without God, His Word, His Spirit, and His host with you, you might as well be wrestling against shadows, or fighting back a tsunami with your fists. Ill-equipped

67

might as well be unequipped. Without God, the enemy knows the opponents' strategies, their weaknesses, and their fears, and will exploit them all.

In the mind of the enemy, victory is all but assured, unless the power of God is unleashed against it. No government on earth, not even the United States government, can blind, bind, or out-mastermind the enemy, because the adversary is ancient, intelligent, powerful, and spiritual, and the creatures that bullets can hit are never without sinister powers behind them. Implicit in the strategy to confront the enemy, there must be the awareness that mankind is already on the adversary's property; the Gates of Hell are here . . . in the sky, on the ground, extending from the center of the earth to the outermost reaches of this universe. The Nephil-Adam (Ne-fil-A-dom), the very spawn of the enemy themselves, along with the Gadarenos and the *MacLaines*, were the only ones that could be engaged on a physical plane, but even so, they could not be overcome without the Spirit. The MacLaines were the ignorant and blind followers of the enemy, and the Gadarenos were the physical possessions of the demons. Demonic spirits cannot be touched by mortal hands unless they choose to be, and that is usually in the framework of sexual congress, abduction, or possession. All demonic interaction causes harm. But the MacLaines and the Gadarenos are to be pitied, and if willing, rescued. They are to be engaged only philosophically and spiritually, unless by reason of obstruction or self-defense . . . but all bets were off when engaging the demon spawn.

Nick had crossed over to the higher side of middle age, but still could be mistaken for 30-something. His hair loss was the only real sign that his age was above, say 35, and that was what motivated him to keep his hair shaved down to stubble. He had a tight beard and mustache that he would shave away only when he needed to act extensively with military credentials. Middle-aged, yes, but Nick was fit and mentally sharp, and his skill and experience gave him a leadership advantage over just about everyone in the agency.

Dominic's Knightlight call sign was "Rock." It was a name not derived, as some thought, from the movie *Rocky*, though Dominic was predominantly Italian. Rock was a call sign that he himself chose from a specific episode of the television series *Mystery Science Theater 3000*, an extremely comedic series that he had become fond of in the latter part of the '90s and beyond. Nick had gained two very close friends while making Knightlight his life's work, and these fellow agents were now in his "trinity," and under his command.

Michael Cavor, one of Nick's closest friends, was an intellectual and did not initially look like a dangerous man. Mike, however, was an explosives expert, a communications genius, and an unparalleled sniper. He gave himself the call sign of "Tick," which some thought related to the "tick" of a time bomb, as was his expertise, but it was actually derived from his favorite cartoon series, *The Tick*, also of the '90s.

"There are some cartoons best appreciated by adults," Mike would often say. Nick agreed. Nick originally wanted to call Mike "Egon." But Mike, rightly so, did not want a moniker that tied him to a worldly "paranormal investigator," because *ghosts don't exist*, at least not in the traditional sense, not as dead humans roaming the planet. Those ideas were merely traditions. When it comes to traditions, Truth always trumps them, making a deep knowledge of Truth vital because the traditions of men err, but Truth endures. The Truth is this: **It is appointed for men once to die, and then the judgment.** This is not negotiable, and there is no coming back for reasons of haunting, or reincarnation, or to have a "redo" at life. The only caveat to *that* Truth is regarding resuscitation, resurrection, or rapture. But those are also Truths consistent and compatible with each other. That is not to say that anyone ceases to exist. The body dies. The spirit and soul, or the very *being* of a man, lives on, either "Coram Deo," before the face of God by individual choice, or "Coram Gehenna," before the lake of fire, after a soon-coming judgment—the alternate choice when rejecting the first. This life is the Great Test for the beloved creation, Man—not for immortality, but rather for location and quality of life eternal.

Mike (Tick) was several years younger than Nick (Rock), but Nick noticed a maturity in Mike beyond his years. It was almost enviable, though often irritating. Mike, a widower by natural causes, was recruited when his sister was abducted by what others would call "aliens." Mike knew what they really were and why they had abducted his sister. Although UFO sightings can happen to anyone, all of the so-called "alien abductions" revolve around those who either have dabbled in the occult or have opened themselves up to satanic forces, often unwittingly, unknowingly, but nevertheless the forces behind them are always satanic. Mike's sister was a member of the old "New Age" movement. And by association she delved into the use of power crystals, pseudo-spiritual meditation, Ouija boards, Tarot cards, and she communed with unknown spiritual guides who claimed to be her teachers, ultimately becoming her masters, and were leading her to the pit of Hell.

The mind of a man has no mass, but is normally tightly associated with brain cells, permeating the organ, governing not just the body, but the spirit of a man as well. By virtue of drug use, transcendental meditation, spiritism, or hypnosis, the mind's connection with the brain becomes sporadic and disjoined. Therefore, the spirit and body of a man is open and extremely susceptible to demonic intervention, even possession. There are those who have had close encounters of the fourth kind, or "abductions," by so-called "aliens," and have seen, heard, and experienced things that are also described by those who have *not* experienced abduction; or they have had the mere suggestion of alien contact, under hypnosis, that yields the same descriptions, the same anti-Christian messages, and the same experiences as actual "abductees." The demonic realm is intertwined with ours, and there are multitudes of demons waiting for permission to inhabit the faithless man.

Mike had been there, in his sister's room, waiting for the next abduction. Leslie, his sister, had discovered that these entities she'd allowed, even invited to herself, were becoming harmful and sinister. She confided in Mike, and Mike knew he had to resist them on her behalf. Leslie had become confused by these experiences and did not know what to believe. She did not know that you should deal with experiences the same way you deal with traditions: compare them to the standard of Truth, and embrace the Author of Truth. All Leslie knew was that she had gotten herself into serious trouble that her New Age friends could not help her with, and would not acknowledge as evil. Nevertheless, Mike knew evil, and knew where it came from. Hell was coming to visit his sister, and demonic forces were out to destroy her. He knew that the key to helping her was to lead Leslie to the Lord Jesus Christ, but Leslie was not ready to take that step, or make that commitment, though she requested that Mike stay with her.

The night Mike lost his sister was a night of horror. Mike was not as prepared for the battle as he had thought. When the beings came for Leslie, somehow Mike was held fast, immobile. He saw everything, heard everything, even smelled everything, but could do nothing. His sister was beaten, violated, and then taken away, and Mike had not seen her since. That night, he was struck dumb, and could not call out to God vocally. The demonic spirits in the room, the *Moronis*, wore the more common disguise of the "grays" or smallish aliens, gray in color, with oversize heads and large elliptical eyes, and slender in build. Though there are, according to UFOlogists, three basic types of aliens, and their various subtypes, the reality is that they are *all* demonic spirits, each able to appear as an angel of light, a human, a horror, or even seemingly mechanical or non-organic. The "ship" outside was no ship at all, but another angelic being appearing as a saucer within a saucer, a disk within a disk, a wheel within a wheel, similar to the angel described in Ezekiel. The grays mocked Mike in strange high-pitched gibberish, and mentally attacked him, placing horrible thoughts in his mind. They assaulted him on a spiritual level that forced him to the edge of consciousness, perhaps sanity. Mike was helpless as they defiled his sister, but Mike also saw that, try as they might, they could not lay a hand on *him*. The entire event took only seven or eight minutes, but to Mike it seemed to last hours. As they departed with his sister in tow, he fell to the floor, not able to move for another seven or eight minutes.

Mike lay on the floor, and while trying to regain his motor skills, he heard a knocking at the front door of his sister's home. Mike found that his voice was returning, and he was able to utter a cry for help. The door burst open and Knightlight Agent Wells came to his aid. It was no coincidence that Agent Wells was there. Over the course of months, Knightlight was tracking reports of "flying saucers" and "mysterious lights in the sky," and had a tip from one of the witnesses that reoccurring sightings had been over, or near, Leslie's home. Agent Wells was staking out the area, monitoring it, but that night they had met resistance in getting to Leslie's home on time. It became evident, while Mike was being debriefed, that he was absolutely a candidate for recruitment. Mike gave the offer to join much thought and prayer before he committed himself to Knightlight. It was a decision he has never regretted.

Eugene Ledford, a strapping young six-foot-four man with an obscure sense of humor, was the third member of Nick's "Bravo" trinity. Eugene was husky and strong, and he was the muscle of the team. His weapon of choice was the shotgun, but Gene was comfortable with most firearms. "The Big Cheese," or just "Cheese,"

was his handle. Cheese was his second-favorite food, and he chose that name because he didn't think "Bacon," "Pork Belly," or "The Big Ham" would be the best of monikers.

Gene thought of himself as a "country boy" though he lived in the city. He loved camping and could best be described as a cheerful loner. Socially, he helped in his church, and offered his talents to those in need, but he never really struck close relationships with any until he joined Knightlight. He was in the National Guard, but had never been deployed abroad. His term of service was nearing an end, and he was considering the possibility of "re-upping." He was an online PC gamer, and his reaction time was excellent, making him one of the best at first-person shooters. But Gene made the Knightlight team because he was a vampire slayer. *His* story was simple: He took one week off from his job at Target, the department store where he worked, and went on a trip to the Devil's Tower National Monument in Wyoming, for purposes of camping. Who knew that there were vampires nearby?

Now these are not movie vampires like Dracula, wearing formalwear and a cape, or like the popularized shimmering-skinned teen heartthrobs of the *Twilight* franchise. These are like no vampires from any movie. They aren't vampire "wannabes" that one might run into at an old Marilyn Manson concert, or "Goth-pyre" posers, or "sexual vampire" perverts. These creatures are tall, gaunt, lean, and stealthy *monsters* that hide themselves in the earth from mankind—their food—until they are ravenous. They hide by day, buried in soft ground in the country, or sewers and subways in the city, and select their prey when it is very alone and quite vulnerable. Not that they couldn't take on several sizable men at once, but they enjoy terrifying and prolonging the horror in their prey as they stalk their victims. They enjoy playing with their "food," especially the isolated, helpless, hopeless persons most easily filled with despair. Homeless persons, runaways, lost people, hikers, bikers, anyone alone is on the menu, and a potential feast, but they wisely chose those who would least be missed. They, being of this world *and* of another, have close contact with both, and are ignorant of very little. They know things because they are always in touch with the demons that run to and fro throughout the earth.

Of old, all demonic hybrids, the Nephil-Adam, were worshiped as gods and demigods, titans and giants to fear. They ruled many distant lands, and were fierce warriors, tyrants, and conquerors. They were judged and destroyed during the Deluge, but returned to plague mankind again and again. They spread from Babel to Gath, to Nepal, to Egypt, to Central America, to Rapa Nui. On every land and shore they would take by fear, ferocity, and force. They've dwelt on the heights of Mount Olympus, as well as the cavernous depths of Mount Aetna, perhaps even on the arguably "historical" Atlantis. And wherever they have tread on this world, they have spread terror and awe. They have created wonders and performed legendary feats, and inspired men to marvel and despair.

All of Nephil-Adam's various taxonomic *kinds* were born with great beauty and strength, besides their magnificent stature, sometimes exceeding ten feet tall. Powerful and charismatic they were . . . for a period of time. Their longevity far exceeded that of mankind, and as they aged beyond the prime of their human half, they went through physical changes, some far more drastic than others. All gradually became hirsute to varying degrees, their skin became rough and thick, and their beauty faded into divergent grotesqueries. Their flesh, bones, teeth, nails, and eyes began to take on the demonic traits of their unearthly parentage, and they lived often beyond their desire to live. Most of them hated God and mankind, with *very few* exceptions.

The Gibbor, first of the post-flood Nephil-Adam, were the natural leaders of all their kind, beginning with Nimrod and beyond. The Nephilim (Ne-fill-em or Ne-fill-eem) were the most powerful and massive of all, often called Yeti or Sasquatch, even Bigfoot. They were intelligent yet merciless killers and the enforcers of the Gibbor. The

Rephaim were the untamable, wild berserkers, much later dubbed werewolves. The Zuzim were the smallest of all. They became feral, misshapen beings, nomadic, solitary, stealthy, cunning, but monstrous creatures nonetheless. The Emim were night stalkers, blood-drinking cannibals, whose prey were the weak or isolated, and they were the ones named *vampir*. And the Anakim were giant *terrors* whose speed and ferocity in combat were unsurpassed. The shadows of other creatures who stalked the earth could also be found in legend. All were products of genetic manipulation by dark spiritual forces in preparation for the imperative coming of the Dark Messiah. All were later dubbed "Bigfoot," "Yeti," "Sasquatch," and much more, by ignorant man.

In the past and with a comparatively small population, these creatures ruled ruthlessly. They conquered much of the earth, hindered only by a people who worshiped God alone, until the time of the Babylonian Empire, the first Global Empire after the fall of the previous Babel. Born over the dust of the great Tower, the roots of the man-made mountain, the Babylonian Empire became the spiritual cesspool of the planet. But the Babylonians did not choose to worship the Nephil-Adam for reasons of self-exaltation. The demon spawn were then hunted and slain en masse, or driven into hiding by the powerful armies of men ever since, as man multiplied upon the face of the earth. But the earth has not been without their spawn since Eden fell, and their numbers have been growing in recent years, as some expected they would. They know that it is not yet time for them to come into power, but soon. They await the Dark Messiah, and as Knightlight noted, they no longer waited patiently.

These vampires near Gene's campsite not only drank the life's blood of their victims, but also ate carcasses and marrow of man and animal alike, though they preferred the flesh of man. These dug holes away from their own dwelling, jammed the bones into the earth, and then covered them with stone and soil, where no trace could be found. They were and are the powerful Emim, the "Terrors" spoken of in Genesis 14:5, poorly translated generically as "giants" in the King James, but one of only a few poorly translated words. These are the *real vampires* related in legend and passed down through the generations of man, in lore. These are monsters, not romantic interests or suave aristocrats. There are a few comparative traits they have besides ingesting life from the living: They sleep in the earth by day, they hunt at night, and there's a visceral gravity to their stare that is so intense and fearsome it can make a man lose bowel control without knowing it, or even caring. The gaze of the vampire can immobilize the victim with the overwhelming and projected spiritual presence of sheer terror.

Eugene had pitched his tent in a nearby camping area, started a campfire, and roasted cheese-dogs for supper. Night was black about him, but for the fire. Then in the warm solitude of the camp, an unnatural, absolutely supernatural *dread* began to creep up his spine. Immediately Gene pulled his 9mm Smith & Wesson M&P handgun from its holster. It was part of his normal apparel, and he had a license to carry. Cradling the gun in his lap so that it would not be easily visible, he began to nervously sing Steven Curtis Chapman's "Great Adventure," and to worship God alone.

But when the fire began to die down, and the smoke to fade, he could see a reflection of the fire in a pair of evil eyes suspended high in the air, fifteen feet in front of him on the other side of the burning timber. Then he saw the faint fire-glow on bare and pointed teeth. It's no shame that Gene wet himself, because he then responded instantly with deadly force, sending three bullets between the eyes of the terrible creature in front of him. Immediately after that, he ran up to it and unloaded the rest of his magazine into the creature's chest, still terrified that the vampire might rise. It did not. The monster was dead before it took the first step in attack.

Gene changed his clothes, calmed down, and then snapped some poor-quality photos of the creature with his cell phone's camera.

When he finally got a signal for his phone, he uploaded the pictures to his Facebook account and added a few detailed comments to the images. It drew much attention among Cheese's friends, and a few others who knew where to look for such breaking news. Within ten minutes, every social media account of Gene's became inaccessible to him and the general public. Knightlight agents were on-site within eight hours, before Gene, who finally fell asleep with his reloaded M&P on his chest, awoke. It was Agent Duncan of Alpha team who roused the groggy young man, debriefed him, and, after a lengthy interview, offered him membership in the elite, yet humble, service of Knightlight. And now the Big Cheese is a loner no longer.

‡⟷‡

Knightlight deployed agents in threes . . . always. A trinity is the bare minimum complement for a strike-team to engage a trophy and expect to survive. If for any reason a covert operation required a single agent to embed with civilians, you can bet that the two other agents were close by. On occasion, in more difficult situations, a pair of trinities were dispatched, forfeiting a degree of inconspicuousness. But if a pair of trinities could not handle the incursion, Knightlight would request the services of the US military's general or even elite soldiers. On missions abroad, Knightlight would work at the request with the support of certain foreign powers. Africa, Central America, and the Middle East were the most dangerous foreign soils to enter, but fortunately in Middle East scenarios the agency would coordinate with the respected Israeli Mossad . . . but only when things really got out of hand. On average, things really got out of hand annually.

Knightlight had twelve trinity strike-teams at any given time and a few reserve personnel in training as substitutes or replacements. They were the field agents inserted once a target was confirmed and the threat was imminent or ongoing. There were investigation teams

77

of various sizes and makeup, analysis teams, forensic teams, logistic teams, command-and-control staff, technical teams, communications teams, political attachés, translators, engineers, code breakers, and then there was the secret weapon: Prayer Warriors. The First Agent, Christopher Griffin, was now the coordinator all of those, with Knightlight's Director above him, and only the President of the United States was above the Director.

The Central Western Knightlight office, code-named Archangel, was in actuality a vast and fortified bunker inside Lookout Mountain, just west of Golden, Colorado. It was constructed far below the grave site of William F. "Buffalo Bill" Cody. The excavation within the mountain was to be the original site for SAC-NORAD, built by the Army Corps of Engineers. Then its location was changed based on proximity of the fast-growing population of Golden/Denver. SAC-NORAD relocated farther south in the Rocky Mountain range, within the more isolated Cheyenne Mountain.

The bunker, "Archangel," was characterized, humorously, by some of the agents as the "debunker," since Knightlight's ministry role had been ever engaged in standing against false doctrine, various false sciences, cults, out-and-out lies, and myths that are woven into the fabric of mankind's vain imagination. It was one of four Knightlight US offices, and was by far the most secretive and secure site Knightlight had. It was the "main office" of Knightlight where the Director and First Agent resided, and was the central support hub for all agents. Archangel had many resources within the enormous mountain bunker, and many departments, which included living quarters, recreational facilities, and a large chapel. It could communicate with and see virtually anywhere on the planet and was tied into most satellites in orbit. It had experimental labs and a hospital, and was the main research and development site with access to all conventional military assets if needed. Today there was nothing out of the ordinary happening, which is to say, it was always in a state of high activity.

Dominic Moreau and Michael Cavor were in the Ops room at one of several computer stations where they could easily access mission data, and virtually any data on the planet. They were researching sightings, and had been for hours. It was tedious but necessary work, and both thanked God for computers. They remembered the stories of the First Agent and how, in the past, he had to gather the data by mail, newspapers, and media reports, and then manually organize it before it could be used. Now, with the aid of cutting-edge technology, satellites, sniffer software, and the Internet, they correlated the data with "missing persons," "ritualistic violence," "pharmaceutical-related homicides," and what some call "paranormal activities," be it regarding man, beast, or worse. There were monsters out there, hybrid-beasts, demons, witches, satanic cults, the demon-possessed, dragons, and more. Whatever Hell spat out, Knightlight was there to engage and return to its pit. It was dangerous and deadly work, and only those fully committed to the task, and the Lord, could hope to live to tell the tale, let alone conquer the evil they battled.

The agents, when researching, would make electronic notes of their observations and opinions, and then send them up the chain of command for potential missions. It was serious business, but serious business could often be less burdensome when one allowed humor to lighten the load. After all, another Truth is that a merry heart does good like medicine. It was during *this* studious and sober operation that a humorous thought occurred to Moreau, while reading about a possible Emim encounter, and the description of the creature itself.

"Where did the Big Cheese get off to? I've got a good one for him," Dominic said.

Distracted, but not looking away from his thirty-two-inch HD flat-panel monitor, Cavor said, "I think he went to the bathroom."

"Oh, well then I'll try it on you. What do vampires use for public transportation?" Dominic asked Cavor.

Cavor, completely preoccupied, looking at the "hot-list" database, asked, "Did you read our sit-rep on Central Indiana? The sightings are moving directly northwest, and there have been several suspicious missing-persons reports stretching from Hoosier National Forest, through Bloomington, all the way up to Greencastle."

"Yes, it looks like a signature trail. Intel-Analysis already flagged it and sent that data to the Director through Griffin as a high probability for an advance investigation team. He'll look at it and all others after his meeting with that *spook* from the State Department," Dominic replied, and then admitted, "I've noticed Intel Tracking has been getting better at sorting out red herrings to prevent wasted trips."

"Agreed," said Cavor.

"But at least we don't get misdeployed as much as the advance scouts do. I appreciate their legwork in front of us," Nick added.

"I've been analyzing our successes all the way back to 2001," Cavor said, "and I'm somewhat concerned. Our teams currently average only 1.983 trophies per year now from each category, and there's just 59.8 real trophies a year from all the teams combined. I've run those numbers and I don't see how we can make a dent against repopulation. I think I'm going to suggest to the Director that we need to update our strategy."

"Well, population size may be growing beyond any hope of containment, but we can only guess at what rate," Dominic replied. "We only act on the cases where there is a clear and present danger, but we do seem to be spread a little thin at times. Perhaps we need a few more strike-teams. On the other hand, I think our strategy is fine, and has the virtue of being time-tested. Nobody said the endgame means we win, because we all know that we *don't win*; we occupy enemy territory in the heavenly realm, and act in the natural realm, when warranted. *We hold the line.* If we simply defend the weak, deliver the "good news" as best as possible, and hinder the enemy, we are serving our purpose, and helping the people we're trying to protect. That's our mission. But feel free to send anything up the chain that you think might help."

"You've basically given the *philosophical* mission statement, but the practicality is that we are losing the war, and I am not sure we have to," Cavor said. "We've embedded before, at least from time to time, on certain Cryp-Trips, but watching the web server feed from the S.I.U. conference gave me an idea. It looks like they have a plan and funding to target their "Sasquatch" on a massive scale. They are collaborating on a unified hunt for Malcolm Carson's Agnostopithecus."

"Yes, I sent you that link after I watched it," Dominic responded.

"Oh . . . right. Well, apart from the fact that Carson is the *glittering jewel of colossal ignorance*, we could use it as cover and insert *all* of our teams into a massive coordinated locate-and-strike effort."

"Well, I agree that it may be an attractive idea, if only to protect *them* from danger, but each time we insert, we risk blowing our cover," Dominic said. "Not that I'm too concerned about them knowing the truth about their Sasquatch, since we offer some of that information publicly in the form of our largely ignored *Internet outreach ministry*. But you know that if we're acting under the auspices of any government agency, we have to be covert and careful about the details we share with others."

"We don't have to act with official credentials . . . we just have to be there, use their intel to help us locate and engage the trophy while they're trying to find their own hindquarters with both hands, and a flashlight. We act as . . . um . . . we act as engaged citizens, or crypto-groupies, or anything unofficial, and join up," Mike suggested.

"But you are forgetting the most important aspect of embedding. When we embed, we expose ourselves to the enemy because they are watching these crypto-zoologists carefully. They may still be blind to our strategy, but they will have advance notice of our presence. That's just a fact," Dominic stated.

"We would still have an informational advantage over the enemy because we'd still have our own gathered intelligence," explained Cavor. "We could just use our credentials to cover any background story that would make us look attractive to have on the expedition. But we'd not act officially."

"Mike, if we embed with *any story* and use government resources to provide background cover, which seems necessary to prove we are who we say we are, then we're already acting in an official capacity, with all the implicit restrictions that go with it."

"Or . . . we could at least tap, or trap and trace, their data communications and use their intel."

"The tap won't fly under the Patriot Act because they are largely Americans and are completely harmless conspirators who are only endangering themselves with their stupid venture," Dominic pointed out. "Another thing about embedding, I've used the 'camera crew' cover twice on Malcolm's retarded TV show, and though I've laid as low as possible, sneaking around their backs to reach the target first is extremely difficult. You've worked, covertly, with John Cosworth's crew in British Colombia, but each time we are risking full-blown exposure if we embed with them. And you can bet that Carson will be visiting every site since he's overseeing all of it, and handpicking each group's complement."

"I'm just saying that time is running out, the attacks are increasing, and our enemy doesn't seem to be too concerned anymore for secrecy. Some of the attacks and incidents are showing up on YouTube, Twitter, and even the *Drudge Report*. We need to maximize our efforts or we risk becoming useless," Cavor said.

"Useless? We've saved multiple hundreds of lives directly, and countless thousands indirectly," Dominic said.

"But we're nearing the endgame, Nick. The Word says that when we see Israel return to their land as a nation, though I am not sure we shouldn't be counting from when Jerusalem became entirely under Israeli ownership, but that *this generation* is at the threshold of the 'catching away of the saints.' Then comes the Great Tribulation, and then the return of Christ. Ezekiel 37 has been fulfilled. This generation is almost spent regardless of when the clock started ticking. You know that the prophecies regarding Christ's return specifically mention that *'as in the days of Noah, so it will be at the coming of the Son of man.'* Violence permeates the entire world, as it did in Noah's time. There is again widespread sexual congress between demonic entities and mankind, and hearts are turning away from God rather than toward Him, and manifold other prophecies are being fulfilled. Knowledge has greatly increased, there are *serious* earthquakes 'in divers places' many times a year now, with increased magnitude in very populated areas, and that includes tsunamis, and nuclear disaster.

"Men travel to and fro over the entire planet, daily," Tick continued, knowing well the timeline of prophecy and history as it concerned the "end times." "There are wars and rumors of wars, globally, on a scale never before seen, beginning with World War I. What is good is called 'evil,' and what is evil is called 'good.' Ezekiel 38 and 39 and Revelation 4 through 19 are on the verge of fulfillment. The whole Middle East region has been openly hostile against Israel since 1948 and it is nearing critical mass. Since they became a nation, they've endured the Palestinians' Qibya Massacre; the Six-Day War from Egypt; the battle of Karameh from Jordan; the War of Attrition, from Egypt again; and the Yom Kippur war with Egypt, Syria, and Jordan. The PLO terrorisms including the Olympic hostage murders. There are bombings and shellings against Israel from Lebanon, with Palestinian, Iranian, and Syrian support, and *that* on a daily basis."

"Then, of course," Tick went on, "these spilled into attacks against Israel's truest ally—*America*—from Iran first, as the Shah was deposed and US hostages were taken under the Ayatollah regime, then from Libya, murdering those on Pan Am Flight 103 in the '80s and other acts of terrorism as Al-Qaida rose behind the scenes. Then we saw Iraq attacking Kuwait and Israel in the '90s and drawing us into a ground war with Iraq. Shortly thereafter, we saw the first attack on the World Trade Center in '93 by Al-Qaida. And don't forget that Clinton *gave* China *Cray Supercomputers* in the late 90's with Sun Microsystems fronting them through Hong Kong, and China then demonstrated their appreciation by launching cyber-attacks against American facilities and interests ever since. Then, of course, the World Trade Center terrorist attack on nine-eleven in 2001. Al-Qaida hatefully murdered thousands and forced us into two theaters of combat in the Middle East lasting over a decade," he gulped a breath and continued.

"And remember the so-called 'Arab Spring' of 2011, where many Muslim nations overthrew their fascist leaders, but instantly turned into Islamic Extremist States and our President did nothing to lead them toward real peaceful democracies, while taking opportunistic credit for his part in the uprisings? The Administration actually treated those nations as 'favored' over Israel at the time, making America look spineless, but still *fiercely hated* by those same Muslim nations now governed by the Muslim Brotherhood. Then, more recently, we gave billions of American taxpayer dollars and many fighter jets to unstable *Egypt,* while we endured puerile whining about the *Sequester. Our nation is actually losing its credibility, respect and its moral authority while enabling and preparing other nations for **Armageddon!**"

"So it would seem," said Rock with a nod. "Add to that - *this* Administration actually calling an act of clear Islamic Terrorism at Ft. Hood, *'workplace violence'* isn't just naïve, it's trend-settingly *stupid!* It practically invited the terrorist attack on Benghazi, 9/11 - 2012 that went undefended, unanswered and was even lied about. The Benghazi attack made us look incompetent to our allies and enemies alike. ***Men died*** because of ***politics, politicians*** and a complete failure in vigilance. I mean, seriously, the entire world watched as ***nobody*** in this Administration took responsibility for, well, ***calculated dishonesty,*** and no justice was served against our attackers. An unanswered Al-Qaida was dumped into Bush's lap from the previous administration's inaction. To his credit, *'W'* kept us safe and strong after their attack, and the buck stopped with him, but those days are gone. Weakness invites other terrorist attacks, emboldens foreign and domestic enemies including Korea's Kim Jong-un, Assad, Ahmadinejad, ***Islamist Extremists worldwide,*** and even evil 'home-grown' terrorists like Nidal Hasan..." Rock sighed, then added, "But, in a degree of fairness... a very small degree... *we* have the benefit of seeing the ***true enemy*** behind it all, and still, the world just doesn't understand evil."

"Yes," agreed Tick, "Unfortunately Boston found that out the hard way... it's unfortunate that others since, have as well. But right after the attack on Boston; exactly two days later, when the Gun-control Bill, forged *against lawful citizens, mind you,* was defeated in the Senate, Obama immediately marched out to the Rose Garden and in sheer arrogance, he *chastised* Congress for the world to see. In the same breath he characterized *law-abiding American citizens* as ***"shameful"*** for protecting their God-given, not government-given *freedoms* – our 2nd Amendment rights – knowing full well that *murder with any weapon is already a crime,* and that *criminals don't submit themselves to background checks or declare their guns, knives or bombs.* The country was still reeling from the terrorist attack in Boston that the Government couldn't prevent. Now I'm not one of those Alex Jones *'see a conspiracy everywhere' types,* but directing that kind of anger and insult towards the *loyal American opposition* is simply... ***wicked. Freedom itself was shamed that day.*** Bridling, burdening and blaming lawful Americans is antithetical to any answer. Less than a week later that lamebrain *Bloomberg* said the Second Amendment should be reinterpreted... as if he ***even understands what it means, now.*** Americans have the *right to defend themselves* from all enemies, in their homes or on the streets, and the *right to remain free* and protect themselves *even from their own government,* should it one day choose to declare itself a *monarchy, a dictatorship... or worse.* That's the very *intent* of the 2nd Amendment. New gun laws aren't needed. Encouragement, fire-arms training, and sharpened eyes against attack are far more valuable. Law enforcement helps, but more often it helps *after the fact of a tragedy,* rarely before."

Tick paused and Rock didn't disturb the silence. Blowing off "steam" is therapeutic and Rock was sympathetic toward it. Tick did notice that he'd completely strayed *off-topic* and was lending his voice to bitterness. It was a rare thing indeed to hear Tick so fervent in his speech. But he was wounded to the heart knowing that his country was crumbling around him, and beyond belief... *it was proud of it.* Too many people were willing to trade their *"freedoms"* for *"security from the government,"* proving that they are worthy of neither. Freedom comes at a price that too many now either refused to pay, or demanded others to pay in their stead. Personal responsibility was dying at the hands of the selfish "gimme" generation. He used to think America - founded on Christian principles - trusting in God: The God of the Bible – the land of the free and the home of the brave - was a *Christian* nation. He knows better now. He knows that anything truly "Christian" is an endangered species within the borders of the country he truly loves. But his passion was grounded in fact, reason and of course, Truth. As he paused, he mentally re-aligned his speech toward prophetic eschatology again. But he decided that a little *patriotic acrimony* could be a good thing. At least it was honest dissent on home soil.

"Today, after the Gaza war, and now that the UN has recognized the statehood of Palestine," Tick continued, "Israel is completely surrounded by hostile Muslim governments and terrorists who want them *exterminated,* and *still* most of America ignorantly believes that if they just go the way of the UN and embrace the Palestinians, the world will be at peace. Meanwhile, Russia, the kingdom to the north of Israel, is working *with* Iran for the first time in history against Israel, just as foretold in Scripture. This administration sees the State of Israel as the problem with the Middle East, and even when we are saying they are our allies, our actions and inaction demonstrate to her enemies that we will not act appropriately to defend her beyond Iron Dome assistance. The dominant branch of Muslims—the Shi'a—are looking for their Twelfth Imam; Genesis agrees that they will have their twelve princes from Ishmael. Israel is looking for their Messiah, not knowing that Jews and Muslims alike will probably accept the same *dark man* as their own savior until he betrays Israel. Oh, there will be three-and-a-half years of false peace in Israel, but then there will be three-and-a-half years of horror. *It's coming soon to a theatre near you!*" he concluded with exasperation.

"You're right," Dominic said evenly, slightly dampening Tick's exuberance without detracting from his point. On the contrary, Nick had more to add to the list. "And we have epidemics and diseases like HIV, mad cow disease, avian flu, super E. coli bacteria, listeria, hepatitis, ebola, flesh-eating viruses, West Nile, cancer, pestilences aplenty. We have droughts and famines in many countries and they're spreading. Since God has been removed from public schools, supplanted by evolutionary doctrines and Earth worship, there has been a great falling away from the Church, and violence within the schools themselves. Children in public schools are closer to being 'government property' than wards of their parents, yet parents give them up freely and no longer ignorantly. They are unprotected from Biblical ethics of right and wrong."

Dominic went on, "We've got a global economy that's tanking, and the movement for a global currency and credit is here, which will logically become cashless for security purposes and stability and universality, but ultimately for control. Then moving that system to a physical 'mark' in the form of either a scannable identifier, an RFID bio-chip, or some kind of distinctive branded identifier mark that will be placed on people's right forearm or forehead if they want to buy or sell anything. That's all laid out in the Gospel, which, I might add, has now been preached in every corner of the world, if not in every language.

"And what about the prophecies concerning the rebuilding of the temple?" he continued. "The temple utensils now exist for Israel to begin daily sacrifices once the temple has been rebuilt, which they are preparing to do, and have been for years. The cornerstone has been waiting to be laid since the early 1980s. With genetic manipulation, there now exist 'red heifers' for the temple's consecration. They've also used genetic tests to determine which Jews are of the line of Aaron, and have instructed men in priestly skills. Once the Antichrist appears, he will make it possible for Israel to rebuild the temple without Muslim intervention. There will be a wall erected between the temple and the Dome of the Rock, dividing the city as mentioned in Ezekiel 40. There will be a false aura of peace for three-and-a-half years while the temple is being built, until the Dark Messiah declares himself to be 'god' in the temple. Since the advent of CNN, all eyes have been able to see, *in real time*, what will happen in Jerusalem during the Tribulation, just as foretold. And then all Hell breaks loose . . . literally. I know how it goes, *but we are not there yet*."

"Still," replied Tick, "I think this is an opportunity that we should exploit to its fullest. Simply being there to protect the cryptos seems worthy enough reason to tag along with them."

"I'm not arguing with you, Mike, I'm just showing you the issues that might prevent that from being a strategic advantage, and compatible with our mission, and within the law," he said, and then reflected. "But to tell you the truth, I feel sorry for Malcolm Carson . . . . I'm going to have to add his name to my prayers. I'd *really*, honestly like to sit down and have a serious talk with him.

He's going to get people killed and he's an obstacle in the way of our mission," Dominic said in all earnestness. Dominic remembered his own faith in evolution prior to God revealing to him the Truth. His heart went out to those blinded with science, or a faith that they believed itself to be *science*. He admitted to himself that he was also deeply angered that the godless philosophy had not been properly put to death by now.

"Well, I'm going to send up a mission proposal regarding this. Do you have any beefs with that?" asked Mike.

"No, go ahead. I trust Griffin can make the correct decision on what course of action we take. His discernment is impeccable, even if I may have reservations about it. Bottom line, I trust the First Agent's judgment."

The glass doors in the hallway behind them parted almost silently, and in came Eugene Ledford, still a young man, and still the Big Cheese. He walked as quietly as he could across the room to come up behind Nick and Mike. He was going to give them a startle, the way Nick usually startled Gene. When off mission, the three were the best of friends and had an extremely lighthearted relationship. Jokes, pranks, running gags were all part of their companionship. But when on mission, they took their job seriously, and professionally.

Gene was almost behind them when Nick said, "It's about time, Cheese. What took you? Did you have Taco Bell for lunch?" which completely blew Gene's stealth approach out of the water.

"Your Mom!" Gene said in jest, as he was foiled again.

The term "Your Mom," beyond the standard derogatory meaning, was a running gag used against Nick, as it pertained to a specific past mission gone afoul. Three years ago Nick had been captured by the enemy and interrogated, and "Your Mom" was the only response the interrogator was given, over and over again. He received blow after blow in response to the answer. "Your Mom" happened to be the correct answer to the interrogator's first question: "What is the password for your BlackBerry?" It was in fact "Y0urm0m." Rock knew that no interrogator would believe his answer; however, he also knew that it would pass a lie detector test. He was beaten efficiently for it, and with alacrity. Had he not been rescued (the odds were always unfavorable for the interrogated), he might have been broken, but Rock had not reached the breaking point before Tick and the Cheese came to his aid.

"Oh my," Mike said with surprise, as a thought came to him that had eluded him until now. "It just occurred to me that we are also in the same position as the world was, when the Tower of Babel was built."

"What do you mean?" asked Nick, putting his attention back to the task at hand.

"The Tower was constructed out of pride and arrogance by the same Mighty Men we are hunting, but it was constructed out of pride and arrogance, against God. They were brilliant architects, scientists, and craftsman, and had amazing ingenuity . . . . Do you remember why?" Mike asked.

"Of course we know. For Pete's sake, Mike," Dominic said, immediately feeling compelled to show Mike just *how much* he knew about the subject. "Nimrod was the great-grandson of Noah, who unified the people as a single great nation with many cities erected at his command. He was their leader and high priest of the occult. He ruled them with ease because he was the first Mighty Man, the first demonic hybrid, a Gibbor, of the *post-flood* world, and he was a tyrant. His followers all worshiped him under his rule, and built the Tower, perhaps a ziggurat, to depose and defy God. And, of course, they all spoke the same language and were united, which placed them in a position to believe that they could be on par with God, and grasp *godhood* in their own efforts. Nimrod's wife, Semiramis, was the Queen of the Babylonian Mystery religion. She and her religion both are the Whore of Babylon compared to the bride of Christ—the Church.

When Nimrod died, she became the "Goddess of the Moon" and sat as a queen who claimed she was no widow, because she gave birth to Tammuz, the incarnation and reincarnation, or rather *rebirth*, of Nimrod, and the second documented demonic "post-flood hybrid" and another Mighty Man, though there were most likely many other than just those two at the time." Nick said this as if he had been insulted by the question that should never have been a question, as if that weren't integral to Knightlight's primary mission. And as if Tammuz wasn't still the highest-value target of their ongoing operation. Osama Bin Laden was an easily found and exterminated "pantywaist" compared to Tammuz. Not that Nick had any disrespect for the Navy Seals or the US intelligence and tactics that finally exposed and disposed of Bin Laden. Quite the contrary. But Tammuz was still alive somewhere, a centuries-old murderer, a puppeteer of men and Nephil-Adam alike. And it is he to whom the Mighty Men are accountable even today. Tammuz is the trophy of trophies.

"So what?" Gene asked. "What is it that puts us in the same position as the Tower of Babel, or the same category as the original Babylonians?"

"Easy . . . . Like then, we now all speak the same language," Mike said with an air confidence. "Genesis 11:1," he quoted. "And the earth was of one language, and one speech." I just realized that today the earth is technically of one language . . . and it is *not* English," he added, as he tried to point them in the direction that his logic had taken him.

"What?" Gene asked, momentarily perplexed. "Any linguist could tell you that we have over six thousand languages on earth. Most of them are spoken by very small populations, perhaps eight hundred people to a tribe. I know that English is required for all aviators to communicate with all airports, and vice versa, and Morse code is nearly universal in civilized countries, but I guarantee you that we all don't speak the same language."

"I'll qualify it then. Anywhere—no, *everywhere*—there is technology, *and there is technology in every country on the planet now*, we all speak the same language," pronounced Mike.

"Ah . . . I understand . . . You're right," agreed Dominic.

"All right, what am I missing?" asked Eugene.

"Tell him," Tick said to Rock.

"Wherever there are computers, in every corner of the globe, there is one language—*binary*—regardless of the spoken language. When you get down to it, all our electronic communication is translated into binary digits," said the Rock. "After that, there is only the question of OS, hardware BIOS, or application compatibility, but it is all fundamentally the binary language.

"I guess it is," agreed the Big Cheese.

"Oh, and Gene," Nick began on a completely different subject, "what *do* vampires use for public transportation?"

"Um . . . oh I got it: the Blood Mobile!"

"Oooh, nice try, but *FAIL!*" Nick said with good-humored vigor.

"Succubus—Suck-You-Bus," answered Tick with confidence, and he received a smile and a nod from Rock. They all began to laugh. Then an e-mail popped up in front of Mike. It was addressed to the entire Bravo Trinity team from Christopher Griffin. Mike read it and relayed it to his companions.

"We've been scheduled for a V-Op next week. It looks like this one is going to be a protracted insertion. We have to report Wednesday at 07:00 hours," said Mike. "Oh great! It's a Black Out mission." he added.

"We better get our game faces on and put some time in before that. We don't want to disappoint the First Agent," Dominic said, and each of them nodded their agreement and resolve.

7

PLANS AND LOGISTICS

(From the notes of First Agent Christopher Griffin)

(Section: Philosophical Thinking)

Insanity was once described by Albert Einstein as "doing the same thing over and over, and expecting different results." It is an overused quote of late, and of course, he was wrong. Einstein's definition was merely identifying a symptom of insanity. Insanity is not being able to distinguish between fantasy and reality, with a variety of symptoms indicating such psychosis. It has been demonstrated that this world does not know the difference between fantasy and reality. The reality of this world is that it was created, and is governed by its Creator. All on this planet are accountable to their Creator and their fellow man. This is reality.

But this world has turned its back on reality, embracing the fantasy of evolution. This fantasy has eroded the culture of Western civilization, and this planet has given itself to this insane worldview. Is it any wonder that violent crime is on the rise? Is it such a surprise that our societies abuse drugs, both legal and illegal? Is it any wonder that hundreds of millions of deaths occurred during the last century due to war and abuse from the tyrannical governance of mankind? Everyone cries out for justice, peace, love, hope, but they cannot find any answers to those from evolution. Evolution is a harsh faith that does not have an answer to the above, because it isn't real.

The choice to embrace reality is still available to mankind, but that offer is obtainable only for a limited time. Soon, even the choice to believe will be gone. There is no life, Truth, or future in insanity. Reality is the only hope for mankind.

⊱──⊰

Modesto, California—Present Day, June 21st

The term "crypto-zoologist" is considered an embarrassing term in the scientific community. Indeed, to most esteemed observational scientists *and* to those indoctrinated in the naturalistic faith of speculative scientific study, it was a "dirty word." The crypto-zoologists themselves were a joke to some, an intellectual hindrance to others, but the term was an unacknowledged contradiction because the subject of the study, being hidden, made it virtually impossible to really study. The study of hidden life-forms is synonymous with research for the evidential discovery of the Boogie Man. Mainstream science does not believe in monsters, even when confronted with evidences of such. This is rightly so when evidence is circumstantial or based solely on the testimony of rattled witnesses. The Loch Ness Monster, Bigfoot, the Chupacabra, the Yeti, the Jersey Devil, fairies and elves, unicorns, etc., are the stuff of study for most cryptos, but some venture out of the zoological (animalia) and step into

94

the paranormal, and as such study evidences for angels, demons, ghosts, and spirits. But most try to manipulate the evidences by employing a naturalistic explanation for such findings. Some cryptos are serious biologists earnestly trying to shed light on heretofore *unknown* creatures and explain seemingly supernatural animals with naturalistic reason and evidences, but there are truly many kooks and certifiable wackos who tag along with them.

Cryptos are looked dimly upon by mainstream science, even though some notables in academia have come from such roots, including Robert "Bob" Ballard, who paid his respects to "Nessie," and also advanced the science in support of the "Global Flood of Noah." He did the former before searching for, and indeed finding, the *Titanic*, and the latter was after his credibility was well established. He and his fellow scientists—William Ryan and Walter Pittman—learned something important about the scientific community when they began to discuss their evidences and conclusions regarding the flood: If there is evidence for any *"thing, or event"* that contradicts the scientific community's "consensus," they will ascribe a naturalistic explanation for that *"thing or event,"* disregard evidences of the miraculous that are contrary to their paradigm, and label the underlying Biblical premise as "myth," in order to discredit both the notion and the scientist, by personal and professional bias, apart from actual science. Those gentlemen learned that belief in the Word of God, and proof backing up the claims it makes, is scientific anathema, being the *antithesis* of the evolutionary model. They also learned that the *Biblical Archaeological Review*, which has revealed countless facts and proven innumerable claims in support of the Bible, had not one ounce of *faith* in their coffers regardless of the Biblical evidences they discovered.

Malcolm Carson's office, a mere twenty feet by fourteen feet with one window, was cluttered with books and articles and news clippings and artifacts from his many adventures. He truly was an adventurer at heart, and loved his field of study. The office was always just a pit stop for him, as he'd rather be in the field, or speaking somewhere . . . at someone else's expense. Between engagements, he'd drop off items of his own interest on his desk, or stack important papers wherever he could, and then be off again, not wasting time to file items or organize his office. When he was married, his wife would often drop by and chide him about the mess, and, irritatingly, start cleaning up his office. She was a neat-freak, and that was merely one of the reasons they ended up parting ways.

The best thing about Malcolm's marriage was his daughter, Crystal. She was now 28 years old, and currently worked with him as his publicist, traveling coordinator, accountant, and anything else Malcolm needed. She received her doctorate in microbiology a year ago, but had actually fallen out of love with the humdrum idea of being stuck in some laboratory for the rest of her life. She both blamed and appreciated her father for instilling in her a sense of adventure by taking her on many of his excursions during her college breaks. Now, while she had time to decide what she wanted to do with her degree, she worked for Malcolm. She wasn't his "Girl Friday," she was his "Princess." And like many fathers, he loved her more than she knew, or would know until she had one of her own. Parenthood changes the heart and one's perspective in a surprising instant. In the past, Crystal was in the field with her father only during school breaks, lightly assisting him. It amounted to familial, nonprofessional assistance. With this project and all the time she'd spent working on it with Malcolm, they had become closer than ever. She was the apple of his eye, and others in the field, rather the *men* with him in the field, knew intuitively that she was not "up for grabs" where any hanky-panky was concerned.

Malcolm sat at his desk and cleared away some clutter, disturbing the dust, which became visible, like tiny fighter jets darting about in the sun rays that spilled through the blinds of his window. He now had room to open his briefcase. As an afterthought, he turned on his desktop PC but ignored it, since it took *forever* to boot up. After opening the briefcase, he retrieved the sign-up sheets that he had collected after his speech in Washington. He meticulously read them and sorted them as he liked. He saw the many familiar names of his associates, several of whom he was barely acquainted with, and dozens of unknowns. He weeded out some of the unknowns and chose team leaders and group complements based on their strengths and even their perceived weaknesses. Hours passed quickly, which was unusual to Malcolm when he spent time in his office. Confident that he would have an army of the best *fellow explorers*, he took the sheets of paper of the men and women he intended to hire over to the copier/fax machine, set the feature to scan-to-e-mail, and began scanning the documents, watching the light move under each page from left to right. When the scan was complete, the documents were instantly sent to his e-mail account, from which he could forward them on to his new employer, CQ Petroleum Corp. Once there, they would be further scrutinized, the candidates would undergo background checks that they'd already consented to, and ultimately they would be contacted for their own employment. The entire process would take mere days since this was a "high-priority" mission for the company.

Malcolm went back to his desk with the original documents in hand and unceremoniously stuffed them into the top drawer of the file cabinet next to his desk. Then he sat in front of his computer, logged into his e-mail account, and began the process of sending the documents on. Once done, he clicked a desktop link, which brought up an electronic world map that CQ had supplied him with. There were many red dots on the map already; each red dot was a location of an intended site for his Agnostopithecus venture. He looked them over, remembering the whys and wherefores for placing them there to begin with. He zoomed in to the section that was clearly labeled "British Colombia," zoomed in even further to Garibaldi Lake, and then slid the map coordinates southwest, right-clicked, and placed another marker in a densely forested area for which the map could not display a name. It was roughly this spot that was considered, more and more, a Sasquatch hot spot. Then he saved and closed the map, which automatically updated CQ's database of intended sites they would need to plan to supply.

Malcolm's pants vibrated, which startled him slightly. He'd forgotten to put his cell phone back on the "ring" setting. He stood from his desk and pulled out the phone, and then took his reading glasses out of his shirt pocket and put them on so he could read the name of the caller. He wished somebody would make a feature on his phone so he could tell by the vibration who was calling him. He did not doubt that there would be "an app for that" sometime in the near future if it didn't already exist. When he recognized the displayed number of his daughter, her ring-tone came to his mind. When his phone rang from her number, it would play the music from an old Ernie Kovacs skit called "The Nairobi Trio." He loved that bit. He had the ring-tone custom-made, and each time she called, he remembered the old Kinescope broadcasts he saw as a child.

He answered his phone with, "Hello, Princess."

"Dad, do you still have to call me Princess?" the voice of Malcolm's daughter asked.

"I'm your Dad forever, and you are my Princess forever, so . . . yes, I have to call you that," Malcolm said, smiling. She had a wonderful "telephone" voice, he noted.

"I've been working with CQ on equipment, and I think we need to lease another small warehouse. We've run out of room here. I was thinking that if we shipped and stored the equipment at small rental garages near the sites you're going to be staging from, we would have fewer logistics problems than having all of it in a few large warehouses far from your sites."

"That's a great idea. But since the sites are not confirmed or staffed yet, let's wait a week or so before we do that. In the meantime, get another warehouse with a one-month lease, and once we are set on the locations, we can move the equipment near the sites. Excellent idea," Malcolm said.

"OK. Do you have a time frame on deployment yet?" Crystal asked.

"I only have to wait for CQ's confirmation on the teams. They are chomping," he said instead of *champing*, "at the bit to get going, so I'd say we will be deploying within ten days. My question is, are you going to be traveling with me, or are you going to pop in and out as needed?"

"I thought I'd join you solid for the first month and make sure everything is going well, and then play it by ear after that. I like the field, but it turns my life upside down before I go, and then immediately afterwards," she said.

"That sounds just fine, Princess. Anything else?" asked Malcolm.

"Mom says you should '*die and be a cheap funeral,*' but apart from that, nope, I'm good," she said.

"OK then. I'll call you when we know what sites we'll be visiting and when, and then I'll meet you at the first destination, and we'll travel together after that. You'll have all the information and can make the travel arrangements, and have the tickets for me at the airport?" Malcolm asked.

"Just like usual. I'll take care of it, Dad . . . . Well, I'll let you go and get on with renting that warehouse then."

"OK. I love you," ended Malcolm.

"Love you too, Dad. Bye." And she ended the call.

Malcolm sighed and put his phone back in his pants, forgetting to set it to ring instead of vibrate once more. He was thinking of how fortunate he was to have a daughter who could basically manage all the details of his business, and actually wanted to spend time with him on his ventures. He sure loved her . . . and he sure wished her mom would be robustly attacked by badgers.

99

THE BLOOD OF THE MOON

(From the notes of First Agent Christopher Griffin)

The culmination of all human history has taken us to a certain day. Every act from the past, every word spoken, every single thought that has been expressed or set in motion, has moved history to this day of which I speak. This day is relevant to all. This day is forged with exacting foreknowledge of mankind's choices, and has been predestined and purposed in advance according to those choices under the boundaries of Providence. This day is where men make that choice that foreknowledge has already engraved in the Book of Life, from the beginning of time. It is a day of great responsibility, and the only day promised to mankind regarding his earthly life. Today, of course, is that day. Ask yourself: "What mark will I leave upon history, and what will be inscribed in the Book of Life regarding me?"

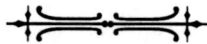

Shades State Park, 18 miles SW of Crawfordsville, Indiana— Present Day, June 21st, Night

Shades State Park is nestled next to Pine Hills Nature Preserve just west of it, where Sugar Creek and State Road 234 separate the two at the Deer's Mill Covered Bridge. Shades is a quiet, forested park that boasts a "nature lover's paradise" for the entire family, with hiking, camping, canoeing, and simple, peaceful relaxation. It is a large oasis in the fields of corn and soybeans that many seek for restful enjoyment and quiet escapism in the land of the Hoosiers. Trails and paths run throughout the forest among the thick stands of trees and brush that produce the park's familiar namesake, though the name "Shades" actually has a different etymological origin.

Everyone who reads the brochure/map they receive at the entrance to Shades Park can easily discover that Shades and Pine Hills Nature Preserve were once a single park. It also informs them that when the two were one, the dark and dense forest was originally referred to as the "Shades of Death." There are many historical tales that explain the reason for this title. One tale on the brochure is in reference to a bloody Indian war, a massacre between two tribes, in which all were slain but for twenty wounded warriors who left the area littered with roughly six hundred bodies of the fallen tribesmen from both warring tribes. There were no winners of the war, and death was the only lasting mark that both tribes left behind.

An account excluded from the brochure concerns the tale of Old Man Moses Rush, a hateful man when sober—and a worse man when drunk. His evil antics were legendary in the county *while he lived*, but were obscured by historical information afterward, and nearly forgotten. He was finally eliminated, or "done in," by his wife while he slept, which, as it turned out, was the first murder trial in Crawfordsville, the county seat of Montgomery County. Since most in the area knew how evil Moses Rush was, the missis was given the verdict of "innocent by means of self-defense," and further, the record shows that it was the jury's expressed opinion that Old Man Moses was dispatched with "commendable promptness." It was the first crime of its sort in the county, but certainly not the last.

Another story, occurring just after Shades and Pine Hills were divided, involved a person who came to be known as the Mad Hermit of Pine Hills. It seems that this man, Lawrence Hasselman, the surviving brother and owner of Pine Hills, kept a vigil to dissuade any who would come near the property. Lawrence was said to be delusional, and when he spoke to the few people he trusted, he spoke of a ghastly *"witch in the woods"* that he claimed was hunting him relentlessly.

To this day, there are some who dispute that the word "Shades" in the designation "Shades of Death" actually referred to the spirits of the dead that are said to inhabit the forest. Whichever happens to be the correct etymology of the name, all acknowledge that there was a foreboding intent in its christening; only time has diminished the fear of the forest, but its legends still live on. Though the State Park boasts of many points of interest, the site called the Devil's Punch Bowl was an allusion to its history, and no doubt all of the above played a part in drawing monsters to west-central Indiana.

Some years ago, Chuck Smith, Pastor of Costa's Mesa Calvary Chapel in California and founder of the Calvary Chapel Church, once commented that while attending a particular Midwest Pastor's Conference in Crawfordsville, Indiana, he could *feel* the demonic oppression in the area. He said that it was almost palpable. The demonic oppression has increased tenfold since.

Crawfordsville, in the heart of Montgomery County, is populated with nice, friendly, God-fearing people . . . mostly. They are honest and hardworking citizens who look out for their neighbors . . . mostly. But Montgomery County on balance has its own assortment of Wiccan practitioners, Crowley Satanists, Occult groups of all sorts, and full-fledged cults that mimic Christianity. These are nestled into a community of very committed Christians who honor the Lord and Biblical authority, social Christians attending as one would a club, and atheists alike. The Bible-believing churches do try to take stands against doctrines containing scriptural error and

Biblical ignorance, and there are warriors who trust in the complete, inerrant Word of God, atonement in the blood of Christ, and the power of His resurrection; but even they do not know the extent of the darkness that they try to illuminate. They do not truly know that there are evil men in the darkness, evil women, and much, much worse.

Nowadays, cable, satellite TV, and the Internet often keep the community indoors and connected to important information, and entertainment. They also have opened the door to all manner of ungodliness and pornography that the world gives away freely, like chlamydia. Things that used to be viewed or practiced in secret, rarely acknowledged in public except as the subject of ridicule, are now instantly accessible and can be invited into each home with the click of a mouse button, by accident, upon request, or on demand. Pornography is so easily accessed and prevalent that it is making deviancy appear "normal and proper." And as in virtually every community in America, a cancer spreads into hearts and minds that either know no better or have forgotten the better. It has been said that men celebrate together, but suffer alone. In Montgomery County USA, many suffer alone.

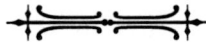

The moon was rising over the thick wall of trees in Shades State Park. Only a few miles away, the large group of Wiccans were practicing, reveling in their sensual rituals on Darlene Campbell's secluded property, while the worst of their practices was about to begin in a glen at the northeast end of the Shades. It was an area that was not open to camping or hiking, but there was a secluded glen there where Darlene's coven practiced rituals five times a year, and it hid them from the world. Only a few of those parties who spied this world with satellites had any interest in that location, and the ones who did noted that "all was going well."

The Council of the Thirteen, under Darlene, watched as Bradley Taylor gathered the rocks that were once again an altar, and all were now before Darlene, listening to her, kneeling before her, waiting for her to finish her invocation to the darkness. Darlene stood behind a table in her Wiccan robes. She had several inner pockets holding many items. The table in front of her was covered with a purple felt cloth that flowed to the ground on all sides, and had an intricate gold-and-black pentagram stitched on the top of it with symbols at each point and in the center. Darlene would never entertain the notion that the pentagram *was* the Baphomet, though it absolutely *was*. On the tablecloth were five lit candles, each a different color, each a different representation, one placed at each point or "station" of the pentagram: water, fire, earth, air, and spirit. Also on the cloth were a book, a silver cup with some sort of herbal liquid in it, and a box containing various illegal drugs. All in attendance were robed and were ready to receive their promised visitor. Darlene spoke the last words of the rite and raised her arms.

"We gather tonight, on this beautiful Summer Solstice, to partake in the spirits of light. We do so, as it is our will to do so," she proclaimed.

"Do what thou wilt, O Queen," came the response from the Thirteen.

"We open ourselves to the light of the masters, the heart of the masters, and the mind of the masters, as with the spirit of the earth and the elements. We open to all but the oppression of the Tsidkenu, the fatherless child," she said.

"Tsidkenu is not the star," they replied.

"Rise, my Thirteen," she commanded, as the full moon breached the wall of trees completely, spilled over it, and bathed them all in the blue-white light.

"The spirits have revealed their will to me, my Thirteen. We have no offering worthy for this eve . . . . Therefore, we were instructed to wait on the one who will bring the offering to us. We wait on an ancient master. We wait on the spirit of illumination, and the wait is nearly over. The light shines down on us, and the timing is at hand," she said; and all were silent before the altar.

Then, one of the Thirteen gasped. Then another, and another, and finally Darlene turned and saw a giant black figure a mere twenty feet behind her. It had come from the dark forest in silence. She too gasped and staggered back a step, almost knocking over the candles on the table. How long it had been there, nobody knew. It was soundless and massive. They were able to make it out only because of the reflected light of the moon glistening on its fur. It was huge and powerful, and it frightened everyone who stood before it, making their knees weak. It held something in its arms, something limp and possibly lifeless, and then it became clear that it was the body of a young woman. Cindy Stroud was unconscious in the arms of the beast, captive, and completely undone.

"Welcome," Darlene barely found voice for the salutation. "Welcome, O Master of the ages. Please . . . ," she stammered, "please . . . if you please, set your burden on our humble altar, as we serve you." She trembled to the core of her being as she spoke.

Silently and with what appeared to be no effort at all, the dark giant took five steps and lay the breathing but unmoving body of the young woman upon the altar, and then stepped back to where it stood before. In a deep, unearthly voice it commanded, "αρχίζουν την τελετή σας," which Darlene surprisingly understood, though not trained in the Greek language. The creature made her hear, "*Begin the ceremony.*"

Darlene, shaking, pulled a flask from her heavy robe and stepped to the young woman's prone side. She lifted her head, unscrewed the flask's lid with her thumb, and poured a potion into the young woman's mouth. The girl coughed and sputtered, but the brew was ingested, making her convulse, kick, and moan. Darlene signaled Bradley to grab the girl's ankles until she became still and completely unconscious again. Darlene lay the woman's head down, releasing her to slumber on the rock altar.

"Bring me the chalice, Bel-ta-bul," she commanded, using Bradley's secret name for all to hear.

Fear was in Darlene's voice. She tried to master the expression of it, if not the emotion itself. She also tried not to turn around and let that monster see the fear that she knew could be seen in her eyes. She was keenly aware that the forces to which she had given herself were powerful and deadly. She felt frail and unimportant before them.

Bradley, as a servant, if not official worshiper, obeyed Darlene's command and warily took the silver cup off the table, careful not to spill the liquid in it, and held it out to Darlene. With one hand, Darlene guided the cup, still being held by Bradley, into position, and then she pulled a sharp knife from her robe. With her other hand, Darlene lifted Cindy Stroud's arm in the air and spoke an enchantment that only she and the menacing creature behind her could understand. When she had finished her incantation, she cut Cindy's arm between biceps and triceps, and let the blood drip into the cup until she was satisfied that there was enough. Setting down the knife, Darlene pulled a small roll of gauze from her robe's pocket. She instructed Bradley to bind the wound she had made on Cindy's arm, which he did, tucking in the end to keep it from unraveling. Darlene stood at the side of her motionless victim on the altar and raised the cup aloft in both hands.

"This night we have a magical creature among us, a high master of the elemental spirits. Before his face I ask a blessing on this cup! Grant us the power you possess, spirits of the universe. Visit us and empower us, spirits of the earth, spirits of the water, spirits of flame, and spirits of the air, and may our spirits be entwined with yours. I drink from this and receive from you all that I ask. Then I pass it to the Thirteen that they may partake in the power, wisdom, and strength you offer only to the bold, the brazen, and the brave. Now visit us and guide us, and perfect our magic," she said, and took a sip of the thick, dark, and warm liquid in the cup. Her fear did not subside, but she knew what she needed to do, and what was to happen next.

Darlene passed the cup to the first of her robed followers, who knelt upon receiving the cup, sipped, rose, and then passed the cup to the next person. She could see that they, too, were frightened; yet they were also determined to partake, as much as she was. Her determination was one of conviction above all, but theirs was inspired by the fear of consequences that would certainly befall them should they *not* partake. Each in turn knelt, sipped, and then passed the cup to the next until it reached the last of the Thirteen, who set the cup on the altar next to the girl.

Darlene walked over to the altar, lifted the head of the girl, just as she had done before, and forced her to ingest from the cup of her own blood. Then Darlene rose and placed the cup on the table.

"Expose the offering to the moonlight, Tal-Rosh," Darlene commanded another of the Thirteen.

The robed man closest to the girl pulled a knife from his own robe and began to obey the command. All who wore robes had knives, antiquated, unique, thrice-cursed, and very, very sharp. The one responding to the command knelt by the girl and cut her clothes asunder, revealing her pale and mostly uncovered skin to the moonlight.

Darlene began another arcane incantation. It began in English, but then it morphed into Latin for nearly a full minute, then changed to Greek and then to something older, esoteric and unrecognizable to all but her guest. It was another language she did not know, but this time she did not understand what she said, and she did not even recognize her own voice as she spoke. It sent chills up her spine in terror and ecstasy. All this was new to her, but she would not let the fact be known to her followers. Then, she saw a dark ribbon of smoke appear out of nothing and hover over the body of her offering . . . just a thin tendril of smoke, at first. It was darker than the shadows beyond the glen. It swirled and twisted, growing slowly, getting larger. Its color turned from black to purple, and became lighter, and suddenly it began to glow.

The Thirteen also beheld the smoke—or was it an apparition? They all watched in awe as it seemed to take on life, glow brighter, and become a being of sorts. They could smell it, sweet like honey for a moment, then bitter like brimstone, and back to honey . . . and now it seemed to be making a small sound, an electrical discharge that sounded similar to that of a distant bug zapper's electrical arc, but much softer. Then lights like fireflies began appearing within the glowing smoke-body. The tiny lights, spherical, at least twenty, chased each other within the iridescent haze, and grew in size as the smoke expanded. Then the smoky entity made sudden jerking movements, pausing for a second, then pulling one way, then another, getting larger with each violent spasm. The lights inside gained intensity . . . they were incandescent and bathed the woman below it in an unearthly glow. The hair on the arms of all attending stood on end, and something very much like Saint Elmo's fire instantly engulfed the area.

Although she did not know how, it came to Darlene that there was something else they must now do. She commanded the Thirteen, "Gather round the altar. Get on your knees and worship the lights, and the darkness," and they began to obey . . . but fearfully she realized that she had never moved her lips to speak the command, and again, the voice was not hers. The Thirteen surrounded the altar and worshiped the creature, rather than the Creator.

And lastly, by what cause they did not know, all of them instantly understood, without being told, what must next be done. They laid hands on the woman, the offering, holding her in place. Then those who touched her legs began to part them, and those who held her arms pulled them tight. The smoke-being and the lights within began to move closer toward the unconscious young woman, extending dark tendrils that caressed her. Moving over and around her, they embraced her, and when her body began to convulse in some sort of seizure, they gripped her and entered her. Cindy screamed but she remained unconscious.

Minutes passed in a blur. None of them could recollect exactly what happened. The lights emerged from the smoke, up and above the group as the smoke entered the body of the woman. Each light grew in size and spun about them overhead like glowing orbs or discs. They grew until each was as large as a man, and then their shapes transformed into that of a man or that of a woman, and they evenly circled the group, and danced and spun over and about the ensemble. They made coordinated pulsing noises that seemed like music, but it was sinister, and no pleasure to the ears. The last thing any could remember was holding the woman down as the swirling cacophony above them reached a crescendo . . . and then . . . all was silent . . . and somehow, the woman they had held down was gone from their grasp. Their hands were now palm-down on the rocks of the altar, the smoke-entity-thing was gone, and they were staring at one another, with Darlene looking down at them. Then Darlene shook herself from the trancelike state and turned her head. All there followed her gaze. In the distance they saw the giant moving away from them, carrying the body of the woman, and both disappeared into the forest under the cover of darkness. Then all looked up, and the lights that were people changed back into small orbs and were silently moving high above them. Then they scattered and flew out of sight. None of them knew that the lights had other business, dark business, elsewhere in the Montgomery County area.

A smile came to Darlene's lips. "We are worthy," she said. The Thirteen repeated her words. "We are gods," she said, and the Thirteen spoke as one, the same as she, none perceiving that they were the furthest from the true God.

9

THE BODY OF EVIDENCE

(From the notes of First Agent Christopher Griffin)

Taxonomy is the scientific and logical method of how we determine the similarities and differences of virtually everything. Naturally, since all creatures live on the same planet with the same environment, gravity, heat sources, and solar radiation, there are similarities between very different kinds and types of creatures since they exist in the commonalities of this world. But the taxonomical process can also cause one to make foolish inferences and construct completely spurious conclusions. As incorporated into the evolution model, it can be demonstrable that many conclusions are not based on science, but speculation made believable by the use of art, and imagination, and compounded by unsustainable blind consensus.

Embryological recapitulation is a glaring example of such. This is where biological organisms were compared superficially with others to manufacture the idea that they were related linearly under "biogenic law," as opposed to being related by branching evolutionary relationships, which are also spurious in nature. The method was to simply take unborn humans at

110

various stages of gestation and compare them to dissimilar animals, and claim, "At this stage we have a tail like a tadpole," and, "Look, here we have gills like a fish," and "Look, we are breathing water like fish do," when clearly the so-called gills were human glands and only looked like gills, being completely genetically different. The "tail" was the formation of the human spinal column and there was never a time when we breathed water, as the amniotic fluid isn't. But, to make things worse, the art depicting these similarities as evidences were forged to make outrageous claims more convincing.

But such are the foolish ways of humanity to postulate and put forth an idea, theorize about it, fall in love with it by means of pride, determine how to support or falsify it, discover grounds for falsification, ignore it as a means of nullifying the theory, then modify the means with a new set of postulations in support of the premise, finding that they also hold no water, yet clinging to the argument because it is inconceivable that the theory one loves in arrogance is incorrect. And that is how the assertion of evolution continues.

The geologic column in chart form, as shown in any museum, is pure fantasy art. It exists in all its beauty and completeness, layer upon layer, epoch upon epoch, nowhere in the natural world. It is still displayed because it furthers the premise in a single picture. Were those the only two examples, it might be forgivable, but that isn't the case. You won't learn of scientific lies and contradictions in public school, most colleges, or any museum of natural history, because naturally, they exclude the possibility of any other origin of mankind beyond evolution. To challenge the theory is academic suicide.

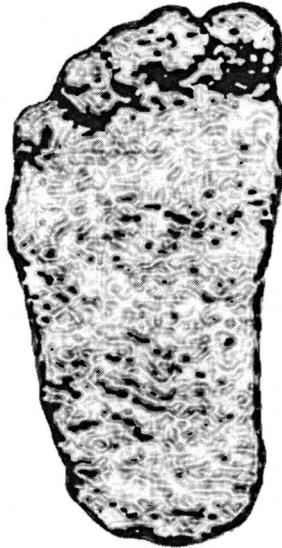

Pine Hills Nature Preserve, Montgomery County, Indiana—Present Day, June 25th

It was just nine days before Independence Day when a group of hikers at Pine Hills Nature Preserve stumbled upon the dead body of Bill Donovan. Sheriff Braxton and all Montgomery County Law Enforcement had a missing persons report on both him and Cindy Stroud, but apparently now, of the two, only Cindy was still listed as missing. It turned out that this was the third death in the southwest part of Montgomery County in one week, and that did not include the missing Amish, the Beiler family. The names of the other two bodies found were being withheld until families were notified, but all information concerning them was in the police database.

The first body was found at Lake Waveland. It was thought to have been a boating accident because the corpse was badly torn up. It had been gnawed on by something with strong teeth, but coyotes will do that to a corpse. The coroner, Dr. Mills, thought the bite-radius measurements had to be two or three coyotes next to each other, certainly not just one mouth because of the size. The death gave no indication that there was no reason to close the lake for Independence Day. Hair samples in the wounds appeared to be animal, not human, so that gave more credence to coyotes. The hair samples were taken as evidence but were not sent to the lab to determine exactly what kind of hair it was, because it clearly had to be an animal's and nothing related to the cause of the death. An entire pack of coyotes would find it very difficult to take down a full-grown man. Wolves, perhaps, but no wolf colony was anywhere near here.

The second body was found near a local dog kennel between the Lake and Shades State Park. According to the coroner, it was a possible homicide, because the bruises and contusions all over the body were not sustainable by a car accident unless the car came back to hit the victim repeatedly, yet there were no tire marks, paint, or undercarriage residues. But the cause of death was even stranger. The only other injury on the completely pummeled body was on the inner thigh. Something big had bitten a chunk of meat out of the victim's leg. And the most confusing part was that it seemed the body had been exsanguinated through the femoral artery, because there was little evidence of blood around the body, and little left in it. They had no suspect or apparent motive, so the case was still an open investigation. The coroner, however, had the body prepped and ready to be delivered to a medical examiner for further analysis in Indianapolis.

Today was a hot and humid late June afternoon. It had not rained since June 19th, but the humidity lingered. It was a typical Indiana summer. Sheriff Braxton drove his GMC Yukon into Pine Hills after he heard the call that a body had been found. His Deputy went ahead of him because he was already visiting Shades with his family, and it was within walking distance for him. Braxton used the Department of Natural Resources' access route that all Indiana State Parks have so that equipment and work crews can reach and manage the park facilities and features. The body had been found deep in the park, and Braxton drove the path carefully near the "backbone" because there were some sheer drop-offs. Ahead, the Sheriff saw his Deputy, Caleb Donner, so he parked the SUV about 200 feet away and walked the rest of the distance.

"Here he is, Sheriff. The coroner is on the way," Donner said, pointing at the lifeless body.

"Your wife and kids still in Shades?" asked Braxton.

"Yeah, I didn't want them getting close to this," said Donner.

"Good," said Braxton.

"Looks like this guy's neck was broken, and by the way the marks on the neck appear, whoever snapped it seems to have only used one hand. And Sheriff . . . it's the biggest handprint I've ever seen. I think we should put out an APB on Shaq O'Neal," Donner said.

"This is getting out of hand, no pun intended. This is the third death in a week . . . . And the second one may have been an animal attack, after the body was nearly beaten to death by . . . something Dr. Mills can't account for, yet."

"Do you think we have a cougar loose around here? It wouldn't be the first time," the Deputy said.

"I don't know. It's been years since that last panther was put down, but it never harmed anything beyond livestock. And they don't beat the living tar out of their victims, and drink their blood. It's going to be a real head-scratcher until we get more information," Braxton said as he moved in even closer to the corpse.

"Step back, I want to get a look at his neck," Braxton said. He bent down and looked carefully at the bruising pattern on the neck, touching nothing. "No, no, no," he said. "Why can't it be natural causes?" he asked in general, not really looking for an answer from the Deputy.

The Sheriff put a rubber glove on his right hand, looked more closely at the neck on the corpse, and swatted flies away. He took note of the position of the body, noticed that the hands were not cut or bloody, and looked for but found no other wounds. Carefully, he reached inside the Levi's blue jeans that the body wore, and pulled the leather wallet out with gloved fingers.

"You take pictures yet?" Braxton asked.

"Several with my cell phone's camera. They're high-resolution, so they should be good. The kids that found the body have been given Voluntary Statement forms. I've got their names and contact information, and I've sent them out of the park," the Deputy said.

"Good," was all Braxton said, as he opened the wallet, found cash still in it, and confirmed that the driver's license was the man they had been looking for. The photo did not look too much like the face on the ground, but four days dead will do that to a corpse.

"You've heard the other calls to the station recently, haven't you, Sheriff?" Donner asked.

"Strange lights in the sky and glowing *forms* don't break a man's neck, Caleb. Let's not get spooked over will-o'-the-wisps. That's an air-traffic controller's problem," said Braxton.

"But the timing's strange. You once told me to rule out *nothing*," the Deputy said.

"OK, now I'm telling you, rule out what's *stupid*, Caleb," Braxton said as he rose from the corpse. "We'll file the reports because that's our job, but none of those calls needs to show up in the *Journal Review*, or *The Paper*'s police blotter."

"Well, I only mention it because it's been on the radio . . . on the morning chat. I'm not talking about a call from the Alamo Hobo either; I'm talking about some upstanding citizens calling in and reporting the sightings of every weird kind you can imagine. And stuff is being reported as missing too. Cars have been vandalized, equipment has been stolen. I'm not sure if they are connected, but strange things are happening all over the county," commented Deputy Donner.

"The second a strange light in the sky is seen breaking any law that *we* have to enforce, you can let me know and we'll arrest it.

Until then, let's try to figure out what's going on without any of that Area-51 *BS*," Braxton said.

"Well, the dogs should be here in a minute. We might find that girl then . . . she could be close by, but the underbrush is so thick, she could be ten feet away and we'd have to trip over her to find her," Donner said.

"I hear Jimmy's truck . . . I'm going to have to find a better way to park so they can get through. Wait right here," Braxton ordered.

The Sheriff started walking toward his truck, when up ahead, Jimmy Jones pulled in behind it. Jimmy got out and started to unload his dogs, so Braxton figured reparking was pointless. He stopped for a second and then shook his head as he remembered that the ME was going to be coming up the same path, so both trucks would have to move. He started toward the trucks again, when the dogs began hollering. Braxton quickened his pace, got closer, passed his own truck, and walked back to Jimmy's truck where the dogs were raising Cain.

"What's the matter with your dogs, Jimmy?" asked Braxton.

"They've got a scent that they don't like, Sheriff. They won't come out of their kennel," Jimmy said.

"What good are tracking dogs if they are afraid to track?" asked Braxton.

"My dogs have gone after cougar, Sheriff. They've never been afraid of anything before," Jimmy retorted, defending his honor.

"Well, leave them kenneled then and back down until you have flat ground to park. Then you can get them out. The medical examiner is going to be coming up this service road soon. I've got to repark too," said Braxton.

"All right, Sheriff," Jimmy said and slammed the kennel door shut. "Can you get a swatch of clothing from the body that Donner found so that I can give them a scent that they may be able to back-trace?" he asked.

"I'll get a shoe for you—just move that noise down the hill," Braxton said. Braxton shook his head and headed back again to where Donner stood watch. Jimmy fired up the truck's engine, but the dogs made the engine barely audible.

Braxton walked back toward Donner, thankful that noise was getting far away. He'd no more than covered half the distance when he heard honking from Jimmy's truck and the dogs barking even louder than before, squealing now, perhaps screaming? Then the honking sound changed to a steady horn blast, and Braxton shook his head and turned back toward his SUV. When he got to it, he climbed in, started it up, and went down the hill in reverse, looking out backward in the rear window so he would not leave the road. The honking got louder as he got closer, and Jimmy didn't seem to want to let up on the horn until he saw the Sheriff's truck back up to him and pull alongside him. Jimmy released the horn, and as Braxton rolled down his window, he could tell see Jimmy was white as a sheet, waving his arms at the Sheriff, with the dogs still barking.

"Did you see it, Sheriff, standing on the ridge? Jimmy shouted excitedly through the vehicle, barely over the dogs.

"See what, Jimmy?" Braxton asked.

"The bear . . . or *something*! It was black, but I don't think it was any black bear though! It had to be a Kodiak or something. It was ten feet tall," Jimmy shouted, still frightened by what he beheld.

"Calm down, Jimmy. There's no black bear or grizzly within two hundred miles of here, you know that," Braxton said.

"Well, maybe it was a gorilla, like somebody's giant exotic pet escaped, or maybe a truck with a wild animal wrecked and it got loose . . . ," Jimmy posed, excitedly.

"A ten-foot-tall gorilla? Jimmy, I know you aren't one to lie, so I believe you saw *something*, but, c'mon, a ten-foot gorilla," Braxton said, bewildered. He knew that Jimmy used to drink, but that was years ago. Jimmy was a teetotaler now, and Braxton considered him a friend.

"I know what I saw, and it was too big to be a normal bear. And it looked different from a bear, but it had to be a bear, or . . .

no, it had to be a bear! And that's what's driving my dogs crazy," he said.

"All right, you're excited and your dogs are excited. Go home and maybe we can try this later." Braxton looked up. "Oh, there's the coroner. Get out of here, Jimmy, I'll call you later."

"Sheriff, I don't know if you're safe out here with that thing running loose in the woods," Jimmy said. "You might just go up and get your Deputy and get out of here too. Call a zoo animal recovery team or something, and let them get that animal out of here. I hate to say it, Sheriff, but it looked mean, maybe even . . . evil . . . it was spooky. I was scared for my life when I saw it."

"I've got my shotgun and a forty-five, and Donner has his sidearm, so don't worry about us. Go home," Braxton said. He moved his SUV farther back and shut it down, to let the coroner pass. Braxton got out and flagged down the coroner, while Jimmy turned around and he and his dogs went the way leading out of the park.

"Rodger," Braxton said to the coroner, "give me a lift up there with you."

"Sure, climb in," Dr. Rodger Mills said, and he waited for the Sheriff to cross to the other side of the car.

"Wait a sec, I want to take my shotgun with me, and get some tape," Braxton said. He went back to his SUV, unlocked the weapon from its station-bar, and pulled it out. He then grabbed the tape from his glove compartment, shoved it in his pocket, shut the door, and got in Dr. Mills's car. "Thanks," he added, and the two drove up to the Deputy.

Dr. Mills drove carefully up the hill in his station wagon that was always ready for transporting a cadaver. He looked over to the Sheriff.

"Is the shotgun really necessary?" he asked.

"I doubt it, Rodger, but my windows are rolled down and I don't want anyone messing with my weapons when I'm this far away from my truck," Braxton said, covering his reason for carrying the weapon. He was not sure what Jimmy saw, but a gun in the hand is better than two in the truck.

Dr. Mills pulled up as close to the cadaver as possible so that they would not have to carry it far. He shut off the engine and the two got out and went to the Deputy's side.

"Hi, Caleb, how's the family?" Dr. Mills shook the Deputy's hand, and then took out his examination gloves and began to put them on.

"Great, Doc. Sorry we seem to be keeping you so busy this week," Caleb said.

"Not at all," Doc Mills said, adjusting his gloves. "Well, let's get to it, shall we?"

He bent over the body and waved off the flies, and if he was bothered by the smell, he made no indication of it. Gently, he touched the throat and neck of the cadaver, studying it carefully. Then, ever so gently, he lifted the head about two inches off the ground, rotating it a few centimeters back and fourth, looking at the scrapes on the face and feeling the broken neck. Then he set the head down and carefully examined the hands and nails of the man.

Deputy Donner had withstood the smell of the dead man for longer than he desired to, so he stepped back and watched from a distance, trying not to disturb anything that he might be blamed for. As far as disturbing evidence is concerned, he'd made several mistakes in the past. Braxton had scolded him each time, according to protocol, but then added, "Experience is made of many mistakes, and you have a lot more experiences ahead of you." And Braxton didn't hold them against him for long. He liked and respected Braxton. Although this was Donner's day off, he was always on call; and with the weirdness going around the county, he was glad he was no longer alone in the forest. He observed the examination of the body and was glad he was now upwind. Then he looked over at the path that must have been at least thirty feet from the corpse.

He carefully walked toward it to see whether perhaps something was dropped while this man was attacked, maybe he was while walking the path.

Dr. Mills made a cursory look over the rest of the body, peeking under clothing for epidermal pallor and lividity. After finding no other indications of injury to note, he knew that he'd be able to give it a much more in-depth study during the autopsy, once he had the cadaver on a table. Having seen enough for the moment, he rose and looked at Braxton with puzzlement in his expression.

"Well, I'd say that the time of death was about four days ago," Dr. Mills said. "The neck is broken and appears to be crushed. With the exception of facial abrasions, there are no other indications of damage to the cadaver. If it was here that long, there *should* be signs of scavengers, but I noticed no turkey vultures in the sky, and there are no signs of a coyote, rat, or other animal mastication. Insects are the only evident creatures taking advantage of the body. I also noticed that there is an odor here that is foul, but not indicative of the cadaver's decay; that is, I smell the cadaver and *something else* that is around this area. Now, the lack of any scavenger sign and that smell are both *very* unusual to me. However, the mechanism of death was by that single handprint on the throat . . . and I'm sure you already know *that* is not the right size of hand for *any man* that I'm aware of. But I noted that the collarbone, jaw, and even the back of the skull were also bruised by the single hand, indicating, well, a huge and powerful hand. It *could* have been some man-made device that did it, but it doesn't look like it. And there are no other signs of trauma to the body, except facial abrasions, and that most likely came as the body was dropped by whatever crushed the throat. On just what I've got so far, it looks like someone with an enormous hand lifted this man up in the air, *as there are no scuffle marks in the dirt*, snapped his neck with one hand, and dropped him where he is. It's unbelievable, actually, but that's what it initially looks like to me," Mills said.

"Can you tell if this is in any way related to the other two deaths?" Braxton asked.

"My first reaction would be no. They *seem* isolated, but I also don't believe in coincidences, so I am just not sure. I'll review the findings on both cases," Mills said honestly.

"Don't take this as crazy talk, Doc," Braxton said, "but could a bear . . . or a gorilla have done this?"

"Definitely not a bear. It's clearly a hand that can grasp, on the cadaver's throat. But why do you say gorilla?" Mills asked.

"Jimmy, the dog handler, who was just leaving as you pulled in, told me before I sent him home that he saw either a bear or maybe a gorilla on the eastern ridge. He, um . . . ." Braxton was hesitant to say more, but then continued, "He said this bear or gorilla was *ten feet tall* . . . . I didn't see anything, and I have no idea what he saw, but Jimmy was serious and very scared."

"I'm not sure what did this, Sheriff, but what Jimmy may have seen, is well . . . ." Now it was Dr. Mills's turn to be hesitant to continue, but he did anyway. "I don't know if they really exist, mind you, but it *could* have been a . . . ." Dr. Mills was almost embarrassed to say it, but then out it came: "It could have been something like a . . . a Bigfoot."

"Are you serious, Doc? A *Bigfoot*?" Braxton questioned.

"I only mention it as a possibility. Like I said, I don't even know if they exist . . . but, look at the size of that handprint on that neck. No human being has a hand that big."

"I don't believe it!" exclaimed the Deputy. "Hey, Sheriff . . . *no way*! Sheriff . . . ." Deputy Donner cursed and shouted from several yards away from the path.

"What, Caleb?" Braxton replied.

"Both of you come here and look at this!" the Deputy exclaimed.

Braxton and Mills walked over to Caleb, who was obviously excited about something. It was just what Braxton needed, more excitement. Caleb was staring at the ground, and pointing to it.

"Could someone with a foot this size," he said, pointing at a footprint in the dirt, "have a hand *that* size?" Caleb was now pointing at the corpse.

All three beheld the giant footprint of a monster. It wasn't a perfect footprint, but Braxton knew that they'd have to cast a plaster moulage of the print, and most important, that his life was going to get very complicated, very fast, when he wrote this up and sent it to the Captain. Braxton hated complications.

"I might be able to contact someone who knows much more about this 'Bigfoot' business than I do, if you want me to," Mills offered.

"This is nuts," Braxton said. "Go ahead, contact the Men in Black if you have to. This isn't my line of work."

"First I want to get a forensic pathologist here, preferably an FBI pathologist. It is clear that you have a homicide on your hands, Sheriff, and this one is giving me the willies," Dr. Mills said.

"Yup," the Sheriff said, resigning himself to that much, and admitting that he was in way over his head.

"Can we go to your office and call it in?" Dr. Mills requested. "I've got the odd feeling that we're being watched . . . and I don't mind admitting that I'm scared."

"Let's tape this crime scene up, Caleb, and get outta here," Braxton said.

"I'm for that, Sheriff," Caleb said, feeling the creepiness begin to climb the back of his neck as well.

"I'll call this in to the Captain and let *him* contact the FBI," Braxton said as he pulled a roll of tape from his pocket and tossed it to his Deputy. "Then I'll get the DNR to close the park until they're through."

"OK, Sheriff," Dr. Mills said, "but let's make it fast . . . . I've never been scared enough to soil myself . . . until now."

The Sheriff and Deputy taped the area quickly, and all three got into Dr. Mills's car until he had backed it up to the Sheriff's SUV.

The police officers got out hastily, looking up and down the wooded hillsides and slopes to see whether they could identify who might be watching them, as they all felt it now. Then the officers entered the SUV and followed Dr. Mills out of the park. They did not stop feeling the unusual sensation of dread until they were two miles away, and halfway to the Waveland-based Sheriff's Office.

10

VARIOUS SHADES OF REALITY

(From the notes of First Agent Christopher Griffin)

For the Agent's Handbook—1956—Chapter 5—
Required Reading

Section: First Responders Regarding Witnesses—Practical
and Philosophical

A single witness constitutes the least reliable of evidences. The human mind is designed to see patterns, formations, order, shapes, in everything, recognize them, and categorize them. This "visual taxonomy" is often a hindrance regarding a witness. When a man looks at a rabbit-shaped cloud, it is never a rabbit, only the mind making order out of patterns and shapes that the mind recognizes as something it may have seen before, or something imagined. The cloud only has the appearance of order, and from other points of view, other perspectives, it does not look at all like a rabbit; soon, even the "appearance" of the rabbit is no more, and is swallowed up in the chaotic clouds where it was spawned. When fear is inserted into visual taxonomy, images and remembered events can be skewed, and may not be reliable.

When questioning a single eyewitness, speak in a calm and even tone and take down the complete statement word for word. Never assist the witness in finding the words to describe the event. Only after the statement is complete should the agent question the witness against the statement. The agent should ask all of the questions provided in the report manual, currently form A-22. Always note the involuntary movement and posture of the witness. Look the witness in the eye and observe where the witness looks when eye contact is broken. Tone of voice and demeanor are important. Compare the answers to the testimony and identify any inconsistencies. Make note of the witness's belief system including involvement with the occult. Record dates, times, names, and locations of every incident/event mentioned. No detail is too trivial to record. Assure the witness that the event is being looked into by a team of professionals. Do not offer any secure information, or lead the witness to unsubstantial conclusions. Do everything you can to corroborate or falsify the testimony with the evidence at hand, but do not take action unless there is a clear and present danger. In that unlikely event, follow the instructions on enemy engagement, beginning on page 156 of this manual. <u>Remember your training.</u>

If the witness seems credible, canvass the witness's neighborhood for opinions of reliability and stability of the witness, and question the immediate family of the witness if possible. Do this also in the workplace of the witness. Be sure to express your own discernment and gut feelings in the comments section. File the report and begin research for historical similarities and patterns, if any. Finalize the report, *then contact dispatch for further operational instructions, or for the next assignment.*

For multiple witness sightings, dispatch will have a forensics team on standby. Compare interviews and data and—only if it is warranted—contact dispatch for the forensics team. At that point, dispatch will have a level-three Trinity support team on standby, and alert designated authorities regarding an Operation Inception. Assist forensics in any way possible.

—✦═✦—

Colorado Rocky Mountains, 18 miles north of Gunnison—December 21, 1984, 7:10pm

Theatre of Combat: Close-Quarters—Underground Mining Facility—Structurally Sound.

Strike-Team Bravo extraction code transmitted. Artillery support ready.

The Knightlight Trinity Bravo had been in the mine for over eight long hours on a "Seek and Destroy V-Op." Insertion was roughly half a mile downhill from the mine opening, where they had parked their vehicle. They had traversed the mountainous terrain to the opening, breached the mineshaft, searched the various chambers, and made a critical mistake. The mine they were currently in was a mineshaft only in appearance. It was the stronghold of a demonic coven where man and Nephil-Adam alike were conspiring and advancing their agenda. Bravo team had been able to defeat all of the early-warning systems they had knowingly encountered. They had infiltrated the hive and were prepared to destroy it . . . until one mistake corrupted the mission. In a deep chamber they were compromised and attacked, and Michael Cavor, "Tick," had been killed in action. Nick and Gene were now running for their own lives.

"How far now?" Eugene Ledford shouted into his headset as he ran uphill in the dark and dusty mining tunnel at full tilt. Eugene had sprinted 20 yards ahead of his partner, Dominic Moreau, with longer strides, carrying a bright signal flare in his left hand and a 12-gauge shotgun in his right. Eugene was sweating despite the cool, dry air around him, and there was no wiping it away. The Big Cheese ignored the sweat and the fatigue of running uphill, and slowed only after he reached the mouth of the storage cavern. That uppermost cavern connected the surface tunnel, with the deeper chamber tunnels that honeycombed the underground facility. They had just come up from the dark depths, on a failed mission, and were being pursued by all that dwelt down there. The two were making an urgent exit, but the third member of their team was simply gone.

Eugene turned around to face back down the tunnel from which he'd just ascended. He saw Dominic's liquid lightbar in motion and the light reflecting off Dominic's balding forehead, but could not see beyond him. Gene held his flare as a torch, looking into the darkness, knowing what pursued them and how much their own lives depended upon getting to the surface first. He noted that the air around him smelled like "Independence Day" to him because of the flare.

Finally, Dominic emerged out of the darkness; his black shirt was visibly dust covered and dirty. He noted that he was raising clouds of dust with every foot impact, and still the thunderings and cacophonous bellows were at his heels.

"Twenty seconds behind me!" Dominic shouted ahead.

Eugene popped open the fill-cap and knocked over the barrel of fuel they had maneuvered there earlier at one side of the tunnel, while Dominic rounded the corner and did the same on his side of the tunnel, allowing the unmarked barrels of petroleum liquid to spill out and down the tunnel path beneath them. The sounds emanating from the darkness below filled large the cavern with echoes.

"Ten seconds!" shouted Dominic, barely above the raucous clamor that was coming up the tunnel to the storage cavern. A rumbling akin to a stampede could be felt beneath their boots.

"Toss it now!" Dominic ordered.

Eugene tossed his flare down the tunnel and the two dove for cover behind a pile of timber support braces, away from the downward mouth of the tunnel. Eugene's flare landed more than three yards too far and off to the left of the petroleum stream. There was no explosion, but the sounds of rage were closing in upon them from somewhere beyond the light of the flare.

The two peered over their wooden makeshift bunker. The rumblings slowed, and then the shouting and bellowing ceased. The pursuers were mastered by a single guttural but commanding voice, one that did not sound human. It spoke "στήκετε" in the ancient Greek language. In their ears it was "Steko!" which translates as "stand fast" or "hold your position" in English.

The two Knightlight agents looked down into the tunnel witnessing only the distant flickering flare illuminating the load-bearing buttresses and exposed wiring that followed the tunnel floor, but their vision stopped at the impenetrable darkness beyond. Then they saw a colossal form begin to take shape in the most distant reaches of the flare's light. The enormous dark mass halted at the outer limits of their view, when two dim, spherical light reflections became visible in the darkness. They were a pair of eyes suspended up high in the 12-foot ceiling of the mineshaft tunnel. Dominic and Eugene judged that the being who owned them must be nearly ten feet tall. The lighted eyes seemed to change slightly from spherical shapes to up-tilted ovals with an inner reflective catlike ring. And then they blinked. The distant but discernibly hate-filled eyes fully reflected the crimson incandescence of the flare.

"I should never have said that you throw like a girl. You overthrew your flare," Dominic whispered to Eugene.

Gene took another flare from his belt and ignited it with a puff of smoke and flame, but Nick motioned for him not to toss it yet.

"Where is Tammuz?" Nick shouted down the tunnel. He waited for a few seconds, but all he received in response was his echo. He really did not expect an answer . . . . *This monster may be piloted, but may not be vocally interactive*, he thought to himself with uncertainty.

"The Andre smells a trap. What should we do, Rock?" Eugene asked cautiously.

"Give them some buck, and then we'll send another barrel down. There's another one behind us. We can light it up while we have time," Dominic said.

Eugene, taking advantage of the hesitation of the pursuers, fired buckshot down the shaft, and sent another volley behind the first. The booming flashes of light offered them momentary cover from what still remained down the tunnel. An angry howl answered the gunfire. Eugene backed up to the midpoint of the cavern where Dominic was now wrestling with the fuel barrel, trying to move it and tip it in the right direction. Eugene, a good seven inches taller and fifty pounds heavier than Dominic, grabbed the opposite side of the barrel and helped drop it in the right direction.

Standing behind the barrel, still mostly out of breath from their sprint up the tunnel, Dominic swapped his lightstick with Gene's flare.

"Go topside and flush this toilet. I'll be right behind you," Nick said.

"Make it fast; the threat of a trap isn't going to slow the Andre down for long. Here, take my shottie." Eugene handed him the military 12-gauge, turned, and got his left foot stuck in a wooden pallet. He tried to move but he was stuck.

"Dang, I'm stuck!" Eugene shouted.

"Happened to me earlier. Crouch and step backward," Dominic advised wisely.

Eugene crouched and then jumped backward and freed himself, and then headed rapidly up the last tunnel toward daylight.

"I'm clear," Eugene said. "Stupid bugs," he added under his breath.

The storage cavern, made visible in the red flickering light, looked similar to an old miner's storage room with wooden supports, dolly carts, rusted tools, crates, pallets, more beams, and supports, some in use and some stacked for future use. It was much larger than a normal mining station and it was intentional that it looked old and abandoned. The tunnel dimensions themselves were nearly twice the ceiling height one would expect in a real mine, and though dusty and dirty, it was of sturdier and recent construction. Its dilapidated condition was strictly for the sake of appearance.

Dominic quickly bent over to pry the cap off the fuel barrel, looking down the tunnel again. Now he could see that a man wearing a National Parks uniform had imposed himself between the flare and Dominic, but he did not obscure the large eyes that held their place near the ceiling of the tunnel, still fixed above and beyond the flickering light. The man was moving cautiously up the fuel-soaked tunnel, leveling his 9mm sidearm in Dominic's direction. The distant hulking shape waited, apparently choosing to observe his minion's success, or lack thereof.

Quickly, Dominic popped the lid off the fuel barrel, pushed it forward, rolling it down the tunnel, and dove for cover just as the robed man let fly a volley of lead. Dark liquid spilled out as the barrel descended, but Dominic noticed that some had spilled and pooled between Dominic and the mouth of the tunnel. He tossed the flare into the liquid and it erupted with heat and brilliant flame that ran downhill trailing the barrel and would ignite the rest of the liquid spilled moments prior.

The cavern was ablaze, but 9mm gunfire prevented Dominic from rising. He aimed and discharged his own weapon in the general direction of the now-completely-obscured man; but he was unsure where the man now stood, and surely the flames had engulfed that man. Then he heard the sound that shook him at the core of his being from directly in front of him on the other side of the flame. He'd heard it before, under different circumstances, and it never failed to incite fear. It was a monstrous roar, whether a battle cry or a curse, he could not tell. It was a sound as if some impossible horror had been unleashed from the pit of Hell, and had been empowered to destroy by the terror of its voice alone. It was an impressive effect. It belonged in Hell, and Dominic promised himself that if his legs would just move, he would send it back there. Seemingly born of fire, a body bathed in flame soared over Dominic's head, writhing as it flew through the air and impacted the far wall. It sank to the ground, motionless, and continued to burn. It was the man in the National Parks uniform, and Nick knew that the Andre had thrown the man once he caught fire. All the while, the Andre continued to bellow. It was a reoccurring roar that was deafening, panic-inspiring, and not of this earth.

Heat and brilliant flame continued to make a seemingly impenetrable wall to any who might foolishly dare to brave it. Dominic was thankful for that. But smoke was filling the chamber, too. Then Nick heard the voice of horror close by, as a giant pillar of flame wielding a gleaming blade, long and heavy, emerged through the inferno on a blind down-stroke meant to cleave Dominic in half. The Andre, afire, wielded an old, arcane weapon from a bygone day. The rock beneath Nick's feet vibrated and stone chips flew up as the blade missed him completely, but only by inches, and embedded itself in the rock. Dominic stared in amazement at the blade, forged by some unknown and long-forgotten artisan, which now had merged with the stone floor, mere inches in front of him. The roar of hate erupted again, now tinged with frustration, as the fiery creature pulled free the heavy blade, lifting it again above the flames and demonstrating amazing strength. The furious voice reached a crescendo as the blade reached its apex, ready for the down-stroke, and Dominic's eyes were transfixed upon it. Simply put, it was awesome to behold.

As Dominic rolled away from the fire and steel as fast as he could, another explosion rocked the cavern, and the blade was dropped by the burning creature. Both were absorbed in the conflagration, lost in the inferno.

Dominic realized that the final barrel must have ignited violently behind the sword bearer, engulfing the monster completely in fire, obscuring it completely. That was the last he saw of it while down below. The ceiling was bathed in roiling flame and smoke. He continued to roll away from the intense heat, and then crawled farther away from the blaze until he could rise and then dash out of the cavern on hasty, but tired, legs. He made his way up the tunnel as best he could, out of the mouth of the mine, and into the waning twilight sky. Another explosion erupted far behind him as he exited the tunnel. Smoke preceded and trailed his exit, but fortunately nothing else emerged in his wake. He went twenty feet to the left of the cave mouth, and then threw himself on the ground, covering his head, which was exactly all Eugene needed to see.

Eugene gave the small lever on his hand-held detonator a single twist that sent an electrical charge down 150 meters of wiring, into the storage cavern below, and another 800 meters beyond that to the first antechamber, setting off twenty pounds of C-4 in each area. The detonation instantly launched brown dust, black smoke, and debris out of the tunnel as if Hell had further vomited its rage upon them. The ground shook and the last light of dusk was temporarily taken from them in a cloud of debris.

Momentarily blinded by the dust and smoke, Dominic crawled to the large rock behind which he knew Eugene was crouching. Neither could see much of anything yet.

"This could have gone a whole lot better," Eugene said, as he heard Dominic sit down beside him. Rocks tumbled down the hill below them and the ground became still.

"At least we're still here, and there's one more Andre down there that isn't. I have no idea how many MacLaines were inside, but they had their chance," Dominic said.

"I wonder what tipped them off? I was sure we had the element of surprise," Eugene said as he rubbed a bruised shin. "We took out all of the IR cameras and the pressure mats. That's all that we detected."

"They could have had several backup security systems that we couldn't detect—a temperature variation sensor, a radio feedback detector, or trembler switch, could be any number of systems we missed, but my money is on the stinking Moronis. They're always there in 'spectator's mode,' but you don't see them unless they want to be seen. Their *abilities* may have been factored in, if not their actual presence. Remember, we aren't smarter than our enemy, even in here."

"The rules keep changing . . . we've always got to be on our toes," Eugene said. "Let's promise never to do a Black-Out mission again without some cheats of our own. We'd better make contact and find out what the satellite is showing. We still have a strike to call in."

"Give it another minute. We don't want a blind descent in this dust cloud," Dominic said. Except for their labored breathing, the two heard nothing, although that could partially be attributed to temporary deafness on account of the explosion.

"Too bad about Tick," Eugene said over his headset, taking in deep breaths.

"You shouldn't have called him a 'Red Shirt,' Cheese. It undermines his confidence,'" Dominic said.

"Yeah, but death builds character," Eugene said.

"I'll build *your* character, Cheese," came a voice over the headset that belonged to Michael Cavor, aka Tick. "You do know that nobody likes you," he added. Trash-talking each other was another way they blew off steam. None of them meant it, and all of them did it to "one-up" the other.

"Cut comms, Tick! You're dead . . . act like it!" ordered Dominic.

"Roger that," Tick sighed, and his comm was silent thereafter.

"I hope we had all the exits blocked. We can't see anything from here," Eugene said.

"If we missed an exit, I'll just blame Tick for bailing on us. Regardless, we dealt them a severe blow, and scored pretty high when we took out the altar. It should be a while before they can reconstitute elsewhere, and we downed an Andre, which satisfied the secondary objectives, though he wasn't alone." Dominic noticed a slight breeze and the dust was beginning to clear. "Of course, the primary objective was FUBAR, and we lost a man. All right, let's make our way down to the Land Rover and e-vac."

"Roger that," Eugene agreed, largely exhausted and still not acclimated to the altitude. He checked his person for his sidearm, gear, and tackle, and was satisfied that he was packed with all he remembered carrying.

"My legs are already starting to feel like two heavy, slow things," Eugene stated.

"*Lost Skeleton of Cadavra* . . . . Um . . . the Scientist's wife . . . Betty," replied Dominic. "Shouldn't be too much farther, Cheese, and then you can rest and I can do science," he quoted, inserting "Cheese."

Eugene and Dominic often quoted obscure movie lines from their favorite shows. This time it was from the Larry Blamire film

The Lost Skeleton of Cadavra. It was one of their favorites. Actually, they loved all the Blamire films and knew them largely by heart. *Mystery Science Theatre 3000* was another series of shows they knew well, but they were known to quote anything from Humphrey Bogart to *The Simpsons*, just to keep each other sharp.

Both men began to sidestep down the steep incline to their SUV, several hundred feet below the cavern egress. As they closed in on the waiting vehicle, they could hear the two-way radio continuing its attempt to establish communication, but until now there was no one around to answer yet. The voice on the other end of the radio was muffled, but became audible as they closed the distance.

"Bravo, this is Spectacle. Do you copy? Over," the voice from the radio asked.

Rock and the Big Cheese rushed to get to the vehicle and give answer. Eugene began to slide on the hill, lost his footing, and chose to ride down the slope on his rear, while Dominic side-jumped all the way down, knowing he would easily beat the younger, faster, but less agile Eugene. Dominic removed the key from his pocket and clutched it tightly in his palm. He noted how solid the small key felt in his hand as he slid to a stop at the bottom of the hill. He then sprinted over to the Rover and unlocked it, and then he opened the door, climbed in, and grabbed the two-way radio's microphone.

"This is Bravo, over," Dominic responded.

"Glad you finally showed up; I've got a dinner engagement tonight," the voice of Spectacle said. With the mic's key still open, he could be heard in the background speaking to someone else on his end, *"I've established contact,"* and then back to Bravo Team he said, *"You are an hour overdue. What's the sit-rep? Over."*

Dominic closed his eyes and mentally went down the list, and then added his voice to it. "Situation is as follows: Bravo L3-SFT is not intact, current status is two. Confirmation of target was positive. Covert infiltration—compromised. Contact—positive. Paper trail is a negative. One Andre is down; all others are MIA. Trophy is negative. Shop liquidation is positive on all known exits. Other hostile casualties are unknown. Over."

"Roger that, Bravo. Are you calling in a fire mission?"

"Affirmative, we are e-vac now. Give us ten, and we're good to go."

"Satellite confirmation is coming up now . . . stand by," spoke Spectacle.

Larry Thompson, or "Spectacle," the generic code name for all remote tactical support operators, had been an active field agent under the code name of "3rdCav," until he had broken his leg on his last mission. He was recovering and offering support to incursion teams from Archangel.

"What do you have for us, Spectacle? Over," requested Dominic. Eugene had just reached the bottom of the slope, a brown cloud nearly obscuring him.

"Bravo Team, sat-scan has smoke plumes venting on the southern slope, opposite side of your current position . . . you'd better get moving. There may be natives also on e-vac."

"Roger that, Spectacle. Any in-bounds? Over."

"I have a few infrared signatures moving in your direction, but with smoke and dust they could be elk as far as I can tell. Best pull up stakes now and make your own dust. Let us know if early extraction is necessary."

"Roger that, Bravo Team is code white and bugging out. Over and out," Dominic said as Eugene entered the vehicle and strapped himself in.

"Spectacle out."

"Plumes to the south? They must be air shafts; we couldn't have missed any other exits," Eugene suggested.

"Do you want to roll those dice? We also have unidentified heat signatures. I suggest the better part of valor," Dominic replied while starting the engine and putting the vehicle into drive.

"Where's my shottie? Don't tell me you left it in the mine," Eugene said.

"You'll spawn a new one next time. Take the sniper rifle in the back seat."

Dominic put his hand on the radio and music began to play. It was Journey's "Don't stop Believin'."

"How'd you do that?" asked the Cheese as Dominic put his foot on the gas.

"Just a little digital magic, a harmless cheat," Dominic said.

Dominic floored it, tossing gravel and dust behind the SUV. Both men moved with the G's while they made a mad dash down the winding hill. Nick drove as fast as was reasonably safe, just shy of fishtailing, but he pushed the envelope whenever he was able, barely aware that both were singing to the music as they recklessly drove down the incline. Then the first boulder landed in their path, making an impact crater where the slope merged with the road, rolling in front of the Blazer, across the dirt road, and on down the mountain.

"*SWEET MERCIFUL FUDGE!* Where'd that come from?" Eugene shouted in surprise while Dominic was occupied by swerving and narrowly avoiding the 300-plus-pound rock.

"There it is! Up the hill!" said the Big Cheese.

Dominic stole a glance at the huge silhouette lifting a second boulder over its head, high above them, up the mountainside on their left.

"The road turns here and back-traces below us several times," Rock said.

"So?" asked Eugene.

"We're going to be directly below him each time we turn back. I'll slow down so you can get a bead on him with the scope. If we drop him in the open, we might yet get our trophy," Dominic said, braking and turning back around as the road descended the mountain before them. A second boulder flew across the windshield, missing them by inches.

"Holy snot, Batman!" Dominic shouted, seeing something blur by, thinking perhaps that it was his life flashing before his eyes, and not a projectile, "That was close!" Then he added, "The trophy's secondary, Cheese, I want to get out of here alive!"

Eugene sighted the thing in the scope, but for only a moment at a time with the bouncing of the SUV. "I got him . . . nope, lost him . . . there he is . . . rats . . . Can't you find a smooth patch?" he asked. But the road was bumpy, and the black form high above them tossed a third boulder. "Incoming!" Eugene shouted.

This time the boulder made slight contact with the tail end of the Blazer, causing bumper damage, shattering the right taillights, and shoving the vehicle's rear to the left. Dominic compensated and steadied the vehicle.

"OK, I've got him . . . ."

"No you don't," Dominic said as he swerved to miss the enormous dark form that was directly ahead of them. An earsplitting roar erupted from just outside Eugene's window and his weapon was snagged out from his hands, lost forever as they passed the enraged creature, the roar and stench were both realistic and nerve-racking.

Eugene looked behind them and saw that the beast was in rapid pursuit. "I hate to say this, but all I have is my .357 and a spool of Det-cord. If you can't outrun this one, we had better leave the road and take our chances straight down the slope."

"We're not ditching yet," Dominic said as he gave it his foot. Although it was nearly dark, he saw the blacktop ahead and knew that he would be able to beat the creature. "Put a couple of slugs in it to slow it down!"

Eugene fired, shooting through the blazer's rear window and maybe hitting the thing's shoulder, maybe not; but, at this speed, it was falling behind them. Soon they did hit the pavement, and that was the last the two saw of these particular creatures. Both Dominic and Eugene were momentarily deaf, ears ringing because of Gene's discharging of his weapon, but neither was complaining.

Eugene waited two solid minutes for his hearing to come back before he lifted the microphone from the two-way and called in, "Bravo Team to Spectacle. We are free and clear. Made contact on the way out, but we didn't want to join Tick, so we are still empty-handed. Over."

The voice of Larry Thompson responded, "Roger, Bravo. Closing."

"All right, close this session and meet in the debriefing room in fifteen," came the voice of First Agent Griffin over all headsets and speakers.

Dominic and Eugene took off the virtual reality helmets and stepped off the multidirectional-terrain treadmills. It took five more minutes to get out of their III (Inertial, Impact, Interaction) suits with the assistance of the VR training techs. Mike, or "Tick," was up in the observation booth waiting for them to unhook as he had previously done when his avatar was killed.

The VR suits had multidermal stimulation points on every inner surface, which served to give them the effect of touch, impact, and inertia. Also, there were micro air-pressure jets to simulate wind and temperature. The helmets gave them the Extreme 280-degree 3-D vision and Tru-Sound audio, and provided olfactory stimuli so they could smell everything necessary in the virtual environment. Taste was the only sense that was not intentionally simulated, though sometimes the smells were palpable, and usually in an unpleasant way. The Simulator could be programmed for any environment and scenario. The VR training room was one of their more expensive training facilities. It provided the most realistic experience one could devise, and some had given it the name "The Vominator" because it could make even the most resilient person sick when it messed with your equilibrium.

139

One unique feature to the simulator was that each team member was full-body scanned into the system, and there was a photorealistic avatar of each of them within the game that enabled them to interact with one another with spectacular detail. If one of them received an injury, say a leg wound, it would realistically be evident on the avatar's body, and the suit would hinder the user's ability to walk. Torn clothing, blood, abrasions, all would be added as incurred. There was only one other simulator on the planet that was as good as Knightlight's. It too was a Japanese creation, but it somehow became the possession of the Chinese government.

⧓

The briefing room was basically a sterile classroom. There were four rows of student desks in the back, a table with four chairs around it at the front, and a large marker-board on the wall that also served as a projection screen. Suspended from the ceiling was a Hi-Def projector. In the briefing room, sitting at the table, were Dominic, Mike, and Eugene. The three were quietly discussing the mission and trying to guess what comments the First Agent might be giving them in his evaluation. They were always wrong when it came to predicting Griffin's comments. They did not know that Griffin always listened to their discussions before he entered the room, and intentionally tried to make comments that they did not already share among themselves. Griffin's philosophy was that if the team already knew what they did wrong, he would always focus on what they didn't know.

"That was *awesome*," Eugene said, still taken with the virtual mission. "The suit modifications made it ultrarealistic. I could feel the G's going down the mountain."

"Yes, but with our experience, our teamwork, and our level of training, we should have been able to beat the simulator easily. But we weren't properly equipped. I call *shenanigans* on this simulation," Mike said.

140

"The Black-Out missions always have unknowns. We're only briefed on the objectives. Tactical information doesn't exist before insertion. It's supposed to keep us off balance so we can improve our skill. And there is nothing linear about the environment. I actually enjoy them," responded Nick.

"Yes, but realism should, by definition, include the current technology we use in the field. Without that, we don't have the proper tools, is all I'm saying," Mike said in his defense.

Agent Griffin, after ten minutes of making Bravo team wait, entered the room and took the last seat at the rectangular table. By then the discussion between team members had degraded to which Doctor Who was the best. Each had his favorites, but all agreed that Matt Smith—Doctor Who eleven, Atheism aside, as unfortunately most actors are without "saving knowledge"—was the best of the recent Doctors. And not just because of his spot-on portrayal, but because the writers finally and intricately began interweaving the plot to reflect the interaction and complications one might face with time travel and destiny. And the truth was they all agreed that the seventh season finale was completely *awesome*!

"Gentlemen," Griffin greeted them as he sat. "Let's get down to business."

"Yes, First Agent," they replied in unison, and straightened up.

"Nick, you lost a man on this mission. How do you explain that?" Griffin asked.

"Negligence, sir," Dominic replied. "We cleared the altar room prematurely. We failed to check our corners completely. We failed to see through the stealth of the enemy."

"Agreed," said Griffin. "Mike, how would you characterize this mission?"

"Unfair, sir," said Tick. "Let me explain: This V-Op was set in a 1984 arena of combat. Today we have some of the most advanced equipment and weaponry on earth, but we could only use what that time period, and environment, allowed. We should have been able to kick butt and take names without so much as an injury if we had our own equipment."

"Perhaps you did not understand the nature of this training mission," Griffin said. "Do you think it was simply to show me that you could complete the mission with skill alone?"

"I assumed we should have been able to, sir. It's not like somehow on a real mission we're going to accidentally *divide by zero* and travel back in time or something," said Mike.

"Or use a TARDIS, or a DeLorean," Cheese chimed in.

"No, *that* is not likely going to happen," said Griffin, shaking his head slightly, with a good-humored smile. He then turned his attention to Eugene. "Would you like to take a stab at the intent of this training mission, Gene?" Griffin asked.

"Well, I think all of the simulations are just to keep us at the top of our game. But I suppose *this* mission was to give us some historical perspective. I recognized it as a variation of one of *your* missions that we've studied in the archives," said Gene.

"Good eye, Gene," Griffin said. He and was going to say more, when Mike jumped in.

"That's another thing—this simulation was based on a past mission, and we all know that each mission is completely unique. Revising a historical event just isn't going to happen," said Mike.

"Also true," agreed Griffin, "but there was specific a reason for my choosing this mission, and this time period with its inherent equipment limitations. Nick, tell us what that reason is," Griffin said.

"It was a test of our resourcefulness," Nick said, after just realizing it himself. "Gadgets can fail, but a drum of fuel will always be incendiary."

"Succinct and accurate, Nick," Griffin said.

"Yeah," offered the Big Cheese, "like Rock always says, 'When in doubt, find something flammable—preferably something that rhymes with *asoline.*'"

"I think I said that only once . . . ," commented Rock.

"Seriously now, we have lost agents"—Griffin paused and corrected himself—"*I* have lost agents because we relied too heavily on technology. Don't get me wrong, I *want* my agents to be the best equipped possible. I'm glad to have you field-test and deploy the newest and most cutting edges of technology available. But you must have the wherewithal to make a weapon or a defensive barrier with anything at hand. You must, at any given moment, avail yourselves of any and all resources, and use them to your advantage."

"*Star Trek* . . . 'Arena,'" Tick said. "I should have guessed." Everyone, including Agent Griffin, understood the reference Mike made. It was an episode of the original series in which the Captain had to use and combine many resources on the planet to defeat a stronger, and equally intelligent, antagonist.

"I am going to mark this mission down as a success, even though you lost a man . . . . When I was on this mission, when it really happened, I alone survived," Griffin admitted, still humbled by the memory.

"We remember, First Agent," Nick said, in an understanding tone.

"That aside, in this scenario," continued Griffin, "we wanted to see how well you could fare when you did not have a taser gun, or night vision, gun-cams, smart-shells, wrist rockets, hot-watches, threads, rail-guns, and so on . . . and your communications to Spectacle were limited to aboveground only. There may be a time that you find yourselves ill-equipped. I trust everyone here remembers Echo Team's disastrous mission when the tornado hit their camp and they had nothing with them but what they were wearing? They were attacked shortly after that, when the whole area was in chaos. We lost Agent Greer on that mission and the other two barely got out of there alive. You need to be able to engage the enemy when plans go wrong, or intelligence is incorrect, or you find yourselves completely unprepared for what the enemy throws at you. It can happen during any mission."

"Understood," agreed Nick. "Still, it is just a glorified combat-sim video game."

From out of the blue, and with a smile on his face, Eugene spoke up: "And if video games have taught me anything, it's that I can use a *cat* as a silencer!"

Nobody spoke for a moment. Griffin and Mike were pondering how a cat might be used as a silencer. Griffin stared at Gene with a raised eyebrow and a slightly open mouth, but then he noticed that Nick was struggling to withhold laughter. Nick knew that Gene was referring to an old video game called "Postal."

"So noted," spoke Griffin, deadpan, and then continued the discussion.

"What would you say was missing from this exercise, Mike?"

"Well, first, simulations, as good as they are, are not real, so *reality* was not represented in our minds. I mean, this simulator is very realistic, *ultrarealistic* . . . but we know it isn't real, so we know we can't actually be killed inside it."

"That is true. What else . . . uh, Eugene?" Griffin asked.

"I thought it was real enough," Gene agreed, then added, "Can we create our own scenarios in our spare time for practice?"

Griffin smiled. "Perhaps, but answer the question, please."

"Well, even the textures were excellent, and the pressure points in the gloves let you feel everything you touched, and the contraction fibers simulate gravity pretty well . . . but interaction was limited because we could not eat anything or taste anything—oh, wait . . . there were no insects . . . when we were outside, there were no insects."

"Interesting. I'll add that to my notes and send it to the programmers. But I am searching for something else . . . . Nick?"

"We had no spiritual interaction. There wasn't any prayer-team support in the simulation, and there was no spiritual attack to defend against," Nick concluded.

"Precisely. The *spiritual* is nothing we can simulate. The best virtual reality experience is still in the mind. We have the best simulator in the world, but it is not even close to what the mind can simulate. It may be able to get your adrenaline going, but we can't convince your mind that it's real. It does serve to hone and enhance your response time and reaction time in the real world. It puts your teamwork skills to the test, and tries your tactics, but in the real world, you would prepare yourselves spiritually, physically, and mentally for battle against demonic presences. Simulations can't give you that visceral terror that you must face every time you confront an Andre, a Chaney, a Max, an Ogle, Jerseys, or whatever."

"Yeah, to me, *that's* the biggest drawback. I can remember the danger, and even *fear*, from past experience, but I can't make myself completely *believe* the danger. I've been surprised and startled, in the V-Op, but I never feel my mortality threatened," Mike offered.

"And there were no civilians to protect," Gene added.

"Very good," Griffin said. "You were placed in a situation where you only had antagonists, and only each other to defend."

"That's why I don't understand why we lost Tick . . . . I think he just got bored with the scenario, saw death as a way out, and bailed on us," Nick chided Mike.

"That's a non sequitur. I'd never do that," Mike said in his defense, and *not* in the best of humor.

"One important thing I noted," Griffin said, ignoring the minor quarrel, "and I have a little speech that I want to give you: I suggest to all of you that you practice the *presence of the Lord*. He *is* with you while within a simulation or without. That is the only "spiritual" assistance you have. As Nick pointed out, there is no prayer-team coverage within, and of course, the monsters are not real. But the Lord can always assist you in reality, and even in a simulator. He can guide you and goad you wherever you are, so listen to the still, small voice wherever you find yourselves. You are a team so act like a team. You are a band of brothers so keep your conduct as such. Remember, you are Christians, even in a simulator, and you

145

may be the only Bible that others ever read . . . . You are part of an elite team, but we're all part of a kingdom—a righteous kingdom, an enduring kingdom, but a humble kingdom, a caring kingdom, and a long-suffering kingdom. And finally, the Lord knows the V-Op system infinitely better than the programmers do, so let your behavior and words be something He would be proud of, stay focused, and know God is with you."

"Yes, First Agent," they all replied.

"Next order of business," spoke Griffin. "It was suggested by Mike that as a strategy for Nephil-Adam interception, we embed with Malcolm Carson's massive crypto-zoological excursion that seems to be under way. I take all suggestions and I seriously consider them, even bounce some off the Director if it requires such attention, which this did. However, though we shall keep a weather eye on them, we will not embed with any at this time. Although our paths will cross, much sooner than later, an embed can get very unpredictable, and it puts others, those very cryptos, in harm's way, as most of you well know. Add to that, the coordination needed for that many embeds would most certainly be difficult. The Director and I have chosen not to add that dynamic to our own efforts at this time. We may select a few that look as if they may need protection, as we have before, but I wanted to let you know it was considered, but we will not be taking on that kind of massive coordinated effort unless such a time requires it. Our agents are being deployed more often lately. We have most of them in the field at the moment. Taking them off their current assignments isn't a good idea at this time."

"Yes, First Agent," said Mike.

"Now," continued the First Agent, "I've e-mailed my performance notations to each of you, and we've noted the bugs you found. I would like your responses by tomorrow, noon, while today is still fresh in your minds. I also wanted to mention that the State Department wants to conduct an audit of all Knightlight activities, locations, and equipment. They want to be satisfied that any 'Government monies' are not spent for religious purposes. I will allow this investigation without resistance, because we never *have* disallowed it; but just a reminder, make sure your requisition paperwork is always in order, and keep your receipts when in the field, and make sure they are from the proper accounts. This is not the first audit and it won't be the last, so dot every *i* and cross every *t*. Next, I have dispatched an investigation team as FBI forensic pathologists to a State Park in Indiana, 'Shades,' I believe is the name. The I-Team reported back while you were in V-Op. They say that the evidence points to the need of a strike-team, and Bravo Team is on the bubble. I've asked them to confirm their findings, get a topological survey, mark it up with data—incidents, dates, times, and evidence. I expect to hear back from them in two days. Be ready to deploy within forty-eight hours."

"Yes, First Agent," they said in unison.

"Oh, I almost forgot." He could tell the three were tired and wanting the briefing to end, so he was trying to keep the briefing well, brief. "The upgrade to your mobile base is complete. It has been equipped with the external SLED, the Seamless Light Emitting Diode, on surfaces over the armor and under a layer of nonreflective Lexan. And your optical window HUDs are now bidirectional, so you will be able to project images on the other side of the windshield for external visibility that are synchronous matches with the SLED panels. The many pinhole cameras will capture the entire environment around the base. When parked, in an unobtrusive and unexposed area, only a trained eye will be able to detect it at roughly ten feet's distance. The SLED itself will run silently on battery power, but the batteries will require charging from the engine. It will let you know when it needs recharging, though the batteries should last a full eighteen hours, and recharging takes only thirty minutes. The wheel-well panels and skirt are retractable, and I suggest you retract them when moving. All mounted weapons deployment systems will emerge from the roof panels now. We are working on the next generation of invisibility, at this time employing meta-material, but there are still a few bugs yet to be worked out."

The team's mobile base was a heavily modified and converted Army M978 A2 Oshkosh tanker truck, with eight big wheels, and could reasonably navigate most terrains. The tank had been rebuilt to be slightly taller for a working and living area, and the techs tried to give it a generic profile so that it would look less conspicuous when imitating various trucks and buses. It had bunks for sleeping, three computer cubicles, a well-stocked refrigerator, an extra-large weapons locker, a water recycler, satellite feeds with telemetry, stealth capabilities, trap deployment capabilities, perimeter defenses, night-vision optics, countermeasures galore, and much more. It was state-of-the-art technology added to a proven ground vehicle.

"All in all, with the help of electroluminescence, you will be virtually invisible in the day, but you still have the *manual* blind for night cover. The scent neutralizer has been adjusted so we hope you will have a zero olfactory presence at your base. Now hit the showers and get some R&R. I'll be at one of the pool tables in the rec room at 21:00 hours, if any of you think you can beat me. I've an old bottle of wine, care of the NRA Wine Club, and three very good cigars for your victory dance," Griffin concluded, smiling. "Good effort, men," he said, and he left the room.

11

EN ROUTE TO THE "CROSSROADS OF AMERICA"

(From the notes of First Agent Christopher Griffin)

*Critical Thinking—Logic Exposes Philosophical
Contradictions*

Contradictions can exist in the mind as a concept, but never in reality. Paradoxes exist, but contradictions do not. I will demonstrate a contradiction as it applies to this poser: "If a tree falls in the forest, and no one is there to hear it, does it make a sound?" Most mistake this for a "phenomenological puzzle" of physics and causality. However, this is an <u>existential</u> question and a contradiction. It seems a shrewd enigma, but it is just more anthropic, post-modernist, inconsistent nonsense.

The group offering this conundrum believe themselves to be thinkers of great depth, whereas the other group believes that the answer can be derived by physics, acoustics, with a yes or no answer and a detailed explanation. Neither seems to comprehend the incongruity. The postulation first assumes that there could in fact be <u>no observer</u> where "man" or at least some natural "being" is the implied observer, and by allusion, that there is no Ultimate Observer who may completely supersede the very possibility of "non-observation." It ascribes the existence of sound <u>only if observed</u>, and there is a Truth in that, but it is not what they think it is. (I'll explain below.)

To see the contradiction, it must be understood that the challenge is not questioning that a sound can be "heard," but whether the sound actually "exists." You must also understand that, at the same time, it already ascribes existence to a familiar universe which at least includes a tree, a forest, perhaps ground, an audio-conducting atmosphere, light (assumed) that makes all potentially visible, gravity, and all the attributes of physics, without requiring an observer for those. Its premise is that without the observer giving reality to the sound, the sound might not exist. But it contradicts itself because if mere observation by a natural being were required for sound's existence (and there is no observer), you would also have to rule out the existence of the tree, and the forest, and gravity, and the existence of physics, and the existence of the question itself, not just the sound. The postulation employs faulty logic, and is self-contradictory.

But what of the observer? I suggest that the question ascribes a limited form of "god-hood" to the unnamed observer, since without an observer nothing exists, and I agree. But now I will explain as I said I would: Nature, the totality of this universe, does not exist just because the natural beings within observe it, nor did it come into being <u>to be observed</u> by natural beings within, as some foolish persons propose. It exists only because the Creator/Observer magnificently made it, and observes it within and from without, moment-to-moment, microsecond-to-microsecond. Our observations are incidental and of allowance.

Nothing exists if the Creator/Observer is not the immediate witness to it eternally, because He has the power for what is observable to "be" in the first place. He thinks, therefore we are; and reality is sustained by His very being. If man were self-existent, Rene' Descartes could have been correct, but reality is not based upon man's philosophical views or his perception. That gives me great confidence and joy, because I know that I exist because the Lord God Almighty is thinking of me and is with me, moment-to-moment, microsecond-to-microsecond. I know that He exists because there "is" something to observe. Conclusion: You must always analyze the wisdom of this world to expose it for the foolishness that it is.

<hr />

Present Day, July 6th, 1:30pm

Malcolm Carson was at the Modesto City-County Airport, also known as Harry Sham Field, and the locals call it that with a straight face. He was rolling his luggage behind him, and holding his cell phone against his ear, while heading for his flight down at the end of the terminal. He was speaking to Dr. Mills of Crawfordsville, Indiana. Malcolm had already gone through Terminal Security. They had treated him respectfully and professionally, but it was always an intrusive act. He was thankful that he'd not have to go through it again at Los Angeles International Airport. Many a time he'd had his person manhandled, and his packages probed, and vice versa, at LAX.

Malcolm had just finished a (somewhat) International Press Conference, kicking off his extended series of explorations. For the first time, he publicly mentioned some of the areas where his teams of explorers were going to begin their "Monster Hunt." He spoke in generalities so that he would not get party crashers to his investigations, and there were many omissions for the same reasons. He'd mentioned some of his team leaders, shining attention on their fields of study and qualifications.

The teams themselves had already been dispatched two days earlier, and were in the process of arriving at their locations and setting up the sites. Most would begin, this very day, to venture out from their base camps to set camera traps and laser tripwires, dig pits for baited traps, etc. This evening, many would begin broadcasting into the wild with what they believed were Sasquatch vocalization calls. It was all so exciting to Malcolm. There would be film crews on standby to record a capture and live Internet streaming from some of the sites. Malcolm just *knew* that his fame was about to be catapulted into the annals of history.

It was surprising to the group of crypto-zoologists how rapidly they were expected to deploy, as it had been less than a month since they had signed with Malcolm. At the time, they didn't know that CQ Petroleum was virtually prepared for them to take the field on the day they signed. The first sights for most of the exploration teams had been picked and prepped, permits filed, permissions acquired, and equipment stockpiled. Also, they were ignorant of the fact that Malcolm had been working with CQ for over a year, and by the time of the Crypto-Zoological Conference, he was only waiting for teams to be staffed. And now, they were in the field . . . ready to find, lure, and capture the first Agnostopithecus.

Malcolm's travel plans had him shuttling to LAX, then flying to Denver International Airport, which he still remembered because of the luggage-mangling transfer system that ate his luggage twice before they got the kinks out of the system. From Denver, he would get a connecting flight to Indianapolis's newer International Airport, where he'd meet Crystal. Then the two of them would drive to Waveland, Indiana, stay at a bed-and-breakfast, and, by tomorrow night, be camping in Pine Hills Nature Preserve.

Originally, British Columbia was going to be his first stop for a site visit. That had changed when Malcolm received an e-mail from an old fraternity brother, now Dr. Rodger Mills, who appeared to have one of the freshest trails of evidence for the hunt. Malcolm, of course, was versed in the many sightings of Bigfoot in Indiana, but this was hardly a historical hot spot. Hoosier National Forest in Southern Indiana had far more sightings than Central Indiana ever had, though he was familiar with the alleged Crawfordsville Monster of the late 1800s, the Roachdale Monster of the 1970s, and several other sightings of various related and unrelated oddities. Still, Dr. Mills, a very reliable source if there was any, had supplied all the needed criteria for a Priority One investigation including sightings, physical evidence, police and medical corroboration, and disappearances—even deaths—that might relate to the sightings. Malcolm continued his conversation with Dr. Mills.

"Yes, Rodger," Malcolm said, "I'll be at the site tomorrow. The fax number I gave you should be ready to receive anything you wish to send to my team and me."

He listened to Dr. Mills, who repeated the number to Malcolm. Malcolm, in turn, nodded his head in response, then realized that Dr. Mills could not see him, so he added, "Yes, that's correct," and continued ambling toward his shuttle's welcome desk.

"Now, the local Sheriff you mentioned, can you contact him and have him meet me at the site, say at 4:00pm local time tomorrow, so I can give him the rest of our permit paperwork?"

Dr. Mills said that he could make the call, but he also offered to contact the Department of Natural Resources, which would also require a copy of the paperwork from Malcolm's team, so that it could give access to the still-closed park.

"Very good, Rodger. Thank you so much for calling this incident to my attention. It is by far the best immediate lead we've received. I mean, we are absolutely stationing our teams at just about every site that historically has been active, and sightings do pick up in the summer, but the evidence you've found in your own backyard is the best actionable information we've received recently," Malcolm said.

Dr. Mills stressed the fact that there have been missing persons and deaths associated with the sightings, and he warned Malcolm to be prepared to defend himself and his investigatory team.

"Thanks for the reminder, Rodge, but trust me, we are prepared for anything. We have strong men, escape-proof cages, tranquilizer darts dosed for an elephant, Kevlar nets, night vision, laser perimeter warning alarms, camera traps, and firearms, should they be necessary . . . . Will I see you there?" Malcolm asked his old friend.

Dr. Mills told him that he was not going anywhere near that park area. He was truly frightened the last time he was there, and he believed that it was a dangerous place. Then the doctor remembered to mention what the FBI had said. They had been on-site, conducting a missing-persons search with local officers and State Police. They didn't give up much in the way of information, but what he was able to glean from Sheriff Braxton was that they advised that section of the park be closed until they had dispatched another team to clear the site and could give assurance that the public would be safe there.

"The FBI is still investigating? That may cause problems for us," Malcolm noted. "Don't you worry about it, though, I've sent my daughter on ahead and she'll take care of what she can. We have permits and both of us will be on-site tomorrow afternoon. None of my team has reported any problems with site permits yet, so we *should* be good. Are you sure you don't want to drop by, maybe meet for dinner in Wavetown?"

Dr. Mills corrected him that it is Waveland, not Wavetown, and respectfully declined. He said something just wasn't right about that whole section of Montgomery County lately, and he wanted to keep his distance until whatever was there was long gone.

"All right, Rodge. Thanks for all your assistance, and who knows, maybe I'll have time to come to Crawfordsburg and visit you. Take care now, buddy," Malcolm said as a salutation.

Dr. Mills didn't correct Malcolm about mispronouncing Crawfordsville, and simply said his goodbye.

Malcolm folded up his phone, placed it in his holster, and walked up to the departure desk for his flight. He was ready to get this show on the road, and he knew that today was the first day of his great adventure. Indiana awaited him, and destiny steered his course.

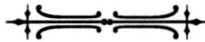

Lookout Mountain, Archangel— Present Day, July 6th

Dominic Moreau stowed his ready-bag in the mobile base next to his bunk. They were gassed up, locked and loaded, and ready to move out. The prayer team had briefed Nick concerning the nearly overwhelming demonic oppression that they'd discerned regarding his team's destination, and assured him that they were being covered continually on their mission, but that danger absolutely awaited them. They had been in prayer ever since the mission destination was known. They were warriors of the Spirit who prayed for all the teams, and actually everyone who came to mind, including the civilians that the team would impact, and they especially asked for the pulling down of demonic strongholds in the locations of deployment. They prayed with Nick's team at the briefing, and informed them that they felt extreme resistance from the enemy. They were almost certain that it would not just be the Moronis and

Nephil-Adam to contend with, but they could not specify what else they might face. When they reached the point where they knew not what to pray, they always ended with, "May Your will be done, Lord," because all agreed that God's perfect *will* was always better, wiser, and truer than that of any man. Only He could empower men to assail the very gates of Hell.

Cheese and Tick entered the mobile base and stored their gear as well. Nick called them to the small table for one final prayer before they launched. They each took a seat and bowed their heads reverently.

"Father," Nick said, "please be with us and work through us to complete our mission. Give us wisdom and discernment so we can do what is right, and not what seems right in our own eyes. Give us strength and courage to face the enemy, and help us to represent you above and beyond our abilities. Send your angels ahead of us to do battle where we can't set foot, and give them victory over the enemy, where our strength is of no help. Enable us to minister to those you put in our path regardless of their religious affiliation, or lack thereof. May our aim be true, and our resolve be unshakable. In Jesus' name we pray, amen," Nick concluded.

The three rose and put their fists together in the shape of a triangle, a trinity, and all spoke, "Hold the line," which was their battle cry of sorts. Only then were all three ready to launch their mission.

"Have all arms been stocked and magazines filled?" Nick asked Tick.

"Affirmative, and the cycle and ATV are gassed and locked down," Tick replied.

"Food stores are loaded, and delicious," the Big Cheese said. "We're ready to Rock," he added. Cheese was ever the *pun-meister*.

"I'll take the first shift in the pilot's seat," Nick said. "Cheese, you have communications; Tick, ride shotgun so you can handle the tech."

"Roger that," said the Big Cheese.

"Copy that," said Tick.

Dominic and Mike exited the rear of the mobile base, which lowered, allowing them to walk out. When Nick pressed the key-chain remote, it raised back into the "closed" position. The two walked around to the front of the large all-terrain vehicle, each to his own side. Rock and Tick both used their remotes to unlock and open their own invisible cab door to the large stealth vehicle. They entered in their respective doors, climbing up into the cab, where they put on their headsets and jacked into their communication console.

"Check, check," said Rock in the headset's mic. They had wireless, stealth communications sets, and Blackberries to communicate when on mission, but they wanted to save the batteries and the vehicle headsets did not need to recharge. Tick gave the thumbs up to show that he could hear Rock in his headset, and then gave the same test, and Rock gave his own thumbs up.

"Wall to wall," replied Cheese in the back section of the vehicle.

"Roger that," said Rock.

"Copy all," said Tick.

"Patch us into Spectacle and tell them that we are ready to roll," said Rock.

"Roger that," said Cheese, as he switched to the correct frequency and set communications that all might hear the mobile base's interaction with command and control comms.

"Spectacle, this is Bravo. Mobile Base Two is manned and ready to launch from Bay One. Initiate localized depressurization. Over," Cheese said. The entire base had roughly twice the normal atmospheric pressurization, or thirty-one pounds per square inch at sea level. The bunker was its own hyperbaric chamber. The reason behind it was entirely related to health issues. The human body heals faster under increased oxygenated pressure, muscles produce fewer toxins, and aging effects are also slightly decreased under those conditions. To enhance the beneficial aspects of the increased pressure, the cafeteria served dietetic and individual specific meals that were geared toward nutrition and tempered by personal taste. Most Knightlight agents and general employees appeared younger and healthier than what their birthdays revealed them to be.

"Firing up the engine," said Rock to all, as he started the vehicle, satisfied at the sound of the engine. A slight hissing sound of air escaping made their ears pop.

The mobile base's power plant was now a highly muffled gasoline engine because the former diesel engine was simply too loud for any semblance of stealth. That was taken care of before their very first mission using the vehicle, and upgrades were routine maintenance.

"Good morning, Bravo, this is Spectacle; Grumbugs, at your service. Bay One is now depressurized and I am activating outer doors," announced the voice of Grumbugs, who was manning the comms for Bravo Team under the generic code name of Spectacle. There were many operators and voices that would be slated for covering as "Spectacle" over their two-day journey to Indiana: Mad Dog, Cannon Fodder, Killer Girl, the Big Shot, Gun Babe, the Surveyor—all from Archangel—as well as Mega-oink, Torso-boy, Killer Dynamo, Flex-my-Pecks, Flo, and Zoidberg—from Halo, the Eastern office of Knightlight. It would be about a twenty-three-hour trip to the site, with no certain way of telling how long the duration of the operation would be once it was engaged.

The large, all but impenetrable outer doors began very slowly to part, letting daylight into Bay One. Rock ran a prelaunch check that consisted of computerized indicators either on his dashboard or on the front windshield's heads-up display. He looked at and confirmed the status of the fuel gauge, tire pressure and tread depth, all engine fluids, and engine temperature, as well as the cabin, trailer, and external temperatures. Countermeasures were full, and "ready" was the indicator of the retractable roof's auto-turret. Rock was about to check the lights, which usually could be seen on mirrors next to the bay doors, and were placed there just for such a check, but, looking at the reflection of the dark and blank vehicle, he remembered that the lights were now handled in concert with the new SLED panels. For headlights at night, there were small retractable panels on the front where, so depending on the configuration of the vehicle image they were going to display, the front panels would retract so that actual headlights behind the panels could shine forward. The LED lights projected from a flat panel could be bright, but they were not powerful enough for driving visibility on the open road.

Tick pulled up the new console in front of him that gave him access and control over the external SLED, powering it on and allowing interactivity.

"What external images do we have to mimic?" he asked Rock. All three men had been to the SLED training, but had yet to actually use it outside the classroom and did not know the range of images available to them. The vehicle would mimic any external environment when they were in stasis at a site, disguising it and blending it into the environment, but it could also display the image of many vehicles while mobile. There were indeed a great number of selections, each with its own registered plates, identification codes, and/or advertisements.

"Well," Tick said as he listed the choices on his console, "apart from stealth mode, we can look like one of several charter bus lines, or a mostly flat-nosed school bus, all with tinted windows. There are several choices of big rigs and tankers, Military Branch—all generics—or private-sector designs of UPS, FedEx, Walmart, or Target trucks with plates and logos, and various Winnebago-like campers. We can alter all of those by color choices and external designs. Or we can go with the default black panel, which looks cool, but most likely would draw attention."

"Not as much attention as we'd get if this thing *blue-screens* on us," said Rock.

"Oooo, the *BSOD* . . . I hadn't thought of that," said Tick. "That would be one butt-splosion of a problem."

"Yeah, a pant-load. But that's just one of a multitude of possible disadvantages when using untried tech in the field. Let's go with Army green. We're going to have to fill 'er up again at Ft. Riley, Kansas, anyway. We might as well drive in under the right colors for the base," Rock decided.

Tick chose the Army tanker selection, and then he engaged the SLED.

"Army Tanker up," Tick said.

Rock watched out the windshield and saw the outer skin of the mobile base go from nearly black, lighting up to a dark gray, and then changing to a very impressive olive-green Army tanker truck. The side-view windows within the truck were flat-panel monitors, using the external cameras to project an image onto the screen so that the driver and passenger could see what they would have seen out there if they had side windows.

"Tanker, check," Rock confirmed. "Wow that looks surprisingly good. But since that's our general shape anyway, I suppose it would."

"Raising wheel panels and skirt," said Tick.

"Skirt, check. Wheel panels, check," replied Rock as he observed them raise and lock into position. "Retracting exhaust hose," he added, disengaging it from the garage.

All vehicles in the bays had hoses for venting exhaust gases out of the bay. Not only did the bays store various vehicles, but that is where they would be worked on by mechanics and techs for oil changes and light mechanical or technical servicing. To the left of the last bay, there was a large tunnel with a flatbed subway train that would shuttle vehicles to a completely different area for major work, such as the installation of the SLED.

"Doors open. You are free and clear to launch," announced Grumbugs.

The large truck exited the mountain and followed the paved road all the way to I-70 and headed east. It followed the interstate through and out of Denver, turning very few heads as it proceeded just below the speed limit. It was hot out, but the truck maintained a cool cabin temperature. Mike was worried that a combination of high temperatures, wind speed, and rough pavement might adversely affect the truck's exterior imaging system, but it seemed to be working flawlessly.

"So," said Tick to Rock, "we're going to stick with the biohazard protocol?"

"No choice, amigo . . . ," Rock answered. "The ball's in play, and that's our cover. Since the investigation team, *as FBI*, found concrete evidence of Nephil-Adam involvement, they've prepared the back story with Ops and Logistic support. And they've informed the local police that a *courier truck* from Blackwater, or some other government contracted service that escapes me at the moment, had been lost in the area years ago. That truck was—supposedly—carrying a hallucinogenic nerve toxin that was to be delivered to the Chemical Depot in Newport, Indiana, for disposal. This truck has been distressed for looks and planted on an Amish property where that family had been reported as missing. That's southwest of our site. Although it's contrary to water flow, the location is perfect for claims of aerosol dispersion in the direction of Shades and Pine Hills Parks."

"I know. That's all in the briefing packet, but there exists evidence to the contrary. Evidence in the hands of law enforcement."

"Most of the evidence can be explained by a leaking canister of QNB causing aberrant or even homicidal behavior, hallucinations, and so on . . . and the rest *could* be explained away by coincidence. I know it's thin, but that's all we've got to work with at this time. Just do us all a favor and don't try to pronounce QNB's full name, or we'll all look incompetent," said Rock.

"QNB *can* explain the missing persons, the murders, even the strange lights and, well, *'ghosts'* that have been widely reported," Tick said, "but the plaster foot casts and the giant handprints on the victim's throat are not going to be explained away by 3-Quinuck, um, Quionuclid, wait . . . Quinuclidinyl benzilate. Ha, nailed it."

"After two fails," said Cheese from the rear.

"Just say 'QNB,' 'BZ,' or 'buzz-nerve agent' or we're hosed, OK?" Rock admonished him. "We're not going to be covering all bases with the story; it's just explaining our presence. At any rate, the FBI team will be leaving the site tomorrow morning and have already instructed law enforcement that the CDC—*that's us*—will be taking over the parks tomorrow afternoon, with the EPA locking down the truck carrying the toxin. The cover is workable, hopefully, if not the best cover. The team will leave one of their SUVs at the Amish site for us to use, and it will by then have CDC decals on it. It should be well equipped, and have their latest notes and data."

"I just hope we can get by without wearing hazmat suits in the heat of the summer," said Tick.

"You and me both. We'll have sniffers preset for 'false-positive' readings on the Amish property, but we'll reset them to negative readings in the park areas," replied Rock. Then the Big Cheese broke in over their headsets.

"This is the Big Cheese." He intentionally sounded *official* now, since his announcement was duty related. "I've just received a message from the advance team. They've located the bodies of an entire Amish family within seven clicks of Shades State Park. Their bodies were found in the forested area a couple hundred meters behind their home. They were buried under the bodies of two horses. Although badly decomposed, it's clear that the cadavers had been masticated."

Rock and Tick looked at each other with furrowed brows. "Roger that, Cheese," said Rock, "Tell the advance team to handle it as discreetly as possible. I'd like them to close that end of the case so we can focus on the hunt."

"Copy that. But they said the news media is asking questions and it's getting out of hand out there. Our cover isn't going to explain all of this."

"If we have to fall back to the truth, then that's all we can do," said Rock. Silently to himself he thought, *That's what we should do anyway.*

"Copy that," said the Cheese.

Rock had never liked hiding behind stories that misled the public, or anyone; few, however, would understand the truth, and fear would likely be the result of it, possibly causing more harm than good. Silently he contemplated the situation, and he and his team rolled on toward Indiana.

<hr/>

Present Day, July 6th, Evening

Darlene Campbell lay on her bed with red satin sheets and dreamed silently of dark things, dark places, and dark doings for most of the night. Sometime just before dawn, she began to toss and turn without waking. Should someone have seen her, it would have appeared to them that she was having a nightmare, but Darlene was the mistress of her slumber, and was wrestling with something that had intruded on her dream. She wrestled with Light. The Light withstood her, telling her to turn back, to retreat, telling her that she had gone too far but it was not too late . . . yet. She resisted more and more, nearly to waking, and the Light, as a gentleman, relented, allowing her will to make the choice herself. The choice was the same that we all face daily: to serve and win life, or to rule and lose it.

Darlene awoke from her sleep suddenly, sensing her master outside. She sat up and slid out of bed, stepping lightly, cautiously, to her open window. The musky smell lit up her nostrils, but she actually enjoyed it, knowing it signaled her lord.

"I am here, O Mighty One," she spoke out her window to the dark figure in the open air.

"Our work is going to be difficult," the deep voice spoke in English, with an accent that she could not place.

Darlene had, thus far, communicated with the being only in tongues that had been foreign and dead. "What do you wish me to do?" she responded, knowing not to ask for many details at this time.

"You will defend my lair," spoke the giant, "against all intruders. The child *will* be born there."

"Yes, my lord," she replied, wondering why the being needed help in doing so. But, assuming that it did not wish to be discovered by the world at large, she did not question its intentions.

"Your coven will obey you unto death?" it asked, requiring assurance.

"Some of them will, the Thirteen will, and perhaps twenty more, but I'll have to hand select those," she said. "Master, when you say, *'obey you unto death,'* do you mean unto their own death, or unto the death of others?"

"I mean both," it snarled hotly, angered by the question.

"I will have no less than thirty at hand to protect your lair, Master," she said, bowing her head in fear.

"I will give you instructions on what to expect, and how to respond to the unexpected," it said, calmer now.

"Yes, my lord," she said.

Darlene grabbed a pencil and a notepad that were handy on her night stand. She sometimes used them to document her dreams, and now to play stenographer. They communed for twenty minutes. Darlene looked down to her notepad one final time, and the creature was gone by the time she looked up. She peered out her window and saw no trace of the being. She looked back at her notepad and studied the plan. She knew now that it was going to be dark and dangerous business.

Darlene wiped some sleep from her eyes and went into the bathroom to shower. Once done, she dressed in a cool green halter and skirt, and picked up the phone. She pressed the speed-dial for Bradley Taylor. The phone on the other end was answered with a sleepy "Hullo?" by Bradley.

"Bradley, this is your Queen," she said.

Bradley's mind was still fuzzy from being stirred out of his own sleep by the call. "Yes, my Qu--n," he said with a yawn, distorting the salutation into something that wasn't a word. "I mean my Queen," he restated.

"We have important work today. I want you to summon the Thirteen for an eleven o'clock gathering in my home . . . eleven o'clock this morning. Tell them they *must* attend. Then I want you to contact everyone on the red list and tell them the same. We have an emergency to deal with and I need all who are trusted to be there, or be cursed."

"Yes, my Queen," he said.

"We will need special equipment, so write this down, and tell Solomon that if there is anything else he can think of that may help, he is to bring it. We must meet today to plan, and be set up and ready by tomorrow at dusk," she said. She then gave Bradley a list of what she knew they needed.

"What do we need it for?" asked Bradley.

Darlene explained to him exactly why the equipment was needed and how it was to be used. She did not understand the interworking of the communications equipment, but Solomon did, and once he was told why it was needed, she trusted that he would know what else should be added to the list.

"I'll make sure we are there," Bradley said.

"I did not say you would be there, Bradley. This is for those who would kill or die at my command," she countered, not so pleasantly.

"But, my Queen, I obey you, and would follow you to the overthrowing of Heaven," he said, with a wounded disappointment in his voice.

"Then you may come. But if I see the slightest inkling of cowardice in you, you will join the bodies under the fire pit in my backyard," she threatened.

"I will die protecting you, my Queen," he said. Bradley was still in love with Darlene. Even though she had used her body only as a way to bring Bradley into the coven, and though she used and abused him, he was blindly in love with her. He believed that his loyalty would eventually earn him a place among the Thirteen, and then, he hoped, as King, beside the Queen . . . . He was a fool. But what passes for love among those who do not know the True Love of God can still make the strongest man weak, or the weakest man believe himself strong . . . even when he is only fooling himself. Not that unregenerate man is without the ability to understand the Love of God as "His children" can, because it can be understood to a degree by those who truly love their parents, and in turn, their children, selflessly. But it is impossible for them to experience that Godly love firsthand, without the Cross of Christ to bridge the insurmountable gap between the two.

There are, in actuality, only two religions in this world, if you boil them down to their basest premise: One reaches to the heavens and says at least one of the following: "I will make my own way to the heavens," or, "I will prove myself worthy," or, "I will make a name for myself," or, "I will earn God's favor," or, "I will be a god unto myself," or, "I will make myself righteous, or wise, or powerful, or important, and I will be like unto God Himself." The other religion, the religion of Truth, recognizes that man is not worthy, not righteous, and knowledgeable but not wise—not so powerful or important, and nowhere near God Himself. It accepts the hand of God Himself, reaching down to us, condescending to us, providing payment for the sin that we did not ask to be born into, and providing a way for man to come to Him, in His righteousness, not ours. Some need to ask themselves this question: "If I were drowning and a single rope were lowered to me with the intent to save me, would I reject it because I did not like the way it was lowered to me?"

"I may hold you to that, Bradley" Darlene said to him regarding his life. "You may attend."

"Thank you, my Queen," he said.

"Lastly, tell Mrs. Haversham that her guests will need observation, and her assistance may be needed," instructed Darlene.

"I will," said Bradley.

"Remember, eleven o'clock. Eleven o'clock—*sharp*," she concluded.

"Yes, my Queen," he said, and all the salutation he received was a "click" before his line went silent.

Darlene set the phone down and began to meditate and chant. All the while in her mind she knew this fact: *They are coming.* In response to that knowledge, she thought, *We must be ready . . . .*

Present Day, July 6th, Evening

Leaving Fort Riley, Knightlight's Bravo Team inside the mobile base rolled out of the gates and headed east on I-70. The Big Cheese rode shotgun with Tick at the wheel this time. They kept a steady pace and were reasonably on schedule for their destination: Indiana. They were going to drive on through the night, when radar indicated rough weather ahead. They began seeing flashes of light ahead of them in the distance around 0100 hours. When they had passed Topeka, they caught up with an intense thunderstorm, which pummeled them mercilessly until they finally pushed through it on the east side of Kansas City, Missouri. It was nature at its worst, but it did not slow their progress much. The MFB was powerful and stout. The thunderstorm had spawned several tornadoes, and though none of them hit I-70 traffic, many residences had not been so fortunate, and the team lifted up all in the storm's path through prayer.

Sometime afterward, the Big Cheese turned off the radio as the prerecorded and "streamed" version of the *Rush Limbaugh Show* ended, and he looked over to Tick. He wanted to get something off his chest that had been bothering him for a while now. Finally, he gathered his gumption and spoke.

"Have you ever had a crisis of faith?" he asked.

Tick broke his own silence with little hesitation. "You might just as well have asked me if I've ever been a jerk, or if I've ever lusted in my heart, or have ever been a hypocrite . . . . Yes, is the answer to all . . . . Why?"

"What was your crisis?" Cheese asked.

"Oh, just a little 'thing' that made me think I was smarter than God," he stated.

"And . . . what was that little thing?" Cheese prodded after a moment of silence.

"Do you remember what Isaiah 34:4 and Revelations 6:14 pertain to?" He answered with a question, which he knew would either "tick" the Cheese off, or "cheese" him off, but only in a good-natured way.

"I hate it when you do that," Cheese said.

"I know," replied Tick.

"No, I don't remember specifically what those Scriptures say," admitted Cheese, as the truck continued in the right lane of traffic.

"Both speak of the end of this world. Here is the condensed eschatological timeline so that you have it in context: After the Rapture, there is the Great Seven-Year Tribulation, then the Second

Coming of Christ, then the Millennial Reign with Christ, and then the Last Battle, as Satan is loosed upon the earth for his last hurrah. Then he'll be defeated, then he, death, and Hell will be cast into what is referred to as the 'Lake of Fire' forever. Then the end of this universe, at which point we will be witness to the end of this universe and the beginning of a new one," Tick said.

"So . . . ," prodded Cheese.

"So those two Scriptures said something that I thought was impossible in light of physics and the nature of this universe, and I had a crisis of faith," Tick simply said.

Cheese waited for Tick to continue . . . and waited . . . and nothing.

"WHAT WAS YOUR CRISIS OF FAITH?" Cheese shouted.

"Can you guys keep quieter on the comms? I'm trying to get some sleep," Rock said over their headphones.

"Roger that," said Cheese sheepishly, and much more quietly.

"Both Scriptures say that this universe, the very fabric of this universe, gets rolled up like a scroll . . . but paper and parchment are flat," he said. "I happen to know that there is nothing *flat* about this universe unless you are considering the ratio between gravity and the expansion rate of the universe . . . and there is no Scripture preceding these that says, '*first God flattened the universe . . . then rolled it up like a scroll and then it vanishes into nothingness . . .* '; therefore, my crisis of faith was because of logic. I could not mentally get past that issue and I began to doubt God's word. I searched all Hebrew and Greek references. But I still found that it was describing exactly what the English text states, and I simply could not see what God was saying when comparing the end of this universe in such a manner. To me, our universe was *nothing* like a parchment, making it an error, and there can be no error in Sacred Scripture, unless the Word of God is incorrect. And if it is incorrect in one single point, then it fails its own test of validity . . . . There you have it."

"Bummer," said the Cheese. "You couldn't just accept it by faith, trusting that He can do whatever He wants to do, in any way that He wants to do it?"

"I could not. Not then, anyway. I thought I knew more than God because I know something about the nature of this universe, and I thought He had made an error that could not be resolved in my mind. And if God is in error on any single point . . . then He is wrong . . . completely. He cannot be God, and err."

"An impasse." Cheese realized he said that too loud, then corrected himself by whispering, "An impasse."

"Indeed," he said. "But I did not see that the lack of understanding was on my end, not God's. I couldn't see, and I blamed God not only for my inability to see, but for possibly being wrong. Now, add to that, 2 Peter 3:10, where it speaks of that specific event as well. It says the elements shall melt with a fervent heat, and all in this universe will burn up . . . and dissolve into nothingness. So . . . this universe will be rolled up like a scroll and dissolve into nothingness. I honestly thought that the concept was, well, ridiculous."

"That is a dilemma . . . . I take it you resolved this issue, then," Cheese inquired.

"Absolutely," said Tick.

"Well? How was your crisis resolved?" Cheese nudged the story on again.

"God put me to the test . . . . In my heart I heard a still small voice speak to me saying, '*Mike, have you ever examined a scroll?*'

"OK, so I guess you took out a piece of paper," Cheese said.

"I did. And do you know what I noticed?" asked Tick.

"That you had a paper cut, I don't know. You tell the story. I'm not gonna guess."

"I noticed that even though thin, the paper was three-dimensional existing in a fourth dimension. *OK*, I thought to myself, *that's a start*. Then I rolled it up like a scroll and examined it . . . . Nothing special . . . . Then I turned the tube and looked down it carefully, and then it hit me like a Dad spanks an insolent child, with authority and compassion: I was not looking at a flat piece of paper . . . I wasn't looking at a roll of paper . . . and I was not looking at a tube . . . . And I remembered that God used a simile, so He meant *'like a scroll,'* and He *never said* 'like parchment,' and that's when I realized just what I was actually looking at. I was looking at a *spiral*. A *SPIRAL*," Tick emphasized.

"Tick . . . , um . . . I don't get it . . . ," Cheese said. *"Splain, Lucy,"* he said in a very poor attempt at sounding like Ricky Ricardo.

"OK, listen up. Space, or rather, *space-time*, is a physical property that can be manipulated by rate of travel, mass, and energy. Space itself is curved, not flat, not straight . . . it is stretched, just like Genesis 1:1 says. Space-time was the first thing created by God, and that is truly logical canvas to begin creating within. But getting to the point . . . when we launch a satellite into orbit, it is not stationary, it is moving, or falling in an arch, still being pulled by the earth's gravity. But unless its course is corrected, what do you think will happen?"

"Well . . . it eventually falls into the planet's gravity well and crashes," the Cheese said.

"Correction, my friend: It *spirals* into the planet, but it also burns up on reentry, or dissolves. A scroll also spirals, AND it spirals into nothingness . . . it just ends. I discovered that a scroll is a *perfect* phenomenological representation, and is explained in an easily comprehensible *symbolic language* to depict the end of this universe, which will apparently spiral into itself and dissolve as it does so," Tick said with confidence.

"Dang!" exclaimed Cheese. "I'd never have put that together . . . ."

"Dang, indeed," agreed Tick. "I was spanked by the Lord's wisdom, corrected by Him, humbled by Him, and my crisis was over. From then on, I took every such issue with faith in Him, and eventually was able to understand the Truth on all issues I encountered. It was *personally* awesome how God opened my eyes, and that crisis gave me faith for all other near-crises. Crises are learning experiences, and growing experiences, and they are all under God's sovereignty."

"I guess so . . . ," said the Big Cheese.

"Rock," said Tick, "have you told Cheese what opened your eyes to the Lord?"

The two heard a sigh over their headphones. Rock really wanted to sleep, but responded anyway.

"I'm pretty sure I did," came Rock's voice over their headsets.

"Nope," said Cheese.

"Now is as good a time as any," said Tick, steering them through evening traffic.

"You say that because *you* aren't trying to sleep," replied Rock.

"I'm all ears," said Cheese.

"Fine," Rock sighed again, knowing "sleep" wasn't going to occur until he gave his testimony. "OK. As it pertained to me directly, God used a completely mainstream and secular *movie* to open my eyes to the Him."

"You're joking, right," said Cheese.

"Nope," said Rock and Tick at the same time.

"How on earth?" asked Cheese.

"The movie's plot underpinnings or the *gist* of the story was that logic is not enough for one's worldview to be sustained and supported, and to be *complete* the individual person must have something more. There is a void, or vacuum, that logic cannot fill, or be a substitute for. I had my entire belief system based on the fact that logic could sustain me. I was proven wrong. I realized that logic is a good tool, but it isn't what separates us from the animals, because they too employ logic and act logically."

"If I get you right," said Cheese, "you are saying that *ants*, for example, will logically behave like ants, nothing else, and they will move about this planet employing logic to overcome obstacles in this world, working logically and predictably within the laws of physics and nature."

"Very much like that," said Rock. "Now, some personal history. I was an atheist, a humanist, and an evolutionist and I was arrogantly proud of that fact. I believed I was reasonable and completely logical in my world-view. But just to broaden my horizons, I had become acquainted with most religions, faiths, and beliefs, and I believed that though most were quite ridiculous, and all of them were affectations that humanity developed to feel useful and hopeful in this world. But most ran contrary to the others, making all diametrically opposed to each other, ruling out the possibility that *all roads lead to God.* By then, if I could pick one, or put stock in any, the Bible seemed the most ordered, reliable, historically accurate, verifiable, and generally "good" for mankind. But logic alone was not going to make me a believer. It could not be accepted by logic alone, because I could not quantify or relate to an invisible, all-powerful, self-existent 'God.' There was a concept that I resisted because it defied my common sense . . . it was something completely foreign to me . . . it was simple faith."

"I see. So how did you bridge the gap between logic and faith?" Cheese asked.

"After I watched the movie, something was spoken to my heart. It said, 'Man alone has the ability to leap beyond logic, and accept that which is . . . *faith.*' I had always looked at faith as a weakness, a frivolity for the less intelligent and the superstitious; but I found out that it is unique to humanity, and vital. At that point, I knew that placing my faith in the Word of God was the only true and right course of action for my life. I thought the power of logic knew no limits, until I discovered the power of faith. Only then could I see that the two work together perfectly."

"Cool beans . . . . So . . . what was this movie that opened your eyes?" Cheese asked.

Tick jumped in and stole Rock's thunder: "*Star Trek: The Motion Picture,*" Tick said.

"Wow . . . live long and prosper, dude," said Cheese.

"I have done both so far. So, Cheese . . . it's your turn. What is *your* current crisis?" asked Rock, resigning himself to the fact that this discussion must run its course before he could get any sleep.

Cheese, big and burly, brushed his hand across his blond hair, front to back—hair that Rock would kill for . . . figuratively. He began to blush and then sweat, though the cabin was cool. Then he exhaled loudly, swallowed hard, and admitted, "I'm . . . scared."

"Ah . . . *scaredy-cat*, eh . . . ? I always thought of you as a mama's boy," Tick said, making fun of him immediately. It was the team's *way*, especially when attempting to deflect fear, or doubt, or even honesty.

"It's not funny, Mike. Every time I come up against the enemy during an actual *event*, I almost can't move," Cheese spoke honestly.

"But you *do* move, Cheese," Tick said. "You *do* move. You are trained to move, and your training kicks in during every event, even when your *mind* and *will* can't get you going."

Several miles passed. Rock waited . . . Tick waited. Both knew they must wait. A full four minutes passed before Cheese said, "I'm afraid I won't move," he confided. "I believe that I was called to do this, but I doubt it whenever we're on mission, or on our way to one."

"I do too," Tick confided honestly, somewhat sympathetically, but diminishing the emotion's importance.

"Ditto," came Rock's voice from the back of the truck.

"I mean, I'm SCARED," said Cheese loudly, angrily but earnestly. "I'm afraid I'll get us killed, I'm afraid I'll freeze, I'm afraid I'll accidentally kill a civilian, I'm afraid that if we lose . . . and I'm captured by . . . by one of *them* . . . I'm AFRAID that if I'm tortured, I'll even deny Jesus, just to end the torment."

Rock breathed out a sigh, and waited a moment to be sure Cheese had finished and was ready to listen. Then he spoke. "Eugene," he said from the back, from his bunk, calmly and with authority. "You are *not* alone. You are *never* alone. You are a mighty man of valor, and if you fall, God will lift you up, and His Spirit *will* give you the strength to *keep* you. The responsibility for the mission is in *His* hands, not yours, not mine, not the First Agent's. *He* is in control. All we have to do is follow as He leads us. The responsibility for what happens is His. He has gone before us *already*." Rock paused, hoping his words were absorbed rather than deflected. "Take comfort in the fact that *if we win*, it's to His glory, and if we lose, He is *still* glorified, and we are still with Him. If you can't move, then just *stand fast* and hold your ground for His glory. We won't leave you while we have breath, and I *know* that nothing on earth could stop you from coming to our aid, if one of us should be taken."

"I know . . . ," Eugene, the Big Cheese, finally said as his eyes teared up. "I know. Thanks," he added.

"And remember," began Rock, pausing to gain their attention. Both Cheese and Tick knew what was coming. It was customary to end something serious with something humorous. It was their way. They expected Rock to begin singing, "Never gonna give you up, never gonna let you down . . . ," a classic Rick-roll, but instead, Rock changed it up and sang the ending chorus to another song: *"Everyone's a hero in their own way!"*

Cheese and Tick laughed at the *Dr. Horrible's Sing-Along Blog* song. If Rock hadn't stopped singing, they surely would have chimed in.

After a moment or two, when the laughter ended, Rock asked, "Crisis averted?"

"Yeah . . . ," he said as his smile began to fade, "for now at least."

"We can talk about this at any time, amigo," said Rock.

"I should be good for a while," said Cheese.

"Good . . . cause I WANT SOME SLEEP, NOW!" Rock exclaimed, in good humor.

"Roger that," said Cheese.

"Copy that," said Tick.

"G'night then," said Rock.

"Night," said Tick.

"Goodnight, John-boy," said Cheese. "Oh . . . and . . . Your mom!"

Rock smiled in his bunk, closed his eyes, and prayed for his team while waiting for sleep to overtake him softly and silently. The truck rolled on toward Indiana, the Crossroads of America, but sleep was still eluding Nick.

Nick lay back in his bunk and allowed his mind to drift and list so that he could pass into sleep. But his memory took him back to the time when he first met Director Bensington Redwood. It was a milestone in Nick's experience. The Director had opened Nick's eyes to broader possibilities concerning the Nephil-Adam. The word "nephilim" literally means "the fallen ones," but he was brought to the realization that they were not only the spawn of the fallen ones, but also the children of man. It was possible that they could be considered the *innocent* children of the "willfully fallen," that is, innocent of direct disobedience of God. When looking at the fact that mankind also qualified as *the fallen* to the same degree, and that they too are born into that condition, it begged the question, "Can a *fallen one* be redeemed?" Christ came to redeem *mankind*. He died once, for all. So if a *fallen one* identified itself with man, by parentage, rather than as the issue of a demon, to the same degree, could a "man-nephilim" claim redemption as a *man*, by faith? It was a question that even Director Bensington Redwood could not answer. But it was Redwood's expressed hope that it *was* possible.

Not all that are Nephil-Adam have obeyed their demonic parent. Not all were a danger to mankind by virtue of behavior. Indeed, Knightlight noted the nonbelligerent sightings of Nephil-Adam, but took no action against those who behaved themselves. Knightlight vigorously engaged the Moronis whenever they were encountered. But the benign Nephil-Adam were not part of Knightlight's mission, because of the possibility of redemption for them. Eradication of their kind was not Knightlight's responsibility, as God is the only wise judge of such matters, and He remains silent on it, a silence which shouts that it is *His* alone to judge.

The Director had instilled something in Nick that alleviated his hatred for the Nephil-Adam in total, and gave him a glimmer of hope that perhaps they should not all be eradicated, as Nick had previously believed. It gave him the possibility of sympathy, or perhaps empathy, for them, at least for those who chose to live in peace with man. However, none of that was in question when their activities were directed against mankind. The war was "on" against those Nephil-Adam.

By and large, Knightlight agents were deadly monster hunters whenever Nephil-Adam chose to be monsters. They were dragon slayers, demon resisters, and assailers of the gates of Hell. But they did have their share of dealings with what others call UFOs.

Most UFO sightings are simply misidentifications of man-made or natural phenomena, even hoaxes, but increasingly, there have been actual sightings as the enemy has become bolder. Sightings themselves constitute a close encounter of the *first kind*. They are the most common, but, again, are usually misidentification of a natural phenomenon or man-made object.

The *second kind* of close encounter is an actual sighting with physical evidence of the event left behind. But contrary to popular mythology, Nephil-Adam and Moronis are not interested in the making of crop circles or other nonsense. On the other hand, radar hits, electromagnetic disturbances, and scorch marks—even foul odors—can be evidence of actual physical manifestations.

The most popularized form of "contact" is the close encounter of the *third kind*. That is direct confrontation with an inhuman being or entity. Knightlight has fought and wrestled with many manifested Moronis. "Moroni" is Knightlight slang for a formerly angelic being posing as a messenger from God, or an alien, a person, a creature, or a spiritual visitant. The Moronis are named so with regard to Joseph Smith's folly in his lack of knowledge and spiritual discernment. It was a fallen angel, calling himself Moroni, who beguiled Smith and guided him to found the polytheistic and un-Christian Mormon religion. If Moroni's message was valid, in and of itself, one must argue that José Luis de Jesús Miranda's message is equally valid, as are *all* others, but validity isn't found in a messenger's (questionable) earnestness, or seemingly good intentions; it is found in comparison with the standard of Truth.

Mormonism is a religion compatible with evolution and many other false teachings that incorporate but taint, rewrite, or diminish the Bible. Although the false angel Moroni's *specific* message— the Book of Mormon—was supposed to be transliterated from pictograms to words through a pair of mystical spectacles, and was also supposed to be *word-perfect and exact*, the message itself has been transformed over the years and it has been edited for content along the way for compatibility with reality, and for error-correction purposes. One only needs to compare any "historical version" of their "book" with its recent counterpart for proof, but all their books should be compared to the Word of God.

Mormonism is a secretive, stressful, and legalistic religion in which one must strive to reach their god by rituals and *works*, and not by God's completed work on their behalf, in Christ. If "sacrifices" and "works of righteousness" made one "righteous," then the Jews would not have needed to offer up yearly sacrifices. Christ, on the other hand, completed the law and fulfilled it, and now no other sacrifice is required, or indeed is even acceptable. Christ's sacrifice, being *perfect*—made once for all mankind, obtainable only by *faith* in His sacrifice, and, of course, in *Him*—is the only way to stand rightly before a Holy God, the provider and imparter of that *perfect sacrifice*.

But *religious works* make men feel secure, even proud, by virtue of deeds performed and rites carried out to offset their sin and perhaps gain favor, status, and, in some cases, *equality* with their god. The religious often compare themselves to lists of right and wrong, and to others for their measure of righteousness, and not to the standard that God has set in His Holy Word. Righteousness is imparted only by faith in the Living Word of God—Jesus Christ—in His completed work, not ours. And above all law that is given, and above all prophets' revelations, we are commanded to hear Christ.

On the other hand, a Christian should feel honored to stand with a Mormon at any "pro-life rally," work at a business side by side with one, or even champion one as "POTUS," as long as the candidate upheld the Constitution and remained worthy of respect, but one should **always part ways with Mormons wherever the doctrine of Christ is concerned**. The truth is that Mormons need salvation as much as any of the "lost" of this world. God loves the Mormons as He also loves Muslims, the alcoholic, the homosexual, or any other sinner, but they need to know the real Jesus—God incarnate, their Creator, not Satan's brother, not just a good man, not just a prophet. Mormons are skilled at proselytizing and wooing Christians from Christianity and into their fold. Their morality, conviction, dedication, and determination are persuasive, even enviable, traits, but as with all other religions, their work-based paths lead away from Biblical authority and Truth. It is religious bondage. Through love, kindness, and a willingness to understand them without fear, anger, or hatred, some Mormons have been led to see their doctrinal contradictions with the Word of God; but those reclaimed, by the nature of the religion, stand as outcasts and even "dead" in the eyes of their Mormon family and former friends. Joseph Smith's close encounter of "the third kind" has led millions to spiritual ruin.

The *fourth kind* of close encounter is indeed abduction by beings who can take any shape. Again, demons, fallen angels,

Moronis appearing as angels of light, or beings beyond this solar system—be they humanoid, reptilian, spiritual manifestation, or other—are all of the same origin, and they enjoy harming and misleading mankind. Abductions often include physical probing, genetic manipulation, and experimentation, causing horrific pain, instilling unimaginable fear, and exercising mental and physical control of the abductees. The beings mark those whom they have taken by their spiritual weakness as targets for repeated torture. Bullets are of no consequence to the Moroni. The power of God, His Word, His Host, prayer, and spiritual confrontation by those with experience are the only offense. These abductees are truly candidates for demonic possession.

When movies portray exorcisms, they are usually Catholic exorcisms. The reality of a *successful* confrontation is not portrayed well on-screen because of the following: Demons are simply *not* Catholic, and directors of such films are largely spiritually ignorant. Of course, the demons in question are not Jewish, Protestant, Eastern Orthodox, Calvinists, or Armenian either. The point concerning Catholicism is that demons have no real regard for the Papacy, icons, crucifixes, holy water, the Eucharist, Sacraments, or Catholic rituals of any kind. If they react to those, they do it as a means of deception and for other reasons of their own. Unfortunately, many Catholics, though perhaps Christian, walk largely in ignorance where their *relationship* with Christ is concerned. They may be very religious and earnest in the practice of their religion, but many are precariously superstitious, evidencing the lack of a solid understanding of the Word of God. Most rely on priests as an intermediary between men and God, and therefore their personal relationship with Jesus suffers. Biblically speaking, nobody sits *"alter Christus."* There is no true "Holy Father" but God Himself. Prayer to Mary or any *patron saint* was never required or suggested in Sacred Scripture beyond prayer *for* the saints who are alive on earth. The Church is the Bride of Christ—God's Bride. Mary, blessed as she was, is merely part of the Church, not Queen of Heaven, not a perpetual virgin or Mother of God. Rosaries, statues, penance, and prayer stations all hinder, rather than help, the Christian. Those ultimately reduce the relationship to a process, or rite, and therefore a "work," whereas real faith should be the practice of "faith and fellowship" with God Himself, daily, and with repentance from dead works, not penance, because the sin is already paid for. However, worshiping in ignorance is always correctable when one *abides in a growing relationship with Christ* and knows His Word, apart from religious teachings and rituals. Christians need not go through anyone but Jesus Himself to obtain mercy and forgiveness, and to have their petitions heard before an engaged and loving God.

Close encounters of the *fifth kind* constitute contact with demonic entities through spiritism, metaphysics, mysticism, and occultist means. This is where contact is ignorantly, shamefully consensual. Communication between humans and the demonic realm can be in-depth, and mysteries can be revealed. Demons know men, their relationships, their history, because **they've been there firsthand** all along. Remote viewing is also included in this type of contact. Spiritual messages are often given in the guise of any type of being the medium requires, and the messages can be anything that will direct the hearer away from Christ. Close encounters of the *sixth kind* have aspects of all the others but manifest physical injury, even death, to the contactee.

Finally, with Nick's thoughts drifting, his mind began to shut down in the way it usually did. Images took over ordered thought and gained clarity, pulling him away from the conscious world around him to the place where he found rest. And then finally he slept.

12

CONVERGENCE

**(The first correspondence from
Bensington Redwood to President Harry
S. Truman, sent September 11, 1947)**

Dear President Truman,

You do not know me, but I am one of the wealthiest men currently living on the planet, and I have vital information to disclose to you. First, I must say that you have shown great courage and restraint with the use of atomics, and this world now needs a leader with such traits because it is about to drastically change, and indeed has greatly changed during your lifetime, but it is on the cusp of a new era. It will be an era unlike any witnessed by mankind, but one that has been declared by God Himself, many times, in the Sacred Scripture of the Bible. Knowledge will increase. But wisdom and the knowledge of God will wax cold, and powers that heretofore have lurked behind the scenes, will begin to flex their muscles increasingly.

It was the French poet Baudelaire, who said, "My dear brothers, never forget, when you hear the progress of enlightenment vaunted, that the devil's best trick is to persuade you that he doesn't exist!" It is a wise saying. Many had thought that Adolf Hitler was the Biblical fulfillment of the role of "Antichrist," until he was deposed, but that was all according to the plan of the enemy. Why? Because if such notions can be fostered, and somewhat validated in the minds of the masses, then dashed upon the rocks, it destroys and demoralizes faith in prophetic fulfillment on balance. Again, I stress that it happened according to plan, and most persons now believe that the devil doesn't exist. However, we have an adversary that is real, ancient, cruel, and wise, and he knows how to undermine even one's perception of reality. Communism and fascism may be evil, but Satan is the father of evil, and he is the true threat and author of the others.

Mr. President, I respectfully request that you receive and listen to a group of men whom I will be sending to Washington in the near future, that I may fully explain and substantiate an imminent threat to humanity, and offer a reasonable and specific course of action, a counteroffensive plan, if you will. There is an undeniable danger that you must be made aware of, and it will begin next year, on the day Israel will be recognized as a nation. Once that prophetic event occurs, we will be living one generation, a single life span, away from Armageddon. Beginning next year, we will be living in the shadow of the Great Tribulation, a span of time which I call a "prelude to the dark messiah"—a prelude to the real Antichrist. Of course I celebrate Israel's statehood, but her enemies will encompass her and eventually the entire world will be against her. But until then, we will have our own campaign to war against the enemies of mankind.

As a token of my earnestness and the urgency of having an audience with you, you should note the enclosed check for fifty-thousand dollars that I donate to the President Harry S. Truman Library fund. Sir, we have trouble on the horizon and a storm will begin building. Although it cannot be averted, it can be managed for a time.

In the defense of humanity, I remain,

Bensington Redwood

SHADES STATE PARK

7751 S. CR 890 West • Waveland, IN 47989 • (765) 435-2810
3,082 acres   Established 1947

LEGEND

=====	Road
-----	Hiking Trail
	Boundary
	Nature Preserve
♿	Accessible
	Connecting Trail

Payphones located at pond and campground

TRAIL TABLE

TRAIL	MILEAGE	TRAIL TYPE
1	.75	Moderate/Rugged
2	1.25	Rugged/Rugged
4	.625	Moderate/Rugged
5	.75	Moderate/Rugged
6	.5	Easy
7	.875	Rugged
8	.25	Rugged
9	.5	Moderate
10	.5	Moderate
Back Pack	2.5	Moderate

SHELTERS

●	Pine
●	Dell
●	Hickory

PINE
HILLS
NATURE
PRESERVE
HIKING ONLY!
No Picnicking or Camping

Indian Creek

Sugar Creek

No Camping Along Sugar Creek

No Camping or Picnicking in this Area

Public Canoe Launch

Devil's Mill
Cromwell Bridge

Parking

Property Manager's Residence

Pine Hills Parking

Assistant Property Manager's Residence

Prospect Point
Inspiration Point
Silver Cascade Falls
Steamboat Rock
Heart Ravine
Maidenhair Falls
CANOE ISLAND
Pearl Ravine
Frisz Ravine
Kintz Ravine
Kickapoo Ravine
Shawnee Canyon
Hemlock Picnic Area
Devil's Punch Bowl
Red Fox Ravine
Pond
Gatehouse
Parking

Backpack Trail
Accessible only by hiking

Campground Loop Trail

Campground
Control Station
Amphitheater

Youth Tent Camping

Entrance

County Road 800S

IND 234

- Stay on marked trails.
- Trails close at dusk.
- All hikers must be off trails prior to dusk.
- Bicycles prohibited on trails and service roads.
- Swimming and wading in Sugar Creek are prohibited within the park.

WARNING: All trails, except 9, 10 and Backpack, have portions that use ravine streambeds as trail surface and sections of trail can become slick and trail tread uneven. Parts of these trails may be impassible during high water and should be considered closed during these times. Use alternate trails during times of high water.

Ladders are used on trails 4 and 6. These can be hazardous for visitors with some medical conditions or disabilities. Hikers with small children and pets should use alternate trails.

Approximate Scale in Miles
0   1/4   1/2

LOCATION MAP

SHADES STATE PARK
Indianapolis

PARK BOUNDARY

Note: Backpack and Canoe camps are not accessible by vehicle.

Backpack and Canoe campers see special information on reverse side of map.

Indiana—Present Day, July 7th

Malcolm Carson's flight was delayed in LA, and then again in Denver. Even with the delays, he could get no sleep while aboard the flights. Excitement kept him awake, but he'd never been able to sleep on an aircraft. He had the belief, and knew it was childish, that his own will was needed to help keep the plane aloft. When the jet finally touched down at Indianapolis International Airport, it was 1:03am Eastern time. Malcolm was tired, and he looked it. He ambled off the jet with carry-on luggage in tow and headed for the baggage reclamation area below the concourse. That is where he spotted his daughter.

Crystal Ann Carson, on the other hand, looked fresh as the morning dew. She was dressed in khaki pants, cuffed just at the lacings of her hiking boots, and she wore a light blue shirt with the long sleeves rolled up just above her elbows. She also had a white neckerchief loosely tied about her neck and an Australian hat atop her head. Her appearance was that of an adventurer ready to head out into the bush, and she stood out in the crowd. The sight of his daughter reinvigorated Malcolm, and he felt a surge of adrenaline and excitement that the adventure was finally at hand.

"Crystal," Malcolm said, walking up to her and giving her a kiss on her cheek. He noted that she wore perfume and smelled . . . heavenly. He knew that she'd not be wearing it while at the camp, so he said nothing about it. "You are a pleasant sight, my dear."

"Hi, Dad. Let's get your luggage and hit the road so you can get some rest," she said. She then assisted him in both finding his bags and lugging them to the waiting rental car. Once the rental was filled with Malcolm's luggage, he took the passenger's seat and allowed Crystal to drive them to their bed-and-breakfast accommodation in Waveland.

Malcolm pulled out a map of Shades State Park and turned the passenger light on so he could read the map, as Crystal navigated their way out of the airport and onto I-70 West.

"So, where on this map is base camp?" Malcolm asked.

"We set up in Pine Hills by the creek and in the lee of the Devil's Backbone. It is a very pretty park," Crystal said.

"Um . . . where on this map is that?" he asked, not seeing the "Backbone" on the map.

"Oh, I forgot. It isn't actually on the map. Do you see where Shades ends and Pine Hills begins?"

"Yes, right here at the covered bridge." Malcolm pointed to the map.

"Actually, there is a covered bridge and a new bridge. They're next to each other. Camp is southeast of the bridge by about half a mile. Sorry, the map has most of the landmarks on it for Shades State Park, but on that map, the Pine Hills section only shows the creeks and the boundaries. I met with Dr. Mills at his office in Crawfordsville just shortly after you called him. I gathered and signed the permits and I even have the DNR waivers, so you won't have to do any of that. There is another map, *a much better map*, which the DNR ranger showed me. It illustrates all their access roads, posts, projects, and buildings that aren't shown on any other map. They made it themselves and the only copy offered to the public is on a wall in their office. That's the best map to use," she said.

"The only copy. On a wall? That's not very helpful," said Malcolm.

"I took several high-resolution photos of it, Dad. I printed them off and you have copies in your room. We have it in *very good detail*," Crystal said proudly.

"That's my girl," Malcolm said.

"Oh, and Waveland's Sheriff—Braxton—agreed to be on-site sometime tomorrow . . . I mean *this afternoon*," she corrected herself. "Just an informal visit so you can ask him anything you need to," she said.

"What's he like?"

"He's seems to be nice enough, and he knows the area well. I believe he's going to be excellent for updating us on the history of the site, perhaps clue us in on details that didn't make the local papers. He may even be of further assistance if we have to leave the State Parks and track on private property. It seems that he was actually glad that Dr. Mills had contacted you."

"Very encouraging news, Honey. Oh, I almost forgot," he added, as he reached behind and pulled out two books from the outside pocket on his carry-on luggage. "I have two photographs that I'd like you to study when we arrive. In the background of each photo, there is a man whose face I need you to study so you can keep an eye out for him at all of the sites. I've circled his face in red marker."

"A man, Dad? You are not trying to fix me up with someone again, are you?"

"Nothing like that, Crystal. This man may be a source for trouble for us, and if we spot him, I want to hire a private detective to follow him wherever he goes. I don't want you to confront him. I don't want him to know that he's been, well, *detected* at all. But I do want him watched 24-7. If he shows up, he'll likely be in our camp as part of a film crew or an assistant of some kind to one of the guides. And his credentials have already passed inspection by some kind of trickery, but he's being tracked by the Feds, and that may bring heat our way by just being near him."

"OK, Dad, spill it," she ordered her father in the way a beloved child can manipulate her parent without appearing to be disrespectful to him, for public appearance's sake, yet blatantly doing so.

"Whatever his current *nom de-voyage* is, the man's real name is Dominic Monroe, or Murrow. He is with a secretive organization called Knightlight, which is under Federal investigation, and his very presence may jeopardize the site or even compromise the entire mission. He is to be regarded as a hostile impostor, or intruder, but treated no differently than anyone else at the site until we can figure out how to get him out of my life. Got that?"

"Yes, Dad, Dominic Monroe or Murrow, and Nightlight . . . got it. But what organization could possibly be interested in a Bigfoot hunt? I don't see the connection."

"I won't pretend to understand it myself, but that is why we will hire a P.I. immediately upon identifying him, if he ever shows up. I want to know everything I can about him, even if I have to grab him around the ankles and drag it out of him."

"Just don't go *postal*, Dad. If we see him, stick to your own plan and whatever you do, *don't confront him*."

"My dear, I assure you that I will not tip my hand in any way."

"Yeah, right," she said sarcastically.

"Now, let's talk about you," he said.

"Yes . . . ?"

"Who are you currently seeing, and has he been informed that we both are proficient with firearms?"

Crystal smiled at that. Malcolm was always overprotective, but it was, she knew, a demonstration of his love for her, and it bothered her and comforted her at the same time.

Crystal was extremely attractive and knew that she turned many male heads as she gracefully walked by them, past them, and outwardly unaware of them. She wanted to fall in love, to be swept off her feet by the man of her dreams. But she had yet to meet a man who was interested in her work, someone shared her values and personal interests, and someone who would wait for marriage instead of trying to manipulate her into the "sack" before her finger had a shiny gold band on it. She was patient and somehow just *knew* that it would pay off in the end. She had faith that her life was going to bless her patience, though she was not completely sure where that faith came from, nor by whom the blessings would come. She was strong-willed, confident, and undeterred from her work, yet she knew that somewhere out there was a man who could make her knees buckle and her heart skip, and enable her to turn her love of life toward him. She just *knew* . . . like most women *just know*. She, however, would save herself for that man, while others would give themselves away for much less than she required. She had many friends who had settled for less than perfect lives, and knew they had regrets about it. She would have no regrets when the right man was revealed to her . . . none whatsoever.

Knowing that destiny was surely ahead, and truly believing in that fact, meant being wise by preparing her life for that event. She wanted to be everything she could be for that unknown man in her future. She wanted to be his partner, a tender comfort to him and a wise counsel when he required it. She wanted to adventure with him, but even adventure would be a second love, after him. It was somewhere ahead of her, and her heart and mind looked forward to it.

"Dad, I am currently seeing *nobody*. But don't worry; should I meet the right man, I promise that *you* will be the *last to know*," she said and smiled at him.

"Careful, Crystal, I may be tempted to put a P.I. on your tail as well," he bluffed in good humor, but his message was clear: He loved her.

The two drove on I-70 westward for half an hour until it intersected with State Road 59, which they took north through Brazil, then through hills and forested areas to Mansfield, then on until the road leveled off, revealing a sea of corn under the starlit night. They spoke very little as Crystal watched the road ahead, and Malcolm, tired and drowsy, began dozing, off and on.

They continued to Bellmore and slowed, seeing the lonesome flashing red light ahead at the crossroads. It was a beautiful and warm summer night, and to keep from getting too sleepy, Crystal rolled down her window. She noticed the bright stars that filled the cloudless sky. It was a breathtaking spectacle for the city girl. She loved getting out in the field whenever she could to experience the sights, sounds, and smells of the country.

As the vehicle slowed at the crossing of 59 and US-36, Malcolm stirred. "How much farther?" he asked.

"Twenty minutes or so from here," she said.

"Good, I'm ready for bed," he said, and then drifted back to light unconsciousness.

They followed 59 until they arrived at the small town of Waveland, and pulled into the drive of the bed-and-breakfast home. Crystal nudged Malcolm awake as she shut down the engine. She then guided him up to their rooms and let Malcolm get to bed before she went back and transported his luggage to her room for temporary keeping.

Crystal's small room had a double bed with nightstand, a small desk, a rocking chair, a television, and a small bathroom. It was comfortable and simple. She had no plans to stay there much, since there was a trailer in the park just for her and her father. They could work and sleep there if they chose, and both intended to spend as much time on-site as possible. But that site had no running water, which made keeping the B&B rooms available to them attractive.

After Crystal washed up and put on her nightgown, she grabbed the two books that her father had called her attention to and began to study the face of Dominic, with the comfort afforded by the soft bed. It was her intention to be able to recognize the man if he had gained weight or lost it, if he wore glasses or not, and even if he was bearded or cleanshaven. She would have put Lois Lane to shame for not recognizing who Clark Kent really was. She examined the photos until sleep gently, silently overtook her.

Not even realizing she had slept, Crystal awoke with the sound of her alarm clock buzzing at 8:00am Eastern Time. She snapped fully awake, shut off the irritating sound, and went to the bathroom. It took her a mere twenty-two minutes to relieve herself, shower, brush her teeth, and dry her hair. She prided herself in her timeliness and efficiency regardless of the activity. When she emerged in her bathrobe, she went to the coffeepot that was time-synchronized with her alarm, and poured herself a cup of coffee, adding sugar and creamer. She sat at the bedroom's small desk and snapped open her laptop computer and let it boot to the desktop as she carefully sipped her hot, invigorating beverage. While there, she Google-searched for Dominic Murrow, but found nothing that seemed connected to the person in the photographs. She searched Dominic Monroe, but found similar and just as unhelpful information. She then decided to switch to an image search but it yielded the same results . . . nothing useful. So she fell back on the remembered organizational name of Nightlight. That too was a head-scratcher for her because she found nothing that might be a suspicious organization, and you can *always* find something on virtually anyone, or any*thing*, if you put in the correct search parameters. And she, of course, believed that she had. Her *Google-fu* was usually formidable.

She then checked her own e-mail account, and then her father's, corresponding quickly with various persons and agencies as she finished her coffee. The time was now 9:30 and she knew that she had better wake her father. She also knew it would still be two hours after he was up before they would be on their way, knowing what a slow starter he was in the morning unless he was actually camping out. So she woke him, moved his luggage from her room to his, and then went back to her room and dressed. She then checked the e-mail accounts again and watched the Fox News channel in HD until Malcolm knocked on her door to announce that he was ready to drive to the site. She quickly turned off all electrical devices and exited the bed-and-breakfast with her father, and the two headed out to the site.

It was a stunningly pretty summer day as they pulled out of the B&B and cruised through the quaint small town of Waveland. Crystal loved the "Heartland," the small towns where people say "good morning" to you and know you by name. She'd heard that Andrew Breitbart was of the same thought, and she wished she'd been able to meet him before his untimely death. As they progressed through town, she noted a redheaded lady artist at work in front of a craft store, painting a covered bridge, for which the area was famous, but it was the strangest painting of such that she'd ever seen.

Artists, Crystal thought. *Who can understand them?*

Crystal drove down the hill, out of town, over the short bridge, crossed SR-47, and then took the shortcut to Pine Hills. Malcolm was poring over the printed e-mail from Dr. Mills that drew him to the site in the first place. The drive was a pleasant one and Malcolm was missing it. He was lost in his thoughts, until he looked up and saw the farmland around them and the line of trees ahead. He absorbed the scenery and allowed his daughter to quietly drive them to their destination. After roughly ten minutes, Crystal broke the peaceful silence.

"This, on the left, is where you would turn to go to Shades State Park," Crystal announced, as they made the northward curve toward Pine Hills on SR-234. "I expect we will be spending the bulk of our time in there."

"Look at all the trees ahead," Malcolm said as the view changed from farmland to forest.

"Breathtaking," Crystal agreed, driving farther north toward the site. "This right turn is the Pine Hills service road that we need to take to get down to the site. It's only about three-fourths of a mile, but it is a slow ride, so just enjoy the view."

And Malcolm did enjoy the view, looking up at the green sky that was held in place by tall, slender living pillars of wood. The undergrowth was not as dense as he had expected, and you could see clearly at least 200 feet in any direction. It was perfect for the need to spot anything, even a "Squatch," from a reasonable distance, and still maintain their own cover. Malcolm cringed at the term *Squatch*, especially because that word came to mind first, as opposed to its full moniker. It was, of course, shorthand jargon for *Sasquatch*. To Malcolm, the term removed the majestic grandeur of the language itself. It was gutter-slang and unscientific. The taxonomical language was specific and descriptive, and the term *Squatch* cheapened it to accommodate fads such as "texting" or "tweeting" and especially for the sake of "arrogance." It tells others "if you don't know our lingo, then you aren't one of us." Still, he suffered it without correction when others used it, but it still bothered him.

The drive was slow and careful, but pleasant, and the forest was beautiful. Malcolm was relaxed yet excited to be in the field, and his outlook on the Agnostopithecus expedition was nothing but encouraging . . . until they saw the campsite, the lights on the police car, and the obvious uproar within the camp.

"What on earth . . . ," said Malcolm.

"Maybe the campsite was robbed, or something," Crystal said, hoping it was nothing more than that. "The Sheriff was supposed to be here later this afternoon, but this looks like he's here for official business."

She pulled up into a clearing that was nearly 100 feet from the campsite and parked. Seeing John Cosworth speaking to Sheriff Braxton, Malcolm exited his vehicle and strode quickly down the hill to the campsite. Crystal shut off the engine, exited, and jogged lithely to catch up to him, following him all the way down to the camp.

"What's going on here, John?" Malcolm asked Cosworth.

"Hi, Malcolm. Good to see you. You're just in time," Cosworth said. "This is Sheriff Braxton, who has just informed me that we may have to abandon the site. He was just explaining why."

Malcolm shook Cosworth's hand, then Braxton's, eyeing him warily, while Crystal stood behind her father and prepared to document the bad news they expected Braxton to begin explaining.

"As you know, there've been several deaths and disappearances in this area, and at least one of them looks to be homicide," Braxton began. "We've had cause to believe them to be linked to the reason you are out here: the sightings. But the FBI has informed me that there may be another cause for the deaths, and that the two might not be linked. *They* think it's just a coincidence."

"Well, I should hope so," spoke Malcolm. "There has never been a verifiable case of *murder* as it relates to an Agnostopithecus."

"Agnosto-who?" asked Braxton.

"A Bigfoot," said Cosworth.

"Oh . . . OK, Bigfoot," Braxton continued. "At any rate, the FBI found an old transport truck not far from here that contained some sort of *nerve agent*. They say it may be leaking and may be the cause for some nearby folks to act in dangerous ways. I'm here letting everyone know that the EPA is involved, and the CDC is on its way and will be shutting down the parks in the area until cleanup and decontamination can be completed. That means your permits will be temporarily revoked until they are done."

"Wonderful," said Malcolm sarcastically. "Can this '*nerve agent*' be the reason for all of the Agnostopithecus sightings in the first place?" he asked Braxton.

"It may explain some of the various things people have been seeing around here lately; I don't know. I do know a hallucination can't leave a sixteen-inch footprint, or handprints on . . . ," he stopped short of saying "on the victim" because the investigation was ongoing, "on some evidence, but supposedly it can cause irrational fear and group hysteria. I was told that it can even cause murderous and suicidal behavior in those exposed to it. That's what the Feds say, anyway. I'll do some research on it."

"Good," Malcolm said. "I mean 'good' that this site will not be a complete waste of our time and money. How soon will we know what our options are?"

"Start packing up now. I am sure they will want you out of here, and it's better to be safe than under arrest or dead. When the CDC's on-site, we'll know more. They'll be examining the truck found on a farm a few miles southwest of here, and then meet here, my guess is around six or seven pm."

"Now that is unreasonable, Constable," Malcolm began. "We're fully deployed here and we have all the right paperwork. If this is miles away, there can't be much of a danger. I happen to know that even weaponized VX gas disperses easily, and is a poor weapon."

"It's a poor weapon if you're upwind of it, or it's raining, but I'm not even comfortable being here knowing that it's even *possibly* in the air. Get packed and be ready to move," Braxton said.

"Thanks for the information," Cosworth said to Braxton, wanting to keep Malcolm from causing trouble between themselves and the law.

"I'll be back here at five-thirty and wait for the Feds with you," said Braxton, who then turned and headed away from the scientists.

Malcolm looked around the campsite while Braxton retreated. The two trailers were here, anchored down, and several trucks. Even the small excavator he knew they needed was present, and it looked as though it had been put to use already. The light generators were there, cables had been run everywhere needed, tents had been set up, and he saw camera traps on a couple of trees and noted that the cages were there, already assembled. It looked good, and that's what really infuriated him. The site was prepped, and this was Day One, and now he and his men were being sent packing.

"Are we *fully* set up?" asked Malcolm quietly of Cosworth.

"Nearly," replied Cosworth, matching Malcolm's diminished volume.

"Good. It appears that we have a few hours to work with, so let's not waste them," said Carson.

As Braxton left the site, high up on the Devil's Backbone, hidden by the overhanging trees, the camp came under observation by a pair of cold, hate-filled, and calculating eyes.

(State Road 47, Parke County, Indiana—July 7th, 6:15pm Eastern Standard Time)

"Yes, First Agent," Dominic said as he adjusted his headset so he could better hear and be heard. "I knew we were busy, but I didn't think we had that many ongoing missions simultaneously."

"We are deployed at 100 percent now. I've even got two advance teams that are going to work together as agents in Florida," said Griffin.

"That's a first," said Nick. "What's going on?"

"Sightings and encounters on a larger scale than we had anticipated, and it's clear that we will need to train new teams. If this is a trend, we'll need to expand our operation significantly. But the scale of high-confidence sightings has the Director and me quite concerned. I want you to be careful out there and watch your backs. Something sinister's afoot, but we can't discern the enemy's strategy or nail down a paradigm yet."

"What about the 'N-contingency'? Are you considering that as an option?"

"Not at this time," replied the First Agent.

"Roger that," said Rock.

"Now, regarding your mission: After you e-vac the locals out of the park, set an extrawide perimeter boundary to isolate your hunt from outsiders, and I recommend you double your snare deployment as well," said First Agent.

"Affirmative," replied Rock. "Depending on who the *locals* are, we may need to interact with them more than usual since that Bigfoot Squad from CQ Petroleum is at the site. Our covers are fragile, and these crypto sci-fi-entists are apt to believe that we are there for the same reasons they are. I may have to break confidence to keep them away."

"Rock, I trust your judgment, but reveal only what you *must*. We walk a fine line where national security is concerned. Make them sign a *nondisclosure* if you have to tell them anything compromising, and Rock . . . ," the First Agent paused for a moment as if he had an epiphany, "be open to an opportunity for recruitment. Atheists aside, there may yet be Knightlight material among them."

"Roger that, First Agent, although my guess is that they are obstacles and casualties waiting to happen. On the other hand, if they can even be simple allies, I would welcome that much," said Rock.

"Perhaps . . . ," said First Agent. "Perhaps. But be careful handling them, and even more careful once they are out of the way."

"Affirmative, First Agent," said Rock, then added, "Permission to say that you sound a little worried, Sir."

"Granted, but *uneasy* is closer to the truth, Rock. Something is building out there, and we're not sure if it means escalation of the campaign, or the endgame, or what. But the evil of Tammuz is spreading. In fact, it's suddenly spiked, and it may be that the enemy and his monsters are mustering their forces. We know that one day they will, but we aren't sure if it's their time yet. I hope it is, because the Rapture is something I truly wish to see, but this could just be an indication that we have a long and hard road ahead of us. Time will tell."

"Amen, First Agent. Let us know anything you can, when you can."

"Affirmative, Rock. Keep your heads down, and watch your backs. First Agent out."

"Out," replied Rock, and then silently he thought, *What on earth is going on?*

Cheese saw the navigational transponder indicate that they were near their destination. As he looked ahead, he saw a green sign declaring, "Entering Montgomery County—Leaving Parke County." Rock saw the sign as well.

"How are you feeling, Tick?" inquired Rock.

Tick, in the back section of the truck, responded, "If you must know the truth, I feel like I want to go out and get drunk."

"Yeah, and I feel like I want to start smoking again," replied Rock. "How about you, Cheese, what's come to your mind?"

"Women," replied Cheese.

"Women," seconded Tick.

"Women," agreed Rock, nodding his head.

"Spiritual oppression is thick here. Keep on your toes, amigos, we are now in the enemy's backyard . . . and they know we're trespassing."

Tick spoke a prayer aloud: "Father, thank you for going ahead of us. Please protect Your sons and keep us from stumbling. Help us focus our eyes on You, and lead us with Your Holy Spirit. We ask that You loose Your angels to do battle before us, and be victorious against the powers of darkness in the air. Fill our lack, show us favor and mercy, and forgive us and cleanse us by the blood of Your Son and by Your Holy Word. Amen."

"Amen," replied Rock and Cheese in unison.

Every county, every state, every country has its own demonic chain of command and a specialized form of oppression against the human occupants therein. Most of that oppression is general and largely indiscernible by the human occupants, unless it is aimed in concentration at a specific local church, evangelist, or worshiper. Although satanic authority is directed against most of humanity at all times, the enemy shows specific interest in targeting the warriors of God. The enemy also outnumbers Christians, but God Himself is matchless, and His angels outnumber the demonic population two-to-one. Whatever can cause Christians to be tripped up will be laid in front of them, to distract them, to rob them, to kill them, and ultimately in hopes of destroying them. But there are rules of engagement, and nothing can be done outside of God's permission. Unfortunately, Satan already has the faithless in his pocket, and it is the faithful whom he keeps his forces directed against, for the most part.

The large vehicle, with the Big Cheese at the wheel, pulled into the gravel drive of the Beiler family residence, directly off State Road 47, just within Montgomery County, Indiana. It slowly navigated the drive back to the enormous Amish barn where the Advance Team had left a black Hummer 3 SUV for them to pick up. It was a Knightlight Hummer, meaning it had many electronic device additions, weapons mounts, countermeasures, and advanced lighting capabilities, including a head's-up display on the windshield and night vision. Ian Fleming would be proud of every vehicle in Knightlight's motor pool.

Cheese set the automated anchor footers on the MFB, lowered its skirt, and shut it down. Slowly, the three dismounted their large truck and stretched their legs, with Tick carrying three MREs.

"I've got our supper, and I know I'm ready to eat," said Tick.

The three sat on the Beiler house's porch steps and ate their rations quietly after a quick "thanks" to God. The meals ready to eat were not bad, but weren't nearly as good as what they were served back in the Archangel bunker. Rock knew they were spoiled at any Knightlight base, and even the MREs were luxury compared to what passes for a meal in other parts of the world. Rock had learned to be thankful even for just bread and uncontaminated water. After they finished their entrées and were almost done, Tick asked whether they were going to eat their corn. Tick always asked for their corn. It was, they knew, his favorite vegetable, but Rock insisted that it was because of its memory-enhancing properties that Tick favored it. In point of fact, Rock jokingly called it forget-me-not food. When the Cheese finally asked why, Rock explained that the next day, when Tick used the latrine, he'd remember what he had for lunch today. Corn is the only way to be sure. After they cleaned their plates, they stowed away the trash and enjoyed the still, warm weather of an Indiana summer.

"So, the Ops team has been here and gone?" asked Cheese.

"Yeah. The vehicle that supposedly has the toxin should be directly north of this position, roughly one hundred feet past the tree line. It is sealed and secure. All photos and paperwork should be in the Hummer, so there's no need to go back there unless the Sheriff requires a look. In that event, full hazmat protocol will be required," Dominic said as he did a couple of leg stretches. "Tick, you'd better change the truck's logo to CDC while we're thinking about it."

"Roger that," said Tick. He reentered the giant vehicle and transformed the external image of the mobile field unit, then closed, sealed, and locked the transport, ready to move on to the site in the SUV. Their intention was to visit the site, speak to the Sheriff, and perform all necessary preliminary park-closure procedures before they moved the field office onto the site. It was expected to be a simple preengagement trip before they actually deployed later in the night.

The team members were dressed in military fatigues with black berets and black jungle boots, but also wore protective plastic micro-thin white covers over their shirts and pants. The shirt had a CDC patch on the breast, and an attached hood with face mask that they allowed to hang down their backs. They had sidearms on their belt, with respirators on the opposite side, but they had no intention of using them unless they needed to make a show of the biohazard.

"Everyone have their credentials handy and saddle up in the Hummer," Rock instructed as he entered the driver seat of the H3. Most of the Knightlight vehicles were keyed the same and had identical transponder chips with them so that the vehicles could be used by any agent at any time of need, and tracked.

All three men entered the black vehicle with dark limousine tint on the windows. In the glove compartment Rock found the update sheet from the FBI investigators and passed it back to Tick so that he could assimilate it while they drove from the Amish farm to Pine

Hills Nature Preserve. Rock flipped on the interactive GPS display on the dashboard, and let it locate their destination. Then he started the Hummer, ready to move out.

"Seat belts," Rock said as he backed the SUV around a tight turn to face them toward the main road. Tick locked himself tightly and relaxed in the spacious rear seat. The Hummer was essentially a very comfortable tank. The base vehicle was spec'd for the President of the United States, *then* modified further by Knightlight. It was rigged, and plated to take the POTUS out of a battle if necessary, but Knightlight utilized it as the tip of the spear when necessary.

The large SUV rolled out onto State Road 47, turning north at Waveland, and headed for Pine Hills. Tick absorbed the data from the FBI, and the Big Cheese just sat back and enjoyed the serene summer evening in Indiana.

"Well . . . ," began Tick from the back seat, "the analysis of the Advance Team points to either a Maxie or a Chaney, but there is no conclusive evidence as to which."

The classification of a "Max" or "Maxie" was Knightlight slang indicating a vampire, classically called an Emim. Max Schreck was the very first screen appearance of a vampire in silent film, and thus the etymology of the term. "Chaney" was shorthand for a werewolf, or a Rephaim. Lon Chaney Jr. was the first to portray "The Wolfman" or (werewolf) in film. There were shorthand names for all of the demon spawn and their followers; and, of course, the parent demons themselves were called Moronis.

"Once it's dead, we'll know for sure which. One smooth stone to the head, and we'll have our trophy," said Rock.

"The crypto-zoologists are currently on-site in Pine Hills. They arrived yesterday. John Cosworth is their team leader," continued Tick, looking at the paperwork. "Relocation to a nearby park, Turkey Run, has been arranged for them. That's the park we passed on the way over here. The details are here," he said as he passed it to the Big Cheese.

"Thanks," said Cheese, and he began to digest the details before they arrived.

After only a short time traveling, the team pulled onto State Road 234, passed the entrance to Shades State Park, and closed in on Pine Hills. The GPS navigator indicated that Rock should turn left in 100 feet, which he did when he saw the park's DNR access road, which showed signs of recent and heavy traffic. The forest swallowed them as they slowly traveled their path northward and down a ravine toward the base of the Devil's Backbone. It was unspoken, but all three felt the short-hairs on the back of their neck begin to rise. They had arrived.

"It's hammer time," Rock said, and then added, "Hold the line."

"Hold the line," Tick and Cheese replied.

Sheriff Braxton, with a clipboard in his hand, saw the headlights of the Hummer approaching Malcolm Carson's campsite. He had asked first whether Carson's group had seen anything yet, anything "strange," and received a negative on that. Then he asked why Carson's group had not packed up and prepared to move to another location. Malcolm gave him a song and dance about proper paperwork and wanting the order to move to come from the "horse's mouth." Needless to say, it was a not-so-veiled act of *disrespect* toward the Sheriff's authority. Braxton, however, chose to suffer it until the CDC arrived, since Braxton had a stake in Carson's group being there and capturing the *thing* that shouldn't exist.

"Here come the Feds," Braxton announced to Malcolm, who was standing by the camper that would act as his field office. "Stay there while I introduce myself and have a brief confab with them."

"Fine," replied Malcolm as Crystal emerged and stepped down from the camper. Both watched as the Hummer approached slowly in the failing light of the forest.

The Hummer pulled slightly off the downhill path to the left, roughly ninety feet from the first tents, where the crypto-zoologists had established their camping area. It seemed to be recently cleared for a parking, so park Rock did, and shut down the engine. None could see within the vehicle because of the black tinting, and it was a bit intimidating because of its obvious girth and inscrutability. After a few moments, three doors opened, the front two with CDC decals on them, and the men inside stepped from the SUV and met Braxton at the front of the Hummer. They were all distant enough, and in the diminishing light Malcolm and Crystal could not clearly see the agents' faces.

"You're late," said Braxton as if there were an actual agreed-on time for their arrival.

"Sheriff Braxton, I presume?" Rock asked, rather than stated, extending his right hand and holding his open wallet, with ID visible, in the other hand.

"That's me," Braxton said as he shook Rock's hand firmly.

"I am Agent Nick Moreau, and this is Agent Mike Cavor, and this is Agent Gene Ledford. We are the CDC Biohazard Analysis detail you were expecting," spoke Rock. With the introductions, Braxton shook each hand extended toward him in turn, while he examined the various IDs they all displayed. "The EPA will be assisting, but only at the wreck site."

"What's the order, then?" Braxton inquired.

"The order is that we secure the area, quantify any danger, decontaminate if possible and necessary, look for your missing person, take samples, and ensure that the site is clear before we open up the parks. The FBI should have given you a prepared statement for the press—is that so?"

"I have it. And the DNR has been notified already. Park services have been temporarily suspended until they hear an all-clear from you. Though we wish this mess had never happened, we're slightly relieved that it didn't show signs of contamination over the Independence Day weekend. Officer Peck of the DNR gave me this for you to sign," said Braxton, extending the clipboard with pen attached.

"What's this?" asked Rock.

"Just an agreement that you will not disturb lying timber, you won't molest any honeybees, or tree frogs, and so on," Braxton said as Rock took the paperwork and looked it over. "I'm told it is a standard form."

"Right," said Rock. "Thank you," he added as he removed the paperwork, handed the clipboard back to the Sheriff, and handed off the paperwork to Tick. "Agent Cavor, please file this under *toilet paper.*"

"What?" asked the Sheriff in surprise.

"Sheriff Braxton, it is my intention to roll over logs, molest any bee, if need be, and startle all the tree frogs in the park, if it helps us locate your missing person and secure the site. My agency places the value of a human life above a few woodland creatures," declared Rock to the Sheriff. Actually Rock did not believe he'd have to kill anything, save a monster, but he needed to let the Sheriff know that their authority was above and beyond that of the DNR's interests. Braxton immediately, if only internally, raised his "respect level" for Agent Moreau.

"I'm glad to hear that," said Braxton. "Now let me explain something to you: These *biologists* are basically here at my request and I want them back to work ASAP. So what's your protocol?"

"We've been to the site of the hazardous release of QNB on the Beiler farm. Precisely how the truck ended up there, we do not currently have intel on, apart from the fact that it went missing from its intended destination of Newport several years ago. It was not found after a search of the route was conducted. It may be that the driver took a shortcut off the predetermined route, but for whatever reason, it ended up where it still sits. Fortunately, the biohazard is presently contained, if not yet neutralized," explained Rock to reinforce the story.

"I already know the back story, Agent Moreau. What are you going to do to get the parks open again so that we can deal with . . . other matters that might not be related to this spill?" asked Braxton.

Rock knew exactly what Braxton meant. Braxton was a no-nonsense officer and Rock esteemed that trait. And he knew that the Sheriff had already been dealing with the serious matter for which Rock was there, to also deal with seriously. But first he was forced to perform the stupid dance of covering up *that* very reason so that Knightlight could then deal with *that* reason, and hope to remain unobtrusive, anonymous, and covert, which is a difficult prospect at best. A city, *any city*, was easier to work in because law enforcement was already strained to their limits and they actually welcomed aid from outside agencies, as long as it did not undermine their authority, or yank a case from an interested officer. The covert nature of doing business worked best against the noise of the city. Small towns and rural areas were difficult at best, because local enforcement actually knew the community and individuals impacted, and often had personal stakes in the matters. Rural areas have few distractions, making it necessary to maintain a working cover, and contrary to popular belief, not all the best and brightest people live in the city.

"While the hazard is being neutralized, we need your cooperation in cordoning off the area's perimeter of effect until the chemical and residuals are rendered inert," Rock instructed. "Till then, we have a potential danger that can spread with prevailing winds, specifically toward Shades State Park and Pine Hills."

"For how long?" asked Braxton.

"I don't foresee it lasting longer than a week, but that all depends on what else we might find. Neutralization of the threat is priority one, but my team will be within the parks hunting for the missing girl, while taking readings and samples of the local flora and fauna. You *will* hear gunfire within the parks, because we need specimens to examine. A couple of deer, a few squirrels, birds, bats, perhaps coyotes, and we *will* capture a few tree frogs. If necessary, however, we will call in FEMA for the administering of antitoxins, and whatever damage has been done *should* be accounted for by the time we are finished. You will receive a copy of our report once the investigation is complete."

"Sounds like a sporting event, but if you would please find the missing girl, I'll be in your debt. I can even have my men assist you," said Braxton.

Of course Rock's team was not there to shoot any deer or other wildlife apart from the Nephil-Adam, but shots fired needed an explanation, and giving that information up front would quell curiosity to a degree. On the other hand, if they had to use explosives, a rail-gun, or any weapon with an audibly *unique* signature, their story and credibility would float about as well as a cannonball does. Although Rock personally had nothing against hunting of animals for food, culling herds when necessary, or killing in self-defense of life or in defense of the Constitution and his country, he wasn't much of a fan of sportsman hunting unless there was a meal at the end of it, or a *monstrously* significant trophy.

"If your men can keep a perimeter for us, we should be good," said Rock.

"Just for the record, this 'toxic spill' was discovered in a very *untimely* manner, and is in *convenient* conflict with the biologists' investigation. Bottom line, they are suspicious of this entire event," spoke Braxton with a degree of suspicion of his own thrown in the mix.

"I've been briefed on that, and the effects of QNB may account for some of the reasons that made this site, well, attractive to your biologists in the first place. But they will have to postpone their expedition until we've finished with our cleanup efforts. That is nonnegotiable."

"I looked up QNB on the Internet, and it may explain some of the things going on here, but it doesn't explain all of them, Agent Moreau," replied Braxton matter-of-factly.

"I won't try to account for all of them, Sheriff. My job is specific. I will execute it and let you know when my mission is accomplished. The biologists will be given an alternate campsite at . . . what's the name of it, Agent Ledford?" Rock asked the Cheese, pretending that he did not already know.

"Turkey Run State Park," replied the Cheese.

"Turkey Run. And they will be allowed back into these parks when I give you the green light," concluded Rock, letting Braxton know that he would be informed, but would have authority in the matter only as far as Rock gave it to him.

"They won't like it," said Braxton, "but I'll make sure they do as you say."

"Would you rather *I* give them the bad news?" asked Rock.

"I'm technically responsible for them, so I'll let them know," said Braxton.

"That will be fine, Sheriff. Honestly, I appreciate and respect your position in the matter, and I'll do my best to keep you in the loop while relying on your assistance," said Rock.

"Welcome to Indiana," said Braxton.

"Thanks. Now I have a question for you," said Rock. "Are there any caves or sinkholes in this area?"

"Caves?"

"Yes, caves."

"None that I know of," said Braxton. "Southern Indiana has plenty, though."

"Well then, you may have a new one in this area, and we'll do our best to locate it," said Rock.

"What makes you think there are caves here?" asked Braxton.

"Because ever since the FBI investigation began, and for the duration of our trip here, we've been using infrared, or rather, multi-spectrum satellite imaging over the entire area. We have confirmation that warm humanoid bodies have been appearing and disappearing in more than one specific area of Shades, and we've ruled out the possibility that they entered a vehicle, cold water, or a known structure."

"Humanoid?" Braxton asked apprehensively. He knew that the term *humanoid* could apply to a monster as well as a man, or the missing girl.

"Humanoid—as opposed to wildlife."

"Oh, OK. So will those be your first stops to look for the girl?" said Braxton.

"Yes, and we can begin our search as soon as we have this site evacuated and locked down," said Rock with finality.

"I'll talk with the biologists."

Rock watched as Braxton walked away and approached the campsite. He knew that he was peeing in the Sheriff's pond, and he took no pleasure in it. Knightlight was there to protect these people, even if it meant that they would not be liked as they carried out their mission. It was a balance that he felt only a fragile grip upon. *"People should know the specific danger around them, and should be prepared and equipped to defend against it,"* was Rock's argument against secrecy. But it was his task to root out murderous creatures covertly, while trying to maintain a plausible cover for public consumption, while also trying to prevent any further deaths, including that of his own team.

Rock and the team began removing the outer clear-plastic covers over their uniforms that were worn only for the Sheriff's benefit. They stowed them in the back of the Hummer, and then slowly Rock, Tick, and the Big Cheese began to approach the campsite. Rock was pacing himself so that his presence would not interrupt or circumvent the Sheriff's explanation to the crypto-zoologists. It was clear that the Sheriff was finishing up, so the Knightlight team moved in closer. Rock saw John Cosworth with Braxton and another man who was obscured by Braxton, and there was a woman behind the man. He recognized Cosworth even though it was the Big Cheese who had covertly worked with him in the past.

John Cosworth was a tall, fair-haired man of about 50 years old. He was somewhat gangly and had a large nose that could have been his most striking feature, but in actuality, his thick hair was the first thing anyone noticed. It was very much like a blond version of former Illinois Governor Rod Blagojevich. It looked almost silly on anyone over the age of 20, but those with that particular view were never of the envious "follicly challenged" club.

Rock nodded to Cheese regarding Cosworth, who also saw him. Cheese shook his head, indicating that Cosworth most likely would not recognize him. Cheese had a long, thick "hippy" beard and mustache and much heavier when he was previously embedded with the cryptos. He was currently clean-shaven and lighter, and it made a big difference.

Suddenly, Rock stopped dead in his tracks, signaled his men to halt, and turned to his teammates.

"Malcolm Carson's there," he said flatly.

"Great," said Tick. "Why did our intel omit hat little fact?"

"I'm not that surprised," said Cheese. "He's probably doing a photo-op for *Animal Planetoid*, or something."

"Oh well, sooner or later . . . might as well be sooner," Rock said, and he turned back and continued to walk toward the group of Sasquatch hunters.

Crystal saw the Feds coming closer. The two in the back were taller than their leader, and her attention moved from her father's conversation to them. She looked at Rock, who was much closer now. The first thing that came to her mind was "handsome." Next, she met his eyes and noticed that those were clearly the most attractive feature about him. Instantly, she straightened her posture and pulled a strand of hair away from her face, unconsciously primping. It was something she'd rarely done. Then, as Rock was roughly twenty feet away, surprise and shock took her breath away. She could feel her face flush and her eyes widen while he still held her gaze, so she looked away. It was *Dominic Monroe* . . . the man whose face she was supposed to memorize . . . and "beware of," according to her father. The pictures did not do him justice, and his facial hair threw her for a moment. But he was categorized by her father as an enemy, so she gently nudged her father to get his attention.

"Yes, dear," Malcolm said. "Just a moment . . . I'm just trying to reason with the constable."

"I need to speak with you . . . *NOW,*" she politely said but firmly, smiling to Braxton and moving her Dad away from him for a minute.

"What is it, Crystal?" Malcolm impatiently asked.

"*He's here,*" she stressed, quietly, but punctuating it with a painful squeeze to his arm.

"Ouch—who is here?" Malcolm asked.

"*Dominic Monroe . . . DON'T LOOK,*" she urgently commanded.

He looked. The man coming toward them appeared to be of similar build to Dominic Monroe, but Malcolm was unsure.

"It might be him, and it might not be him . . . . I don't think it's him," Malcolm finally said.

"It's him, Dad. Now act normal. We'll hire an investigator in the morning," she said.

The two turned back around. Crystal was still flushed but was trying her best to act normal. They waited with Braxton as the three men strode up to them to join in on the conversation.

"Good evening, lady and gentlemen. We are with the CDC. I am Agent Nick . . . ," Rock began, and was cut off by Malcolm, as he finally was recognized.

"Ah, the *infamous Dominic Monroe,*" finished Malcolm with contempt, and to the surprise of all.

"Infamous?" asked Braxton.

Cheese jabbed Tick and said, "That means he's *more than famous,* El Guapo," in homage to *The Three Amigos.* Rock heard it, recognized it, and ignored it.

"It's *Moreau*, actually, Dominic Moreau," corrected Rock, not sure whether Malcolm recognized him or whether the Sheriff had told him his name.

"You know each other?" asked Cosworth. And with that question, Rock perceived that the Sheriff did not give them his name, so Rock chose not to play ignorant.

"We have been acquainted, in the past," Rock acknowledged. "But I was not with the CDC back then."

"No, you weren't. You were with . . . ," Malcolm spat.

"*DAD*," interrupted Crystal, grabbing his arm tightly. "*Ow-nay* is not the *ime-tay*," she punctuated to him in front of them all, not having the slightest clue as to why she said it in pig Latin. She flushed again after realizing it.

"Oh, it's the time, all right," Malcolm insisted, paying her no mind. Then, to the surprise of all present, himself included, Malcolm took a swing at Rock.

Malcolm Carson was roughly four inches taller than Rock, and had a good seventy pounds on him. He was not a violent man, per se. But this was supposed to be the greatest day of his career, and it seemed to be flying exactly like pile of horse manure doesn't, right in front of his eyes; and he knew that if it could be attributed to anyone, it was the man in front of him. So, as some men do when they confront an issue beyond their ability to immediately cope with, Malcolm lashed out at it with a speed that was akin to a mentally challenged garden slug that had been drinking heavily.

Rock saw it coming. Actually, everyone had the time to see it coming. In retrospect, when the ham-handed fist came toward Rock's face, Rock believed he had time to order Chinese, in Mandarin, even though he didn't speak Mandarin and would need to refer to a dictionary, before the fist got near him. But still, Rock reflexively grabbed the meaty thumb of Malcolm's fist in flight with his left hand, while it was missing his face, and placed his own right thumb on the nerve center between Malcolm's neck and shoulder. The action drove

Malcolm back, taking the large-framed man down to the ground quickly, and reasonably gently, almost as if the two were "dipping" in mid-dance. Then Rock stepped back from the downed Carson.

"You monster," Cheese said to Rock, with a smile on his face, suppressing laughter.

"Secure that, Agent Ledford," said Rock. "I'm sorry, Carson, let me help you up." Rock offered a hand to the downed man.

"Sheriff, I want to press charges," Malcolm said, slapping Rock's hand away and slowly getting his body up off the ground with Crystal's assistance.

"My suggestion is that you refrain from embarrassing yourself further and begin getting this camp packed up," said Braxton. "Assaulting a law-enforcement officer is a felony, Carson. Since it was only an *attempt* at assault, I assume Agent Moreau won't be pressing charges of his own?"

"I consider the matter closed, Sheriff, and again, sorry, Mr. Carson," said Rock. Then he felt something strange. It wasn't embarrassment at taking down Carson. It wasn't the beauty of Carson's daughter, which he only just then noticed. It was something foreboding and he wasn't sure of the source. He wanted to speak to Tick and Cheese in private.

"We will be glad to assist you in getting your camp moved," Rock said. Then he turned and motioned his two teammates to follow him out of earshot.

"Boy, Malcolm was *cheesed*, and *ticked*, but you *rocked* his world," the Cheese said.

Rock sighed and rolled his eyes at that pun.

"Sorry. What's up Rock?" asked the Big Cheese.

"We need to get these folks out of here. I don't like the lay of the land," said Rock.

"Well, while we're here, and there's twenty other men, I don't see anything to worry about until it's just down to the three of us," assured Tick.

"That's *probably* right, Tick," Rock said with some doubt. "Maybe it's the fact that Malcolm not only recognized me, but knew my name. That much was a surprise," said Rock.

"That *punch* wasn't, though. '*You should have gone with option B: taken the claw to the face and rolled on the ground, and died,*'" Cheese said, smiling as he paraphrased a line from Kung-Pow: Enter the Fist, a Steve Oedekerk movie.

"Secure that, *Master Tang*," Rock said, also referencing the movie, and matching the challenge of the "*obscure quote*."

"Sorry," said Cheese with a smile.

"I doubt that," said Rock, matching Cheese's smile. "All right," he continued, addressing the matter at hand, "until we are deployed here, Cheese can lead the most-ready members of their party to Turkey Run, taking them to their site, while Tick and I get the rest ready to go."

"Now seems to be the best time to have that *talk* with Carson," said Tick.

"Not here, and not now. He's visibly angry and in no mood to listen to anything I've got to say after what just happened," Rock said.

"Now *might* be the best time—while he's still hot about confronting you. He may want a rematch on an intellectual level. That's where he thinks he can take *you* down. If you run into Waveland for, say, *coffee*, I bet he follows you . . . that is, if you telegraph it properly," continued Tick.

"Sounds like a plan, Rock," Cheese said, agreeing.

"He's an evolutionist—an arrogant one at that—and we've just ruined his plans. He's not going to want anything from us except our absence," said Rock.

"It may be the only chance you ever get. One chance is better than none," said Tick.

"Fine. I'll give it a try, but I don't think we should split up," said Rock. "It breaks protocol."

"*That* protocol is for *after* we deploy, Rock," said Tick. "We're still in the site-prep phase."

"Enemy territory is still *enemy territory*," said Rock, and then he relented after a moment's thought. "But I guess I'll give it a go. If either of you can get the group's communication frequency, do it unobtrusively. If not, we can scan for it from the MFB."

Rock noticed that the darkness was consuming the forest, bite by bite, and night was almost upon them. Campfires and electric lights made the campsite bright, but it did not seem to be penetrating the darkness encompassing them. It was a thick darkness . . . oppressive and nearly tangible. It was if the darkness were pushing against the light, restricting it. But Rock shook off the foreboding, and he and his team turned again to the campsite and the trio moved purposefully toward the Sheriff, Cosworth, and the Carsons.

"Anything I should know about?" asked Braxton.

"No, Sheriff, I was just deciding how we'll do this," said Rock to Braxton. Then much more loudly he said, "Who in the group is ready to travel to the new site?"

"We are," spoke Crystal on her and her father's behalf. She was hoping that Dominic would be taking them. In her mind, the hope was that Nick and her father could mend fences during the ride over, but in her heart, it was to find out why she was becoming attracted to the handsome CDC officer. He was obviously older than she was, but she had always been attracted to more mature men.

"Good," said Rock. "Agent Ledford will ride with you to Turkey Run and get you admitted with his credentials, and all costs incurred there will be on us."

"I'm not ready to go," said Malcolm, correcting his daughter. "And I'm not leaving **my camp** in your hands," he said directly to Rock.

"**My camp**," corrected John Cosworth firmly, letting Malcolm know that although a higher ranking officer was onboard his ship, he was still the Captain.

"I didn't catch your name," Rock said to Crystal.

"She is *my daughter*," injected Carson.

"I'm Crystal Carson, Agent Moreau," she said with a smile, "and *I can speak for myself, Dad*," she asserted, firing a glance at him that she knew he'd understand.

"*Agent*," repeated Malcolm with distain and disbelief. He rolled his eyes at the statement, but did not exacerbate it further for his daughter's sake.

"Crystal," began Rock, "if you will allow Agent Ledford to accompany you to Turkey Run, I'll let Agent Cavor work with Mr. Cosworth in getting this camp mobile. As for me, just to allay your concerns, Mr. Carson, I'll go get some coffee in Waveland and stay out of your hair until you and the camp have moved. Will that work for all?" Rock asked.

Rock waited, and although John Cosworth nodded, Carson kept silent, which was accepted by Rock as assenting to the proposition.

"We might as well take the tents and sleeping bags with us, since they can be broken down and stowed pretty quickly," Crystal said to the Big Cheese.

"Sure," Cheese replied, and the two moved over to the tents and got a couple men to assist them. As she walked away, Crystal stole more than a couple of glances at Nick discreetly.

"Very well, I'll be back in an hour and a half or so, and pick up Agent Cavor, and then we'll pick up Agent Ledford at the new site," Rock concluded.

"Thanks," said Cosworth to Rock, not happily, and knowing that the CDC's rationale and authority were unassailable. Also of note was that the agent did appear to be trying to make the move as painless as possible.

"Thanks for nothing," Carson murmured in visceral disgust. He wanted to tell the "*agent*" off, but he knew that it was an inopportune time.

"Mr. Carson, we're here for your protection," responded Rock with authority. He gazed at Carson in all seriousness, and held his gaze on the one that met him and matched him. "You underestimate the danger you're in. You need to be careful because the way things are, you stand a good chance of getting yourself killed, and none of us wants that."

Malcolm narrowed his eyes and furrowed his brow, but said nothing. Rock could see Malcolm working out something in his head. Whether it was his next response, or something else, Rock wasn't sure.

Rock shook hands with the Sheriff, who nodded his approval that Rock had handled the situation well enough. Then slowly Rock worked his way to the Hummer, where he sat for a minute or two, observing the activity in the camp, before starting it. He saw the Cheese with three or four bedrolls in hand, walking with Crystal Carson to a Land Rover, but they were stopped by Malcolm, who had a few words with them. Then there was a key exchange between father and daughter, and Cheese and Crystal changed course and headed for a Subaru Outback, while Malcolm climbed into the Land Rover.

"Good," thought Rock. He started his engine. Then he pressed a button on his navigational dashboard system so that it would recognize his voice commands.

"Head's up right," he commanded, and the display on the passenger's side came to life.

"Internet. Search. Malcolm Carson crypto-zoologist," he commanded and in a split second many links popped-up for him to choose. "Scroll, scroll, select. Audio output." It was time for a quick refresher course on Carson.

The vehicle read the information aloud so that Rock could listen to select excerpts of Malcolm own writings while he made his way to Waveland.

"*Know thy enemy,*" Rock thought to himself.

13

PUTTING THE WORLD IN CONTEXT

(From the notes of First Agent Christopher Griffin)

(Section: Cause, Effect, and Perspective)

The law of causality says that there is neither an effect without a cause, nor a cause without an effect. Causality is truth and law. Nothing happens by chance, and there are no coincidences. Perspective can reveal the cause, or can blind one to it.

There are three aspects of this vast but limited universe within which we exist, but only two of them are eternal. One aspect is physical, which includes all matter and energy including space-time. This is the transitory, entropic aspect.

The second is the mind, known to some as the soul, or "the person, the heart," which is eternal. The mind is without mass, and as such, it exists in a timeless state, though still enclosed in flesh, and is influenced and impacted by the other two aspects of this universe. Eternity is written upon the hearts of men. The heart intuitively knows and can almost taste eternity, even when the mortal body cannot.

The third aspect is the spiritual realm where our Creator and extrauniversal beings beyond current comprehension exist, and where we exist as well. Though the transitory, finite "flesh" largely separates us from the spiritual, it is still accessible to a degree, and impacts all other aspects of the universe. The spiritual is more real, more substantial than the physical, and it too is eternal. The physical is the shadow cast by the spiritual. The tangible "effect" pales in comparison to its spiritual "cause."

But all three have something in common: They all exist because God Almighty does. He is the Cause; everything we can sense or measure is merely an effect. The assertion of "evolution" exists and persists because the Cause is hated, and His Truth is rejected. Without knowledge of the Cause, one limits his own perspective. One then must try to explain reality by effect only. Wish him luck.

A compass needle has two points. Though all of creation points to the Creator like the needle of a compass points to true north, from a wrong perspective, a backward perspective, it points the opposite way as well.

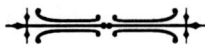

Carson headed south and followed Dominic's black H3 SUV at a distance without losing sight, all the way to the tiny town of Waveland. His rented Land Rover—LR5—had a bumper sticker on it that read, "Constitutional Amendment 28: Congress shall pass no law without knowing what it is first!" If he'd have noticed it, he'd have ripped it off the vehicle. A fog was rising in the cool air, and banks of it were suspended over the cornfield in soft pillows of floating mist under the starry sky. Malcolm noticed the serenity about him. The air smelled of fertile land and sweet corn. It became a pleasant but cool summer night across Indiana. It was wonderful and almost distracting to Malcolm. He crossed State Road 47 and turned onto State Road 59 at the gas station. SR-59 began at Waveland and terminated in southern Indiana at another tiny town called Sandborn. It ran straight through "Covered Bridge" and Amish country.

Malcolm's vehicle traversed the small bridge that spanned the Little Raccoon Creek before going uphill to the center of the town. He saw brake lights flare on the Hummer that he pursued as it reached the top of the hill. Carson slowed his own SUV, not wanting to look like he was intentionally tailing Dominic, which he obviously was. As he reached the top of the hill, he saw that Dominic had parked in front of a little diner, the only diner in the small town. Parking his Rover in front of the hardware store, Carson was just in time to see Dominic enter the establishment. He could see through the window that several people were out of the chill of the darkening evening and enjoying their dinner. He observed that Dominic had chosen to sit in the back, apart from attention, and without company.

Carson decided to confront Rock again, but not *quite* the way he had before, which ended abruptly back at the nature preserve. He wasn't going to take another swing at Dominic, but he did want some answers. Carson crossed the street and opened the door to the quaint diner, hearing the bell ring upon entry, announcing him. He noticed that the old-fashioned restaurant was decorated with a rustic motif of antiques and old photos of the town adorning the walls. He was a stranger and received several looks registering him as such. He proceeded straight to Dominic's table and helped himself to a seat across from Nick unceremoniously. Dominic made no sign of objection, or for that matter, acceptance of Carson's presence, but Dominic definitely expected Carson to show.

"OK, Mr. CDC . . . . First, I'm not accepting your B.S. story about a hazardous toxin released in the area; I know you are just here for *a coverup* . . . . And exactly what did you mean when you said that I was going to get myself killed? **Was that some kind of a *threat*?**" he demanded, as if on some level it was *he* who should be on the defensive regarding Dominic's authority, and acting as if his own credibility and stature were gravely diminished by the commandments of "Fake Agent Dominic Moreau."

"You are free to believe what you want. You will still obey the site restrictions," Rock said calmly.

"That's not an answer. What did you mean?" Carson spat.

"You should calm down, Mr. Carson," said Rock with no emotion or intonation.

"I'll calm down when you're out of my life. Now answer me," spoke the crypto-zoologist.

"What do you suggest I'm covering up?" Dominic asked as if he didn't already know.

"*The Sasquatch sightings are obviously being covered up!* Now what did you mean about me getting killed?" asked Carson.

Dominic calmly signaled to the waitress that he wanted coffee and turned up his cup without looking at Carson. He observed that his fingers were still a little oily from cleaning his gun earlier in the back of the mobile base, so he wiped them with his napkin, and then, in a lowered tone, Rock responded to Malcolm.

"I meant that you, and your team, frolicking through the woods trying to trap a mythological beast, would *very likely* endanger yourselves before you were able to capture anything. Is that plain enough? It is not a personal threat, but a clear warning."

"So, for argument's sake then, and ignoring your 'toxic release *story*,' are you suggesting that a myth can kill? It seems to me that by way of denial, you have inadvertently admitted the Sasquatch's existence."

"Then I will clarify it for you," Rock responded. "I deny that your Agnostopithecus exists. My admission has nothing to do with your *silly idea* of a Sasquatch. To put it bluntly: **There is no such animal.**"

"Well, at least you admit that something is out there, Mr. Dominic Moreau, of **Knightlight**," he said with a singular smugness. "Yes, I know who you are. *Knightlight* is the organization you work for, isn't it? I also know that it's some kind of government-sponsored *religious* organization that may or may not be guilty of violating *Separation of Church and State* laws. You may be able to fool the local law enforcement with your CDC badge, and cock-and-bull story, but I know who you are."

Dominic was visibly unmoved by Malcolm's obvious intentions to surprise him with seemingly esoteric knowledge. Over the years, and with much training, he had learned to harden his emotions against most forms of insult because they were only means of distraction that baited one from the matters at hand into a mindless reaction to the provocation. There was a time when adrenaline alone in any confrontation would get him keyed-up to a point that he called "*Barney Fife Anxiety.*" Every once in a long while, *Don Knotts* would surface, but it wasn't going to happen today.

"If you knew who I was, then you'd know that my credentials are valid," Dominic said. "You know my name, and perhaps a little about the organization, Knightlight, but I assure you, you don't know who I am, because if you did, you might be just a little afraid to be near me, and you would certainly be terrified of whom you are hunting."

"**Whom I am hunting?** My dear Mr. Moreau, you give me more information each time you open your mouth. Now I am hunting a person?" asked Malcolm in open derision.

Dominic had experiences with men like this before. He loathed the type of man Carson was. He loathed Carson because he'd been such a man himself. It discussed him. Then a voice resonated inside his mind saying, "*Apart from Me in your life, are you any better than*

Carson?" Dominic recognized the gentle Schoolmaster's voice, and inwardly admitted the answer was no. Dominic bowed his will to the rebuke, and silently repented.

"Yes," Dominic yielded. He knew it was time for Truth, at least a measure of it, if not the complete Truth. "You are hunting a person, and it knows who you are. It knows what your plans are, but more to the point, it knows me, and my team. It knows we are here, and our very presence is as much an attraction to it as blood is to a shark. It thinks itself to be the top of the food chain, and I'm here to prove it wrong."

"A person is not an 'it,' Mr. Moreau. You are obviously confused. And do you suggest that the animal, or 'being' you describe, is . . . clairvoyant, or are you even sure *you know what you're talking about*?" Carson mocked.

Dominic could tell that this would not be easy. Carson was intentionally antagonizing him. It would be much simpler to launch an ad hominem attack of his own, but that was not an option. Instead, he reminded himself of the virtue of meekness. Meekness did not mean that he would stand for just anything. Meekness is "power under restraint," so he restrained himself . . . for now. And, yes, he wanted this opportunity, if not in this specific *way*. Carson was in danger, and he didn't wish that kind of harm upon him or anyone, friend or foe. He wanted to open Carson's eyes, but he knew that Malcolm Carson would hear him only as long as it suited him to do so. In order to get Carson to become engaged and actually *listen*, he'd have to allow Carson press him for it.

"Ah . . . are we at a loss for words, *Knightlight*? Don't be afraid, I'm not going to *blow your cover*." He said the last words loudly enough to turn many heads in their direction.

"What I know is not for public consumption unless there is a grave need requiring it," said Nick seriously, but quietly.

"Oh . . . I get it . . . a *need-to-know basis* . . . . I've heard that B.S. before from many bureaucrats. It means you get to lie and I have to swallow it . . . . Well, I'm not biting this time. I want it straight and clear, you got that?" Carson challenged.

Carson was absolutely right. It was personally shaming to Nick. Knightlight was sworn to be truthful, even if that meant to say nothing if the truth could not be said. But when working with or for the Government, certain "cover stories" that stretched the limits of truth were forced upon them. Agents had leeway . . . a degree of it anyway. Silently, Nick asked the Lord for guidance.

Carson waited for a response, intentionally baiting Moreau for an argument. His eyes drifted down to Moreau's sidearm. He'd forgotten that he was picking a fight with an armed man. Never a good idea. It was then, in the silence, that Carson realized that his tone was a little bit *too irritating*, a little too "in your face"; so he chose to *dial it back*, if only a tad. He didn't want to let himself get to a point where Moreau might actually draw on *him*, or take a swing at him. He was angry at Moreau, and he did demand answers. On the other hand, he knew he wouldn't get anywhere unscathed with out-and-out belligerence.

"Seriously, Moreau . . . ." Malcolm still heard anger in his voice, and forced a calmer tone. "Seriously, if you have any real information on what's out there, I suppose I would be a fool not to listen," Carson said in an effort to sound sincere.

Both of them paused as the waitress poured their fresh and piping-hot coffee and then moved on.

"Mr. Carson, it would be a great relief to me if you knew and understood what was out there . . . *I kid you not*. But if I explained it to you, which I'm not *technically* authorized to do, I guarantee that you won't believe me, and the knowledge I imparted would be used foolishly."

"Why ever wouldn't I believe you, if you told me the truth?" asked Malcolm.

"You won't understand it because of your learned bias. You are set in your ways, which makes you inflexible in your beliefs, rigid in your thinking, regardless of evidence that might change your mind. At this point in time, what I know is not for you to know, and honestly, it would be a waste of our time because you lack the ability to comprehend the **Truth**," Dominic said earnestly, but hoping he'd alluded to enough *mystery* that Malcolm would press him for more information.

Malcolm's bias was a fortified wall. Under the best conditions it would be difficult to breach. Add anger to the mix, and the difficult verges on the impossible. Sometimes you can't even get a peaceful conversation going in a "spiritual" direction unless it is requested. There are many excellent ways to share the Lord with someone else—by example, by word and deed—and all conducted peacefully, respectfully, and lovingly. Rock knew that the route he was on was not going to be *excellent, peaceful, or easy*, but sometimes, on rare occasions, confrontation needs to be met when confrontation is demanded.

"What is *truth*, Moreau?" Carson asked. "Is your perception of truth somehow above mine?"

Nick saw his opening. His reply was one of necessity.

"Jesus is Truth, Mr. Carson," Dominic said bluntly, but honestly. "The Word of God is Truth, and if I said anything different, I'd be a liar. It was Pontius Pilot who asked the same question you just did, not even knowing that he was staring Truth in the face."

"I don't want religious mumbo jumbo, Moreau, I want the facts."

"Facts are not the problem. I could give you facts. It's the interpretation of those facts that you're not equipped to handle."

"I suppose *religious* facts are what you mean. You have your facts, I have mine, but you obviously know mine, so why don't you just tell me yours?"

"No, Mr. Carson. What you don't seem to get is that we've always shared the same facts. We share the same world. We share the same universe. But you see the facts through the filter

225

of evolutionary pseudo-science, through a naturalistic worldview. And you are steeped in humanistic *dogma*, while I see the same facts but understand and interpret them through the revelation of their Creator, which is always complemented by *real* science. It gives me an enormous advantage over you. I have the testimony of both the *Witness* and the *Cause* of creation, which always surpasses the guesswork of mankind. All you have is the greatest hoax ever perpetrated upon mankind: evolution. We definitely have different starting points when we examine the same facts. We absolutely have different biases when we scrutinize the same evidences. However, the facts, when complete, always verify what I already know through Scripture, whereas you and those with your way of thinking have to continue to revise your faith just to make it limp to the next series of facts that contradict your worldview. Always limping, and always remaining in willful, stubborn ignorance."

Malcolm looked at Nick with a deadpan stare, letting his mouth hang open just a bit to emphasize his utter disbelief. He blinked, and then spoke with as much disdain as he could muster.

"*You've got to be kidding . . . . Scientific fact* is my bias, nothing more. If I have any faith, it's in the ability of science to discover and reveal the true nature of this universe," Carson said.

"Faith is faith. Testable, repeatable observational science has never contradicted anything I believe, Mr. Carson. But when you cross the line into *speculative science*, without all the facts, you fail to come to the correct conclusions . . . every single time," Dominic said.

"You're dancing around my questions. I want pertinent information. I want to know the facts you know, and then I'll come to my own conclusions regarding them. But I'll not be led into some theological debate with you, so I suggest you just give me the facts I need," Carson retorted.

"Here are some facts for you: This world is going through planetary PMS beyond man's control to do anything about it. It's on the threshold of devastating turmoil. This is a short slice of time that precedes a seven-year 'new world order' of horrors. This violent planet is reaching the boiling point that was foretold 2,500 years ago, and thereafter, and you don't even recognize it. You want facts, but what you need is the Truth *in context*. You want information, but you want it *without* context. You want pieces of a jigsaw puzzle, but you want them without the picture on the top of the box to compare it to, even when you are offered the picture freely. And worse, you and your fellow evolutionists mock the picture and the offer, like a child ignorantly mocks a foreigner simply because of his *accent*. Then you force the pieces together when they clearly don't fit, making the puzzle into whatever you want it to be, and you proudly boast that it's complete, when it isn't even close. You can't know what I know without also knowing the *meaning*. And you can't comprehend the meaning because in your world, there is *no meaning*. You believe that this world came into being by unassisted chance, not providence, but you don't understand that chance is nothing, it can do nothing, and it produces nothing. It is neither a cause nor an effect."

"Oh, and I suppose your *truth* shall set me free! *Praise the Lord!*" Carson mocked.

"I said Truth in context, Carson, and that was a perfect example of your lack of knowledge. What you misquoted was from the Gospel of John, chapter eight. Jesus qualified His statement. He said '*If* you continue in my Word, *then* you are my disciples indeed, and you shall know the truth, and the truth shall make you free.' So, *no*, the Truth shall not set *you* free, Carson. Truth *can* exist in a vacuum, but it lacks meaning if it is not in context. Context qualifies and quantifies Truth, and you are completely ignorant of the proper context."

Carson knew at that moment he would not get anything out of Moreau unless he allowed him to place his funda-*mentally*-challenged religious *spin* on the information. So, in his own form of wisdom, he chose to yield to the informant.

"Fine, Mr. Moreau, I understand that we're not going to see eye to eye. I'll grant, and even entertain, your theological slant to the facts you impart. I'll listen to whatever you have to offer."

"*Oh, the pomposity of this evolunatic,*" Moreau thought to himself, and then once again, he repented. Inwardly, he weighed the possibility that there could be the slightest of chances that Malcolm would actually listen. Dominic doubted that. It was likely that it would be a waste of breath, but the opportunity was before him. If he was really being offered control of the discussion, and he was able to share the Word of God, he knew that in some providential way, it would not return void. Nick decided to put the offer to the test.

"All right, Carson, I'll give you *some* information that will not compromise my mission or my oath, and I may even answer a few questions you ask. But I'll do it *my way*, in proper context, and only because to me, you are like a puppy who is fascinated by a wagging tail, not realizing it's attached to a ravenous lion. I'll tell you what I can. But I'll tell you *in my own good time, in my own way*, and only because I am trying to save your life."

"I'm listening." Carson said.

"Well, before you commit, let me tell you a little about myself. That alone may change your mind."

"Fine, go," said Carson.

"As you obviously know, I am a firm and complete believer in God, the Creator of this universe, and His Word, the Holy Bible, which *He sets in reverence even above His own name.* I believe in the Biblical authority of Sacred Scripture, again, the Word of God. I believe in God's only begotten Son, Jesus Christ—the Living Word of God, the incarnation of God, my Savior, and the One whom I try to obey as my Lord. I also believe in God's Holy Spirit, who is my comforter, my schoolmaster, and the third part of the Triune nature of my God, who is One God. All three persons are expressed in the first three verses of Genesis chapter one, in the Bible. I am also a sinner, saved by the Grace of God, and nothing more. If I sin, it is because I am a sinner, just like you. If I am able to do anything truly good, or righteous, that's Christ in me, enabling me. And with that *spiritual mumbo jumbo*, I also have a healthy trust in any observational science that can be scrutinized, peer reviewed, tested, tried, and repeated, and that produces verifiable results. I am also a fierce enemy of false sciences that claim they are 'keepers of facts and knowledge.' But said facts are based on blind speculation, incomplete data, or faulty backward extrapolation of said data, and completely biased against alternate but valid evidences that lead to complete misinterpretation of the evidences, and intentionally tries to undermine, falsely discredit, and lie about every foundation of what I *know* as Truth.

Malcolm was about to speak, but Dominic gave him no time.

"Also, *before* I share any real information with you, I want it clear that I will have to bring you up to speed by demonstrating that speculative science is a *faith*, and not *science*. And I will have to deconstruct what you believe in order to give you the context of what I believe, and why. So, with that in mind, are you sure you really want me to continue?" Dominic asked.

"OK, you've made it plain where you stand, which is fair enough for me, but I eventually expect information from you that's pertinent to my expedition," Carson replied, knowing he was heading for a sermon, while wishing to glean whatever he could from it.

"Well then, I promise you that this *will* try your patience, and it *will sting* because I am going to unload on you . . . but in fairness to me, *you asked for it*," Dominic said.

Carson acquiesced.

14

The Big Cheese

The Big Cheese assisted Crystal in breaking down the tents and packing them in the Subaru Outback, which went fairly quickly once the contents of each were set outside the tent. Within fifteen minutes they had a full load. Cheese and Crystal left Tick and the campsite, and the two drove out of the park, heading for Turkey Run State Park.

The Big Cheese rode silently with Crystal Carson as they backtracked down 234, then took a county road to Waveland, turning on State Road 47. Cheese thought Crystal was very attractive, and because of that, he could not think of any small talk that would not make him look like an idiot to her. Every time he thought about saying something, he stopped himself and simply blushed because he knew it was something that would make him look stupid. So he sat there, next to Crystal, blushing and sweating, and he was self-conscious of both. He took out his Blackberry, which had just lost reception due to a lack of tower service in the area, and he pressed buttons and pretended to be doing something important with it, in order to pass the time. Then he became self-conscious that his red face could be better seen in the glow of the LCD.

"I'm surprised you have service out here," Crystal said. "My Blackberry's been out of range since we turned onto this road."

230

"Yes," Cheese said, blushing and sweating even more. "I, um," he stammered, "I've got a backlog of e-mails that I haven't read yet," which was true, so he moved the cursor to the e-mail folder and began looking at his backlog of e-mails, as if he had been doing so all along. He noticed that he would acquire cell service every other minute or so, then lose it again, off and on. He also noticed that all received e-mails were prior to 17:00 hours. They'd been in communications blackout for three hours now. They traveled in silence, by the glow of the Blackberry's LCD screen.

Then the Big Cheese opened his mouth: "So, are you from India?" He meant Indiana, but India was what came out. *IDIOT!* he thought. *Stupid, stupid, stupid!*

"India? No, California," she said, perplexed, wondering what on earth made him think she was from India.

Inwardly, Cheese was smacking himself in the head repeatedly. "I'm sorry, I *meant* Indiana."

"Oh. No, California," she said. "My father and I travel a lot, though, when it relates to his business."

"So, how's business?" Cheese asked.

"Well, it's sucked ever since you guys showed up—what do *you* think?"

More internal head smacking ensued. "Sorry," was all he could come up with, apart from the head smacking. Cheese remembered his youth, and many embarrassing moments flashed before his eyes. In second grade, he was to lead his classmates in the Pledge of Allegiance. So he mustered up his bravery, stood upright, placed his right hand over his heart, and boldly spoke, "I *spledge* allegiance to the flag." Yes, he accidentally said "spledge," instead of "pledge," and his mind went, *What the heck is spledge?* He couldn't reconcile the word, and then he'd lost the rest of the pledge, so fumbling, he continued with "my country 'tis of thee . . ." and concluded with "with truth, justice, and the American way . . . . Amen." The subsequent laugher turned him to tears because it was full of belittlement from his classmates. That was just one of several embarrassing stories that came to mind, and continued to haunt him, usually when he had to speak publicly, which was rare, or to converse with a beautiful lady, which was even more uncommon.

"So, what exactly is QNB?" Crystal asked.

"It's technical. Even I have difficulty pronouncing it right." Cheese said honestly, sheepishly.

"No, I mean where does it come from? What are the symptoms?" she asked.

"Oh. Well, it's a chemical weapon, a nerve agent invented in the early 1950s, but it has distinct *markers* compared to other nerve agents."

"You mean like . . . what?"

"It was designed for nonlethal engagement of enemy forces to disorient and inhibit hostile responses. Unlike other nerve agents, this one cause hallucinations, compulsive behavior, drunkenness, and for some reason it breaks down inhibitions in those exposed to it. Did you ever see the movie called *The Crazies*?"

"I saw the trailer to it a long time ago, but I never saw the movie," Crystal said.

"Well, it is something like that," Cheese said.

"Oh, you mean it turns people into zombies and murderers?" asked Crystal.

"Um, not really. But it's a euphoric, and for some reason seems to make a percentage of exposed people want to take their clothes off," he said, then blushed again. *Smack, smack, SMACK!*

"Oh . . . , well I hope it's contained," she said.

"Actually, we just passed the farm it was found on. That's where our *field office* currently is parked," Cheese said.

"Great. You could've just said it was *contained*. Now I'm going to be wondering which one of us will go crazy first," she said. "If you shoot yourself, I'll know, and if I drive us straight into a tree, then you'll know."

"We're safe, ma'am. There's no harm at this time," Cheese said, as he locked his Blackberry and put it in his pocket.

"From what I understand, the damage has already been done," she countered with an accusatory tone.

Cheese's mind yelled an expletive. He didn't say it, but he sure would have if Crystal hadn't been with him. After all, he didn't cause the QNB release, and there really wasn't any QNB released, and he *was* there to protect her, or them. And they really were safe from the QNB, but he couldn't say they were really safe with certainty because what *was* actually dangerous was still out there, but not in the slightest bit related to QNB. He sure wished they were at Turkey Run so he wouldn't have to talk anymore.

15

ROCK AND A HARD-CASE

(From the notes of First Agent Christopher Griffin)

Most men don't understand nature at all. They see nature as a friend, a home, a comfortable place to live. Before the fall, that much was true. But nature is a fuse and time is a flame. Nature burns in time. Those who seek refuge within it are nothing but ignorant kindling. Men who do not worship their Creator worship the incendiary that will end in ruin. Nature exists as proof that it was created while it testifies that it needs to be abandoned for a safer haven. It holds all captive as it consumes even itself, and it sheds no tears for the dead.

Graph showing tenths of a degree above and below 14C World Average

1997
.05 C

2012
.05 C

Data from Met Office UK study from January 1997 to August 2012.
No aggregate change in global temperature. Posted October 15th 2012

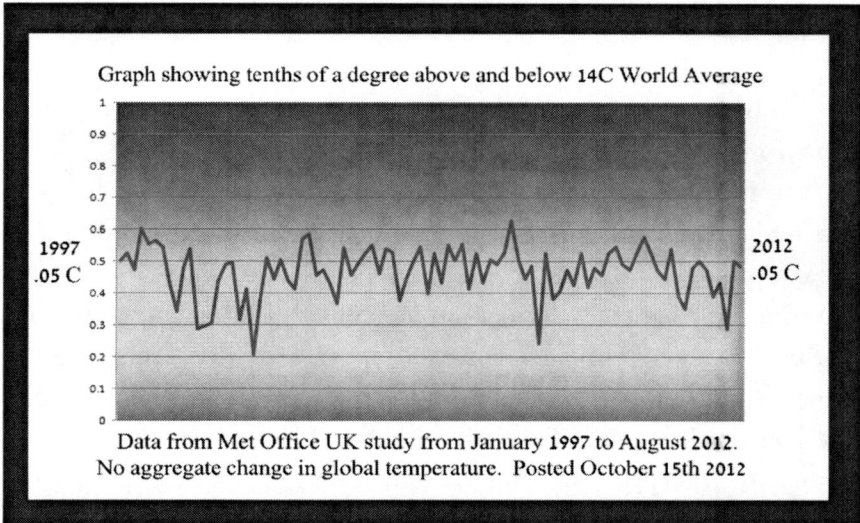

The small diner's crowd, if it could be called a crowd, was thinning out as Nick and Carson continued their discussion.

Nick was practiced at apologetics, the art of the *"Defense of the Faith."* He believed that all Christians must know what they believe, and why. He agreed with Paul of Tarsus that those who have the name of "Christian" should be ready to give an answer to questions about their faith. They should know how to stand against false doctrines, should they be found within the Church or other faiths, which unfortunately includes discerning duplicity and deceit in the halls of scientific academia as well. Yes, there are lazy and carnal Christians, ill equipped and unprepared. And Nick acknowledge that he had a long way to go himself before he could say he was even near living a perfect life before God, but *that* is where mercy, grace, repentance, and growth come in. So he knew he had to show mercy and grace to others who struggled in their Christian walk, and especially to those who did not know Christ. To condemn or confront an unrighteous act, teaching, or idea is *right,* but it should never be an occasion to condemn the one who committed it, because *all men fall short of the Glory of God*, the court of law notwithstanding.

"To begin this, let me reiterate, *context is critical in everything related to Truth*. For me to correctly impart what I know, it must first be framed in proper context, or you'll discard all I tell you and make the same mistakes currently attributed to climatology. For example, I'll bet you are a *'save the earth,' 'man-made global warming will kill the planet'* type of *believer.* I'll bet that you're on *that* bandwagon because you have *some* information regarding the climate, and you trust your speculative scientist friends and peers. But you don't realize that you and they have a complete lack of context to interpret the information," Dominic said, knowing the answer to his question already. He was armed with, perhaps, *unfair knowledge of Carson* in advance.

"Global warming is scientific fact, and—"

"*Don't answer.*" Nick interrupted, "You'll get your rebuttal when I've presented my premise and have demonstrated how speculative science, in every form, is a faith. Next, you'll need your understanding of history updated, because as it stands, you've got nothing within you to deal with anything *out there*." He pointed due north, toward Shades.

"*Fine*, get on with it, then," replied Malcolm, already impatient but remembering his agreement.

"Fine. Let's look back to the 1970s when it was prophesied by the speculation of your secular Climatological Scientists, and spread by the negligent news media, and pushed by opportunistic politicians, that we were heading into another *ice age* because of man-made jet contrails in the air, aka *'chem-trails,'* and that we were doomed by *acid rain* because of sulfur dioxide from automobile emissions. And oh my goodness, *killer bees* were migrating northward and were going to take over America, and we were all going to suffer and die from a lack of oxygen because we were destroying the Amazonian Rain Forest, which embarrassingly still exists. Let's not forget the oil spills of the 70s destroying our oceans. That was frightening stuff, Malcolm. There were people actually afraid to go outside. You're old enough to remember it."

"I remember," Malcolm replied in a huff.

"It scared the poo out of the trusting masses, but it was irresponsible alarmism. Yes, the forecasts of the prophets of doom turned out to be false, but for the first time in its history, the American population responded in an unexpected way, and many observed it and took advantage of it. The populace was not angry or mistrusting of the irresponsible opportunistic alarmists . . . they were *relieved*. That relief was transformed into gratitude instead of anger toward those who had deceived them. They were *glad* to find out that jet contrails weren't harmful, and that their catalytic converters had stopped the dreaded acid rain, which never really existed. They were happy that by planting a tree in their yard, they'd averted disaster and now everyone could breathe, not knowing that our greatest oxygen-producing plants reside within the oceanic plant life that no series of oil spills could possibly hinder. *The people were relieved that they were safe.* Their relief was turned into activism, and they demonstrated that they would gladly *trade freedom for that feeling of participatory salvation.* They were conned into believing that *they were part of the solution to an averted crisis.* Many were children in the 60s, and were envious of the civil rights movement that they weren't able to participate in. The Vietnam War's end left little else for these easily swayed liberals to protest. The next generation, the yuppies— the spiritually bankrupt children of the hippies—also wanted to feel good about themselves, so 'saving the earth' became the new civil rights movement, and protest, even though the prophesies of horror were groundless. Their intentions may have been purer than the narcissistic "Occupy Wall Street" malcontents, but they still believed in a lie."

"The wild guesses of the scientific community had been joined by the panic-mongering news media and championed by politicians who take advantage of fear and ignorance, and together they learned that they wielded *wolfish power over sheep*. They also found that they could turn their sheep upon those who would not swallow the lies of the wolf, demonizing them, and crushing all opposition, because they could convincingly put up a straw-man argument and say that *only 'evil people' are against saving the planet*. It really wasn't a *new concept*, but it had never worked so well before, because *Americans used to measure facts against Truth*, but Truth had been removed from the classroom for an entire generation by then."

"That only proves that societies are evolving, nothing more," Malcolm defended.

"Devolving is closer to it. It proved that our government run public education system, and the liberal news media, had successfully dumbed down the populace to the point that intellectual liars could rise in power, spin so-called 'inconvenient truths,' partner with the masses to avert counterfeit dangers, gain the trust and support of the unwitting, and propagate new falsehoods to feed back to those being bred for obedience to the lie. It turned into a self-perpetuation system of retarding America for purposes of control through fear. It worked far better than Rome's governance by bread and circuses," Dominic said.

"Ridiculous! We're all intelligent free thinkers," said Carson.

"Yes, and you're allowed to remain so as long as you freely think *what you've been trained to think.* So let's jump ahead a decade to the eighties where we were told that we're going kill the planet by CFCs causing a greenhouse effect and melting the polar ice caps, and we'll all either drown because of impending *global warming*, or burn up because of the heat, inspiring such Hollywood propaganda films as *The Fire Next Time* and *Waterworld*, and cartoons like *Captain Planet*, and, more recently in theaters, Spielberg's *A.I.* and *The Day after Tomorrow*."

"Most of Hollywood is sympathetic to our cause . . . heck, most of the *world* is. I applaud them."

Ignoring Carson, Nick continued.

"Remember the Cold War? The Communists were watching American behavior closely, all the way to the end, and they learned a brilliant strategy. They learned it from us. They discovered that it's much easier to lead the people by convincing them that the Government was protecting them against global disaster *with their assistance*, rather than ruling them by making them fear the Government itself. The Communists knew they were losing that battle. Ronald Regan and Margaret Thatcher were instrumental in ending the Cold War, but even *they* didn't know that there was something bigger set in motion behind the scenes. Mikhail Gorbachev was the pioneer activist of Russia, claiming peace, glasnost, perestroika, but it was just a façade for changing their domination and control tactics toward the tactics they saw in America."

"I have had nothing but respect for Mr. Gorbachev," Malcolm offered.

"I assumed as much. Now, jumping ahead yet another decade, we find climatologists coughing up a new slogan: ***man-made climate change***. They engineered the term so they could have it both ways, and to make the argument altogether ambiguous, since there was so much contradictory evidence for either death by UV radiation or death by ice. But now both extremes can work together in harmony under one term in order for a single stampede of human sheep, and so the real freethinkers can be quashed if not squashed. *Man-made climate change* means that in any climate boneheads like Al Gore can shout, 'The sky is falling!' Now we can enjoy being in danger of burning up, or drowning from man-made climate change, or we might just as easily freeze to death because of it. But here's the genius of it: It can now be claimed that we just might die from too much *good weather*. One thing is for certain though: No matter what the climate, the poor polar bears are going to die! And thanks to men like you, the populace believes it and marches in step with

239

it just because they've been told that it is scientific. Not because of the evidence. Not because of facts. But just because their *faith* in the fact that *scientists have a consensus.*"

"About the only thing you just stated correctly is regarding polar bear extinction," said Carson.

"Oh, right . . . . By the way, the polar bears have declined from just 5,000 in 1970 to over 25,000 today . . . oops, that's quintupling . . . but who's going to notice facts? History, reality and Truth are at issue here, and neither you nor your scientists understand it. Do climates change? Yes. Have they changed in the past? Yes, many times. Will they change in the future? Yes, but mankind has no say in the matter. It is about a relevant as ants claiming responsibility for causing 'morning dew,' and ants taking it upon themselves to stop it from happening. It is ludicrous."

"That analogy is ludicrous," retorted Carson.

"*Man-made climate change, like your theory of evolution,* is ludicrous because Truth is sacrificed to for it, reality is distorted by it, and history is re-written to accommodate it. Beyond that, your trusted scientists ignore the fundamental fact that *the nature of science is to question and challenge the prevailing ideas of mankind, including the ones currently held dear.* Instead, they browbeat opposing evidences and ignore the fact that if the global temperature has risen only 'point eight degrees Celsius' in the 150 years prior to 1997, then the planet's temperature and climate is *very stable*. One might argue that we have more data since then, *modern data . . .* very well. But then they ignore and lie about the modern data even though it is concrete proof *against* man-made global warming. I refer to the indisputable British 'Met' Office's data *demonstrating, not guessing*, that the aggregate global temperature—that is, the average temperature of the entire world—has not increased or decreased at all since 1997. There is NO global warming—*ZERO. It does not exist.* Yes, there may be changes to the distribution of heat, but that is not outside of the norm of this planet's history.

Warming may even be a good thing, since more people die of exposure to cold temperatures than of heatstroke. But don't miss the salient point: This planet is not suffering from global warming or global freezing, and if it was, you couldn't prevent it."

"Ridiculous," said Malcolm. "If what you claim, that is that the government and the scientific community are panicking and manipulating people for control was true, why didn't they jump on the December 21st, 2012, *'end of the world, Mayan calendar'* bandwagon? That put a scare in folks across the world," said Malcolm.

"They couldn't. If the world ended then, they'd not profit by it. If it didn't end then, they'd be exposed as the liars they are. It's like the mistake Obama made regarding the Sequester," said Rock. "Control by fear works only if they maintain the fear of an unspecifically dated *'future man-caused doomsday scenario,'* knowing that if tomorrow never comes, then the day after tomorrow is less likely to come, and they can never be called on it."

"Our planet *is* in danger, and men like you are ignoramuses or ignorami, I suppose is the plural," said Carson.

"It isn't even our planet, Carson. *The earth is the Lord's*, not man's, regardless of who holds the title deed to it," Dominic stressed.

"Here's that religious mumbo jumbo again," said Carson. But then he remembered that he'd promised to suffer through it, so he did not immediately deride it further.

"Even in earth's current condition, its *fallen* condition, the earth is a dynamic planet that, by design, *self-cleans* the atmosphere *with* the largest greenhouse emission of all: ***water vapor***. The earth releases its heat into space efficiently and consistently—that is tested, proven scientific fact. The sun is the ultimate generator of our global temperature and various climates, and trust me, it isn't always going to be our friend. But over its eleven-year cycle it produces powerful sunspots and faculae, which man exerts *ZERO* control over, and which increases the standard heat radiated from the sun, and all the while creates ozone within the bounds of the magnetosphere. Water vapor, the magnetosphere, and climate-altering ozone-depleting volcanic emissions are completely outside of mankind's control and are the greatest lower, upper, and extra-atmospheric disrupters of the sun's radiation. A single volcanic eruption can cause more air pollution, *toxic emissions of many kinds*, in one day than the sum total of all mankind's production in a year. And there remains a minimum of 20 to 40 active aboveground volcanoes at any given time. Volcanoes can alter the global temperature on their own, and you can't stop them. Openly ignoring those facts, your wise-by-half climatologists—an evolutionary/humanistic theological subgroup— have the audacity to blame dinosaur flatulence as the explanation for historic climate change and their subsequent extinction. They *embrace and champion the ridiculous* every day because it keeps them in the news, promotes their cause, and above all, maintains their *funding* for such causes from private and public coffers. Politicians accept those idiotic stories because they are also the generation of the brainwashed masses, and because the perpetuation of the narrative increases their control on mankind's everyday activities. But since it happened in the past with dinosaur farts, *they say*, then **our extinction is threatened** by methane from cow flatulence, even though termite-produced methane is a contender with any of the above. But you don't see the environmentalists blaming them, and rightly, they should not."

"Mankind disrupts the delicate balance of nature and you know it," replied Malcolm.

"Oh, it's balanced, and finely tuned, but there is nothing delicate about it, Carson. These are forces of nature that are wielded by a power infinitely beyond ours. What few ever notice is that this entire universe operates with *precision* and stands as evidence of *careful design in that precision*. But there's nothing man-made that comes close to impacting the climate of this world, apart from the historical judgment for his sin, and the one that's soon to come."

Dominic knew that, but for Christ, he was as guilty as any who are soon to be judged. But he also knew that Christ in the life of a believer changes everything. *Everything.*

"Our carbon footprint is crushing the planet! That's not even contestable!" interjected Malcolm.

"I contest it, and you mock real science by blindly accepting it. Mankind's impact is insignificant and laughable in comparison to the magnificent functionality of this planet. Historically, all speculative scientists *know* that we have had many and varied *warmer* climates in the distant and not-so-distant, past, and *colder* ones as well, but they base their global warming *scare tactics*, their *fear mongering*, on incomplete information, bad interpretation of data, omission of data. And because of it, they speak lies which men like you propagate with slogans like the one you just spoke. Even prestigious agencies like NASA have spinelessly participated in subversive disingenuousness because of peer and political pressure, not because of science."

"Together you shout, 'Save the world *from* mankind,' and it stems from a complete lack of belief in our Creator, and because of the general acceptance of godless Darwinistic philosophies. You've corporately turned this world into what Michael Crichton correctly called a 'State of Fear.' But not even Crichton had it completely right. The 'State of Fear' stems directly from Darwinism because it utterly removes God as being the agent in charge of maintaining this universe, and foolishly places mankind as the responsible entity in charge of the climate. Our original responsibility was to manage the planet under *Truth*. But we can't even come close to controlling nature. It is 'godless religion' that you preach daily and celebrate on Earth Day."

"I assure you, I don't have a religious bone in my body," said Malcolm.

"I suggest that you do, but instead of 'Jesus Saves!' your religious slogan is '*Save Gaia—Mother Earth.*' Where evolution is your 'creator-goddess's' doctrine, entropic *time* is the powerless force she employs, blind *chance* is her feeble savior, and *'go green'* is her primary law, but one she enacts with vengeance. But touching on evolution, you, my friend, must *know* that almost every evidence and conclusion Darwin authored has been discredited, or needed to be significantly altered, and is laughable compared to what you think you know about evolution today. Yet you don't realize that fifty years from now, everything currently published will be discredited and laughable. That same pattern will follow forever as the assertion of evolution is modified because secular science does not understand what really happened in the past. Why? Because they weren't there, and they assume they can judge the past by the present, even though everyone knows the distinct and diametric differences between the present and the past."

"A difference which makes no difference *is no difference,*" countered Malcolm. *"It's science, history, and archaeological fact* that we convey to the public. We enlighten them!"

"That isn't true, and it never was. You and your friends are a gang of **liberals** who indoctrinate the youth with your speculative science *so they never question it*, nor are they allowed to question it. You punish and ridicule *thought itself*, and *we've* lost the hearts and minds of generations of children, now adults, because of it. You employ the time-tested way of controlling populations, as Adolf Hitler attempted—by controlling the perception of **history itself**. His 'Hitler Youth' was a brainwashing school of ignorance and hate, and we've begun down that path already. People wonder why violence in schools has increased. I do not. Our schools now impose Biblical ignorance with no standards of truth and no authority higher than the word of man. At the same time, they instill baseless fear while fostering hatred for any opposition to their narrative, especially where Judeo-Christianity is concerned."

"Christians and Jews need to be dragged kicking and screaming into the twenty-first century. It's for their own good. That's why evolution is the accepted teaching in our public schools," said Malcolm.

"Oh, but your invasion is so complete that not only is our educational system corrupted, but many Conservatives, even fellow *Christians*, are duped by your liberal lies. You don't even see that the *teaching* devalues human life by calling *life itself* an accident. You tell mankind that they are pointless, meaningless, and antithetical to nature, when the Creator Himself gave **His own life to save ours**. 'Save the whales and abort the humans' is a heinous maxim, yet you embrace it. You corrupt all doctors' Hippocratic oaths, men and women who have vowed to '*do no harm*,' by having them kill children in the womb, even out of the womb, and with Obamacare you've move them closer to accepting euthanasia as an adequate convenience. *Your kind* are traitors to your Creator and to humanity because of your *version* of history. You don't have the barest grasp about the nature of reality or Truth, yet you wage war against them in ignorance, and without knowing what *power* is really behind your deceit. Darwin didn't invent the idea of evolution, nor did his grandfather Erasmus. It has been a satanic ideology throughout history in order to deflect accountability to God and advocate a philosophy of '*do what thou wilt*,' without guilt . . . But guilt still exists, and it will be accounted for."

Dominic paused to take a breath and a sip of his coffee, while holding up his right hand to prevent Malcolm from responding.

"You are free to *personally believe* your fairy tale." claimed Rock. "This is America. But you lose all moral authority when you force it on others as fact. By exchanging *Truth for a lie*, you've brazenly suppressed *Truth itself*. You claim yourself to be the '*Right Hand of Authority*' regarding the nature of this universe, while condemning the real Authority. You lead men to their doom by your false authority."

"The climate *is changing and we are finally taking charge*. It is the fault of men like you, and it is my duty to sound an alarm. That is morality in action." contested Carson.

"But you *know* there have *always* been changes in the global climate, and you don't think that *we know better than to litter or intentionally pollute*. You think you are the righteous keeper of that knowledge, and more to the point, **the enforcers of it**. But what you don't seem to know is that where we cut trees for timber, we replant, and where wildfires used to rage uncontrolled, sometimes engulfing multiple state-sized territories, we now put them out and hinder their pollution. Trees are the greatest renewable resource on the planet. They are truly a 'wonder crop,' yet loggers are treated like diseases that need to be eradicated. I truly enjoy your side speaking of tolerance when you've no clue what the word means. We were created to care for this planet, but not above caring for mankind. We were created to subdue this planet the way one tends a garden, but not at the expense of the gardener, and not forgetting Who we tend it for. But above all, we were created to know our Creator, and to know that *He* is in control. Here is the **Truth** . . . He gave a resolute promise to mankind, just after the flood of Noah: *'As long as the earth remains, seedtime and harvest, cold and heat, and summer and winter, and day and night shall not cease.'* Genesis eight, verse twenty-two. That is the Truth that you are up against, and you will not have a victory over it because it will outlast you and your humanistic doctrines."

Malcolm shook his head in disbelief.

"Though there may be colder and longer winters from time to time," Rock continued, "and warmer and longer summers, from time to time and though the regions may vary, God has promised us that *He*, not mankind, is in control of the climate. He has kept His word. So you can be sure that when you go outside, regardless of the weather, if the earth is still here, the climate is stable and under God's control, at least until judgment comes upon it. If mankind believed only *that much* of God's Word, then they would have no fear of 'man-made' global warming."

"Well, I don't believe it," Carson stated, still clinging to his unfounded premise if only for opposition's sake now.

"Then, conversely, *you* should be the first to admit *that if this world were billions and billions of years old*, the sum total of all climatological study has occurred in less than the wink of an eye compared to your assumed the age of this earth, then all our Climatological data is laughably anecdotal. You have absolutely no context to determine what a good climate is compared to a bad climate. That fact should make you recognize that the global warming movement is based on conjecture without contextual information. But you continue to make misinformed judgment calls and claim it to be science and fact, persuading mankind to accept it, and forcing all opposition to bow before it."

"They should bow before it *or they should get off this planet*," Malcolm huffed.

"Why? In contradiction to your own beliefs, you aren't trusting in *evolution* to resolve any problems of its own creation. If mankind is a product of evolution, and pollution is the byproduct of man, dinosaurs, cows—then *evolution* is responsible for this crisis you claim, and *evolution* should correct its own mistake. You should logically just let it, by physical adaptation or extinction. Why? Because if evolution were true, then your life, all life, *is pointless . . .* so why should you or anyone else even care about global warming, or anything else? The answer is, because it suits self-interest to do so. You mistakenly call it the 'survival instinct,' and 'concern for mankind,' but it is *'amoral'* sanctimonious control packaged as 'love for the planet,' giving you license to dominate mankind. At best, it is misdirected do-goodism for the more witless followers, perhaps even for you, but for those pulling the strings, it's insidious."

"Insidious? Saving the planet should be every man's goal, Moreau. What you don't like is that our way of salvation flies in the face of your religion! Our morality compels us to do what me must in order to breathe and survive another day," he boasted.

"You really believe I'm against clean air and water? I can think of very few who would want to live in a poisonous environment, and nobody wants their children to. I suggest that *you* are blinded by the misuse of science which murders and enslaves men and prevents you from exercising any right to question it. Real morality has been subverted, supplanted by humanism. You've been denied reality for so long that you believe you are no longer accountable to your Creator. Trust me, evolution will not save you, and it doesn't even like you."

"The universe is using evolution in order to save itself. Evolution is our creator. We are instruments of evolution to sustain what it has produced. It *is* logical." Carson affirmed.

"No. What is logical is that if life is pointless and detrimental to the survival of the planet, then it is not sane or wise for you to survive. But your philosophy is neither sane nor wise, so perhaps it makes some twisted sort of sense to you. Evolutionary Science is much like the Roman Catholic Church during the Dark Ages—control by fear mongering, keeping the populace ignorant of what I like to call *reality in context*, because you can't face the fact that it isn't the planet that needs to be saved . . . it's you."

"My god, man, here's some *reality in context for you*: We have a hole in the *ozone layer* that can potentially kill all life on this planet, and you spout religious garbage as if *that* will prevent it! That's what I call **insane**!" shouted Malcolm.

"And there's the proof of fear mongering, straight from your mouth. You regurgitate it without thought, just like the schoolchildren your compatriots condition. Malcolm, there is no **hole** in the ozone layer. You've been lied to, and you've swallowed it. There is a seasonal thinning at best, and depending upon the year, it has been thicker at times and thinner at times, smaller and larger, but it does not just get thinner and bigger in systematic progression. You tell everyone that the ozone layer protects against UV radiation, but what you don't broadcast is the fact that the ozone layer is

created by the UV radiation from the sun in the first place.
We'd have to destroy the sun if we wanted to destroy the ozone
layer. The thinner location of the layer was discovered way back in
1985 near Antarctica, hardly an industrialized area, but one with
active volcanoes, and being a polar region, it is no discomfort to
mankind. But we were so frightened by the thinning that you call
a hole, that we banned products that produced lower atmospheric
chlorofluorocarbons, halons, and carbon tetrachlorides. All CFC
emissions dropped dramatically by 1993, so the sun should have
been replenishing the ozone layer since then, right? Yet in 2000
your dreaded ozone hole broke area records, and again in 2003
and then in 2006. Wait. Didn't we save the planet in 1993 by
cutting CFCs? On the other hand, it broke no records in 2001,
2002, 2004, or 2005, and hasn't since 2006. So what's your panic
really for? The truth is that we've had the briefest of times to really
study it, and since ozone depletion can be caused by sulfuric gasses
vented from volcanoes, the thinning could be as natural as the
volcanoes themselves. But you believe we should be scared. You
incite panic, make demands on mankind prematurely, and force a
manufactured doomsday scenario upon us as incontrovertible fact.
That is a dangerously irresponsible practice, Mr. Carson."

Carson sighed. In his own mind, he'd sat quietly enough before
the Moreau. He'd given him plenty of leeway to make his case.
Now, Malcolm decided, it was his turn for a counterattack. It was
time to throw a monkey wrench into his adversary's religious
ignorance. He believed that he might be able to catch him by leading
him into admitting that the age of the earth can't possibly be as
young as Creationists must believe. *Yes*, he thought. *Catch him in a
contradiction of time.*

16

ON THE MOVE

Darlene Campbell's backyard was brightly lit by a fire pit set ablaze with fragrant timber. Tiki torches outlined the fire in a large pentagram, better observed and identified from an aerial view than the ground, but the rulers of darkness in high places required no marker to find them. Darkness devoured the last of the failing light, and it was time for things to get underway, on and off her property. Fifty or so partiers were in attendance. Most were lower casts in the coven's order, attending just for a good time, but the mosquitoes were having a banquet. The alcoholic beverages flowed and needleless drugs were passed around, freely shared, freely partaken of. Dancing and cavorting ensued, with loud death-metal music filling their ears, while the deleterious elements inflamed their senses. Shadowy entities moved with them unseen by their glazed eyes, though the flames occasionally made even their silhouettes appear on the lawn and the semicircle of forest behind Darlene's home. They were not alone, but of course, nobody ever is.

As their revelries gained momentum, Darlene moved away from them, and their raucous bacchanalia, joining her chosen Thirteen plus one. Proudly, regally, Darlene stepped before her faithful inner circle, confident in their mission, determined in her cause. Yes, she was still under the authority of her master, but eventually, she believed, her rise to power would break through all barriers, gaining more power, greater than that of her master's *masters*. She believed in the *Grail* that united nations, the *Stone of Destiny* that many before her had knelt upon. She knew that one day she would touch the stone herself, and afterward, behold others kneeling before *her* upon it. She believed that the backwater county of her current residence would become a new spiritual Mecca, not that she wished to stay in Indiana any longer than necessary. She had designs on foreign lands, promised lands . . . knowing that she would have to stand in line, but she had no clue who was at the front of it.

"It is a night for resistance against unbelievers," Darlene said as she addressed her small group. "When the master appears, he'll lead us on the offense. I'm told that our part tonight will be minor, but a mere spark, in time, can kindle a forest fire—and make no mistake, we *are* going to set the world ablaze."

The robed coven members bowed to Darlene and responded with the obligatory, "Yes, my Queen."

Darlene did not know it, but there was already fear of reprisal within the ranks of her coven. Fear that the police and the FBI were getting too close, fear that the towns nearby were becoming aware of dark forces unleashed, and fear that the coven was stepping dangerously into a fire that it could not control, knowing completely that a fire doesn't care who it burns. They dared not discuss it with their Queen, for they knew that she would risk anything and sacrifice everyone for her advancement. But they *had* discussed it already among themselves.

"Solomon, you will place your equipment where you've been told, and then hurry to join us upon the sacred high pass. Make certain that all is working before you leave it, and make certain it is shut down when I require it."

"I will, my Queen," said Solomon with an uncomfortable bow. "I've spliced into the transmission lines for wired remote access to the generator's control. I can shut it down within five minutes of your order."

"That will be acceptable," she said.

Of all Darlene's followers, Solomon was the most fearful. What he was about to do could be pinpointed and traced, and because it was illegal to begin with, his career and livelihood might just be on the line. Still, the *master's* appearance validated everything he'd been promised by Darlene. It truly amazed them all to have witnessed the creature, and to behold the seeding of the surrogate. Strange things had been happening ever since, all over the county. He knew that Darlene's power was real, above and beyond that of his own. Where power was concerned, he *too* enjoyed wielding it when he could, and liked the benefits of manipulating others by his subtle and artful skills. But it was dangerous business now, and on a scale at which he'd never believed he'd be involved. He knew that he was getting in over his head, and it wasn't *water* into which he was wading.

"Bradley," Darlene said as she moved on.

"Yes, my Queen."

"Has Mrs. Haversham's role in this been prepared?"

"Yes, my Queen. Regardless of her condition, she is available to serve. What needed to be done has been done."

"Good," she said, and as the word escaped her lips, she sensed that they had been joined by a powerful presence. Her master was now near them, waiting just within the dark forest behind her home. "We are ready. Does everyone have their glow sticks?"

They responded by producing them, knowing only to activate them when she commanded.

"Follow me," she commanded. "It is time to remove all obstacles that are in the way."

She led them silently past the intoxicated group that were so self-consumed with lust and riotous behavior that they did not notice the fifteen darkly robed figures leave. Darlene knew that the party would last only another hour, as she had three sober followers there ready to put out the fire, extinguish the torches, and power off the stereo. They were ready to drive those who could not drive away to another location, where they could sober up before returning to Darlene's home in the morning to retrieve their vehicles. They were also tasked with cleaning up before Darlene returned home, so that no evidence could be found, and Bradley could be her alibi should she need one. She knew the risks she was taking, and trusted the forces at her master's disposal to make up for any lack she might have.

Darkness was a door between the trees ahead of them, as the perimeter of the forest baptized them in blackness. Darlene was the first to step into the forest and disappear from her backyard. She could not see her master yet, but knew he was nearby. A few steps in, she sensed which direction to turn in the dark, but snapped her glow stick so that she would not stumble. The same point where Darlene had lit her stick was the point where each person following her lit theirs. It was not their first night excursion, but they suspected that it would be their last.

Darlene saw the reflection of her light glinting off two round eyes, high and ahead of her, and knew they had joined the master, but something was different about it this time. She could not see it clearly, but something *felt* different and the scent it produced was not as it had been before. It stood there silently, motionless until the line of followers had stopped.

"We are ready, Master," Darlene spoke, trying to keep her own fear at bay.

Without a word, the massive creature turned and lumbered silently ahead of the witch, knowing where it was leading them without benefit or need of light to guide it. Fourteen of her coven followed Darlene several paces behind. The coven members were excited, expectant, and completely afraid of whom and what they followed.

They took a route where property lines met and where tree lines covered their visibility. They traversed more than one fence, but they kept pace with the large silent strides of the monster ahead. They did not believe that it would slow down for them if they did not. A light fog was beginning to rise, conveniently adding to their cover. They arrived at their destination in only half an hour's time. All knew where they were, and all knew what was expected.

One hundred feet above the valleys on each side, the creature stopped, and the party also ceased their advance. Without turning, the creature spoke one word to Darlene.

"Kha-lal," it commanded in a voice that Darlene did not recognize, but somehow she knew that the language was Hebrew, and that the meaning of the word was "begin."

17

WRESTLING DARWIN

Malcolm Carson was more of a showman than a debater. To his credit, he knew what he believed, if not exactly why. Evolution operated in variables, unknowns, and unspecific processes that could not always be quantified. Lacking definition never stopped the assertions of the evolution proponents. Nobody could define the composition of the presumed "singularity" from which the "Big Bang" originated, or where the singularity itself came from, or what it and space-time exploded *into*, if space-time did not already exist. They could not define what made something stable, like a singularity, become unstable and explode without outside influence. Those were just the initial questions to cosmological evolution that the model *must* explain, but they were unknown still. It started with a premise that can't be resolved, but they ran with the story, called it "science," without letting things like ignorance slow them down.

"May I ask a question?" Carson inquired. He had a few counterarguments to propose, but he also needed information from Moreau to see which were valid to bring up.

Dominic nodded and he took a sip of coffee.

"Do you believe that there have been ice ages then?" Carson posed.

"I believe in, perhaps, a super-glacial period. Immediately after the global flood of Noah, there was so much water aboveground—water vapor, volcanic, possibly meteoric debris in the atmosphere, since the fountains of the deep and the windows of Heaven were opened simultaneously—that there could have been a proliferation of ice on the earth. But it was, comparative to your conjecture of ice ages, a rapid event, and there were still seasons on this earth, if, perhaps, extended winters for the duration. Again, climates change. They have and do."

"Actually, I wanted information pertaining to your historical, *Biblical* perspective so I could understand what specific points I should make. It isn't just regarding global warming."

"Fair enough," agreed Nick. "According to Genesis, before the flood there were only high hills, not mountains or canyons. It was a different world, different from the first, and different from our current earth, and it was cursed. When the 'Windows of Heaven' opened, the world was reshaped by it, perhaps contaminated by it with extraterrestrial ore, and certainly exterminated by it. Simultaneously, whatever the fountains of the deep were—water, or water and magma, perhaps even including petroleum and other elements from within the crust of the planet—they erupted through the earth's crust. That is the only documented historical example of 'man-caused climate change': the Deluge."

"Then hold on a minute." Malcolm was singularly proud of his wiliness. "I see a huge flaw in your *Biblical facts* . . . petroleum is a fossil fuel. As a Bible-thumping Creationist, you *know* that your side believes that the imaginary Flood of Noah *caused* the fossil creation and fossil fuel, so oil *had to have been made after the flood*, and couldn't have erupted from the earth's crust," Carson stated smugly. "There, I've shot holes in your *religious model.* So let's get on with why you are here."

"I didn't say that. Yes, most fossil creation and petrifaction was a result of the Flood, and organic material under pressure can make oil, perhaps did. Coal is a fossil fuel, but crude-oil may be more than you think. Oil *can* be made with organic material in a matter of hours under heat and pressure, it's been tested and verified with observational science. The process is called thermal depolymerization. In point of fact, Noah himself used *"pitch"* to seal the Ark watertight, from within and without, prior to the Deluge. Pitch is a type of petroleum that varies in composition from area to area. It can seep up through porous earth, on land or in the sea, through fissures in the crust, or if found before it can depressurize, one can obtain it by drilling for it. No man knows with certainty where the balance of oil comes from, to this day. There are currently three major theories about its genesis, but all may partially be correct."

"Oh, and pray tell, what are these other theories? I am not aware of more than one," Malcolm stated.

"One theory proposes that petroleum came from algae, organic matter, animals and plants buried in sediment with extreme pressure creating pressure-volume heat and perhaps in concert with geothermal heat, turning it into hydrocarbon liquids. Another is that oil is an *'abiogenic'* compound naturally occurring in the planet's crust. And yet another is that petroleum is produced by massive subterranean bacteria that excrete oil, and there is precedent for that theory as well. The theory that evolutionists largely hold to is the first I mentioned. They claim that organic material, largely plankton, buried under sedimentary rock, slowly, over millions of years, was cooked under pressure, eventually turning the material into hydrocarbons and gas. That first proposal fails on a couple of key points. The first point is the *creation phenomenon*—that is, the life-forms required to produce the quantities of petroleum we find needed must be buried *rapidly all at once*, if not, the life-forms would rot, and decompose on the surface. So it must have been rapidly sealed under multiple layers of sediment and placed under great pressure, as the fossils were. Regional mudslides and

257

floods cannot explain it. Only a global flood would do. Next is the *containment phenomenon*: Oil pressure would have dissipated in mere *thousands* of years forcing itself through the porous earth. It also must have been a recent phenomenon, based on the fact that much of it is still highly pressurized until tapped from beneath the earth and beneath the oceans. Therefore, the evolutionary model of oil creation does not work for the first theory, but a global flood does."

"I've never heard of those other two theories, so I'll not acknowledge them without further study. At any rate, if petroleum erupted from the earth during the flood, there would be oil lakes and oil oceans on the surface of the planet because everyone knows that oil floats," Carson chided.

"Don't you remember the 'BP,' the British Petroleum spill in the Gulf of Mexico back in 2010? It was in all the papers. It was supposed to be the greatest man-made disaster in history—one with potentially planetwide consequences. All the environmental scientists said so, as did the news media, so it must be true! So where is it and where is the global catastrophe? It harmed a few aquatic creatures, birds and coral, but the damage was negligible when compared to *natural disasters*. At any rate, millions and millions of barrels of crude oil *sank* and may yet be able to be reclaimed, or it may recede back into the ocean floor under the pressure of the water above it. Believe it or not, oil is *part* of the ecosystem of this planet, regardless of origin," Nick answered.

"That's ridiculous, Moreau," interjected Malcolm. "Petroleum is a poisonous blight against life and humanity. It is an abomination. We'd be better off if it never existed."

"Like carbon?" Nick asked sarcastically with a smile to his *carbon-based* fellow human. "Perhaps if sin did not exist, then there would be much less petroleum to complain about, but I don't see you asking the government to outlaw either yet, and I see you and Al Gore profiting by the existence of both."

"I trust the Government to consider those things that I lack the power to control," said Malcolm, "at least under *this* administration. The US Government is the only entity outside the *scientific community* that has the interest of the people at heart . . . unlike the *capitalistic society* that is against the best interests of this planet. Government prevents a stupid populace from killing itself."

"The populace is stupid only because they are raised to be stupid, including you and me, Malcolm, but I've stopped drinking the proverbial Kool-Aid. But it was not always so in this nation. It's changed, and continues because *your kind* wishes to impose warped ideas of godless morality on others while telling them that good and evil, right and wrong, Heaven and Hell don't exist. You don't see that it's *your kind* who are traitors, against people, their freedom and their Creator, and you spread panic and fear while manipulating the law to crush all sane opposition."

"All right, finish your dissertation on global warming, the flood, evolution, life, the universe, and everything!" Carson demanded, not realizing he'd quoted Douglas Adams. "But please throw me a *stinking bone* about how that pertains to my excursion."

"Soon I promise. But first there are a few critical points to cover regarding the Deluge because this is the *real history* of the world. It is *Truth* as testified by the Cause and Witness to the event. And note, there are as yet **no witnesses for evolution.** When the flood waters dissipated, the mountains ascended—geological upheaval—and the valleys descended- massive erosion- and the layers of stratum which were laid down during the Deluge can be seen all over the planet to this day. But right afterwards, God Himself gave another promise that this type of event—the global flood—would **never happen again.** That was promised in Genesis 8, and after the flood, the water boundaries were *ordained*, as expounded upon in Jeremiah 5. When the earth is judged next, it will be by fire . . . not because of climate change, but because of the global rejection God. Only *then* will you see man-caused global warming . . . by men's hatred for his own Creator . . . and just prior to that event, is where we are *right now.*"

"All right, you're what I call a *'flat-earther,'*" said Malcolm, "and then, a global warming *denier*, and a global-flood believer, since you seriously believe that Noah existed and survived during a *global* flood. But you still have not given me any information that I've requested."

Dominic chuckled for a moment at the "flat-earther" comment. He was about to relent, and give Malcolm more details regarding *"where we are right now,"* and about the danger he faced in the forest beyond, but this time Malcolm turned the conversation back. His loss.

"Mr. Carson," rebutted Rock, "there was *never* a Jewish, Christian, or *Biblical* doctrine, or scripture that even alluded to a 'flat earth.' The Book of Job declared a round earth before the Greeks were a people, and Isaiah chapter 40 verse 22 clearly calls the earth a sphere. But you can't know that unless you take the time to study and understand the Bible, rather than ignorantly ridiculing it. What's more, there is another interesting verse I'll share with you. Not only does the Bible faithfully communicate and reveal the nature of this world, conveying it in phenomenological language when observational science was in its infancy, but Job chapter 26 verse 7 tells us something that no man at the time could know. It tells us that the earth, the planet itself, is suspended in space. The verse goes like this: 'God stretches out the north over the empty space, and hangs the earth on ***nothing.***'"

"Interesting, I'll give you that. But back to global warming, I'd like to say that you will stop being a denier when the ocean's water level reaches your lower lip. Then the denier will join the choir," Carson said, adding a smile to the statement, and rhyme, as someone "in the know" might say to a child with an added pat to the head.

"Do you realize that you've just stated that you *believe* that a global flood is possible? Interesting . . . . *Waterworld* faith. You don't believe that a global flood could have happened in the past, regardless of the Bible's detailed record of it, even though about every tribe and people in the world tell stories about global flooding, as well as creatures like *monsters, demons, dinosaurian-dragons*, and like *giants*," Rock hinted, but Malcolm did not make the connection.

"On top of that," Rock continued, "the fossil record clearly shows massive extermination, *not extinction*. I reject that term. And these fossils are found in regular layers of *sedimentary* rock strata, according to buoyancy, ability, and wherewithal to seek higher ground, and initial physical location during the inception of the Deluge, *all over the face of the planet*. Those are the 'facts' that we share. But you fail every time trying to make them fit your evolutionary model. Yet you believe in ice ages, which involve massive amounts of frozen *water* on much of the earth, and that if mankind does not stop using gasoline and letting cows fart, we are going to all drown in a global flood. It is a contradiction. It is foolishness called science. Do you still not know how *sedimentary* rock and fossils are formed? And second, do you own any beachfront property?" Dominic asked, but knew the answer already.

"Beachfront property?" The question had taken him aback. "Well, not really *own*, but I have a time share at Panama City Beach in Florida's Gulf Coast, for an entire week every spring. That's a great beach with white sand and is a wonderful vacation spot. Um . . . now, why would you ask?"

"Because regardless of the fear your side has generated, I've never seen anyone move the hotels back from the beach because the water level was rising, since they stand to lose the most in a 'global flood' that you believe is coming. They may be concerned with beach erosion, hurricane damage, tidal surges, and tsunamis, but if the water level were drastically rising, don't you think they would be moving the hotels back? I happen to know for a fact that they continue to build hotels right along the beach. Why do you suppose that is?" asked Rock.

"The oceans are rising. That is a fact," said Carson in all seriousness.

"Yes. They seem to be currently rising, by the estimation of many short-term studies, but it hasn't been the first time, and it isn't because the global temperature is rising. It isn't abnormal, and it's an excruciatingly slow process. If you stood at the beach waiting for the flood to cover you, your great-great-grandchildren would die of old age before the water reached *your lower lip, as you say*; and that is only supposing that it will *continue* to rise. There are other factors that are not completely accounted for within those studies, such as the effect that new seamounts have on the displacement of water, and the total impact of underwater and polar volcanism. Almost all of our climatological data is taken from above the ocean surface, but there is a vast amount of important data that we don't have beneath it, and beneath the ice-caps. They claim that landmass erosion is a symptom of climate change, but erosion has been part of the normal processes on this planet since the flood. Erosion and river deltas displace water, and fresh-water rivers emptying into the ocean impacts the sea level. But are all the glaciers really melting? No. Many are growing rapidly. Antarctic sea ice keeps setting new records for growth. Sea ice displaces water. Did you know Greenland was once green, but the climate changed since then? Antarctica was once ice-free and forested, but yes, the climate has changed. Man needs to expect it, adapt to it, quit panicking and controlling mankind with fear, and move on."

"At least you admit that the ocean levels are rising," said Malcolm.

"I'm just surprised that *you* actually pay for a place that you believe will soon be underwater. Perhaps a *still small voice* is urging you to see reality, at least peripherally?"

Malcolm went back to offense, trying to pitch it toward time contradictions. "Do you know nothing about scientific dating methods? Your '**young earth**' flood model is easily disproved by isotopic dating methods," Carson said, giving a good thrust against his opponent.

"Well, I know quite a bit about radiometric *assumptions* and how dates are calibrated," Dominic countered. "The sum total of carbon-14 dating can be tested only on something that once lived, and to calibrate the dates, it must be tested against historically verified time frames, and those can be done to only roughly 4,000 years in the past. All other radiometric dates are *complete assumptions* based upon the half-life of the isotope in a closed system. But this planet is not a closed system. Heat alone can reset a radiometric clock or speed it up, but many other environmental factors can, and do, alter any hope of defensible results. Did you know that if dinosaurs were just 10,000 years extinct, their petrified fossils would be nothing but mineral through and through? Yet we've found spongy tissue— *unfossilized tissue*—inside T-Rex bones. It isn't just a weird find, *it's an impossible find* if they became extinct 65 million years ago. The only reason that it's treated like an anomaly is because nobody looked specifically for soft tissue in previous finds. Why? Because *it's completely impossible that soft tissue would exist.*"

"Don't you get it? Anything is possible in this universe given enough time for chance to work it out," said Carson.

"No. That's a faulty logic, Carson. Anything is possible, but only if it *can* happen. It remains impossible if it can't. Here's another historical factor your scientists ignore: Everything created by God in the book of Genesis was created with *complete maturity*. God made adult man, not sperm and egg; trees, not seeds; birds, not eggs. God was there in the beginning, not Job, and not Darwin, not me, and not you. Fully formed creatures, a fully formed environment, a fully formed universe was there by the end of day six. Man was created unique, above the entire animal kingdom, and he still is. Animal kinds differed from each other. Aquatic animal kinds differed from land animal kinds and insect kinds and bacteria, and plants differed from all of the above. God also fashioned different sexes, abilities, behaviors

I could go on, an on. He programmed His creation intricately with care. Evolution can't explain or demonstrate the 'hows' and 'whys' because the missing link isn't a monkey; the missing link is between the creation and its *Creator.* Just because you can see nature doesn't mean nature formed what you see. Nothing is self-created."

"Fine. What about the speed of light and the distance of stars?" Carson asked. "Surely you know it takes billions of years for light to reach us from the farthest reaches of space."

"I know that *you* believe that it would take that long. However, I know that *space-time* and all forms of energy are alterable, malleable physical properties, and I'm also familiar with many aspects of quantum physics and the concept of *relativity.* I know that space-time was 'stretched' like a tent—the universe within it—on the same day that light was created. I also know that **time itself**, as it applies to the subatomic, can be said as not to really exist, beyond our practical level of reference. Believe it or not, in all its wonder, majesty, and complexity, *this universe barely exists.* It is mostly space even between teeny-tiny particles and energy fields; even in the most dense elements, atoms are spaced extremely far from each other, but all are held together and ordered by power and wisdom beyond this universe, just to keep ours barely existing."

"Are suggesting that I don't exist?" asked Malcolm with derision born anew.

"I'm suggesting what you *should already know and* **question**, but you haven't put two and two together. Compared to 'Heaven'—the place beyond this universe—ours is akin to a virtual environment, or an interactive movie projection. Our limited human perception tells us different, because this universe is supposed to be tangible to us within it, and so it is. But what we perceive to be real is incredibly finite and borders on the infinitesimal."

"Ridiculous," Malcolm commented.

"Cosmologists admit that 95 percent of this universe is *missing*. Do you understand the gravity of that statement?"

"Very funny," said Malcolm.

"That's the point, not the funny part. Here's the funny part. OK, over 95 percent of the universe just isn't there, so 'science' *imagineered* the term '***dark matte***r' to explain something that they don't understand, but the term might as well be 'voodoo,' because that explanation is just as scientific. Here's another one. Comets should have been long gone from this universe, given your assumed '*evolved*' age. So they imagineered the 'Oort Cloud' beyond our solar system with perhaps a double Jovian gravity planet in it, without any evidence, they run with it and '***blammo!***' the term is adopted as an acceptable scientific rule, and is related as fact every time it's presented for public consumption."

Malcolm, having nothing of this, pressed on. "The speed of light is a constant in this universe, and it takes millions of years for it to travel from one galaxy to another. Deal with it," he said bluntly.

"We both know that the speed of light can be manipulated by transmission medium, Carson. You assume all is as it was when it was created. It is not. And I've seen calculations demonstrating that light could have reached us from the outer boundaries of the current universe in only six days, *relative* to the *perspective* of the earth. I might also remind you that according to Genesis, light—in all forms, all energy by implication—existed before its main *sources* were later restricted to celestial bodies. And there are actually several possible ways that light from stars could be visible here. And all these are within the context of God's revelation regarding how and when He established them, their properties, and their laws, as opposed to their coming into being from nothing, then exploding, becoming orderly out of chaos, simply by chance. Light, stars, galactic distances are no problem from a Biblical Creationist viewpoint, and I add no 'gaps' to the Word of God that would corrupt it in order to accommodate billions of years."

"Yes, the 'Gap' theory. I was hoping you would at least be reasonable enough to meet evolution halfway by allowing that premise. I, however, knew from the start that you most likely would not," said Malcolm, displaying at least a little understanding of his opposition.

"A fundamental flaw with cosmological evolution," Rock continued, "is that matter is never naturally converted from energy, *ever*, without also creating an equal amount of antimatter. It would take something *supernatural*, beyond nature, to accomplish that. It is always a one-to-one ratio, no more, no less. So where is all the antimatter in the universe? Also, equal parts of matter and antimatter would likely annihilate-slash-convert each other back to energy if they came in contact with each other. But the particles would have to be attracted to each other first, and the attraction would have to overcome their velocity during the mythological Big Bang expansion away from the event center. They'd have to behave differently than how they behave now. The hydrogen atom, for example, the first element said to be produced in your 'Big Bang' model—as plasma then as a gas, the model does not take into account that hydrogen gases *and* excited plasmas tend to *expand in a vacuum*. The atoms expand away from each other in a vacuum, even if your *Big Bang* had not first propelled them away from each other to begin with. With the purposeful, industrial efforts of man to compress diatomic hydrogen in canister, it still expands the second the opportunity arises, even within the existing gravity field of earth, and even under 15-pounds-per-square-inch pressure at sea level, *let alone in a vacuum*. Even traveling at nearly the speed of light, a hydrogen atom's mass and resistance would only approach the 'infinite' relative to particles that are not moving or ones that would collide with it. But all matter has a fifty-fifty chance of immediate annihilation, and a much greater chance of not-so-immediate annihilation eventually, because of the equality in antimatter required to exist. But let's say that the atoms somehow managed to form stars, contrary to probability. That star would be a Population III Star, having no metals—no elements heavier than helium—and we should be able to see them today because of the probable longevity of that type of star and because of the conservation of energy. They would be the first and most prevalent type of star. Guess what? There are none we know of today, nor have they been witnessed at any time in the past. Your speculative scientists invent terms like the Big Bang and the Planck Epoch, yet have no working model for them, all the while daring to declare that *that **IS** the history of the universe.* They dare call it fact, and you never ask ***why***. Oh, wait! I forgot the wisdom of Cave Johnson: *'Science isn't about asking why, it's about asking **why not**,'*" offered Rock, knowing that the reference would be missed by Malcolm and most others unfamiliar with Portal 2.

"I can't believe it. You seem to be an intelligent man, but you cling to your religious affectations and hide your eyes against scientific fact. Here are two modern examples of evolution for you which clearly demonstrate evolution: the virus and bacteria. Both evolve right in front of virologists eyes with regularity and with repetitiveness. Viruses are becoming resistant to antibiotics because of that fact. If you really were CDC, you'd know that," said Malcolm.

"They do not, and cannot," parried Rock. "Bacteria like the E. coli have been witnessed and studied for thousands and thousands of generations in an attempt to prove that very thought, but regardless of how many generations are allotted them, the bacteria is still the same kind of bacteria. E. coli is still E. coli, and the antibodies designed within the human body are still the best defense against both the virus and bacteria. Antibiotics can treat an infection, but they don't kill a virus, which is a foreign organism. You should know that a virus can't even reproduce on its own. It requires a highly complex, and already living *foreign cell*, a genetic *factory*, in order to reproduce within it. Viruses' DNA doesn't gain any information to become resistant to antibiotics."

"Actually," he continued, "they often suppress or lose genetic information, and that's a big danger: Imagine World War Two—for argument's sake, and your job is to genetically engineer a poison to kill **only** Nazi soldiers. Your poison needs to be specific to kill your enemy based upon their genetic disposition, say, targeted to the ones with blond hair and blue eyes and eat sauerkraut. Your poison kills most of them, most of the time, but that only makes the ones it didn't kill the new danger. So you now have to face a smaller population of the blonds but those were already immune to the poison, and still are. And you now must face the red-, black-, and brown-haired members who are now the strongest and most prolific, and are now the most dominant in the population. Though they may look slightly different, it's only superficial; they are still the same enemy, and you can no longer use that specific poison against them. Antivirus and bacteriological treatments have this dilemma. The virus never evolves into some new virus; it was never completely at risk from *that* form of attack to begin with. Survival of the fittest isn't evolution; it is just a demonstration of innate diversity within predetermined genetic boundaries. Living organisms do what they were designed to do: be fruitful, multiply, and tenaciously cling to the life we've all been *endowed with by our Creator.* A diversified gene pool can lose or repressed their genetic Achilles' heel, by design."

"They mutate and become airborne. Everyone knows that; it's clearly evolution in action," said Carson.

"Really?" asked Rock. "So when a virus goes airborne it is because it evolved little wings and feathers?" Rock chided him, but many ignorant people have succumbed to the insinuation that the virus had changed into some new organism. They bought it hook, lie, and sphincter. But Rock reminded himself that those were the casualties of the war, not the inventors of it, per se. So he removed all hints of derision from his speech, and continued.

"Here is the rule about mutations, Carson: They are dangerous and should be avoided. Can X-rays cause mutation? Yes. Is it good to be exposed to them so that we can evolve? No. That's why you protect your groin at a dentist's office. While it might be a benign mutation, more often it scars, cripples, maims, and kills. One thing mutations **never do** is *increase information*. But if a mutated *virus* lives to become an airborne strain, it's only because it is able to infect the respiratory tract or mucus membranes where a sneeze or cough will send small infected droplets into the air. It's still the same virus. It is not a better killer. In fact, most have an unfavorable survivability rate because they've left their host, a reasonably closed system, and must now face an open system. It is easier for the parasitic organism to dry up with the droplet, be adversely impacted by rain, heat, or cold; and now it has no living cell in its immediate proximity to infect, like it was when *within* the host."

"DNA itself is proof of evolution," said Carson. "The first amino acids organized themselves by chance to make proteins, and the proteins adhered to each other and formed DNA, and the living cells organized the proteins to build more complex life, with more complex DNA, and today we have great complexity from those primitive beginnings," Malcolm insisted.

"Malcolm, DNA is highly complex even in single-celled organisms. Viability within potential DNA combinations has an **extremely** low range of tolerance because the order in a strand has its own designated purpose, **designed purpose**," Rock emphasized before continuing. "The complexity of human DNA even contains error correction codes to *prevent mutations* from harming the detailed construction process. It is designed for adaptation and variation within its kind, but also designed to a level of specificity as to *prevent* it from becoming something that it is not. The code is designed specifically to avoid becoming something that cannot live. But the salient issue is DNA—*the instruction code*, the physical *software*, if you will, cannot replicate or manufacture anything without an already-living CELL—*the machinery*, the *hardware*, and the complex single cell has no purpose or abilities without DNA to instruct it in construction and replication. The legitimate conclusions of genetic science affirms the fact that for all the 'diverse kinds of living creatures' that we have on this planet, their progenitors *MUST* have had a much richer gene pool—***more actual usable code*** in their DNA, or least ***far less recessive information in the code***—than currently exists in them. But the foundational rule of biology, which drives a stake through the heart of *abiogenic* evolution is: **'*Life comes only from the already living.*'** We *were* originally mineral compounds all right, topsoil from the earth, that much is true, and that much we agree upon. But we had ***life*** imparted to us from a Living Creator. Just like the Word of God, we too are God-breathed."

Malcolm was getting angry at the obviously "thick-headed" agent. He believed he'd had just about enough of this CDC *poser*, and he was about to let it be known.

18

TICK

(From the notes of First Agent Christopher Griffin)

The greatest lie a man can tell is the one he tells himself—that he's OK without a savior. It is a trap a man sets for himself and he blindly steps into it while mocking those who have learned to avoid it, or strive to avoid it. There are many roads a man can walk, but there is only one that will bring fulfillment. Man struggles daily to feel fulfilled and fails. He spends much effort on that which he believes will bring pleasure, only to find it unsatisfying. When will he try the road not taken: the narrow road that leads to fulfillment by the gift of righteousness?

The greatest harm a man can cause is to be a lukewarm, or middle-of-the-road, Christian. Christ says to be either hot or cold in your relationship with Him, but He will spit out those who are lukewarm toward him. Be "full on" for Christ, or be against Him, but don't be a noncommittal ignoramus and call yourself Christian. Those who do not wish to live for Christ, but call themselves Christian, smear Christ's name before those who already mock Him and those who need Him. Let Christ into your entire life, not just your Sunday-morning life.

271

The greatest madness a man can fall prey to is a similar time-tested trap which the enemy sets. First he entices man saying "God is denying you of (*variable*)." Secondly the enemy enslaves the man to an unending pursuit of that *variable* which he believes God had denied him of, and which he continually believes will fulfill him if only he possessed it. Lastly, the enemy condemns the man before God and men for the same *variable* which he enticed the man to pursue in the first place. The enemy wants to destroy men and wants to beat them to death with the very thing he first enticed them to pursue.

Tick worked with John Cosworth and Sheriff Braxton in organizing the crypto-zoologists' exodus from the park. Braxton, satisfied that all was going well, took his leave from them and contacted the Crawfordsville Police Department to confirm the CDC directive and corroborate the validity of the CDC agents themselves, since Malcolm had called them into question. Afterward, he contacted his deputies and gave them instructions. Then Braxton chose to drive into Waveland just to make sure that Malcolm didn't try anything stupid again with the CDC agent.

Tick saw that the rest of the camping equipment was stowed, campfires were extinguished, cookware was removed, and most of what they had deployed was packed into the five SUVs and the two small trailers, one used as Carson's quarters. The other was John and Malcolm's office, with the tracking station, testing lab, and comms console. He made his own sweep to be sure that no stealth cameras were left behind. All that was left to do, as far as Tick knew, was to take down the camp's lighting, reel in electrical cords, and shut down the silenced generators. Fortunately, the three generators had fold-up lighting on them so they would still be able to see once they had the other lights down and packed.

"I understand that you're using quiet generators so you don't scare away your intended target," Tick said to Cosworth, "but all the light pollution you generate can be seen for miles. I'd think that alone would send your Agnostopithecus running in the opposite direction."

"How did you know we call them that?" asked Cosworth, knowing that the term had not been brought up at any time when the CDC was on-site.

"We were briefed by the FBI, and they know more about your group than you might suspect," said Tick.

"That figures," said Cosworth. "I bet they've run background checks on my grandchildren too."

"Very likely," Tick said in jest.

"Well, to answer your concern, when our camp is set up again, any of us can, at a moment's notice, turn off all the visible lighting, and switch to IR with a remote control. We all are equipped with night-vision goggles that are packed away now."

"Ah, very good. But are you sure that your quarry can't also see in the IR spectrum?" Tick asked. He was not asking in ignorance, but was giving Cosworth a hint that could save his life someday.

"We're not concerned since no *mammal* we know of has ever evolved the ability to see in the infrared wavelengths. If they did, it would not be a very useful adaptation since anything and everything that is warmblooded emits IR, including the mammal itself that would be using such vision. Any warmblooded creature would have to be able to control its own body temperature, in the cranial area at least, for it to be able to utilize such an adaptation," explained Cosworth.

"Indeed," agreed Tick knowingly.

"Wait, you aren't suggesting . . . ," Cosworth asked.

"That is all I am doing, sir. Just suggesting," said Tick.

"Oh, OK," said Cosworth. "It is an interesting discussion point. I mean, that would change the entire dynamics of any kind of current hunt for these creatures. But we aren't searching for Superman, just an animal that we know little about, and one which we could be related to."

"Perhaps more than you might expect," said Tick, hinting again with the knowledge that the Nephil-Adam are birthed by humans.

"Yes, well, yes," said Cosworth. "Yes, perhaps a close relative, but until we have a specimen to examine, we are basing it all on conjecture."

"It's a very dangerous proposition, Mr. Cosworth. What if you were not as prepared to capture one as you think?"

"We are specifically prepared for the capture of this animal, Mr . . . ."

"Cavor," offered Tick.

"Mr. Cavor," finished Cosworth. "We have traps, bait, calls, weapons, hides, scanner webs, remote cameras with telemetry, listeners, and other devices that should ensure success. We are very prepared for this, I assure you."

"What about communications with each other? This area is largely a cellular black zone."

"That's easy," said Cosworth. "We have shortwave communications with hands-free equipment."

"Very good," said Tick. "What frequency are you authorized to use?"

"That's the tickler," said Cosworth, "CQ Petroleum has obtained access for us to use a Tibetan frequency of 7240. Apparently, CQ pulled some strings, and they were willing to lend the frequency to us at a nominal licensing fee, since they have a distinct interest in how the Agnostopithecus relates to their Yeti. It is a scrambled signal, but we have descramblers as well."

"That *is* interesting," agreed Tick, making a mental note of the frequency. Tick was a detail man, and if there was ever a devil in the details, he was the one who could spot it. He looked around the camp, noticing a fog moving in on them. It was thick and dense, and while he was watching it, it began to enfold the campsite like a tide rolling in, rising, and then engulfing the camp. It was cool, wet, and thick, and the entire site was set aglow under the bright generator lights diffused by the vapor.

"Generators are shutting down in one minute," a voice called out behind them.

The SUVs had tow packages and were all hitched up. When the lights shut down and the light towers were folded down, they would all be ready to go. It was about two seconds before the lights went out when Tick smelled something out of the ordinary from within the fog. At that moment, he knew something was very wrong. He had only a moment to remember that he should have listened to Rock about his earlier concern. Then the lights went out, and the attack on them began.

19

NO SUCH THING

"That's enough, Moreau. *I want to know what Knightlight is and I want to know what it has to do with my Hunt!* I have a job to do and you are hindering any chance of success. I want you to tell me what you think is out there, and I want it straight," Carson demanded. Carson was beginning to lose his temper again, but Dominic was not about to let that hinder him in the least.

"I've already hinted many things about it which you are unwilling to grasp," Dominic responded, "so I'll explain further because what you are hunting is *not what you think.* You're hunting physical and spiritual manifestations of a Biblical nature, beyond your willingness and current ability to comprehend. Your quarry is much older, much deadlier, and a far more intelligent being than any *missing link* you hope to find. It is not an animal, unless you're comparing it to a mineral or vegetable. *It won't let you contain it if you are able to ever capture it*, and the only reason you can get as close as you have, and remain alive, is that it actually wants you to continue to believe and propagate the evolutionary lie about it. It has a vested interest in your lies, that is, unless you get too close and threaten it by proximity. As long as you try to get near it, or even near my team and me, you're in danger."

"I am a scientist, Mr. Moreau, not a liar as you've accused me of being. And as such, I still believe in the science of evolution. I've brought other scientists with me because most are credible and published biologists, primate behavioral experts, crypto-zoologists, and professional trackers. We are well equipped to sustain and document our excursion. We're not your 'garden variety nuts' who might hunt these animals just for a thrill."

"Belief in a fantasy does nothing to *validate* a fantasy, nor excuse the purveyors of it. You should know that quote, since *you* said it in your book, *Monsters of Myth*, regarding Christianity. And before you say that *scientific consensus* is on your side, I remind you that just as 'Truth' is not attained by consensus, neither is speculative science validated by consensus."

"Touché," Carson replied, somewhat amazed. "I'm glad to see that you have done some research on me. Maybe some of it will rub off on you."

Dominic ignored the false flattery. He had been near Carson in previous missions, and heard his buffoonery from a distance, while secretly, or perhaps not so secretly now, trying to protect the ignoramus and his troupe of clowns and while concurrently trying to remove the threat and keep his own team alive.

"To know what you hunt, you have to step away from your worldview or you'll never understand it," Nick stated.

"My worldview has not let me down yet," rebutted Malcolm.

"Malcolm, evolutionary science is *illegitimate*. I know what breakthroughs the science of medicine has demonstrated. I've witnessed the creation of intelligent machines that computer science has produced. The science of physics is a testable, demonstrable science with substantial contributions to humanity. Aerospace, mathematics, botany, chemistry, thermodynamics, microbiology, optics, herpetology, economics, criminology—all these sciences are tangible, testable, and substantial, and contribute to mankind in manifold ways. They are legitimate. They produce real things, verifiable things, Mr. Carson. But when any science extrapolates from, or is impacted by, "evolutionary science," there is nothing gained but a story. *Nothing* is enhanced but the perpetuated fable. *Nothing* is built by it, *nothing* is cured, *nothing* is nurtured, *nothing* is comforted, no equations are resolved by it, and no benefit can be measured with it. In fact, it is a noose around the neck of science. You are blinded by a science that is falsely called *science.* Truth and wisdom *are* sacrificed for it and hindered because of this *'nothing'* that evolutionary science produces. Evolution fails in its attempt to defy this simple law: *ex nihilo nihil fit, or from nothing, nothing comes.* Creation *must* have a Creator, or nothing is created and nothing exists. Life must exist for life to exist. Nothing lifeless lives. Energy can create matter, but not life. Nothing lifeless can evolve, and if something lives, it already knows genetically what it can be and what it can't. But how many scientific laws is this false science allowed to violate without losing its credibility? How many predictions has it accurately forecast? How many elements did it define? How does it contribute to new surgical techniques? How does it demonstrate itself to be anything beyond a silly *story* that continues to evolve just to make it palpable to swallow?"

"Fine. You've had your say. Fine. I call your sermon to an end. I'm here to capture an Agnostopithecus, Moreau. *What facts do you have that I need?"* Carson demanded, putting the brakes on the lecture that was making him weary.

"Very well . . . ," said Nick, who knew that his time with Malcolm had expired. "Here is a fact for you: Not only are you going to battle in ignorance, but you are playing the role of a pawn against spiritual powers that exist in this universe, and beyond it. The forces you are trying to expose yourself to are deadly. You are not facing a product of evolution, you're facing a being that is a product of genetic manipulation . . . old-style."

Malcolm smiled, almost chuckled. "Be that as *you* may see it, I assure you that we know this animal, and we know what we are doing.

We know creature attacks are on the increase, but so is mankind's ever-encroaching population. I see nothing to be frightened of, though precautionary measures are always being factored in. I've been on bear hunts, for tagging purposes of course, in the Sierras and the Rockies, just to gain knowledge about what might be required in tagging or capturing our hairy friend. But if I were to analyze your scare tactics for motivation, I'd say you just don't like the competition. I think you're afraid I'll capture it before you can."

"Afraid? I'm as afraid as *you* need to be. If you find the creature in your bullheadedness, and you threaten it, you and everyone with you will be dead and lost to this world before you can even wet yourself."

Carson almost said, "I can wet myself faster than you know," but instead he forced a smile and said nothing. He took a sip of his coffee that had cooled down beyond enjoyment.

"You are on a quest that will end poorly, Malcolm," Dominic said.

"I know my quest Moreau. I've been preparing for it for a long time. I seek the Holy Grail of the animal kingdom," said Malcolm

"You are only prepared to track and find an evolutionary cul-de-sac, a curiosity of chance and nature, an animal with surmountable intelligence, but unlike others, you aren't content just to experience it vicariously, or merely study photographs of it, or take castings of its feet, or obtain hair samples, and move on with your life confident that you know enough about your Sasquatch. You want to capture it to become famous and justify your field of study. That's why I warned you, because you believe you are smarter than your intended prey. But the beast you seek is not just dangerous; it's brilliantly deadly and vengeful."

"Brilliant? Vengeful? You are describing Arthur Conan Doyle's *Moriarty*, not an animal. How do you come by this new mystical information? What makes you the wizened custodian of Sasquatch knowledge?"

"Firsthand experience, Carson. Historical knowledge, sound theological discipline, and lastly, complete faith in the Word of our Creator. I know exactly what they are, I know where they come from, and I know what they are trying to accomplish—and I know how to stop them."

"Finally we get to the right topic. Now tell me what they are, and what they're doing here," Carson demanded.

Rock contemplated having Malcolm sign an electronic document of "nondisclosure," but now just wasn't the right time because Carson still was not willing to understand. Providentially, before Rock could say or do anything further, the front door to the diner opened and Sheriff Braxton entered. Several patrons said their hellos to him and he made his way over to Dominic and Malcolm, seating himself at their table. Both watched him as he joined them.

"Well then," said the Sheriff to Dominic, "I've confirmed that you *are* CDC and that you are running the show wherever you say the show is. I've been told by my Captain in Crawfordsville to cooperate, and I am glad to do it if it will get this mess out of here. We've blocked off State Road 234 at the Deer's Mill Bridge and south to the Shades State Park entrance, and we're in the process of evacuating those few homes that are within the perimeter. I've been contacted by Carson's apparently powerful *sponsors*, who all but bribed me into letting Carson's '*monster squad*' stay. But I explained to them that the permits are being temporarily revoked and Carson's group is being moved to Turkey Run until you give the all-clear. Now, I need you to tell me what the danger may be for my deputies so that I can equip my men with appropriate hazmat protection."

"Actually, I need you to move the north roadblock up the hill to where 234 and County Road 879 intersect, just before the turn to Alamo," Dominic said. "I'll also need you to close Sugar Creek to canoeing between the Jim Davis Bridge and the Narrows Covered Bridge that borders Turkey Run. The QNB contaminant is secure, so as long as your men stay at their posts. No hazardous materials will accidentally come in contact with your men, but make sure your deputies are armed, and no man should be stationed alone."

"*QNB*," chuckled Carson. "Sheriff, this man's *contaminant* walks on two legs. He's there for the same reason I am. He's just pulling bigger strings than me. Make him tell you what the contaminant really is."

Braxton looked at Carson for a moment. Carson had rubbed him the wrong way since he showed up. Carson was a self-important celebrity. Braxton had seen his type before, many years ago, when the movie *Hoosiers* was being filmed in the area. He'd met a few of the celebrity types then, and realized that once was enough. Apart from the attention they received from the public, they did not care much for, or about, the local people, or about the fact that they disrupted the lives of thousands. They were interested only in doing their own work and then moving on to the next catered location. Oh, some at least put up a show of being "nice," and perhaps some were, but most were just businessmen caring only for the product, not the people. But Braxton was curious about the reason the CDC chose to show up at the same place and time as Carson's roadshow. So he turned to Dominic and said, "Well?"

"The contaminant is deadly if there is direct contact, Sheriff," spoke Dominic firmly.

"And you can assure me that you will get rid of it all?" asked Braxton.

"That is why I am here," assured Dominic.

"Yeah, removing any sign of it, I'd say, then covering your tracks and making my excursion pointless," Malcolm chimed in.

"Again, we should be finished with this incident within a week, if there are no complications, and Carson's *sideshow* is the first and *foremost complication*," continued Dominic.

"You are cheating me out of the find of the century, Moreau. I'll pull whatever legal strings I can to keep you from stopping me and my work! And I'm gonna find it first," exclaimed Malcolm.

"I am here to dispose of it, Carson. I know your investment in your project, and I know you don't trust me, but I'm doing what has to be done," Dominic said matter-of-factly.

"You're going to kill it! You son of a—" Carson began, but Dominic's cell phone rang out an audible warning. "Bravo emergency distress signal has been activated." Dominic pulled it from its holster while it added, "Thirty-nine degrees, fifty-six hours, twenty-nine point five-two minutes north, by eighty-seven degrees, two hours, fifty-nine point six minutes west. This message repeats."

Dominic cursed to himself, unlocked his Blackberry, and pressed two buttons, putting the phone to his ear and listening. "C'mon, answer!" he said. No answer came, just voicemail, so Dominic canceled the call and pressed two different buttons for speed-dial. "Gene, Mike has initiated a *Code Red* from Carson's site. Move!"

A barely audible voice replied, "Copy that. I received it too. OMW." Then Dominic replied, "Out."

"What on earth?" asked Carson.

"We have an emergency," Dominic said hurriedly. "Sheriff, are you a believer in Jesus Christ?" Dominic asked unabashedly.

"Yep," replied Braxton, with a puzzled look on his face.

"Do you believe in His atonement at the cross, and His resurrection?"

"Yep . . . ," Braxton said again. "Why?"

"Because if you can believe in something that is possible only by the power of God, then I assume that you can trust the rest of His Word as well. What that means is that you may be able to believe in the stuff you have only read about, when you face it . . . . And I expect you'll be facing it soon enough."

Before Braxton could ponder the statement, Nick continued, "We need to get back to Pine Hills now. Chamber a round in your Glock if it isn't already. You lead, sirens all the way," Dominic instructed.

The Sheriff took a deep breath and nodded, getting up and heading for the exit.

"What about me?" Carson asked.

"Pay the bill. Leave a tip." Dominic tossed him a five-dollar bill. "You may follow us to the first roadblock, then stay there until you hear back from me."

"Like that's going to happen," Carson replied, pocketing Rock's five and pulling a ten from his wallet and tossing it on the table, following them out the door as fast as he could.

20

THE AMBUSH

(Excerpt 2 from *History of the Conflict*, by Knightlight Director Bensington Redwood)

As godlessness and the Nephilim prevailed upon the earth, they dominated it, and all but completely corrupted the gene pool of mankind. It was coming close to corrupting the very gene pool which was to produce the Savior of Mankind, and the seed of the woman was required to be spotless before the Lord, acceptable as a pure sacrifice for mankind. But there was one family still genetically pure . . . the family of Noah. Therefore, God pronounced extermination upon the entire world by a composite flood of elements, from above the earth and from within the earth . . . upon all but for that one family that was unpolluted by the issue of the sons of God. God had Noah build a huge ship. After 120 years of building and preaching righteousness to the world, the ship was as ready for the Deluge as mankind was. God, not Noah, chose the representative animals according to their kind. God led them to the ship and instructed Noah to board it. God closed the massive door and had Noah wait seven days in the ark before the Deluge. Nobody was refused passage on the ark, but nobody requested passage, for it had not so much as rained on earth prior to that time. It was the end of the second era on earth, about to give birth to the third. The first was perfect, the second, cursed, and the third, that is the era in which we now exist, and we are feeling the birth pangs of the fourth.

After the seventh day on the ark, with no others desiring salvation, God opened up the Windows of Heaven. That which was in the sky fell, and the deep fountains of the earth burst open, spewing out water, molten rock, and other minerals. The second world died, like a seed does. It germinated under the Deluge, giving birth to a new world, our world. This is the new battleground.

Humanity is at war, immersed in death, and cannot extricate itself from this existence. None are excluded from the field of battle. For humanity's part, there are combatants and casualties, but all are ultimately casualties. The war has raged for several millennia, with many years of combat ahead to endure . . . and few truly understand why. To comprehend the present circumstances, humanity's role in the war, and the origins of it, one must obtain a proper historical context, one must know the story of mankind's existence, what preceded it, how events shaped it and brought it to what we continually refer to as the present. Understanding the past frames the perspective of the "now," and that is a requirement if one is to survive the war, let alone be victorious in it. I have the perspective of centuries, but not I alone.

It has been said that this universe is an unfolding story. It is much more, of course, but it is indeed the grandest of stories where we find ourselves as participants or pawns within. As with all stories, the Author is in complete control, knowing the beginning of the tale and the end, and all events are shaped by the Author. Establishing the rules of engagement, the field of battle, and accommodating free will, the Author affords a modicum of self-determination to the combatants, and has instituted a way for victory and allowed paths for defeat. That single "way" is to consult the "Author" of all, to listen to what He states about it, and most importantly, to trust Him at His Word. To know the Author's design requires that one only listen, and believe.

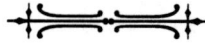

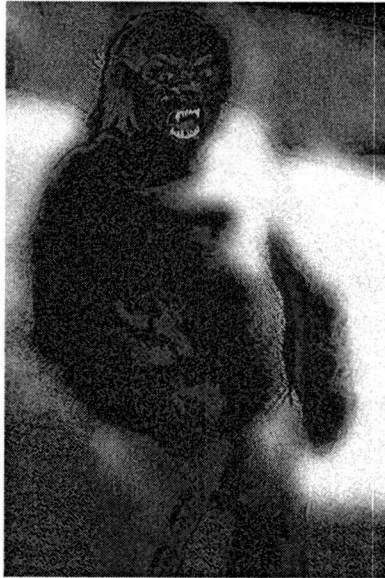

On the way back to Pine Hills, Dominic noticed that the fog had increased greatly, making Braxton's police strobes fill the area around him with dazzling light, nearly blinding Dominic to everything but the vehicle he followed.

Though conscious of the road and the lack of visibility, Nick's concern for his teammate was grave. The EDS was used only in critical rescue/emergency extraction situations. Tick had never issued an emergency distress signal before. He knew he'd beat Cheese to the park by ten minutes or more, so the Sheriff might have to take his place for a short time after they arrived. Then, Rock was sure, the Sheriff would have a *"need to know."*

Carson followed Rock closely, and was blinded to nearly the same degree. Fortunately, the Hummer in front of him blocked the immediate sight from Braxton ahead, but only mostly.

When the three vehicles reached SR-234, they saw that road-closed signage had been posted, only because they were highly reflective signs. They headed west on the State Road and around the curve to pull up next to the Deputy's vehicle that was blockading the road at mid-turn. Braxton stopped and told his men that he and Rock were proceeding to the park. Carson turned off his headlights as he stopped.

"I heard some pretty distant shouting and banging, but you told me to stay here no matter what," said Deputy Caleb Donner.

"You did fine, Caleb. Next time, radio me if there is anything unusual, though. Now, keep with the blockade; we're moving on," was all Braxton said, and they proceeded.

Carson was still following without benefit of headlights, in order to prevent Rock from seeing him follow. It worked, as Rock could no longer see Carson and he kept his attention on the vehicle ahead, while Carson stayed in the shadow of the Hummer. Braxton rode the center line because the road was blocked at both ends, thus no oncoming traffic.

The three vehicles slowed down and made the right-hand turn into the park. It was then that Carson's Land Rover became visible to Rock. That sent a flash of anger across Rock's mind, but because he did not have time to stop and force Carson back, he just continued and hoped Carson would be smart enough to stay in his SUV when they stopped. The longest part of the trip was the five-mile-an-hour ride down to the base of the Devil's Backbone. It was slow and Rock wanted to push Braxton to go faster, but he knew Braxton was going as fast as was safe.

Finally they reached the camp, or at least the area where they had parked before, which was *near* the camp. Men in the dark, thick fog flocked to Braxton's lights shouting and yelling. The three vehicles stopped. Braxton and Rock exited their vehicles and Rock walked up to Braxton as the panicked crypto-biologists swarmed him. Rock heard the slam of a car door behind him and saw that Carson has snuck in under their radar.

"What's going on here?" Braxton shouted as he drew his sidearm and aimed it groundward. Rock, with his Smith & Wesson M&P in his left hand, also pointed to the ground, brandished a bright LED searchlight as the rest, moved beside Braxton.

There were several voices shouting, trying to tell the Sheriff what was happening, but one was John Cosworth, who took over as the other men gathered around the only source of light and safety.

"We were attacked, Braxton. A woman's voice shouted from the top of the Devil's Backbone—I don't even know what language she was speaking—but as soon as she started shouting, rocks were thrown at us from many directions," breathed Cosworth. "As soon as the generator lights went out, and we were just about ready to break camp, we were attacked. We have several injured."

"Where is Agent Cavor?" shouted Rock with the utmost concern.

"I don't know. Until you came we couldn't see anything. They took out our vehicle's lights at the same time it was raining rocks on us! We had to hide under the trucks because even the truck windows were being smashed!"

"Get to the back two vehicles," Rock said, pushing them behind himself. "Move it! Get into Carson's SUV, and mine!"

Braxton reached back into his vehicle and grabbed his black Maglight, turned it on, and closed his door, leaving it unlocked. If need be, he wanted to get to his mounted shotgun quickly.

Then Rock turned to Carson. He was angry, but in complete control of himself. He gave Carson the keys to his Hummer and then he reached into his shirt pocket but didn't find what he was looking for.

"Take everyone back up to the deputies stationed at the south roadblock. Turn left when you hit the road! Tell the deputies to wait for further instructions!" Rock ordered Carson.

Turning back to Braxton, Rock asked, "Do you have hearing protection in your vehicle?"

"No, my shooting bag is back at my office," replied Braxton.

Nodding, Rock motioned to the Sheriff to move, and the two left the group and moved farther down the hill slowly, being instantly swallowed up by the fog, and out of sight.

Malcolm Carson turned to Cosworth, "Here. These are the Hummer keys. My keys are in the Rover. Get everyone in, and go up to the roadblock and stay there. Tell the deputies that the Sheriff instructed them to wait there till he calls."

Carson watched as they all mounted up. It was a tight fit, but all there were able to get in. Malcolm's count was fifteen men, which meant five more were still down at the camp, and another CDC agent was with them. Malcolm stayed behind, climbing into the Sheriff's vehicle, closing the door after him and locking it up tightly.

Rock and Braxton moved down the hill slowly, cautiously, not able to see more than a meter in front of them.

"Turn your flashlight off, and your radio," Rock told Braxton, indicating his shoulder communications radio. "We'll need both in a few minutes, but not now."

Braxton, not really wanting to, complied anyway, not sure why, as two lights are usually better than one . . . perhaps because of the reflectivity of the fog? Braxton was still not sure, but he clipped his torch to his belt.

"Bravo Two," Rock shouted ahead with a commander's authority in his voice, "Sound off!" The order Rock shouted was actually a message to Tick, based on this type of contingency. It was instructing Tick, if he was conscious or within earshot, that he should remain quiet, verbally. If he truly wanted a response from him, he would have yelled out, "Tick, Sound off!"

Rock then began to move at a right angle to the camp. It was a path that was away from both the parked vehicles and the camp. Braxton motioned to him, barely visible, that he was not going in the right direction.

"I know. Follow me," Rock ordered in a lower voice, not wanting the sound of it to carry. The Sheriff complied with that as well, as they continued, making the vehicle, the camp, and themselves become three points of a triangle.

"Bravo Two, sound off!"

There was still no sound ahead, and no false replies.

"Bravo Two?" asked Braxton, following closely.

"A code name for Agent Cavor," said Rock quietly to Braxton. "I'm Bravo One, Ledford is Bravo Three." Then shouting again, "Bravo Two, sound off." And once again as he stopped. Nothing. No footsteps, no distant movement. Traveling about as far as Rock judged was right, he set the spotlight down, and pointed it at an angle from the direction they were going to head next. The tactic was to let a potential enemy believe that they know where you are, while you move elsewhere. Now their lives depended on tactics, unpredictability, and grace above all. The fog muffled all sounds, and at the moment Rock was glad for that much. He knew they were heading into a trap.

They had moved away from the glow of the vehicles and were almost completely away from the glow of the spotlight as well. In the distance, both heard the two SUVs begin pulling out and heading away from the camp. *Less to worry about*, both men thought.

"This is not an ordinary fog, Sheriff," Rock whispered, keeping Braxton near himself so he would not get lost in the darkness.

"What do you mean?"

"Sniff the air," instructed Rock.

The Sheriff sniffed. "Smoke? The campfire?"

"A hint of sulfur—brimstone," Rock said, glad Braxton was keeping his voice down.

"What's that mean?" asked the Sheriff.

"Later," said Rock as the two moved into the camp. Ahead there was a very quiet "ticking" sound, much like one hears when a vehicle's engine is cooling down. That was when Rock identified it as an intentional "rapping" sound, and it wasn't Eminem. It was Morse code. Rock grabbed the Sheriff's wrist with his right hand, pulling him to a low-profile "ducking" position, and made a barely audible "shhhh" sound, indicating that they were finished talking for the time being.

Rock slowly, quietly moved closer to the sound of the rapping. The code heard was a message from Tick. "Ambush," was the first message Rock made out. "Coven, on ridge," was the second message, referring to the danger. "Not hurt," was the third, again referring to himself. "Careful," was the fourth, and then the message stopped, and then began to repeat, then stopped after the message repeated twice.

Rock ignored the last message. They were being as "careful" as possible, and that wasn't always achievable, especially when you have no idea from which direction the enemy might attack. A fallen teammate takes first priority after the danger has passed, so Rock knew that Tick wasn't going to expect him to make a beeline to him, though getting another team member back in play greatly increases survivability.

Rock and Braxton continued to make their way stealthily toward the source of the tapping sound, when Rock stopped. Waiting there for a few moments, Rock began to sense an irrational fear creep up within himself. Fear would have already been present for most people, as he had felt Braxton slightly trembling when Rock had grabbed his wrist. That was a normal response, and for Braxton, it might have also been attributed to his age. But Rock sensed the ancient enemy. It was close, and it was invisible in the cover of the fog. He grabbed the Sheriff's arm, noting that it was trembling greatly now because of the presence of an unseen monster, and pulled him to the ground, and then whispered in his ear, rapidly but distinctly.

"Holster your weapon. Don't move. Don't make a sound. Stay down, and hold your ears shut," Rock commanded the Sheriff, who was beginning to reel from the sensation of fear. But he stayed on the ground and covered his ears as ordered.

Back at the parking area, Malcolm was still in the Sheriff's SUV, crouched down and shaking with a fear he could not explain. It reminded him of his childhood when he slept in his room alone and he'd tuck in the all the blankets at the foot of his bed under his mattress so that a monster could no climb up through the sheets and grab him. He could not remember another time he had been nearly this frightened. He could see nothing in the brightly lit fog around him, and he'd never felt so alone and helpless. Logic and science were of no comfort when there is a paralyzing terror encompassing you, oppressing you, even regressing you to childhood fears. He had never felt spiritual forces of evil before, and though he did not believe in them still, his terror remained.

Back down the hill, Rock rose up from the prone Sheriff and took a practiced side step away from him. Then he outstretched his arms with both hands on his weapon and aimed it to where he perceived he'd left his spotlight, making that his "12-oclock" position. It was very dark, but Rock had an excellent judge of direction, for agents often practice in the dark for that very purpose, and he had steered their course true. Rock steeled himself against the sudden terror he knew was approaching. He wished he had time to impart the details of what they were facing to Braxton, but at least Braxton was down, and had his ears covered.

"Father, be with us," Rock whispered as his prayer.

Immediately, there erupted out from the darkness an earth-shattering howl that made even Rock's knees weak, and chilled his spine. But he resisted it and did not allow his frame to bend or buckle. At almost the instant the howl erupted, there was a loud crash from the same location. Rock, aiming as true as possible to the sound's origin, shouted something that the Sheriff could not understand, and fired at 12:00 then 11:30, then 12:30, then 11:00, then 1:00, then three more back at 12, very fast, very steady. In his mind, within a split second, he knew that was eight shots from the 17+1 load in his 9mm M&P, and he knew he now had 10 HP rounds left before he needed to eject and replace the magazine. He rapidly shot again in the exact same pattern, all of it taking place in a total of six seconds, leaving two rounds in his weapon, one of them chambered.

Rock then, in a fluid series of movements, released the magazine, placed it in his shirt pocket, removed a fully loaded mag from his belt holder, and slapped it home. With one still chambered, he need not rack the slide. Now he was back to 18 rounds aiming into the darkness.

Rock's ears were ringing. He was momentarily deaf, but the Sheriff, who then removed his shaking hands from his ears, was now listening for return fire or retreat. High above them, barely audible, there were sounds of movement, and the sounds did seem to be in retreat. Then, in the direction of his gunfire, the Sheriff heard the heavy thudding of something massive crashing into the woods, breaking branches and tearing through the underbrush, but thankfully in the opposite direction, away from them.

Rock, still holding his weapon out and ready, felt the Sheriff's palm on his shoulder, and his other hand on his extended arms, pressing down gently as a sign that the danger seemed to have passed. He then holstered his weapon.

Knowing that Rock would have trouble hearing, the Sheriff spoke directly into his ear. "They're gone."

Rock nodded, ears still ringing, but very glad for the Sheriff's cooperation and assistance.

He paused a moment, allowing his hearing to return.

"Tick, Sound off," Rock called out.

"Under here," came Tick's muffled voice about forty feet from them.

Miraculously and startlingly fast, the fog became much less dense. Whatever had been accentuating its density was gone. Braxton pulled out his flashlight and the camp was reasonably visible. Behind them, the headlights of the Sheriff's vehicle were also detectable in the still-foggy distance.

The camper that had been Malcolm's office was overturned and had been ripped from the smashed truck's hitch. It lay on its side. Firewood stacked next to it prevented the trailer from crushing Tick, but his leg was still pinned. Others who were remaining still and silent on the ground, at Tick's instruction, began to get up or call out. One had a broken arm, and all of them were bruised and bleeding in various degree from lacerations from the sharp shale stones that had been hurled at them. Fortuitously for their sake, as soon as Tick detected that they were under fire, he shouted for all to get down, stay down, and remain silent until he gave the all-clear. Only five of them obeyed, while the rest of them scattered, running every which way, into limbs, vehicles, generators, trees, and each other. It was total chaos with incoming rocks, a shouting maniac on the ridge spewing incantations, and blind men running all over, with a monster in their midst. It appeared that the monster was there just to scare away the crypto-zoologists, and draw the

Knightlight team into a trap, or all would easily have been killed by the beast. It made no sound as it moved among them, and the horror it generated was stifling. Nobody saw the beast, and perhaps nobody besides Tick knew it was in their midst.

"Let's get this off you," said Rock to Tick, who could now be seen under the trailer.

Rock and the Sheriff went around to the pinch point and lifted it a few inches so that Tick could pull his leg free, which he did. They then went back around and saw that Tick was able to crawl out from under the trailer.

"You came in the *nick* of time, Rock. Thanks," said Tick, hoping his own pun wouldn't be missed. Not being the Big Cheese, his attempts at wordplay usually fell short.

"That's the last time we split up once we arrive at a site. Let's check out the others," said Rock. The Sheriff went to a crypto, while Rock went to another, and then all in turn, making sure all five were accounted for and not seriously hurt.

It was then that Malcolm, somehow now able to move and finally over his great dread, unlocked the Sheriff's SUV and exited the vehicle. He could see better now, and he made his way down toward the destroyed camp, but stayed in the shadows to eavesdrop on the other men.

"Make a call to one of your deputies," Rock instructed the Sheriff. "Have just one of them come down and collect these men and determine who needs to go to the hospital. I don't think anyone needs an ambulance, and I don't want one down here anyway."

"All right," said Braxton, still trying to shake off the event he had just been subjected to. "Do we need the State Police here?"

"No. But this site should have been cleared out minutes after we arrived," said Rock, shaking his head. "This never would have happened if they'd been elsewhere."

"I told Cosworth and Carson to prepare to move this morning. But they had *expanded* their camp by the time I got back, as if they expected their eviction to be overturned. But they were told," said Braxton, who then turned his shoulder radio back on and called his deputies.

"Are you good, Tick?" asked Rock.

"Good enough," said Tick while dusting himself off.

Rock moved away from the camp, pulled out his phone, unlocked it, and made a call into Spectacle. "3rdCav"—shorthand for Third Cavalry—was manning the desk. Rock requested accommodations at the Turkey Run Inn for 20 men, and asked that four FEMA trailers, well stocked for twenty-two men with at least a week's rations, should be delivered to Turkey Run State Park for Carson's team to stay in tomorrow night. He also asked for an on-site cleanup team to be on standby in order to salvage their equipment and supplies and take them to Turkey Run sometime tomorrow. Afterward, they'd have an assessor out there to survey the damage and reimburse Cosworth's expedition for the lost vehicles and equipment at Knightlight's expense. Once on-site, Knightlight takes full responsibility for damages incurred. The attack wasn't the fault of the Crypto-zoologists, even though they should have been gone, but they had yet to be removed from the park, and CQ Petroleum's insurance investigators would not be allowed admittance until the park was reopened. When Rock finished his business, he walked back over to Tick.

"Where's your Blackberry?"

"I dropped it within a minute of the attack. I was using the LED to see, then it was knocked from my hands, and I lost it in the commotion. And I was pinned on top of my weapon and couldn't draw it."

"I'll call it," said Rock. He dialed. It rang four times in Rock's ear, then went to voicemail, but Tick's phone was not heard. Rock locked and pocketed his phone.

"Maybe the battery was knocked loose, or it's broken," said Tick.

"That generator over there," Rock said as he pointed to one of the generators that seemed undamaged in the commotion, "get it started and throw some light on us."

"Q.E.D," said Tick. He walked over to it and unlatched the light armature, raised it, and pressed the start button. In moments, the area was again flooded with light.

"Now you should be able to find your Blackberry," suggested Rock, as he turned to hear Braxton finish instructing his Deputy. Rock then had a thought, and he pulled out his Blackberry again and ran an app on it. It was a limited range point-to-point communications locater with a recently updated map of the area. It showed Rock's position in the center. He pressed the number programmed for the Big Cheese, and since he was apparently within range, it showed his position as well.. Then he selected Tick's number, but because the locater did not report the position, he decided that Tick's phone must be either unpowered or broken.

Malcolm Carson was still shaking. It was horrible, the "primal fear" he had experienced. Nothing had ever given him such an intense emotional reaction of *that* type. He tried to convince himself that it was because of the gunfire that had been blindly expelled in his direction, and not because of the visceral call of the beast, just before it.

"Yes," he told himself, "it was *Knightlight* that had put him in danger from indiscriminate gunfire. That was what caused the fear: mortal danger. The creature's roar was because it too sensed the danger Moreau brought with him."

Malcolm believed at that moment that he must work around, even against, the agent. That belief was what gave Malcolm the strength to move again. And then sudden realization came to him: He *had* heard the creature! It would have been visible if not for the fog. It was *here*! His mission must continue because his prize was there to grasp. Now that the lights were on, he stepped out of the shadows and approached his injured biologists, asking whether they were all right, and suspiciously watching the agents as well. Then he looked over the trucks that had been damaged in the attack and judged them to still be roadworthy after his brief visual inspection. After that, he walked over to Rock, steeling himself against his anger at the agent, and shaking the last of the fear that still held its grip.

"What happened to my equipment?" Carson asked without belligerence.

"The question, Carson, is what are *you* still doing here?" asked Rock.

"I sent the others away, and they were packed tight. There was no room for me unless I rode on the luggage rack. I sat in the Sheriff's car and waited," said Carson.

"Fine," said Rock. "Braxton's called in his Deputy to ferry the rest of your men out of here. Those who are in need will be taken into Crawfordsville, since that's the nearest hospital. Fortunately, nobody was seriously injured."

"Injured by *what? That's what I want to know.* What was going on down here? Who attacked them?" asked Malcolm.

"We'll talk about it with the Sheriff, shortly. First we have to get your men out of here for medical attention," said Rock, knowing now he'd absolutely have to get signed non-disclosure agreements for Carson and Braxton. Now *explanations* were in order.

"Well, I'm going to stay with the Sheriff. Until he goes, I'm staying," said Carson, all the while plotting a way to proceed with his capture of his Agnostopithecus. He did not have a complete plan, but he was working on it. He knew that Crystal and Agent Ledford would be here in moments. Ledford could drive the Land Rover out for them, and Crystal and he could each drive a truck, taking them to Turkey Run and making sure that the biologists had transportation. The plan required mobility, and that much should be easy to accomplish. The plan needed more thought and more information, but it was a necessity, for there were things that Knightlight did not yet know about the site and its surroundings. And there were absolutely things that he didn't want the agents to know about it.

The Big Cheese and Crystal in the Outback arrived at the parking area, and Cheese ran down to the campsite, noting that Tick seemed OK. Crystal followed and met with her father.

"What happened?" the Cheese asked Rock.

"We are evacuating the camp. Explanations will follow when the Sheriff is back here."

Then the Deputy's car came down the trail, stopping just behind the Outback; the five injured men climbed in, and the Sheriff waved the Deputy on, telling him to get out of there. Then Braxton came back over to Rock, Tick, and the Big Cheese, and the Carsons also moved over to the trio.

On his way to join the CDC three, Braxton detoured toward the place where he and Rock had set down Rock's spotlight. It was the very place where that unearthly howl roared forth, with the sounds of destruction that had followed. He shone his light ahead of him, and he saw that one of the lighting generators had been smashed. Braxton knew that no single man could lift one of those, nor could several strong men lift and toss it with a force that would destroy it as completely as it clearly was destroyed. It was frightening as he realized that he and Agent Moreau were obviously the intended targets of the attack. All of this, all the events going on here, was completely foreign to him and had sufficiently scared the tar out of him. But Agent Moreau seemed to know exactly what was happening and how to respond to it, while confusion, fog, and sheer terror prevented Braxton from being useful at all.

"OK," said Rock. "You all want an explanation, so let's caravan to the Sheriff's office, where it's safe—just the Sheriff, my team, and the Carsons. Understand that what we disclose to you is classified."

"I should have known you were B.S.-ing back at the diner. This had better be good," said Carson.

Ignoring Carson, Rock continued. "At the roadblock, where Carson's crew has been taken, any who are not injured can ride to the Turkey Run Inn, where they'll have rooms already available for them."

"Crystal and I will each take one of the trucks—the two that still have the windshields," said Malcolm. "Agent Ledfield, if you please, follow us in our Land Rover."

"No problem," said Cheese, ignoring the mispronunciation of his name.

"Then let's roll, and you'll get your explanation," said Rock.

"Good," said Carson, "because I want to know what's happening!"

21

NO TIME TO LIE

(An excerpt from *Darkness Now*, a published work of Christopher Griffin)

Authenticity and Validity.

Question: How can one discern Truth among all the religions in this world?

Answer: Because only one has the very signature of God.

The Bible is unlike any other document on this planet because its Author is not of this earth. The Word of God is Holy, but was given to be handled by and to wash the tarnished hands of man. It is simplistic in revealing the Creator to persons of little understanding, yet unfathomable to those who do not believe. By design, the humble can comprehend what the self-exalted cannot, and the corporate intelligence of the world is confounded by the faithful.

Beyond the explicit and candid testimonies of the many writers of this book, there is a more sure way to trust the authorship of the Bible, and the Author Himself. Prophecy is the signature of God. Prophecy is the speaking forth of Truth, in a way that man cannot. God exists above and beyond this universe and knows the past, present, and future from all perspectives, since He was, is, and will be there already. To God, our lives are as a tale told. Conversely, mankind can barely discern the present from his own limited perspective. He knows even less concerning history beyond his life span, and cannot foretell the future beyond educated conjecture. The only way one can speak of things that have not yet happened, with accuracy, is for the speaker to exist beyond the here and now, where such things can be known, and by Someone who has the power to know it, command it, and relate it to us. Although demons can reveal the present, and the past, with great detail and accuracy, only God knows the future—perfectly.

God authored the message of His prophets. He sent them to relay His Truth with His signature on it. Israel was instructed by God to discern whether a person calling himself a "prophet" was indeed a prophet, by whether or not his sayings came to pass exactly as foretold. If he was wrong only once while claiming he spoke for God, he was branded a "false prophet," and his judgment was severe. We may feel free to use the Word of God as the standard against any fortuneteller, soothsayer, psychic, false science, politician, or teacher, and any who would attempt to pervert and subvert history itself. Above all, it is a fixed "yardstick" to be held against any person claiming to have authority to speak of future events—including the future of our global climate—but especially those claiming to be a spokesman for God.

The Bible has prophetic messages throughout, and one-third of the text on balance is prophetic. The most outstanding evidence of God's authorship is where prophecy can be accurately dated in origin, and incremental periods can be documented toward fulfillment. Several of these amazing examples are found in the prophetic book of Daniel, including an in-depth foretelling of Alexander the Great, but I'll focus on chapter 9 and couple it with history. Following is a study of it with just a little prophetic knowledge. (Hint: 70 "weeks" equals 70 "7-year periods" totaling, as it unfolds, into a nonconsecutive time period of 490 years, remembering that a 360-day Babylonian calendar was contemporary when it was written, and lastly adding a history book for reference. Those are all the facts needed to understand the discussion.) The prophecy is divided first into a period of 7 weeks, or 49 years, for the Jewish temple to be rebuilt, from a specific time mark: the day the decree goes out to rebuild the temple. Next, add 62 weeks, or 434 years, until the Messiah was to come to them to remove their sins, and for Him to be cut off. So 69 weeks have passed, or 483 years, and that took us straight to Christ's Triumphal entry, and crucifixion—atonement for the sin of Israel, and all mankind, where "Messiah was cut off." That is where the prophecy breaks its consecutive order. Now there is only 1 week, or 7-year period, left to be fulfilled. It will happen in your lifetime, perhaps mine. It will begin when the true Christians aren't able to hinder this "world system of evil," by reason of absentia. It will begin at a time of contractual peace between Israel and Muslim nations, lasting half of the prophetic week, 3.5 years, and during that time, the Jewish Temple will be rebuilt, and consecrated, and a wall will separate it from the Dome of the Rock. It will usher in a new religion, a new economy, and a new way of identification. Then the Dark Messiah will call himself God, from the Jewish Temple, stopping further sacrifices, at which point, all Hell literally breaks loose on the earth. The wrath of God will be poured out on the earth, and in the heavens, culminating in

Christ's return. Although no man currently knows the year of Christ's return, He nevertheless is coming.

Then the dead, great and small, will be judged, and the faithful will be rewarded, but the unfaithful will get their wish: eternity apart from the Love of God. Are you ready, my friend, to face a Righteous God with the works you have wrought in your life, or are you trusting in the provision for your sin—the Righteousness of Christ Himself? He is coming back, but don't take my word for it . . . you have His signature on it!

It was a full hour coordinating the transfer of Carson's crypto-zoologists to the park's hotel, getting them settled in, checking up on the injured (none had serious injuries), and then returning to Waveland and finally arriving at Sheriff Braxton's office. Tick quietly told Rock and the Big Cheese what had happened, but spoke as little to others as possible for that hour, waiting for the privacy of Braxton's office. The Sheriff knew he had to say something to the other crypto-zoologists to explain what had happened, so he said that a biker gang was suspected and were currently being rounded up, assuring them that there would be prosecutions once arrests were made. Malcolm bit his tongue until he had heard the Knightlight trio's "story," but promised nothing beyond temporary collusion.

The Sheriff's post was a series of adjoining rooms leased from a local lawn-mower distribution company. It had no jail, and usually no more than two officers at any given time.

At the office, Braxton allowed Rock to connect his tablet PC with the wireless network for access to his laser printer while Braxton himself gathered chairs around his desk, taking his own seat behind it. After three sheets were printed, Rock put the tablet away and handed a sheet to Braxton, one to Crystal, and then another to Malcolm.

"What's this?" asked Malcolm, looking at the nondisclosure form even after he recognized it for what it was.

"The price of admission," said Rock. "You can wait out in the truck if you don't want to sign it."

Crystal grabbed a pen off the Sheriff's desk, signing the paper immediately, returning the pen, and handing Rock the completed form. Braxton followed suit and then Malcolm reluctantly did the same.

"Now, Agent Moreau, what happened at the site?" asked Braxton.

"I know I was being shot at," exclaimed Malcolm.

"Carson, shut your mouth, and show some respect in my office," said Braxton. "Agent Moreau was the only one firing his weapon and it was not at you, or even in your direction. As near as I can tell, the only reason you're still alive, *after we told you not to even be there*, is because Moreau knew what he was doing, while your 'highly trained team of biologists and trackers' were running around like the Keystone Cops. Now shut up and listen to Agent Moreau."

Rock was really beginning to like Braxton. Braxton was beginning to detest Malcolm. Crystal was even more interested in Moreau now. Tick was hungry, and for some reason had a craving for corn, and was still somewhat shaken, while the Cheese was still mentally banging his head.

"First, Sheriff, we *are* CDC as we've claimed, and you've verified that our credentials are valid, but we are detached to a National Security organization called Knightlight. That's Knightlight with a *K*, just to be clear," Rock said.

Crystal rolled her eyes at her own ignorance. She spent the morning searching for Nightlight and Monroe. She slapped her own inner forehead.

"Problem?" asked Rock of Crystal.

"No," she said, realizing her facial expression had drawn Moreau's attention. "I was thinking of something stupid I did earlier. I mean, nevermind. Sorry. Go ahead and continue," she verbally stumbled. She slapped her inner forehead again, but this time not externalizing it.

"Anyway, Sheriff, we work within all Federal agencies, even the military, and are credentialed within each. We are professionals, and our job is to protect and defend everyone possible from precisely what has been happening in this area, and eliminate the threat. What you *need to know* is that you have a coven or cult '*cell*' in the area. Agent Cavor heard the leader of the cell casting spells from atop the Devil's Backbone, and whoever the followers were, they were devoted enough to attempt homicide on command. Are you aware of any Wiccan or Satanic cults in these parts?"

"We've been briefed on how to identify their existence, and there may be a few individuals who would fit the profile," said Braxton, "but until now there hasn't been any clear evidence of criminal activity. But we haven't done much in the way of investigating them. Witchcraft is technically a protected practice under the Constitution."

"Until they cross the line, you are correct, Sheriff. But I'm fairly certain that with a little work, you may even be able to link past crimes to these members. At any rate, they are now an overt danger to this community," said Rock. "Anything to add to that, Agent Cavor?"

"Their leader is a woman, from the sound of the voice, and must be between the age of 35 and 50. I'd also guess that there were fifteen to twenty followers with her tonight, by the degree of the rock barrage," Tick said.

"I'll talk to my Captain and we'll get something going on it. I've got a few names that may kick the door open. We can try to get prints off some of the rocks and maybe sweep for fibers on the ridge."

"That won't be necessary," said Rock. "I need you to handle what you can *outside* the park. We'll handle the interior and let you know what we find."

Although Braxton only nodded, inwardly he was relieved that he would not have to oversee a forensics team within the park. He'd go back in *if* it were *absolutely necessary*, but he wouldn't like it. Not after the fright he'd experienced that evening.

"That's all this is," Malcolm asked in disbelief, "a bunch of New Age hippies throwing their crystals at the camp? And we need the CDC for that? Give me back that nondisclosure form. This is ridiculous and a waste of my time."

"And which New Age hippy do you suppose let out that *howl* while using a 500-pound generator like a club?" asked Braxton.

"Maybe your *Wicked Witch of the West* is dating a werewolf," said Carson, rolling his eyes and not taking any of this seriously.

"Dad, just quit it and hear these men out," Crystal said. She loved he father, but he sure could be a mule.

"All right, maybe she got her followers to knock over the trailer, and hoist the generator up in a tree and drop it to scare us outta here. They could have been using the same kinda night vision we use to coordinate the attack. Maybe the *howl* was a recording," Malcolm suggested.

"I wish that was all it was, Carson; however I know the smell, the sound, and the *feel* of what I was shooting at, and it wasn't any man or group of men," said Rock. "Sheriff, I'm sorry to say that it appears you have what we call a Nephil-Adam loose in the parks."

"Neffil what?" asked Braxton.

"It's a *monster*, Sheriff, plain and simple. Let me explain," said Rock. He knew that the word was nothing Braxton would recognize, and certainly the Carsons wouldn't have that in their lexicon.

"What you felt and heard earlier was a creature that is not a part of nature. You were gripped by a *spiritual* fear, a supernatural attack, and the howl that you felt nearly liquefying your vertebrae was straight from Hell," said Rock.

"So, Carson is right then?" asked Braxton.

"Of course I'm right. It's been about my Agnostopithecus all along! Moreau is just trying to scare you with his religious nonsense, but if that howl was anything monstrous, it was my Sasquatch," said Malcolm.

"Then we shall find out who is right, and who is dead," the Cheese chimed in, quoting a line from *The Princess Bride*. Then, seeing Rock's stern look, he added, "Sorry."

"No, that's not what I meant," said the Sheriff to Malcolm. "You were right about the toxic gas being a coverup. I was just pointing that out for your benefit."

"That too," said Malcolm, confidently relishing the fact that it was he, not Moreau, who the Sheriff acknowledged was correct.

"Yes, Sheriff," Rock admitted. "The gas *was* a cover story, a lie, to clear the area so we could put the beast down as secretly and securely as possible. I don't like the lies, but they are part and parcel of our covert deployment." Then to Carson he added, "But you are *still wrong* about the creature, Carson. You are *completely wrong about it*. I told you the truth earlier, but you weren't listening."

"Then enlighten me, please. Convert me to your *religion*, and I am sure I'll understand it. Don't forget that I'm just a stupid scientist. What do I know about *anything*?" Malcolm spoke sarcastically. Crystal nudged him to let him know he was being a complete jerk.

"Are you an ass, an idiot, or what?" asked Braxton. "The fact that we signed the nondisclosure form was an admission of the cover story, nothing more. Shut your face-hole and listen to the man, or I'll put you out in my car and handcuff you there until we're done."

Malcolm, being verbally slapped like that, was speechless, and that was the best thing for him, because the Sheriff wasn't bluffing.

Braxton intuitively knew that Rock and his men were experienced, skilled, and knowledgeable about what was going on. He had actually tried to be nice to Carson, letting him know that perhaps for once in his life he'd been right about *something*, but he certainly didn't want to fan the flames of his ego.

"Please continue, Agent Moreau," said the Sheriff.

"You might start at David, Agent Moreau," Tick suggested. "That's a good starting point since even this *scientist* must have heard about it . . . it was in all the papers."

"Roger that," said Rock in agreement. "The account of David and Goliath in the Bible isn't a story; it's history. Goliath of Gath was a Philistine warrior. But he wasn't just a man, as he was only *half*-human. His stature was at least nine feet and he was mean and fearsome. He challenged the entire Hebrew army, and his very presence terrified them. King Saul, the *giant* of Israel, who though completely human stood a whole head higher than any other Israelite at the time, was dwarfed by Goliath's stature and was sent cowering in his tent at the sound of the giant's bellowings. None in the Israelite army dared meet Goliath's challenges, and all in the army were afraid of him. But David, the youngest son of Jesse, a shepherd, was not afraid. He had faced lions and bears and protected his flock with great skill and fearlessness. David convinced King Saul to let him face Goliath. The King allowed it. David picked up five smooth stones and went out to face the giant. The giant boasted and cursed David's God, but David faced him in the name of the Lord of Hosts. Goliath challenged him, and David ran at him and launched a single stone at the forehead of the giant, felling him. David then took Goliath's sword and removed the giant's head with it. This is history, not a parable, not a metaphor, not a fable."

"It's a mildly entertaining story, nothing more. I heard these stories in Sunday School as a child. I didn't buy them then, and I'm not buying them now," said Malcolm.

"David was real, regardless of your ignorant denial. Even secular history corroborates it, like it corroborates the Bible on balance. David needed only one stone to kill the giant, but he took five stones with him. Do you know why, Malcolm?"

"No, but I'm sure you're going to tell me," Malcolm replied.

"Goliath was only one of five giants in his family. By the practiced tradition of the time, if you slay a man, the family has an obligation to avenge the death. David went out that day prepared to face five giants, not just one. Now, the word used for 'giant' in Goliath's family's case is the Hebrew word 'Rephaim.' It is not a term for a normal human being. These were fierce giant creatures that were human/demonic hybrids empowered with great strength, and as they aged, if they were allowed to age, they became monstrous in appearance as well as in demeanor. Even now they live very long, are very strong, and are very intelligent, but their strength and longevity comes from their demonic parentage, and the terror they inspire is *spiritual*. They are real. They have been of old, and were exterminated in the Deluge of Noah. They came back, though, and even spawned entire tribes. When Moses was to lead the Hebrews into the Promised Land of Canaan, after leaving Egypt and receiving the law, spies were sent into the land and they came back with a report stating that it was inhabited by *giants*. The word used there is 'Nephiyl.' The word for man is 'Adam,' or 'A-*dom*," which explains the term I mentioned: Nephil-Adam, or a half Demon, half man. With very few exceptions, they are *all monster*. *That* is your Agnostopithecus, Malcolm, not an evolutionary misfit—a powerful demonic force in the flesh. It is related to mankind more than you could even have guessed. You are up against something dark, physically and spiritually dominant, that loves to kill and terrorize mankind. This one is being assisted by a local cult, and that means it is intending to use this area for procreation of more Nephil-Adamic monsters."

"Horse hockey," said Malcolm, and for once he quoted something he was aware of: Col. Sherman T. Potter of *M*A*S*H*.

"And you can kill it?" asked Braxton.

"In the name of the Lord of Hosts, the name of Jesus, the Christ, and by the power of God's Holy Spirit, we mean to," answered Rock honestly and surely to Braxton, as a brother would express his certainty to his own kin.

"Good," said the Sheriff. "How?"

"As David did: with one smooth stone to the head. We are specifically trained and skilled for this work. We can get the job done if we don't have to worry about casualties. And, like David, we remove the head afterward, then cremate the body. These monsters are hard to kill . . . *very hard*. And even if they have a head wound, they are not above playing dead long enough to rise, seemingly from the *dead*, and kill you while you're celebrating your victory. Removal of the head ends all possible doubt. The stones we use against them are often hollow-point bullets, but we have an arsenal of many weapons at our disposal. We are well equipped for this business, and it looks like business is booming here," said Rock.

"In point of fact," chimed in Tick, "we are at war with them, the ones who prove themselves to be murderous anyway, and we do it on your behalf," he said, nodding his head toward the Carsons.

"And at our expense, no doubt," ridiculed Malcolm. "Our government pays you to exterminate the Sasquatch, and to keep me and other scientists under control. You are like a bunch of jackbooted thugs, following your marching orders to exterminate an entire species of primate that is the great mystery of the past century. And you justify it with religious myth."

"Actually, the money comes from a private foundation," countered Rock. "We rely on our government for accreditation, fuel, and as a store for weaponry trial, and purchase, but your tax support is roughly one dollar for every ten thousand dollars from the foundation. It's negligible. We allow it only because it keeps us on the books as an accredited agency."

"You've told us *where* they came from," spoke Crystal Carson, "at least according to the Bible, but you didn't mention *why* they are here. I am not a believer, so don't get me wrong, but doesn't the Bible tell the *why*s of things? I mean isn't *why* the point of it all?" she asked in earnestness.

"Very astute of you, Miss Carson," Rock said in appreciation of her honesty. "You are quite correct, and I might add, a refreshing change of pace compared to your father. The fact of the matter is that the Bible *does tell us why*. There is much, much more to the story of the Nephil-Adam than what I've said, but I don't have time to tell you *everything* I know, or I would. But regarding *this* particular event we are investigating, it is pretty clear why. Its M.O. indicates that it intends to assist in the rape of a human or humans, by demonic forces, in order to add to an army for future deployment. An army is being built at this very moment all around the world. This is by design and it has an ancient orchestrator, but even he will step aside for the final Emperor who will soon be arising. There will be one last empire that will subjugate all of mankind. The Nephil-Adam are being bred to be warlords, generals, commanders, and captains who will lead an array of armies for the final *world ruling government*, and they mean business."

"I'd like to point out, if I can," said the Big Cheese, "that these beasts won't allow themselves to be your father's captive 'mascot.'"

Crystal did not know what to make of this. She too was a scientist, and believed that the Bible and all religions were nice, as long as they were not taken too seriously. She knew wars often resulted from religions clashing with other beliefs and practices. She did not see that only one of them could be the True and Righteous Faith if any of them could be. She wanted peace on earth, and goodwill toward men, as long as she wasn't forced to partake in the faith itself. She believed that she was too *evolved* and educated to be taken in by such nonsense, but she didn't have the visceral dislike for Christianity that her father obviously had. His hatred actually made her sympathetic for these agents' obvious faith in the *why* of these creatures' existence. *Why* was the only answer in life that eluded her. She understood causality, but nothing in her scientific belief system even answered the simple *why*s in life, let alone the complex ones. It left her with a sense that something more was out there, but she could not grasp it, and in truth, she never actually *tried* to grasp it.

"Well, suppose," Crystal began to Malcolm, "just suppose there is an explanation for the Sasquatch kind within legends and myth. Often we find the facts behind the stories by examining them and finding a common thread. Even you give credence to tribal history . . . so why should we exclude Biblical history if it assists in giving us more insight into our anthropological investigation of the genus?"

"Because it's just stupid. A couple references in the Bible could be interpreted many different ways and probably has nothing to do with what we're hunting," said Malcolm.

"Agent Moreau, why would a God of Love allow such creatures to exist? If they are dangerous, and He is all-powerful, why doesn't He simply rid us of them?" asked Crystal. The question was a classic. Rock was surprised that it did not come up when he spoke with Malcolm earlier.

"Why does God allow bad things to happen to good people?" asked Rock as confirmation.

"Well, yes," she replied.

"Simple, Ms. Carson. There are none good but God, and that includes you and me. Man is reprobate, and though he can do good, from time to time, he is impure. Impure is unclean, and therefore misses the standard of righteousness required to even approach a Holy God. If we are not good by that standard, then we are evil . . . to varying degrees, but evil still. God is Love, but Love hates evil. Sin is evil. Mankind is governed by sin. This world bears the consequences of mankind's sin. It tends toward death and sorrow now, whereas it used to tend toward life and joy. It can be seen in nature—animals killing each other—but is best seen in the heart of mankind. It separates us from direct contact with Him. Righteousness cannot tolerate unrighteousness, and vice versa, but those abiding in unrighteousness can still be saved. He's made provision for that by coming to us in the form of His own Son, because of His love for us. And . . . beyond that, He allows some good to come to all. We have air, food, shelter, family, life. He has even provided my team to protect and defend all men, regardless of degree of sin, should they allow it." Then he turned to Malcolm. "And even to protect sinners who would not willingly allow it."

"Sin," replied Crystal, "seems to be a subjective term, and can have many interpretations."

"I'll define it. It's missing the mark. Here is a metaphor explaining it: You are an expert archer for a king. The king makes the rules, and even he abides by them. And the king loves you, treats you like his daughter, and says that your duty is simply to shoot a target. You must hit the target in the red, but the target is all red and is fifty feet in diameter. If you hit the target every time, you continue to be treated like family, but if not, you are out of the kingdom, doomed to die. Though if you miss, you are at fault, because the target is only one inch away from you. You are able to hit it every time. But then you tell the king that you don't want him anymore, you want to find your own way in life, and you choose to miss the target, finding yourself naked, outside the kingdom. If you try to enter it again, you are to be slain. That is his law. The law shows you that you cannot reach the king no matter what you do, and now, you cannot even hit the target either because you are no longer in sight of it. Remember, unless you hit the mark every time, you are not welcome, and you've already missed it. However, since the king loves you, he condescends to become an archer on your behalf and hits the target for you. But still, you cannot enter the kingdom under penalty of death because you already missed the target. The king sends a messenger who gives you a letter telling you that you may come back to the kingdom, *if* you receive the missive given to you. Next, the king takes the penalty of death for you. He dies for you, and now you, after claiming the message sent to you, are welcomed back into the kingdom. Since the king is actually stronger than death itself, he greets you as you come back into the kingdom. That, in essence, is the entire Gospel."

"Gospel Shmospel. It is **MY HUNT**, *Knightlight*. I have the permits, I have the equipment, I have the training, I have the **RIGHT**," shouted Carson angrily.

"I am sorry, Mr. Carson," Rock said with authority, "I thought you would understand by now that you are no longer hunting *anything* here. You are off the reservation until we've finished, so you are welcome to stay at Turkey Run at our expense, but your part in *this* hunt has ended," said Rock.

"I have permits and the law on my side, *Knightlight*, and CQ has all the lawyers it needs to force the issue," Carson spat. "This is still a free country, and my scientific pursuit is above reproach, and above *you specifically*. I'm not only going to get my Sasquatch, I'm going to show this animal to the world and discredit your organization without having to say a single word about it publicly."

Rock felt the old adrenaline rush and began to get the shakes, but he fought against them. Some might call it a form of stage fright, but Rock knew it was pure adrenaline, and it came from Mayberry. Barney Fife was not welcome, but somehow, the Deputy always seemed to get in. He clenched his teeth against Fife, and furrowed his brow . . . it only served to make him look very angry. Rock could teach others without a problem. He could say whatever was on his mind, casually, with his brothers, but confrontations seemed to be an ever-living source of frustration for him. He was fine earlier with

Carson's confrontation at the diner, which is why he was wondering why he wasn't still "fine." He knew that confrontations happen: it's just a fact of life. But he sure wished he'd never have to feel the spirit of Don Knotts creeping into his veins. It was a specific "thorn in the flesh" for Rock, Biblically speaking, but he still had to finish his business with Malcolm, Crystal, and the Sheriff, so he pressed on.

"If you were to encounter a nonbelligerent Nephil-Adam for capture, you would find out exactly how rapidly it can become belligerent," Rock promised sternly, still shaking slightly. "Then it would tell you just how it was going to rip off your head and shove it up your poop-chute, and lastly it would demonstrate it. I've now explained all you *need* to know about them, but I can't *understand it for you.*"

"I think we're done here," said the Sheriff, seeing Moreau's shakes and believing them, incorrectly, to be a precursor to violence. "Mr. Carson, you and your team will be allowed in the park when these men have given me the all-clear. Are you staying with your team at Turkey Run?"

"No," said Crystal, "We're here in town at the bed-and-breakfast on Main Street."

"OK, then," said Braxton, "Agent Moreau, your team has full control of the parks, and I would appreciate it if you would give me periodic updates to let me and my deputies know whatever we need to know. I don't want my deputies to be in any danger without them knowing why."

"Agreed, Sheriff. Thank you for your time and professionalism," said Rock, as the Sheriff rose and shook his hand. "Mount up," he said to Cheese and Tick. The three of them left the office and headed back to the Beiler farm, while the Carsons followed them out but went the opposite directing, driving up the hill and over to their B&B. Braxton saw them out of the office, and then returned to his desk and sat for a moment. His hands, he noticed, were also beginning to shake and the effects of the evening began to unsettle him physically. He had been terrified this evening and he realized that his office was only five miles from the park. The thought was less than comforting to him. He pulled his desk drawer open and pulled out a bottle of Pepto-Bismol, taking a big pull on it. Then he got up and his stomach began to churn. He rushed to the small bathroom in the back of his office, and vomited.

22

Make Ready the Hunt!

(From the notes of First Agent Christopher Griffin)

There are but two races on this planet, and they have nothing to do with skin color. They have everything to do with parentage. Humans are one race, one blood, one creation in the image of God. In contrast to the above, the human race wastes its time in this world dividing itself against itself, and all suffer for it. But the enemy is pleased by it. Racial feuds about melanin content are the most childish of disagreements between humans, but the focus men place on mere appearance occupies and distracts them efficiently. The content of one's character no longer matters once racial strife is engaged. If the world knew what was happening behind the scenes, they would choose sides, though sides are already chosen without regard to their awareness of all choices. Ignorance of the law does not excuse the lawless—the Law of Grace abides still. Sides are chosen each day, every day, changed and even rechosen, though choice is a gift, not a right. One day soon the choices men make will be irrevocable. That day may be today for some, but one day soon it will be too late for any to change sides. Choose this

318

day whom you will serve—as for me and my house, we will serve the Lord.

╬══════╬

The Knightlight Hummer stopped on the gravel drive of the Beiler house, letting Tick and the Cheese out to follow Rock back to the park to set up the mobile field unit. Tick piloted the huge vehicle, while the Cheese rode shotgun. The fog was still omnipresent, but it was light compared to what they had previously encountered. Rock pulled out of the driveway, with his team chasing, and they made their way past Waveland, past the Deputy station at Shades, and into the Pine Hills entrance. Since there was a clearing made ready by the crypto-zoologists, Rock parked his Hummer there and pointed the way for Tick to park the mobile base near where the crypto camp had been, but off toward where the demolished generator lay. Rock rationalized that it already smelled like human traffic, gasoline, and gunpowder, so they wouldn't be adding any new smells to the area.

The truck was parked, leveled, anchored, and almost completely camouflaged within half an hour of their arrival, but they were rushed, so no traps or threads were deployed around the vehicle at the time, as they usually would have done. However, the mobile base's self-defenses were quite ample, so nobody worried. They wanted to see whether there was a blood trail to follow, and if so, the faster they followed, the better their chances were. Rock had no way of knowing at the time whether he'd actually struck the monster with his weapon's discharge earlier, but if so, they were prepared to track it with ultraviolet lighting and optics. And if not, there still might be a residual pheromone trail to follow, if they were lucky.

The Cheese was getting energy drinks for the three from the truck. Cheese chose a Red Bull for himself, though Rock preferred the Monster—Green—and Tick liked a Starbucks "double-shot." He called it his "Beverage of Justice."

"You called us just in time," said Rock to Tick, while placing the final anchor on the camo. "The Sheriff and I almost didn't make it back to the park in time."

"I what?" asked Tick.

"You sent out the distress signal none too soon, amigo," said Rock, helping Tick anchor the huge vehicle's camouflage.

"I didn't send one out, Rock, and I haven't located my Blackberry yet," Tick said honestly.

"Oh, no . . . hold on," Rock said, taking out his own Blackberry, bringing up the point-to-point tracker and looking at the mini-map overlay on the small LCD display. "This shows that your phone is now on, and it's about a mile away from here. Great . . . someone not only took your phone during the attack, but whoever it was must have been the one who sent in the Code Red. That means three things have happened, and all of them are bad news."

"No way," said Cheese, who was within earshot. He walked over to the other two with the drinks.

"The first thing it means is that they know our protocols, and how to send a valid Code Red," said Tick.

"Yes," said Rock, shaking his head. "That alone tells me that we have a *mole* in the organization, and *this group* that attacked us has direct ties to our mole," he said. He now knew that it could jeopardize the entire mission and had already put them all at grave risk. And not just themselves, but perhaps the entire organization.

"Well, I'll be dipped," Tick said. "They're sophisticated and organized MacLaines. OK, what's the second *bad news* thing?"

"They want us to follow them into another ambush. Just us specifically," said Rock, holding his phone so that the other two could see. "The transponder tracking signal is still active. If they know our protocols, they know we can track them by your Blackberry. It was off last time I checked, but now it is on."

"And the third?" asked Tick.

"They know exactly where *we are*," he said. "I just tracked your BB, but made it possible in doing so for them to trace *my* BB. Fortunately, they don't have Tick's MFB password, which means they don't know how to disable the defenses on our mobile base to gain entry, so we should be safe while we're here, and we should still be mostly invisible if they show up on-site."

"Who would betray us?" asked Cheese.

"I have a thought about that," said Rock. He selected the two-way channel for Knightlight HQ at the bunker.

"Spectacle, this is Bravo One. Patch me through to First Agent," he said into his phone.

He waited, but nobody answered him.

"Spectacle, this is Bravo One. Do you copy?"

Nothing.

"Cheese, you try," ordered Rock.

Cheese pulled out his phone and tried his comms.

"Spectacle, this is Bravo Three. Do you copy?"

Nothing. Cheese tried again. Still nothing.

"Get in the truck and use the satellite comms, Cheese," Rock said.

"Roger that," spoke the Cheese, already moving to the truck.

"Are we being jammed, or is Spectacle being jammed, or is it that communications just suck way out here?" asked Tick.

"No way to be sure, but I am reading your phone, so point-to-point is still working locally. If we're being jammed, we are being *selectively jammed*," said Rock.

"If they are throwing that much signal out, it should be easy to pinpoint them," replied Tick.

"Agreed, but I bet it's near the location of your Blackberry, just southwest of the park. Let's suit up and get ready to walk into an ambush while Cheese tries to make contact."

The two went inside the back of the truck and closed the gate behind them, sealing themselves from the outer world. Rock and

Tick suited up in their cool suits. These covered all but the eyes, but could cover them as well with mesh, by the pull of a flap. The light and thin cool suit was designed to mask body heat so that they would not appear visible in the infrared spectrum. Over that they put on their light armor suit, gun belts, and holsters. Lastly, they donned their steel-plated gumboots, as well as their Kevlar helmets, which had both UV and IR, with retractable optics, lighting, and comms.

Rock placed his reloaded S&W M&P in his left holster, and placed its sister in his right. He added extra mags to his shoulder pockets, two on each side, and an M&P silencer/suppressor in each hip pocket. Then he took a suppressed AR-15 from the gun rack, checked the "star-light" optics on it, and was ready.

Tick was armed similarly, but he preferred the 1911 sidearms, and he grabbed the suppressed sniper rifle from the case. They were entirely black-clad, in nonreflective gear, and they looked like a pair of deadly, armored techno-ninjas who were armed to the teeth.

The Big Cheese entered the room shaking his head, while the other two sprayed liberal amounts of scent neutralizer on each other.

"Nothing's getting through," Cheese announced. "No cell, no sat, no SW, only point-to-point local. We're being jammed professionally. The broadcast *is* near the ambush point on the Blackberry. They're throwing up interference across all spectrums for everything I've tried to connect with. In short, we're being spammed aerially out the wazoo."

"OK. After this mission, we'll use a landline to contact Archangel and First Agent. Until then, we're being manipulated, maneuvered, and isolated. So, since they are expecting us, we don't want to disappoint. We stick together on this and keep our heads in the game. Cheese, suit up," said Rock.

"Just an FYI..I checked the satellite earlier," Tick offered. "Remember that nasty thunderstorm we outran in Kansas City?"

"Nasty indeed," Rock ruminated.

"It's still following us," said Tick. "We should have good weather for several hours, but the National Weather Service has issued a severe thunderstorm warning for this area for around 4:30am."

"My hope is to be back at base by then, but if we have to, we'll push through it," said Rock.

"Well," said Tick, moving out of Cheese's way and getting back to the mission at hand, "what's the call?"

"They've set this trap, they've got our playbook, and they're ready for us," said Rock. "First thing, we sweep this truck for bugs. I doubt they are quite that coordinated, but we'd better make sure. Then we blind the enemy. I'll tell you what the game plan is after that."

With that, they took out sensor-sweeper wands and scanned each other, and then walked the length of the vehicle, up and down, nook and cranny, inside and out, until they were sure they were not being monitored. Back inside, with the external defenses activated, the three gathered together and prayed.

"Father, we are here, in the name of Your Son, standing ready to take the battle to the enemy. Please blind and bind the adversaries encompassing us. Please loose Your angels to do battle before us. Give them victory in the air and keep the enemy from trapping us. Protect us. Give us wisdom and discernment and strength. Bless us and keep us, and move with and before us. Give us the victory that we may glorify You. If we fall, may it be to Your glory. If we succeed, may that glorify You. We are your children, and your servants. Help us be mighty men of valor in the name of our King, though we admit we have no strength apart from Him. We ask this in the name of Jesus and by the power of your Holy Spirit. Please keep us and let us abide in You and in Your fearlessness. Amen."

"Amen," echoed Cheese and Tick.

Fear is contagious in the face of danger, but so is bravery. Rock was intentionally going to be an anchor of bravery for his men, and would resist the fear that was palpable, but by the Grace of God, surmountable.

Rock revealed his strategy.

"Here we go," said Rock, "by the numbers: One, we get my Blackberry away from here so the enemy thinks we've moved, or that we are *on the move.* We'll take it northeast, over the backbone, and plant it a good distance from here. Cheese, close all network connections on your Blackberry so it can't be tracked. Two, we're going to circle to the south of Tick's Blackberry signal, since they should expect us at least from the north. Third, we attempt to set sniping positions at any vantage point along the way and see if we have any targets of opportunity. If not, we go to active shooter formation and spiral ourselves in toward the trap. Fourth, if we spot the origin point, we snipe it and get that tool out of their hands, perhaps springing their trap from a distance. Fifth, we see how they respond and meet them with appropriate force. Watch for traps or triggers on the way. Slow, easy, and silent will be our approach. Any questions?"

No questions were forthcoming.

The "active shooter" formation was a technique developed by law enforcement after a study of the Columbine High School shootings at Littleton, Colorado. It works best in tight locations and with a five-man team, but accommodates as few as two team members. With three men, it keeps advance and rear coverage with a commander in the middle to give orders, and ideally allows for door-to-door room sweeps and entry. It can reverse course and change formation tactics at a simple command. An in-depth study confirmed the mind-set of the shooters and demonstrated that they all had a commonality: The active shooters did not really care whether law enforcement was coming. The shooters were not concerned with anything but controlling those in their immediate vicinity and killing them indiscriminately. It is a power trip overshadowing any self-defensive instinct. With a composite analysis of other subsequent studies, it was discovered that the shooter *could* see an advancing officer but was deluded to the point that his self-preservation instinct was disconnected, almost as if the threat on his mortality didn't even register. In this case, however, the enemy would be lying in wait for the team, unlike an active shooter, but by slowly spiraling in, the team should be able to make a target, even if it is expecting them. At least, that was Rock's hope.

Rock knew that the issue with active shooters, like cultists, was a spiritual issue. They are blinded, first, by their own will, and they also become manipulated by sinister demonic forces. They are given self-empowering delusions and completely compassionless mind-sets. It has happened historically at the decline of any nation that has cast God out of their lives, embracing anything but godliness, opening the many doors to Hell and allowing entry into their hearts and minds. They forfeit the balance of their "will" in doing so. To some, the road to Hell is disguised as utopia; to others, an avenue of power, wealth, esoteric knowledge, fame, or the fulfillment of all manner of wants and lusts. But death is ever in the inviting arms of Hell, regardless of the promises it makes.

The pathology of a falling civilization has been evidenced throughout history, most often by the *progeny* of rulers and powerful men, who never earned their authority, just inherited it. We have inherited freedom, but few today have actually fought for it. The example and attraction of ungodliness trickles down to all layers of the civilization, breeding ignorant, self-important societal leeches and infantile, arrogant moochers, of the likes that were the "Occupy Wall Street" movement of 2011 and beyond. Conversely, the bulk of those uninformed ne'er-do-wells believe the sovereign nation of Israel to be "Occupiers of Palestine," and look upon that embattled nation with derision. A growing number of uninformed *taker's* want their *fair share* of money which they'd never earned, while an ever decreasing number of patriots want their fair share of *freedom that they'd laid everything on the line to obtain.* But pitiable and misdirected fools make the perfect recruits for Satanic cults, New Age Socialism, and Wiccan covens. They recruit all manner of persons who are selfish at heart, ignorant of God, and simply the spiritual cannon fodder of a master whom most do not even believe exists. That is just a slice of the mentality that Knightlight is up against, beyond the clear and present danger of the Nephil-Adam, their lords.

Rock also knew that the prescribed operation for the counteroffensive was now compromised because the enemy likely knew Knightlight tactics and protocols, so his hope was to be unpredictable. For that, and truly everything else, he needed the help of the Lord of Hosts.

"Check your backpacks to confirm their loads," instructed Rock. It was a discipline that all knew, but it was always wise to be reminded. The backpacks all had similar equipment in them and were purposely packed that way so that each could easily access another's equipment. Rock also wanted to confirm the contents of other necessities that might be dissimilar in the pockets. "Flashlights," he intoned.

"Check," the two other men spoke.

"Med-kit," said Rock.

"Check."

"T-blanket," said Rock.

"Check."

Rock went through the entire list, and received checks for all the equipment and tools.

"Ready up!" commanded Rock.

"Ready," they replied.

And then a sudden awareness hit Rock like a snowball to the face. "Feces!" exclaimed Rock. "I'm such an idiot."

"Roger that," said Cheese. "We've known that for years," he said with a smile.

"Secure that," said Tick.

"Give me a minute," said Rock, sitting down and clearing his overactive mind.

The two stood there wondering what Rock was thinking. They didn't wait long.

"Change of plan," said Rock.

"Why?" asked Tick.

"Because they *are* expecting us," said Rock.

"Well, *duh*," said Cheese.

"They *know* that we'll go to them *even if we know it's a trap*, ***especially if it's a trap***, *because that's what we do*," said Rock. "But trap or not, *we* need to act under the assumption that Knightlight HQ has been infiltrated by the enemy. If that's the case, the trap isn't just a trap, it's misdirection," said Rock as he removed his Blackberry from his holster. "Our monster's throwing his MacLaines at us in a *shotgun approach* to try to kill us, which is normal, but the bottom line is the creature is trying to keep us from itself."

"They *are* leading us away," said Tick, nodding. "But away from where?"

"Roughly the opposite direction, the direction where the satellite IR imaging showed warm bodies appearing and disappearing. We are being led away from the nest," said Rock.

"So we're heading into Shades, then?"

"Shades," said Rock, nodding.

"OK. That sounds better to me than springing their trap," said Cheese.

"I don't think so," said Tick. "The Werewolf's den's before us. I'd rather face fifty cultists than a Chaney in the dark."

"Well, with the cult behind us, it won't take too long before they realize we're a no-show. I'm sure they're not wanting to attract the FCC, who will eventually pinpoint their jamming location and investigate it," said Cheese. "Eventually, they'll come for us too."

"Eventually," said Tick.

"We'll face that in due time if we have to, but the monster is our objective, and the MacLaines are a distraction. *He's the head.* Strike the shepherd and the sheep scatter," said Rock with new confidence. Rock downloaded the satellite coordinates to his Blackberry, and then shut down the mobile connection so that it could no longer give or receive a signal.

"Let's do it then," said Cheese, spraying himself with scent neutralizer.

"Hold the line," Rock said.

"Hold the line," Tick and the Big Cheese said.

"Move out," Rock commanded, and they began their mission.

Malcolm and Crystal went upstairs to their rooms, and Crystal got ready for bed. She was conflicted in the way she felt about her father and the man Moreau. Moreau seemed to know exactly what he was talking about, but the Biblical references made him seem like he was what her Dad called a "Bible-thumping funda-*mental* case." But Moreau and his team were the real deal, as far as his governmental ties were concerned, anyway, and that gave credence to him and his story. Not to mention that his eyes—they were . . . well . . . just "dreamy." She shook that out of her mind. At least she tried to. Moreau seemed macho, and commanding and confident . . . and dreamy, and perhaps dangerous, she noted.

Enough! she shouted to herself in her mind and tried to change the subject of her mental stream of thought. But this night was weird and something substantial had happened in the park. There were cultists there, attacking the camp and injuring her father's men, no doubt, and something *wild* was there, something powerful. And apparently it *was* dangerous. Perhaps Dad's Agnostopithecus was truly there . . . perhaps it was a monster, a Nephil-Adam. She couldn't say, but something *was* there. She was truly conflicted about all of this and it made her restless.

She powered up her laptop while she went to brush her teeth, and then came back to do a search on the Bible and David and Goliath. It was a story everyone knew, but Knightlight portrayed it as true history. She noted some key Bible references on a piece of paper and moved on. She searched for Knightlight, and came across several hits for it: a foreign lighting company . . . nope; a superhero . . . nope; paramedics and firefighters . . . nope. She kept searching and found a hit that said "ministry." She clicked it and found what she was looking for. The organization is a ministry that specializes in the investigation of the occult, with an apologetics ministry and with a Bible-based historical archive. It seemed to deal specifically with Creation science as it addresses evolution, relating to the past worlds, the present, and even Bible eschatology.

She became interested and spent a considerable amount of time looking at the site, gaining much information. She was not sure how to assimilate it yet, but she was gaining a context and a respect for Moreau's position. Yet she could not find any "governmental" information at the site, which she believed legitimized their claim of covertness where that was concerned. She did, however, find many papers listed that were predominantly authored by two men, one called First Agent Christopher Griffin, and the other called Director Bensington Redwood. But several of those links required a password to access them. Yes, it did allow public access to information that addressed the Nephil-Adam, and the Bigfoot phenomenon, UFOs, angels, demons, dragons, Satan, and God . . . and to her surprise, a few even mentioned her dad. She read and absorbed much from the page . . . and there was much to absorb.

Then she realized the time, and how it had slipped away from her, so she shut down her laptop, after bookmarking the Knightlight page, and readied herself for bed. As she put herself lightly under the covers and was about to turn off the light, she noticed the Bible on the lamp stand. Had it been there before? She couldn't remember. She picked it up. It was placed there by the Gideons, she noted. She opened it and began to read Genesis. As she did, she tried to apply scientific reality to what was reported to have been accomplished by God. Something strange began to happen to her. She looked it over again . . . just Genesis chapter one. There was a logical continuity there, that is, assuming you believed that God actually did what it said He did. It was interesting nevertheless.

Then she was startled by a knock on her bedroom door. *Must be Dad*, she thought, but somewhere in her mind she was hoping it was the mysterious agent from Knightlight.

✦══✦══✦

When Malcolm got to his room, he went straight for his phone. He called John Cosworth. There was a lot of static. Malcolm thought it must be solar flares, sunspots or something, forgetting that the planet was nightside of the sun at this time. But he got through to Cosworth on the third ring.

"John," Malcolm began, "I had an extensive conference with the Sheriff and the CDC. Some of it is confidential, but the skinny of it is they officially kicked our rear ends out of the parks, except the one you are occupying. So . . . what equipment do you have set up? That is, are you still connected to the traps?"

"No. They could be tripped and we wouldn't know it. Something is blocking communication with them, and the only way to check on them would be on-site."

"I understand, and I agree," said Malcolm.

"The Squatch is there, Malcolm, I didn't see it, but I heard it, I smelled it, and I *felt* it. I was terrified at the time, but it's there. We need to get back in the park, if for nothing else than to check the traps," said Cosworth.

"How is our night-vision equipment?"

"We lost a few headsets, but we are still well equipped. We've been supplied with twice the equipment that we really *needed*. A good percentage is still in the trailers back at base camp. But your daughter made sure we had everything that we needed in spades! She's good at managing your excursions, Malcolm," said Cosworth.

"Yeah, yeah, she's the best," Malcolm said hurriedly, wanting to keep on topic. "What about tranqs and guns?"

"We have all we need," said Cosworth.

"Good. I looked at the other trucks that were damaged at the site, and though the windows are broken, most of them should be operational, and the excavator you rented is undamaged," said Malcolm. "We still have all that we need on-site, and what we don't have there, you've got."

"Why? What are you planning?"

"You *know* what I'm planning," Malcolm said. "What I want to know from you is if you're *in*, and who else on your team is."

"Well," Cosworth said hesitantly, "let me get back to you and I'll tell you what we might be able to get going."

"For Pete's sake, Cosworth, what the deuce do you think you're here for?"

"I know why I'm here, Malcolm, but you're asking me to do a completely *illegal thing*!"

"Fine, fine," said Malcolm, "Sorry. Check on your men, and then get back with me. But remember, the on-site equipment and vehicles are going to be moved in the morning, so it has to be tonight, or nothing. My number is—"

"I have your number. It's displayed on my cell phone. Why didn't you use your cell phone?" Cosworth asked.

"Because it's a piece of junk! I'm getting zero bars here, and even the landline is giving me static," Malcolm replied.

"OK, I'll talk with the guys and get back to you. Just calm down, Malcolm," Cosworth said. Then he added, "Goodbye."

"Bye," said Carson and then he hung up the phone.

Malcolm passed the time examining the DNR map Crystal had printed for him. She captured it in perfect detail as a whole, and then she had it broken down in sections that revealed better detail of every area. It was perfect. He found exactly what he was looking for, took a highlighter from his briefcase, and colored the features he wanted. Then he collated the pages and put all in his briefcase. And so, to pass more time, he spent the remainder of it flipping through the channels on his room's TV. He was wondering why satellite TV was so static-ridden. He watched about half an hour of PBS until he realized that it was on a fundraiser, so he switched to the Weather Channel for a few minutes, then he switched to CNBC, but found the newscasters to be talking-pinheads, so finally he settled on SpongeBob Square Pants, and left it there. At least it had good humor, and he actually enjoyed watching the episodes that paid homage to Tim Conway and Ernest Borgnine as "Mermaid Man and Barnacle Boy." It brought him back to the more simple era of *McHale's Navy, Gilligan's Island, Bewitched, It's About Time, The Munsters, The Addams Family,* and of course *The Andy Griffith Show.* He had no idea how much he had in common with Dominic Moreau where a number of those were concerned.

He sat and watched, and then he looked at the time and wondered, *Why the heck haven't I received my call back?* But then the phone rang.

"Malcolm, we're in, with provision," Cosworth said. "We'll have to get past the roadblocks undetected and that isn't going to be easy. They won't let us down to the site, even with an escort, and we will need some time down there—*unobserved* and *unobstructed* time."

"I know, and I've got what we need to bypass the roadblocks. But you and I know **it's there**! We've the opportunity to turn this around for us, but if we don't get this done by first light, this site will be of no further use to us. And I expect the CDC agents will make it impossible for us to proceed at any of our other sites. It's now or never," said Malcolm.

"OK. You've already convinced me. So, what's the plan?" asked Cosworth.

"There's a DNR entry point to the park on the northwest side off State Road 234. It's before the roadblock on 234 by several miles, and north of the Narrows roadblock. We are going to meet in half an hour at the corner of State Road 41 and 234. Do you know where that is?"

"I have a map, just a second," Cosworth said, and there was paper rustling in the background. Even Cosworth's Magellan was not picking up a GPS signal at this time, so he fell back on all he had left—printed paper maps. "Got it," he finally said.

"We are going to turn off 234 at 1150 East, then onto Lime Pit Road. That will take us to a DNR access road and into the park. Make sure we have bolt cutters. We'll follow that across Shades, where we'll cross 234 again and into Pine Hills, but nowhere near either police roadblock. We should be home free after that," Malcolm said.

"All right, 234 and 41 in half an hour. We'll be there," said Cosworth.

"See you soon. Bye," finished Malcolm as an adrenaline rush of excitement hit him. Quickly, he gathered his briefcase and keys, and he exited his room, crossing the hall to Crystal's room, where he knocked on the door.

Crystal opened the door and Malcolm went in hurriedly.

"Crystal, you were with the big Knightlight agent when you unloaded at the other park," he said rather than asked.

"Yes, Dad. So what?"

"Did you overhear where they were staying the night?" he asked.

"Actually, Agent Ledford said they had a trailer on the Amish farm where the fake toxic spill was supposed to have happened," she said.

"Perfect," said Malcolm. "Now listen. I am going to go see Cosworth, but you don't need to come. In fact, if anyone calls or shows up, tell them I'm in bed and I don't want to be disturbed. My door is locked and if anyone asks where the Range Rover is parked, tell them that Cosworth borrowed it to run into Crawfordsburg to pick up a prescription at a drugstore there."

"All right. What do you have up your sleeve?" she asked, and then instantly knew. "You're going back to the site, aren't you?"

"Not as far as you know," Malcolm said.

"Dad, don't. Just, don't," she said. "You're meddling in government business and they already told you to stay out. You're going to get yourself arrested."

"Sure. They're going to arrest a scientist for doing science? *I don't think so.* Besides, I know a way in and out that they'll never suspect. We'll be out before dawn."

"I'm coming then. If you get caught, you'll either say or do something stupid and land in jail for sure. If I'm there, I can help keep you from making things worse."

"No," Malcolm said. "No. I've come to believe that this creature *may* be dangerous, perhaps it is protecting its young, but I don't think it's safe for you in the park. Stay here and cover for me. If we get lucky, I'll call you on the way back and you can get our stuff together for a fast getaway."

"Dad, don't do it," she pleaded.

"Gotta go now," he said. He kissed her cheek, exited the door, and closed it behind him.

Crystal, on the other side, put her hand on the knob, and then slowly placed her forehead on the door and sighed. She knew at that moment that it wasn't going to end well at all.

23

BEFORE THE FACE OF THE ENEMY

(From the notes of First Agent Christopher Griffin, 5/6/2012)

A Commentary on the Modern and Future Culture

This world has fallen in love with evil. Vampires are the new superhero that men wish to be, and the new romance that women desire to experience. Torture, graphically portrayed on the screen, is now the favored "horror" genre—a splatter-fest. Magic and wizardry are made beautiful and attractive to the modern moviegoer and those with satellite high-definition TVs. They differentiate black magic from white magic, not discerning that there are only degrees of black, and no such thing as white magic.

Talk show hosts are worshiped and people hang onto their every word, believing they are somehow anointed to be spiritual leaders, while they remain fools and lead fools with false doctrines that sound good to the ear. Movie stars are idolized yet they are self-important show ponies, and the bigger the scandal they can generate, or shock the public with, the greater their popularity becomes, until the populace gets bored and demands a new destroyed life to gawk at. And there is no shortage of fools in Hollywood.

Politics is no less sordid. The current President and his allies in the liberal press deride the patriotic. The truly grass-rooted "Tea Party" is branded by them as racist hatemongers when it is clear to all reasonable men that they merely want leaders who are honest, trustworthy, and accountable to their countrymen. They want a leader who has respect for the Constitution, and individual freedom, who will not bow to the social pressures of "political correctness," and who will not allow the Supreme Court or lower appointed judges to bastardize the Constitution. They hope for a leader who will defend this nation against all enemies, both foreign and domestic, who defends her allies without yielding to the pressure of other nations into doing abandoning them. They want a President who will limit the Government's power and intrusiveness, and promote, but not provide for, the general welfare of this nation, as that is the job of good neighbors, who currently do not have to do so when Government takes that responsibility, unjustly.

Americans want equal opportunity under the law, while recognizing that it isn't government's place to guarantee an equal outcome of success. They want a leader who recognizes that faith in God is the heart of the nation, not what divides it, a leader who believes in the One True God, and doesn't just give Him lip service for political reasons. They want a Congress that will use the money lent them wisely, and give back what does not need to be spent. They wish the best for this nation and will work for it, fight for it, die for it, as long as it is worthy of such devotion. But not all who speak against this present darkness belong to the Lord, and that is a weakness that impacts all. Some will compromise their trust and lose it for all. It is only a matter of time.

This country is running headlong into a wall that they will not be able to breach. On its present course, it will fail. And then there will be confusion, hopelessness, hate, panic, rioting, and devastation. And then, as that which hinders is removed from this earth, the Dark Messiah will rise. He will be an eloquent man, speaking peace while raising an army. He will not look like Lucas's Palpatine, but he will similarly act. He will bring peace even to the Middle East, and all will stand in awe at his wisdom, wonder at his presence, and bow to his superiority. And he will hate them, use them, and abuse them. He will establish his own monetary system, his own religion, his own kingdom. Men will fall at his hand for their faith in Christ, and the crowds will hail him for doing so. And when the temple in Israel is finished, and the Dark Messiah stands in it, he will declare himself to be a god. And then, for three-and-a-half years, God Himself will pour out his wrath upon the humanity that hates Him. It is close, it is imminent, it is certain. It has been nearly seventy years since Israel was born anew. Perhaps by strength we will see eighty . . . perhaps.

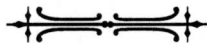

Sheriff Braxton drove the short distance, four miles, from his office to Darlene Campbell's home, but "at least it wasn't inside the park," was his thinking. He reasoned that if anyone in the area was practicing witchcraft, Darlene would either know about it, or possibly be involved in it, without a doubt. Braxton knew her only slightly, just enough to say "howdy," when he felt like saying anything at all. She was attractive, but strange. He would see her at the post office from time to time or occasionally at the diner, but he knew her best by her reputation. Dr. Mills wanted to file a lawsuit against her once for giving people false hope in her homeopathic cures, only to have to treat them in the advanced stages of their illness when her cures did not meet their hopes. Some suspected her of splitting up families and even putting curses on others. But *that* was largely hearsay and he'd heard rumors about himself that were mean-spirited and far from the truth. Thus, he took most rumors about anyone very lightly.

As he pulled up on onto her gravel drive, he saw candles, at a distance in the windows. And since they don't light themselves, and nobody leaves them burning when they're away, he was pretty confident that she was home, and awake. He parked by the house, exited his vehicle, and saw the dashboard clock change from 11:59pm to 12:00am. *That's just great*, he thought to himself, *the witching hour.* He closed his door and then walked up the drive as the gravel crunched beneath his shoes. He traversed the three steps onto her recently painted porch, and strode to her doorstep. He then knocked, not seeing the doorbell in the dark, waiting a full 30 seconds while looking around at the property and into the window, before he knocked again. Listening carefully, he thought he heard voices, though muffled. Then he heard someone on the other side of the door approach and the door opened up to him.

"Miss Campbell," Braxton started. He noticed that she wore a robe, and nothing suggested that there was anything else beneath it.

"Sheriff Braxton. What a surprise. Come in," she bid him. She fully expected him. He was going to be trouble eventually. She knew that much ever since she was visited by her master. But trouble is simply a challenge, an obstacle to overcome. She was prepared . . . ready to overcome this and many more obstacles to come.

"I know it's late, but I was wondering if I could—" Braxton stopped, realizing that while he was asking if he could come in, she'd already invited him to do so.

"Thanks," he said and stepped inside. The place was a little smoky and he immediately inhaled the thick smell of some strange incense burning somewhere. It was pungent, almost stifling, but he was sure that whatever it was, it wasn't marijuana. He knew that smell well from burning evidence after court convictions, but whatever this was, it made him feel a little lightheaded nonetheless.

"Now, what can I do for you?" she asked. She could sense that he was uncomfortable, and that gave her the upper hand. She was ready for any eventuality, and knew well that it might mean that she'd have to remove the Sheriff from her path. Ever so subtly, she employed her abilities for misdirection and seduction.

"I've received some strange reports of . . . disturbances in the area, and I was wondering if you have seen or heard anything unusual in the past few days," Braxton inquired, ignoring the presentation of her endowments.

"Strange reports?" she asked, smiling while furrowing her brow to express confusion in an amused way. "What exactly does that mean?"

"Have you read the papers lately or listened to the news? They're full of reports of people seeing floating lights, glowing people, moving shadows, spooky sounds, maybe monsters and whatnot. People have disappeared, and there has even been a confirmed murder, maybe more than one . . . ."

"Oh dear," she said with a hint of sympathy, but only a hint.

'So, have you heard or seen anything out here?" he asked, noticing a newspaper and several others in a stand by a table in the far corner of her home/store.

"Sheriff, I don't read the paper much. Beyond reading the headlines, I use it to line my cat's litter box. But I know there are rumors floating around about me, living out here all alone, selling the wares I grow and make. But I assure you the rumors about me are false," she said, smiling and touching his arm, petting it, nearly stroking it. Braxton didn't pull away from her; it was an unconscious sign of weakness to do so. But he was not used to being touched in that manner, and he was completely uncomfortable with it.

"I'm not here about any specific rumor, Miss Campbell. May I ask if you were here all evening?" he inquired.

"Yes, I was. I'm growing medicinal mushrooms in the basement, and I had to place some new soil down so the fans will blow the spores onto the new soil. They'll grow a better quality of mushroom in the future. It is all botany, and quite legal, I assure you." Her voice was almost melodious, almost as if she were singing to him. She stroked his arm again. He felt dizzy.

"Are you here alone, or am I interrupting you?" he asked as he felt a prick on his skin from where she was touching him. He pulled back his arm and noticed she had a thimble on her thumb that had some sort of barb on the end.

"Oh, how careless of me," she said, apologizing, "I forgot to take that off. I was doing a little sewing as you came up, and I forgot to take my thimble off. Let me look at that."

"It's nothing, I'm fine," he said, noticing a single drop of blood spreading laterally under his tan cotton uniform.

"At least let me get a moist cloth so your shirt won't stain," she offered.

His head began to ache mildly and his mind was getting fuzzy, while his vision was also beginning to blur. There was no pain from the wound on his arm now, as it was strangely and completely numb up to his shoulder.

"I'll skas agin ar yu lone or m interrupt yoo?" He was seeing two Darlenes and both of her mouths were smiling at him sinisterly, while four eyes narrowed their gaze at him. He tried to ask the question again, but instead, he fell forward and hit the wooden floor like a felled tree.

Darlene saw him falling and stepped out of the way lightly on her toes, to accommodate gravity in bringing the Sheriff down cleanly. She smiled at how easy that was.

"Bradley, you can come up now," she called her toady. "Wheel this thing to the fire pit and dig a hole for his bones. I'll take it from there. Then drive his car somewhere and abandon it as inconspicuously as possible. Oh, and remove the battery cables so his radio won't call attention to itself, and for pity's sake, wear gloves and a cap so prints and hairs are not found in his car."

"Yes, my Queen," Bradley said, still glad to have been allowed to be with her that evening.

"That's all I'll need from you tonight, but do check on the group and see if those CDC men have been dealt with yet. Call me with an update, and then get some sleep. You've finally earned it," she said, giving him praise that she never meant. But as long as he believed it, and obeyed her, that's all that mattered to her.

Bradley Taylor took a hand truck and sat it next to Braxton. Lifting and rolling him onto it with some effort, he strapped the Sheriff down tightly and wheeled him outside with a bump, bump, bump as he went down the porch steps. He took him far out back to the fire pit and rolled him over and next to it. Then he went to the back porch, grabbed a spade, walked back, and found a good place for the hole. He dug as commanded. He was confident that he'd be able to conceal the body well, as he'd done to others several times in the past. It took nearly an hour to finish digging the hole and he had worked up quite a sweat in doing so. Afterward he allowed himself a break to cool down before completing his task. Once he'd gotten his second wind, he fished the car keys out of Braxton's pocket and left him "as is" for Darlene to decide how he would be put to death under the night sky. He sniffed the air and thought, *What a beautiful summer night.*

As instructed, Bradley walked back to the Sheriff's vehicle, and with gloves and a cap already on, he started the SUV and drove it away from his Queen's property. He thought that he'd drive it just south of Waveland and ditch it near Waveland's own covered bridge. He drove through the sleeping town on State Road 59, following it to the right turn, where Main Street ran along 59, then beyond, where it turned left, down and up a hill and into the southern S curve. Next, he proceeded down the hill, where he would be turning right again for his two-mile journey to the covered bridge. He realized it would be a long walk back to his house, where he'd get his motorcycle and then complete his mission that required him to check in on Solomon's trap for the federal agents.

In his attempt to hasten his pace, he depressed the accelerator, not being familiar with the power he was engaging, and the vehicle leapt forward nearly uncontrollably. Then, to his surprise, he found that he'd reached the right turn to the covered bridge unexpectedly quickly. He tried to make the turn but slid on the gravel road; then, as he oversteered to compensate, the Sheriff's vehicle left the road, plowing through weeds and ending its uncontrolled drive by slamming into a hill thirty feet off the road. The impact crashed Bradley's head against the window, knocking him out cold, and causing blood to begin to flow from his temple. He sat there, unconscious, for roughly four hours. Eventually, he was picked up by a DNR officer and taken to jail. But that wouldn't happen for many hours.

Knightlight "Bravo" was moving slowly to the north in Pine Hills under cover of dark. Tick was the first to find the sparse trail of monster blood from the gun wound inflicted by Rock earlier in the evening. The blood showed up moderately well against the carpet of leaves when exposed to UV. There wasn't much of a trail, so Rock's shot was most likely just a flesh wound. They stealthily followed the trail out of Pine Hills, which led them up to SR-234 across the newer road bridge, and then circled back at the canoe store. Now they were moving south, across the covered bridge, toward Shades State Park. Rock was walking point position because if he drew out the enemy unawares, he was more agile and might be able to get out of the way, allowing the Big Cheese to take the first shot. Tick was unrivaled with long-range sniping, but Cheese was the best and fastest with iron sights.

The Big Cheese greatly preferred to be in the middle-man position. He trusted Rock to lead them true, and Tick to back him up. He was comforted by that, yet always a little nervous until the hunt was engaged with the hunted. Being the middle man made Cheese less fearful, if only a *little* less. Rock always said a little fear was healthy, because it kept a man on his toes. "If that's the case," Tick had once suggested, "that makes the Big Cheese a professional ballerina." They all laughed at that one. Cheese countered with, "Your Mom goes to college!" a *Napoleon Dynamite*-ism.

To a degree, Bravo team—the Mighty Warriors of Archangel—had become entertainment trivia "nerds" in their spare time. They watched movies and TV because they were largely socially isolated in the bunker. "Testosterone Theatre" was a name coined by Tick, which meant just about any action movie . . . anything that wasn't a romantic "chick flick." Oh, they were in the Word of God daily and trained often. They kept it to "family appropriate" viewing, mostly. But movies, TV, computer gaming, and genre trivia were a way to blow off steam, and distractions of that nature not only deepened their bond with each other, but also helped keep them sane.

The trio began to cross the covered bridge, listening to the sound of the rushing waters of Sugar Creek beneath them.

"This reminds me of Serbia," whispered the Big Cheese.

"Savanovic, yes, I remember," replied Tick.

Sava Savanovic was a legend in Western Serbia. He was their local monster—a vampire with a long history of killing outsiders, but on occasion he preyed upon the townsfolk of Zarozje. Not too long ago, November of 2012, the mayor of Zarozje, a modest village, had publicly warned the townspeople of an imminent attack because the mill, a very old structure Savanovic was said to haunt, had collapsed. The mayor knew that this would mean Savanovic would be angry and vengeful. The story received little attention outside Serbian boarders, but it was all a false alarm. The old wooden mill on the banks of the Rogacica River was actually brought down during combat between Knightlight and Savanovic—or rather, the creature that was allowing itself to be named so. With great effort, Savanovic was destroyed in the process of leveling the mill.

Rock brought his fist up in the air, for "hold position," signaling the men to stop. He then turned his head, held one finger to his lips to quiet his men, and then signaled that they proceed silently.

They tracked their quarry across the old, yet strong, wooden bridge, then farther south, and into the dark and dense forest that was originally called the Shades of Death. There was still a fog, but they were able to negotiate within it despite the limited visibility; and it acted on their behalf as a noise baffle, making them nearly silent. Crickets, cicadas, and other insects made up the various background noises, undisturbed by the advance of the men. Even the tree frogs did not seem aware of the men's quiet movement. The trail of blood was increasingly difficult to spot because the creature must have been holding the wound shut, perhaps staunching it with leaves, knowing very well that it could be tracked.

Rock wished he could turn on his Blackberry to see how close they were to the point of heat-signature appearance and disappearance, but he wanted to try going by memory for as long as possible so that the LED backlit display would not attract any cultists or the attention of the Chaney. He judged it was less than a mile due west from their present location, so they continued, barely able to see the stars above that told them their heading. And the canopy of leaves above them rarely gave way to the starlight. There was spiritual oppression here, dark and burdensome. Each felt it dogging him, but it wasn't going to slow them down tonight.

They continued silently onward for another twenty minutes, when Rock raised his arm and made a fist again for "hold position."

Rock then turned and noiselessly went to Cheese, while Tick advanced on them to meet.

"Time," whispered Rock to Cheese. Rock did not wear his hot-watch, relying on his partners for the time. The "hot-watch" had a steel cover that popped open. It told accurate time in programmable zones, as well as the date, and it had an alarm. But if you were to pop off the cover, slide it over your fist, and strike it against anything hard enough to break the crystal, barbs would push outward from the watch mounting and lock themselves to the impact area. Then phosphorous inside would mix with air, the watch face would detach from its strap, and it would burn an excruciating hole in whomever or whatever it became attached to. It was considered dangerous and debilitating, but nonlethal. It was, however, highly effective in causing the target such anguish as to make an opening for a lethal follow-up. It would also start a campfire in a pinch, and, as Cheese commented, "it breaks the ice at parties."

"One-thirty-two," responded Cheese quietly. "Are we late for something?"

"The blood trail stopped about ten minutes ago so we're just guessing now where it's headed, and the cultists behind us should be getting restless soon, since we're a no-show. There's no telling what they'll do when they decide a change in plan is necessary. Keep your ears peeled," said Rock.

"Should we pick up the pace, maybe travel abreast to cover a larger swath?" asked Tick.

"Yes," said Rock. "The fog seems to be getting fainter. Five meters apart and keep a wary eye out. The cave may even be a hole in the ground, and we don't want to fall into it. Shoot at anything larger than a deer, and use hand signals or a barn owl call for any other warnings."

The cardinal is Indiana's State Bird, and knowing details like that made "whistle signaling" work effectively. For example, a meadowlark call would be out of place in Indiana, and as such, would audibly call undue attention. However, even a State Bird calling out in the night could automatically be suspicious, since nighthawks and owls are the only nocturnal birds in this particular forest, and *that* knowledge was of even more value at that specific time.

"Roger that," the two said in a hushed tone. Rock took the north, Cheese the middle, and Tick the southern position, all heading west.

The area of the park they were silently traversing was the least traveled in the park since there were no nature trails running through it, only DNR access roads now and again. They were making better time and, by all estimates, nearing the target location. There were no sounds anymore beyond that of their very light tread on the ground. Rock noticed that, and slowed his pace. The others noted and matched his. He sniffed the air carefully—nothing yet. Then Rock, hearing that they were coming up on the winding Sugar Creek again, took in another sample of air through his nostrils, and signaled the others to come to him. He knew that they were quite near their target, and he drew both of his matching sidearms.

"I'd say that we're within about a thousand square feet of it, but I haven't spotted it yet," said Rock quietly.

"How do you know?" asked Cheese.

"No background noises of insects," offered Tick, receiving a nod from Rock.

"Sniff the air," Rock said, and quietly they sampled it.

"Feces, animal decomposition, and a hint of sulfur," Tick reported, and the Cheese corroborated.

"The creek is its water source; the trees, brush, deadfalls, and hills are its cover; and this seems like a good choice for a hide-out," Rock quietly explained. "Wait . . . you hear that?"

The two nodded. There were distant vehicles traveling south of them, and it seemed that there were at least three, perhaps four of them. They were moving reasonably slow from the southwest, and closing. All of them prepared for a possible attack and waited silently for the vehicles to get closer. Then, by the Doppler effect, it was clear that the vehicles were no longer closing in on them, but moving east. Their hunters either were moving away intentionally or were lost, or the drivers were not hunting the team at all. None of them was sure, but the three remained silent until the vehicles passed out of audible range.

"We're clear," said Rock. He figured he was close enough to confirm the satellite coordinates, so he holstered his weapons, removed his Blackberry, and cupped his hand over the LCD screen to sneak a look. Then he locked it down again. "We're almost there."

"Which way?" asked Tick.

"That way," he pointed. "I'm point. V formation; one meter. Watch for tripwires, pits, or any trap, but remember the hostage. We have a damsel in distress. Slow, silent, and weapons free on the trophy. Survival is primary, interrogation is secondary. On me."

Rock rose and the two followed, Tick on his 7:30, Cheese on his 4:30. They only had to walk a short distance when they saw the large tree-laden hill that served as the werewolf's lair. The cave entrance was covered in freshly broken limbs with leaves still on them. Above it was a slide of many stones, also concealed with brush, which appeared primed and ready to seal the cave when a tripwire was triggered, and which would also act as an alarm to the occupant. Farther down the hill were mounds of earth and stone, also covered by fresh branches to conceal the massive excavation of the cave. Even in the daylight, should someone wander off the paths of the park, the cave wouldn't have been noticed by anyone not looking specifically for it.

Silently, the three worked together to move the branches, taking them away from the mouth of the cave and setting them quietly aside. They noted the trip line and Tick tied it off, then cut it with his knife, so that they would not accidentally snag it while they moved the branches away. After five minutes of work, the team was ready to enter. Rock opened his shirt pocket and pulled out a fizzcap packet, offering each member one.

A "fizzcap" was a rapidly dissolvable oral infusion of caffeine, nicotine, and codeine. Just before an actual, as opposed to simulated, high-stress close-combat event, it was better to force your heart rate from condition white to red before you relied on adrenaline to do so. It gave you a little more stamina, a little more focus, and during combat it helped flush muscle toxins produced by strenuous activity out of the system more rapidly. The codeine in the mix prevented a "head spike" or instant headache, which often resulted when just caffeine and nicotine were used. And while it diminished the effects of the caffeine and nicotine combo only slightly, it dulled other imminent pain as well. They each popped one, held it between cheek and gum, allowing it to fizz in their saliva, and then swallowed it to enable it to become absorbed into their system. Each turned his star-light optics on, and looked into the cave.

It was nothing for Nephil-Adam to carve out a den of great proportion in just a few days. They were strong, smart, skilled, and determined. The only thing that would slow them down in the least was to be doing it stealthy, if and when stealth was required. It is believed that they were the muscle and brains behind most of the seven wonders of the ancient world. Not that man was incapable of those feats, or lacked the arrogance to build monuments to himself, but the children of the Sons of God were bred and uniquely suited for such business, and they were not bogged down with warring between one another, for the most part, anyway. There was no love between the clans, but their mutual enemy, small and frail man, the vessels of His very breath, was the focus of their hate.

The mouth of the cave was roughly six feet high, but ten feet inside, it rose to double that height. The slope of the cave was downward, and about twenty feet inside, it turned to the right. At the bend they could see a water trap that was common for collecting incoming rain, and then with the sloping of the tunnel upward after that, it would be dry for the occupants from there on. The three slowly entered the monster's den. Only ten feet inside, it was discovered that they had been outsmarted. The trip line Tick had cut outside the mouth of the cave was only a ruse. There was a car battery inside, and to the left it was connected to an electric eye crossing the floor with some kind of release device above it. The moment Rock broke the invisible beam of the eye, whatever was holding the slide of rocks above the cave entrance gave way. With a mighty thunder, the stone avalanche just outside the cave began to seal them in. It lasted only perhaps thirty seconds, but it completely removed any hope of a quick exit, sealing them into the den. And it resulted in a monstrous roar erupting somewhere farther down the tunnel. All felt the fear biting in the pit of their stomachs. It was clear to all that they were now up against an alert, angry, and deadly beast, without an avenue of retreat. They had reached the heart of danger.

Crystal Carson was looking out her window onto Main Street wondering why her father was so driven that he was going to break the law and risk jail. He reminded her of Captain Ahab from Melville's *Moby Dick*. He would not rest until he came back with victory over his life-controlling "god," as the white whale represented, or in this case, as the Agnostopithecus did for Malcolm. She saw him as one who was becoming doomed by his own ambition, and she simply could not reason with him or steer him from his course. He had been gone at least two full hours, maybe more, and Crystal Carson was very worried, very tired, and very alone.

While turning those thoughts over in her mind, she was surprised to see the Sheriff's vehicle pass by below, but noted as the streetlights played over the driver, it wasn't the Sheriff at the wheel. Perhaps a Deputy was using it. She did not pretend to know the inner workings of the local police, but was glad not to have seen her father handcuffed in the back of the vehicle. The SUV passed out of sight down the road as she remained standing by the window in her quiet room. In the distance she heard the mournful cry of coyotes calling to each other in the night. They were nearer to the town than she would have guessed.

As she was about to move away from the window to begin to pack her clothes just in case they would be heading out on short notice, out the corner of her eye she saw movement beyond the house across the street. She turned to look and she saw a faint blue-white light at horizon level. *A helicopter, perhaps? A low-flying jet?* She wasn't sure, but her attention seemed to be drawn to it. When she looked directly at it, it was difficult to see, but if she looked next to it, it was visible. It seemed indistinct at first, but increasingly its shape changed, forming what looked more and more like a glowing . . . person. It moved slightly, back and forth, almost as if it danced at the corner of her eyes. It moved gracefully to and fro, and then it stopped completely as if it knew it was being observed.

Crystal took a step back as if she'd been caught spying on someone from her window. She gave it a moment and eased herself closer again. The shape, still unmoving, seemed to dissolve from that of a human form and coalesced into a disc, or a sphere.

Ball lightning, perhaps? she thought.

She'd never witnessed ball lightning, but she'd heard that some who see such a phenomenon mistakenly believe it to be a will-o'-the-wisp, an apparition, or a ghost light. She heard herself giggle at it for reasons she couldn't explain. Through the window, she saw the single ball divided into two balls of equal size, both brighter and clearer, and they danced around each other. She giggled again at that.

The lights were mesmerizing, and just staring at them made her want to laugh like a child does when filled with wonderment at the performance of circus clowns. Her eyes were transfixed upon the mischievous lights for many minutes, without even noticing the time moving on. And then, as she watched the lights bob and weave before her, she saw something else, a dimmer but larger light that did not move like the others did. It appeared to be just above them. It didn't move at all. It was a darker, paler light, and it floated in the air but was completely motionless. It was closer to her than the others, perhaps twelve feet away from her window. Then she realized that it wasn't a dimmer light, it was a reflection! The window she was looking out reflected the light—and it was behind her, inside her room!

Crystal was startled out of her formerly enjoyable trance. *This isn't right at all*, she thought, and she turned around to see a blue-white light hovering motionlessly above her bed. It was right in front of her, and she was no longer safe behind a window now, as she was before. She was feeling something from this one, something sinister, and it immediately frightened her. It was like being alone in a funeral home, locked inside with a corpse in the room, and somehow believing, no, *knowing*, that the corpse was going to wake up and attack you; but finding that you were not able to move away from it because you *must* watch it move, you *must* watch it rise, and you mustn't ever turn your back on it for even a second . . . *because that's when it grabs you.*

She could feel that the light wanted something from her, wanted *her* . . . she could sense it. It was a malevolent light, but it just hung there in space, daring her to look away *so it could grab her.* It wanted her to watch it rise, and then it wanted to feast upon her. She tried to move her legs, only to realize that they would not move. She opened her mouth to scream, but nothing came out. Then she heard the light begin to *sing* to her in her mind, while her heartbeat pulsed in her ears. It was an old nursery rhyme she remembered from her childhood. "**Ladybird, ladybird, fly away home**," began the singsong rhyme, "**your house is on fire and your children are** *gone*," it continued. She knew where the song was going, and she felt horror grip her, as surely as she knew that her middle name was Ann. "*All except one, and that's little Ann*," it continued, "*and she has crept under the warming pan*." Then the song began to repeat with a vicious intensity, and the voice was menacing her.

Her entire body shuddered and she realized that she could move, but only if she really, really, forced herself to. She strained for each leg to move, one at a time, only inches at a time. It was slow, and difficult, and it was as if she had to pull each foot out of thick mud to take each small step. Still, she could not look away from the light, and it continued to sing—no, now it was *chanting*—the poem to her as she skirted the room toward the bathroom.

"*Ladybird, ladybird, fly away home*," it chanted to her. The voice deepened and became ferocious, "*your house is on fire and your children are gone*."

She moved two more feet, slowly, horrifyingly slowly. Then, *Finally there*, she thought, and even her thoughts were a whimper. Fighting for every inch of movement, she backed into the bathroom and shut the door against the cold, dead orb above her bed. Her legs gave out as soon as the door was closed, and as she fell to the cool bathroom tile, she hit her head on the bathtub. Immediately she forced herself back up, feeling a trickle of blood from her forehead leaving a crimson trail down the side of her face. She was only able to manage a hushed moan out of her mouth.

There was nothing natural about the light outside her door, and there was nothing in her education that could explain it to her. At that moment she realized just how alone she now was. Her father was away, and she knew nobody in this small town except the elderly lady who ran the bed-and-breakfast. Mrs. Haver-*something* who lived downstairs on the other side of the house had specifically said, "Don't worry about making noise because the building is *quieted*, and I sleep with earplugs." Crystal's cell phone was on the other side of the bathroom door on her nightstand—no help there. She didn't know whether she could fit through the bathroom window and onto the roof outside, but she thought that it was worth a try. She unlatched the window easily and pulled upward on it. It didn't budge, but the movement drew the attention of the two lights that had been dancing across the street. They moved toward her, and now were just outside the bathroom window. She backed away in terror. They jumped around, dodged each other, and looped-the-looped right outside of it. Then they stopped dancing and rushed up to the window. They surprised her so much that she let out a high-pitched scream and fell backward, away from the window, back onto the floor.

The lights ceased their dance and were still, and cared not about the sound of her scream. They hovered next to each other, then moved in, almost pressing up against the pane of glass. Like a pair of cold, dead eyes, they peered in on her, staring her down, looking into her soul . . . and then, to Crystal's horror, they blinked exactly like eyes do. Crystal let out another scream and the two eye-lights pushed through the window without breaking it, and stared down at her. Crystal lost consciousness.

✦═══✦

Malcolm Carson led the caravan carefully and cautiously through Shades State Park, in the direction of Pine Hills. The park rangers, and the DNR in general, had very good access roads and they were well cleaned of fallen branches and reasonably well marked for Malcolm's needs. Cosworth suggested duct-taping the headlights and taillights in the manner of WWII. This was to allow visibility ahead, but prevent the headlight's signature from being excessive. Malcolm thought it was an excellent idea.

Malcolm was already confident that they were going to easily bypass the road blockades, and Knightlight for that matter, ensuring that they would be able to get in, get their business done, and get out with nobody being the wiser. In point of fact, Malcolm believed that there was nobody truly wiser than himself, at least where crypto-zoology was concerned. Since he had a handpicked and experienced crew and knew beyond a shadow of a doubt that the creature was nearby, he had complete confidence that he could turn this Moreau B.S. back on itself. He wanted to show not just the scientific community but even the Government that his theories, his conjecture, his very field of study had been worthy and true all along.

"We're putting a lot on the line for this, Malcolm," said Cosworth in the passenger seat of the Land Rover.

"I'd say that we've been given an opportunity to be saved from the embarrassment of failure," suggested Malcolm.

"I'll apologize profusely if you are right," said Cosworth. "The camera traps will probably be useless, though, considering the fog. I just want to make a smooth getaway even if we come up empty."

"I was with the federal agent when they instructed the Sheriff exactly where to place the blockade. I know we will not even be within a mile of any of his deputies," said Malcolm.

"And you are certain that that biohazard is not anything we should worry about?"

"Although I cannot give you the details, I can assure you that none of us is in danger. If I even thought we were, I'd be the first to decline an invitation to the park," said Malcolm.

"Very well," said Cosworth, feeling like a criminal, but committed to this venture.

Cosworth was a believer in the Squatch. He'd been on a very many excursions, interviewed hundreds of eyewitnesses, studied the Patterson film, and hunted the Yeti, the Yowie, and the Skoocooms—at least until Mount St. Helens erupted. He'd tracked the Wendigo in Canada, the Grassman in nearby Ohio, the Doolagahi and Yahoo in Australia. In fact, he'd been on every continent except Antarctica looking for proof and chasing evidences.

He'd lost his wife because of his drive to find this unknown and elusive creature. And the truth was, he was getting tired. He had been published and received accolades, though not quite rivaling Malcolm's. But he'd lost much on the way, and was truly considering moving on from his vocation, at least where Bigfoot was concerned. That was until Malcolm came up with his "Big Plan" to exonerate them all. But now he was acting outside the law for this man, and nothing had gone right since the Sheriff had shown up today. But, he kept telling himself, *Malcolm is right . . . it* was *here.*

They rode the rest of the way in silence as the caravan slowly traveled all the way through Shades, reaching 234, where they drove just a little south until they saw the familiar DNR entrance that they'd been using the past few days. The rest of the trip was now to carefully navigate back down to their old camp. It felt like days, not hours, since they'd last been there, and all again relived the fear in their minds of the early-evening attack.

Then Malcolm saw it! He swore under his breath and hit the brakes, and then he authored a novella of profanity on the spot.

Cosworth had seen it moments after Malcolm did, and was sure it spelled the end of their illegal activity; for just ahead of them sat the CDC Hummer like an armed security guard standing at a bank's open vault, preventing them all from the treasure ahead.

"What do we do now?" asked Cosworth.

"Well, it's too late to backtrack and we can't turn around here. We'll go down to the site and tell them that we didn't want the equipment we left out here to be pilfered by who-knows-what, and that we just wanted to get it out of here," said Malcolm, instantly coming up with a plausible lie.

"OK," said Cosworth, preparing himself mentally for a jail cell in a small town.

The troupe moved slowly down the hill past the Hummer and came to a stop at the old campsite. Malcolm emerged from his ride and looked around. Nobody. He looked up the hill at the Hummer that had impenetrable tinted windows and walked back up the hill. When he got there, he knocked on black SUV's door. Nothing. Then he decided to announce himself to anyone nearby.

"Calling all CDC agents," he said loudly enough to be audible to Cosworth, still down the hill, but not so loud as to carry any farther. "This is Malcolm Carson; we're just gathering equipment . . . ."

There was no answer and no sign of Knightlight's Three Stooges.

"Knightlight agents are morons!" he said, but not exactly giving a shout and certainly not as loudly as before. "Cultists are bathrobe-wearing pansies!" he added, remembering that they might be there too. There was nothing indicating anyone was nearby, so Malcolm walked back down to Cosworth and the rest of the crew who were now standing beside the trucks.

"The game is afoot," Malcolm said, and with that, the crew went to work checking equipment, setting up communications, and deciding which traps should be looked at first.

Most of the camera traps were not even worth checking, even if the micro SD cards were full of photos. On the other hand, *before the fog rolled in*, some may have captured *something*, and since some were IR cameras, they'd at least have picked up the heat signatures of anything that had passed near them. Cosworth had a map that showed placement of the cameras, but Malcolm was not really interested in them.

"I want to check all four cages," said Malcolm. "If we've caught anything on film, I'm not confident that it'd be anything of note. Still, the pits don't care about fog, and the cages within don't require batteries."

"Fine. Take Jake and Travis with you, and carry your tranq rifles and radios," instructed Cosworth, who was still in charge regardless of what Malcolm thought. He wasn't about to relinquish his authority even if this was all Malcolm's show. Jake and Travis were basically the "roadies" of the group. They both were in college and studying under

Cosworth—Advanced Behavioral Evolutionary Anomalies—and both were good students who loved to be in the field. The most attractive thing about having them come, though, was that they worked with enthusiasm and required nothing in salary. Cosworth was able to move their funding into his own salary for extra site expenditures, less room and board for the two, of course.

"Jake, Travis, you two are with me," Malcolm said to them, not sure which was which, as he grabbed his rifle that was loaded with enough tranquilizer to bring down more than one elephant. He was a fair marksman, and he had the load he wanted in order to make sure that the dart would bring down the creature in one single shot. However, just to be sure, he placed four other darts in his gun belt's holder, not admitting to himself that he wanted the benefit of "*five smooth stones*," just in case.

All three had flashlights, guns, and radios. They moved somewhat quietly, trying to be stealthy, but clearly they were untrained in stealth. After about five minutes, they reached the first of the hidden pits. It was undisturbed and unoccupied.

"Next one's that way," said Malcolm. He chose that moment to test his radio. "This is Malcolm, test, test, test."

"Roger, over," said someone from the group they'd left behind, and it was clear that whatever was preventing their communications earlier was no longer blocking their transmissions.

"Good," said Malcolm to the two men with him. "Over that hill is the second trap."

"I hope we didn't accidentally trap a deer," said Travis. "We could be in trouble if it was hurt in the fall."

"Don't worry about anything like that now; just follow me and be ready to shoot anything that looks bigger than a man," said Malcolm. He almost said "shoot anything that's shaped like a man," but Knightlight might shoot back. On the other hand, he'd not mind at all tranqing one of those dangerous cultists . . . or *Moreau*, if he could get away with it.

The three plodded onward, over the hill and to the next trap. As they closed in, they noticed that the trap had been sprung. As stealthily as possible, they approached the pit, and with their guns aimed, they peered down into the titanium cage. Trapped inside, to their amazement, was a very large and very angry tom turkey. Malcolm had heard that angry turkeys were dangerous birds, so he shot it and instantly the turkey was down, extremely overdosed, and dead within ten seconds.

"Why did you shoot it?" whispered Jake.

"Turkeys are noisy and dangerous when they are mad. I put it down for all our sakes," said Malcolm.

Actually, Malcolm was reasonably correct about the turkey's aggressiveness, but all he really had to do was cover the trap against the noise it would make. Later it could be released with care, but he chose a more convenient course of action. **Perhaps I could give it to Moreau for Thanksgiving and put him down until Black Friday is history**, he thought to himself. *That stinking man is dominating my thoughts!* he acknowledged inwardly in frustration.

Malcolm reloaded his weapon and made it ready for the next trap. The three moved on through the trees and up a hill that was behind the landmark called "the Slide"—a slanted shale wall that people—mostly teens and youth—were no longer allowed to climb, but climb they did, nonetheless. Navigating over the Slide, they found a patch of marijuana growing near the third trap, and as they passed it, both Jake and Travis grabbed as many leaves as they thought they could get away with, without Malcolm noticing that they were stuffing it in their pockets. Malcolm couldn't care less. These two were hired *grunts*, burden bearers on safari, basically, and if they got a bit "high" while they had downtime, he didn't mind. But if he ever caught them doped-up in a needful situation, he was prepared to go ballistic on them. Then he remembered another danger: Some drug dealers farmed cannabis in secluded areas of state parks, and they used real weapons to defend their claim. Malcolm gripped his rifle tightly and trotted onward with a bit more haste.

The third trap lay before them and they approached it, as the others, with caution. The trap was unsprung so they passed it by. Malcolm was getting discouraged. If the fourth trap was sprung, he mentally reasoned it could just as easily be a cultist caught inside, making all of this worthless and wasted. They moved onward and dejection was settling into Malcolm's heart with a heaviness that began to make him sleepy.

"Three traps down, negative capture. Someone will have to clean out the second one, though," said Malcolm over his radio. He received a "roger" from what's-his-name, Malcolm didn't remember, and didn't particularly care to. They moved on quietly, slowly, to the last trap. It was dark and humid and Malcolm was weary trekking up and down the preserve.

Suddenly, Malcolm stopped and crouched down. The other two did the same next to him. In the valley below, they saw what must have been fifteen people in robes, and they were standing around the last trap. It was sprung.

"That's just *great*," whispered Malcolm sarcastically. "We've caught us a stinking cultist!"

"Awesome," whispered one of the other two men, agreeing with Malcolm.

"What do we do?" asked Jake.

"They have stones," said Malcolm—not actual stones in their hands currently, but referring to the previous attack—"but we have rifles. They don't know our load, so they should have no reason to believe we've anything other than bullets in them."

"Right," said Travis.

"OK," said Jake, "What do we do?"

"We walk down there with our guns aimed at them, like we own the place. We tell them to get their carcasses outta here, or we'll blow a hole in each of them."

"Wa, well, what if they charge us?" asked Travis.

"If they even *move* toward us, we take the first three down, and stare the rest down with our guns pointed at them."

"You mean our *empty* guns pointed at them," corrected Jake.

"Do you really think they'll know that? I mean to scare the tar outta them. Once we take three down, I think they'll scatter with poo in their pants, and I don't mean Winnie the . . . ," said Malcolm as forcefully as possible under his breath. He wanted to inspire courage in them, and he was actually pulling it off, but somewhere, he began to notice, was fear. It wasn't rational, but it was there.

"OK," said the two men.

"Should we call it in to Dr. Cosworth, though?" asked Jake.

"Forget Cosworth! You two stand shoulder to shoulder with me and we'll make sure those dangerous idiots know we mean business without us having to fire a shot," said Malcolm.

"OK," they both agreed, and the three of them rose from the ground, stood shoulder to shoulder, and walked down toward the group as if the Duke himself were going down to confront Morgan Hastings.

"Hands up, everybody," shouted Malcolm, with all three men aiming a flashlight down at the cultists as they approached. Malcolm, Travis, and Jake advanced on them with renewed strength, and Malcolm put every effort into making his voice authoritative. "These guns are loaded. ***Don't make us have to put you down!***"

Malcolm had never seen a crowd run away so fast. It was like shining a light in a roach-filled room and seeing them scatter for cover. Only these did not just go for cover; they ran, scrambled, scurried, and climbed away as fast as possible in all directions away from the three. Malcolm really enjoyed watching them go.

"***Get outta here or you're all dead men***," he shouted. But it was overkill as they were already going, nearly gone.

"Dang," said Travis, "I feel like Indiana *stinkin'* Jones!"

Jake laughed, also enjoying the feel of raw power. Malcolm said nothing, but he was smiling, and silently he acknowledged that he felt *ten feet tall*.

"Why were they standing around the trap?" asked Jake as they moved in closer.

"Obviously, one of them fell in, and once you are in, only someone with the keys can get you out. Those cages are about as unbreakable as my heart is," said Malcolm. "**Let's see who it is, and see if we need to put *him* down!**" Malcolm said the last with gusto so that the trapped cultist could clearly hear his intent and tremble. Still, something was gnawing at him, telling him he was in danger.

The three approached the trap cautiously because the cultist could still have a weapon, even a rock that he might toss up through the bars. They peered down the deep hole, expecting an angry Satan worshiper that they were going to scare the poo out of, but as they looked down into the cage, there was a huge, dark, and powerful *thing* in it . . . and it was very angry.

Suddenly, they were confronted with a gut-wrenching stench and an earsplitting **HOWL**. All three men fell backward instantly as if they had been physically hit with a mighty and evil force. All three lost bladder control, and their guns fell out of their hands, landing next to them. Malcolm came to the realization that he was in the throes of a heart attack, but the other two did not know that yet. All three were speechless, struck dumb and petrified with fear, except that Malcolm was clutching his chest with both hands, feeling a stabbing pain, and reeling from it.

The monster, only a few feet away, reached out of the top of the cage. It was barely able to get its forearm through, but forcing it through, it grabbed Travis's leg.

Travis screamed. He was in a grip unlike anything he'd ever felt before. The nails of the monstrous hand embedded themselves in his calf muscle, tearing into it as one might tear into an angel food cake with bare hands. Then it pulled Travis to the edge of the pit as Travis raked his hands into the soil to try to stop his advance, but it was no use. His screaming continued.

Jake, shaken by Travis's screams, scrambled backward and saw Travis at the lip of the pit with a powerful, hairy arm growing out of the darkness. With much less thought than gut reaction, Jake grabbed his gun and moved to the edge of the pit and shot the monster in the neck. The monster roared and released Travis for a moment, grabbing its neck. Travis pulled himself backward and rolled away into a fetal position, grabbing his injured leg and shouting profanities for the pain of it. He could feel the dark, wet blood that now soaked his pants, and the smell of the beast and urine filled his nostrils. He was struggling to remain conscious.

Jake grabbed Malcolm's gun and moved over to the edge again and quickly fired once more. He hit the creature in the eye, bursting it and causing the monster to scream and writhe in pain, shaking the heavy cage and causing the ground around to tremble. Jake backed away again and this time grabbed Travis's gun. He moved quickly, not even looking when he was ready to fire, but merely aiming downward, he pulled the trigger and then backed away again. The dart hit the monster square in the forehead between the eyes, and with a tremendous howl of rage and pain, Jake could feel the monster collapse in the cage, and then it became still.

Jake sat down and shook all over uncontrollably. He held his knees to his chest and rocked back and forth in the soft earth of the valley. Then Travis cried out.

"My leg's broken and I'm bleeding! Help me," he pleaded.

As Jake looked over at him, still shaking, he noticed Malcolm there, writhing on the ground in pain, grabbing his chest and shuddering.

Jake was a card-carrying Medic First Responder, and he recognized Malcolm's problem. He somehow overcame the shakes, pulled Malcolm's arms off his chest, and delivered a hammering blow six inches above his sternum. Then he began pressing on Malcolm's chest in regular beats, forcing Malcolm's arrhythmia into regularity.

"Help me, I'm bleeding to death," shouted Travis in a voice of agony.

"Malcolm has had a heart attack," said Jake. "Take your shirt off and wrap it around your leg and tie it tight over your wound. Apply pressure to the area that is bleeding and then get the radio out of your pocket and call for help, for cryin' out loud!"

Travis, knowing he was not going to get any actual aid until he made the call, forced himself to do as Jake instructed. He removed his shirt, shuddering and whimpering all the way through the process of removing it. After wrapping it tightly around his wound, while screaming in pain and almost passing out because of it, he lay down on his back and pulled the talkie from his cargo pants pocket, lifting it to his mouth and pressing the comm button.

"*HELP!*" Travis screamed into the radio. "*We're at trap 4. Get us help now!*"

"Did not copy. Is that you, Malcolm?" the voice asked on the radio.

Malcolm, eyes shut against the world, was beginning to come to his senses and felt his chest being pushed on, pressed upon by . . . someone. He opened his eyes and saw Jake straddling him, compressing his chest again and again. He felt weak, but he wanted this stupid teen off him, so he took a swing at him and smashed his knuckles into Jake's nose, making it instantly bleed, but successfully getting Jake off him.

Jake, holding his bleeding nose shut, rolled off Malcolm and shouted, "What are you doing? I'm tryin' to save *your stupid life*!"

"Keep off of me, you freak of nature." Malcolm cursed him, albeit weakly, and slowly rolled over and took his own radio out of his holster. "Cosworth," he said, no longer in quite so much agony, but feeling as though he'd been hit by a truck. "This is Malcolm," he said.

"Copy that," came the voice from the hand-held communicator.

"Get over to trap four. Bring the four-by-four with the cage trailer. And bring the backhoe so we can lift the cage onto the trailer! Over," he finally said, while choosing his next words carefully because he was certain that they would go down in history.

"Copy that. We're coming! Over," said the voice of whomever. Malcolm still did not know or care whom he was talking to since everyone had a radio, and it could have been any one of them.

"Tell them I need a stinking ambulance!" yelled Travis, panicking.

Malcolm angrily allowed himself to relay the message about Travis, even though it postponed his historic broadcast. "Bring a med-kit. We have an injured man. Over."

"Tell them we need a defib unit too. You just had a heart attack, you jerk, and you're not out of the woods yet," said Jake, nursing his throbbing nose.

Then it came to Carson like a flood of knowledge: *He'd done it. He'd actually done it!* The Agnostopithecus was his and the next words he spoke would go down in *history*. He thought for only a moment, because he'd rehearsed this possibility many times before in his mind. He knew the words he wanted to say, and he knew they'd be credited to him in the annals of time.

"This is Malcolm Carson," he spoke into the radio, ignoring all of Jake's comments completely. His voice was now that of the convention speaker—authority and dignity were finessed in his tone.

"We have all strived to find the truth behind the unknown. For centuries we have heard stories of monsters and giants, and most believed them to be myths, many even believed them to be lies based on *a primal fear* that we all share concerning the night . . . ."

Jake, looking at Malcolm's hand, almost said something to him, but stopped himself and waited for Malcolm to finish. He'd had about enough of Malcolm and his pompous, self-important ego.

"We have searched the world over to see if there are other creatures out there, creatures of legend, creatures of lore which have been hidden from us. Our efforts had been disparate until now, but in scientific unity, we have pushed the envelope of discovery. This day, I am proud to say that there *is a Bigfoot*, there *is a Sasquatch*, and until now, it was an Agnostopithecus because we did not know for sure *what* it was. But now we will know exactly what it is, because my friends, my colleagues, I am proud to announce that we *have captured a living specimen* and all doubts have now been quelled! Yes, today right before me, ***I have captured the Sasquatch***!"

Malcolm concluded his historic speech in a vocal flourish, and then sighed, completely content with it. He relaxed his muscles and reveled in his victory, holding the radio to his chest in elation, and as he just noticed, in *pain*.

It was then that Jake chose to mention to Malcolm, "Mr. Carson, you didn't hold that talk button *in* during your speech." To which Malcolm proclaimed a violently loud and lengthy curse.

24

BRAXTON

Sheriff Braxton lay tied and unconscious on a large hand truck in the back of the witch's yard. The air was still, the fog had dissipated, and the stars shone down on the land. Trees surrounded Darlene's land in a horseshoe pattern, circling around the back, making it visible to nobody unless they were behind her home.

Sheriff Braxton twitched. His eyes fluttered and then opened. He tried to move. He could not. He had no idea where he was, but the stars . . . the stars were beautiful. He watched them, not knowing anything at the moment, not really knowing who he was. He was floating, he thought, floating to the stars. He continued to float without any real thoughts in his mind. Then flashes of memory came to him like sunlight sparkling in a stream: flashes of pain, of friends, of family, flashes of his life, and then back to pain. He was Braxton . . . yes, Braxton. He was . . . he could not remember more than that at the time. He watched the stars. Then after a few moments he realized that he had an office, a duty, he was working on something . . . something important . . . it . . . it . . . it eluded him. Sheriff. Yes, he knew he was the Sheriff. Then he started to notice his discomfort as feeling began to return to his body. He tried to move again. He could not. His back was hurting dully. He felt his arms and legs were tied to something, and the stars were watching his helplessness, offering no aid, no comfort. He was thirsty, so very thirsty.

"Knightlight," he spoke aloud, not even knowing he could. His own voice was weak and it didn't even sound like his voice. But then again, he was not sure what his voice was supposed to sound like. "Knightlight," he said again, and then remembered Agent Moreau. There was an attack on someone, he thought. Knightlight rescued them and showed Braxton what he was facing. "Monsters," he whispered barely audibly. He shook his head, and it banged against the steel cart he lay upon. "Witches . . . Satan worshipers . . . attacked," he said, not meaning to say anything aloud, but not able to control it either. His inner monologue was no longer silent. "Darlene Campbell," he breathed, and remembered everything. The memories became a deluge in his mind. He reeled from them, but now he knew where he was and he knew *everything*. He realized that he was going to die.

"Father, forgive me," he whispered from his parted and parched lips. If these were going to be his last words, that was what he wanted them to be. Then he moved his fingers. *PAIN!* His body was now becoming wracked with pain. "What did she stab me with?" he wondered aloud. He fought to keep his mouth closed, to keep his thoughts to himself, and he won that small battle. *She's a witch and she knows how to be one*, he thought, *silently* for the first time. As the numbness wore off, the pain increased and he nearly passed out again. It felt as if his blood had crystallized and was tearing through every vein like shards of glass, through every artery, through his very flesh. It was agony. His breathing became erratic, and his body started to convulse; though still bound tightly to the cart, he rattled it and shook it.

What did she shoot me up with? he wondered through the blinding agony. And his body shook as the anguish persisted. Sweat beaded on his skin but the coolness of it did nothing to calm the pain. Every beat of his heart, every pulse drove the pain through him. It coursed through his body and back through again and again, tearing, searing, and cutting its way through him. His consciousness was about to leave him again, but then, as if God Himself saw that Braxton had endured enough pain as well as reached his personal limit to suffering, the pain began to diminish. Slowly, it subsided, taking minutes, painful minutes, and then his body began to relax and his eyes filled with tears that could not be produced earlier. He was tied down, but he was himself again, body, mind, and spirit. He had never experienced anything like that before, and now he believed that he knew what a moment in Hell felt like.

He tried again to wiggle his fingers, and they did move. He tried to move his hips and wiggle free. He was able to move slightly, but he was bound well. He tried to force his body upward, and the cart budged, but not by much. He tried to roll, and that seemed to be successful. He rocked the cart, but then thought that if he rolled it over, he'd be on his face and wouldn't be able to breathe well, so he stopped short of that.

Wait a minute, he thought. His hand was almost on his gun that apparently was not confiscated from him. *Why would they leave it on me?* he thought. He tried to draw it but could not even get his fingers on it to pull the weapon free. *Oh . . . that's why*, he thought. He'd left a note on his desk stating where he was going, as he always did, but his deputies were either home in bed or at the blockade. There would be no rescue until after the shift change at 7:00am when the incoming deputies signed in, got their orders, and moved out. Braxton knew he'd be murdered before dawn, and by the looks of the stars, that was still a few hours away. The stars were fading now, as if a blanket of dark cotton were moving slowly upon them, tucking them in for the night. Then a thought occurred to him: Knightlight *could* try to check with him for some reason, but immediately he dampened that hope as he realized that they'd likely call only if necessary. Or if they ever visited his office, he was pretty sure that it wouldn't be soon enough.

Braxton's heart froze as he heard the backdoor of Darlene's house open and close. He heard her light footsteps down the walkway that ended at the fire pit, where he was. Her approach was slow and measured, as if time was of no consequence to her. He turned his head slightly to see, but he kept his eyes mostly shut, down to the merest slit, to appear as if he wasn't conscious yet. She was loosely robed and moved stealthily, stalking him like a deadly serpent. She stepped closer and closer. It was then that he saw that she brandished a sharp stiletto knife, holding it and petting it. She was saying something under her breath as if speaking to it, no . . . singing to it . . . but what she sang, he couldn't hear. *She's going to cut my heart out and eat it*, he thought.

"So," she said aloud as she came closer to him. She was beautiful, radiant, evil, desirable, and horrid, all at the same time. "I see we're awake, my Sheriff."

He did not want to betray himself by answering. He continued to lie there pretending not to be awake.

"Too late, my Sheriff," she said, "too late. I was watching you for the last half hour. I know you are awake and the potion has worn off. I know the pain you endured for a quarter of an hour. I created it, and I know how it works," she boasted. "Usually it causes the most beautiful screams, and has been known to stop the heart. You should be proud that you survived it."

Slowly, Braxton opened his eyes to the beautiful terror that hovered above him.

"Why are you doing this?" Braxton asked. He truly did not understand the mind of a cultist.

She lowered her beautiful face down to his, and whispered, "Power. I simply desire *POWER*, and as you can see, I have it."

"Power has many forms, lady," Braxton said. "And you'll never have the power to rival the One you're working against."

"If I don't, my master will," she said. "I have power, but of course, there's a chain of command. I'm sure you understand that much, being an officer of the law," she said, toying with him, teasing him with the proximity of her body. "I know that you're attracted to me, my Sheriff. I can tell those things quite accurately. I know what men want. It's a . . . gift. So . . . would you like a long kiss goodbye, my Sheriff . . . a last kiss?"

"Just because I'm tempted doesn't mean I want anything of yours. I say no to temptation every day," countered Braxton.

"Ah, perhaps," she teased, "but since this is your last night on earth, don't you want to go out with pleasure before you end in pain?"

"Lady, I aim to outlive you. You offer pleasure for a moment, but you don't offer it for eternity. If I die, I'll still live, but when you die . . . you'll just be in line to stand before my God's judgment, and after you bow before Him, you face a second death that doesn't end. You choose to live apart from Him . . . . *Well, toots, your wish is granted.*"

"You *really do* believe that wives' tale, don't you?" she whispered. "How sad you must be, never enjoying the pleasures that are available to you, in hopes of a place next to your crucified king. I can offer you *so much happiness, so much pleasure*, but you choose to deny your lusts and leave this life unfulfilled. I pity you, poor Sheriff." She licked his ear, and then bit it.

"Happiness comes and goes, with *happenings*. But then you need more, different and better *happenings* to *keep you happy*," he said knowingly. "Life with my God is Joy regardless of circumstances. Joy is the reward for virtue, and Joy is with me even now."

"Enough!" she shouted and rose above him. She sat on his chest and placed the knife next to his throat. "I'd ask you how you want to die, if I didn't already have designs of my own. Would you like to hear my plans for you?"

"I'd like you to shut up, lady, and do whatever you're gonna do. Just get it over with!" he said, and she lost her temper . . . something she prided herself in being able to keep.

"*You peasant! Who do you think you are?* You're under my complete control and *your life is in my hands*!" she screamed. "I'm going to summon my master and watch him eat you alive!"

"Sum—summon a psychiatrist," he stuttered, feeling fear, trying to push back at it.

Rage took its grip on Darlene, and with both hands, she plunged the knife into his right shoulder with all her might. It went in deep, all the way to the hilt, and an inch of it came out the other side of his shoulder, stopped by the steel of the cart he laid upon.

Braxton let out an anguished breath. It hurt extremely, but it was not as painful as coming out of the drug he'd been poisoned with. It was not even close to that agony.

Darlene's hands were bloodied, and she licked her middle finger that was coated in Braxton's blood. Then she rubbed his blood on her cheeks, somehow enjoying and reveling in it. After that, she grasped the knife again and tried to pull it out. Her hands slipped from it and she failed to extract it, as if it had become part of his body.

"Nn-not so easy to pull it out, is it?" Braxton said through intense, blinding pain. "Better go get someone more powerful than you." It was a struggle to say it, but he verbally slapped her sufficiently.

Unfortunately, she slapped back. She hit his face for that remark, and pounded his chest and then slapped him again and again in her rage. Then suddenly she stopped, took a deep breath, and cocked her head to the side as if she just realized something.

"Now, that's the first thing you said right." Then she laughed, got off his body, and stood facing the trees in the back of her home. With raised arms she began her demonic invocation to summon her master.

"O mighty one, O Master of Ages. I have an offering for you. I have a sacrifice that is pure! Come to me, O ancient one! Come and feast upon this righteous sacrifice!"

She waited . . . nothing. She waited longer and still nothing. She lowered her arms, which were getting tired, and she waited a little longer . . . embarrassment crept into her mind. He wasn't coming as promised. *Something must be wrong*, she thought.

Then, distantly, there was a rustling in the trees. Darlene smiled, instantly raising her arms again as if they'd been there all along. The rustling came closer, louder, and it became a rush like a powerful army was advancing. It sounded almost like a stampede.

Braxton turned his head to see what he too was hearing; it was coming closer, coming for him, presumably. In a way, he wanted to see it. If it was his last sight, he wanted to look on the face of the monster and defy it to the end. And if he somehow could get free while the beast was mauling him, he had a weapon in his shoulder that just might be usable to hurt the creature enough to remember who wounded it.

Then Darlene and the Sheriff both saw what burst through the trees. It was fifteen or twenty robed people running out of the woods, as if fleeing something that had been chasing them. They saw Darlene and all of them ran straight to her.

"Solomon, what are you doing here?" she asked.

Solomon's real name was Tim. Tim Beavers, and he'd had enough of this.

"Darlene, I'm done . . . we're all done. It was fun, it was real— but we almost got gut-shot tonight and that's not my idea of a good time. Throwing stones in the fog was a hoot, but getting gut-shot isn't going to work for me."

Darlene just stared at him, and he could tell her anger was building. Tim had been in on the impregnating of Cindy Stroud and, truthfully, most of the other atrocities orchestrated by Darlene. He'd been a party to animal sacrifices that turned his stomach, and worse. He'd done things that he never would have thought possible, never thought he'd do . . . he'd done just about everything imaginable. But he was beginning to realize that he was on the losing end of life. It was enjoyable for a time, being part of the coven, gaining rank within the order, but he was never satisfied, and he had guilt . . .

heavy guilt. He wanted out. He began to notice that no matter what he did to fill his life with pleasure, it didn't satisfy him. He always wanted more . . . always more, but he found that more did not satisfy either. It was as if he drank from a fountain that did not sate him . . . it just made him thirstier. He hated himself. He hated who he'd become. He didn't want to live like this anymore.

"Darlene . . . ," he said, "I really can't do this anymore. I'm out . . . I'm done."

"You're not released from me. I say who stays and who leaves. We have work to do, and you'll obey me," she said commandingly. "The master should be here. Something's wrong and we're going to find out what."

"*I am **done**. This has gone far enough. We've jumped the shark. It's over. Oh . . . by the way, the scientists . . . they captured one of your **masters**, and *he can't get out of their cage*. He's a zoo specimen now, and we're not going to jail or getting gut-shot for your sake. Not anymore."

Darlene stood there in the moonlight, and an evil smile crossed her face as if she were really going to enjoy demonstrating the consequences of crossing her. It seemed that the light around them was fading and being pulled into Darlene like a black hole. The air smelled of ozone, and all sounds seemed to become still. Tim knew that Darlene was calling upon the powers that she alone in the coven was able to wield. It always gave him the willies.

"Come to me, spirits of the air! Give me your strength!" she shouted, and a dark light coalesced about her. It sparked faintly and flashed subtly, and her hair lifted itself as each strand separated and pointed in all directions. It was something akin to static electricity, as if she had one hand on a powerful Van de Graaff generator. An electric glow emanated from her like St. Elmo's Fire. It engulfed her . . . but whatever it was, it wasn't saintly. Her tattoos shone the brightest as her skin glistened in the unearthly light. Then, in a flash, Darlene stepped forward and slapped Tim very hard. It lifted him off the ground and made a static *crack*. It was the strongest slap he'd ever felt, and he flew sideways in the air and then to the ground in pain and surprise. The entire group of disgruntled followers backed away from her in utter dismay and awe.

"I have the power of many souls! Defy me at your peril," she shouted. She moved toward two other members, grabbed them with each of her hands, and tossed them both into the air, seemingly effortlessly. They landed a good ten feet from where they had stood.

The rest backed away farther, now fearing their former Queen, not knowing what she was capable of, but certain that their entire company could not match her strength.

Tim regained his footing and grabbed a sturdy tree limb that was meant to be burned in the fire pit. He wielded it like a club, seeing that Darlene's attention was no longer on him. With all his strength, he swung the club at the witch and hit her solidly across her back, squarely on her shoulder blades. As soon as he made contact, he felt as if a lightning bolt had shot from her, running up the limb, shattering it, and then traveling into his arms. But the tree limb broke across her back with all Tim's strength, and she fell forward to the ground, remaining still. Tim dropped what was left of the limb, shaking his hands to bring feeling back into them. It was as if reality had been redefined to him. Evil was on the ground now, and he was breaking away from it.

All coven members looked down upon Darlene's still body, fearing she might try to get up, but Tim had fortunately knocked her consciousness completely out of the park. The group then saw the Sheriff, and their eyes widened at the realization of what they were now likely to be implicated in. It was decision time and they knew it.

"Tim," spoke Braxton weakly, "I don't know what you've done, but it's not too late to make some of it right. Untie me and we'll figure it all out, and I promise I'll treat you fairly. I'll even stand before the judge on your behalf and tell him how you stopped me from being murdered. I'll stand with all of you on that," he said.

Tim and the others just stood there. Each one of them knew Braxton, and Braxton knew each one of them. The choice was before them: Run, finish Darlene's work, or face the music of the Indiana justice system. Each choice would permanently change their lives for the worse.

"Tim . . . there is still hope for you. But you know that there's no hope for a cop killer. You *know that*, don't you?"

Tim looked down at the woman who didn't care whether he lived or died, then to the officer who offered hope in getting him out of this mess. Tim wanted out. The others wanted out. It was no longer funny. It was no longer happiness. It was no longer his life.

Tim stood up straight, went to Braxton, and untied him. The others followed and helped lift him off the cart, and braced him as he stood. Tim almost tried to pull the knife out of Braxton's shoulder, but the Sheriff stopped him.

"Leave it there. I'll let the doctors remove it later," he said through teeth clenched against the pain.

"What do we do now?" asked Tim.

"First, we'd better cuff that mad cow." Braxton pointed to Darlene. "Cuff her from behind with these," Braxton said as he removed the cuffs from his belt with his good arm. "I need a ride to the jail in Crawfordsville, and then to the hospital. Where are your cars?"

"We always park them over there," he said as he pointed to the left side of the horseshoe woods, "out of sight so we won't draw attention. I'll give you a lift," said Tim. "What about the others. What should they do?"

"We need a little help getting Darlene in the car, then you all go straight home. I meant what I said. I don't know what you did last night, but this morning all of you saved the life of a police officer. That will count for something. But don't try to run away, or all bets are off," Braxton said. He then said to Tim, "Now, did you say somebody caged the thing, the Bigfoot?"

"If *that's* what it *really* is, then yes," Tim said. "It was in a strong steel cage in a hole at Pine Hills. The trappers came down and scared us off, threatening to shoot us. But the Bigfoot, it looked different from the way it looked before, I mean different than the other time I saw it. It was thinner, more vicious, and it reminded me more of a vampire that had turned halfway into bat form. It scares the feces out of us just to see it, but this time it looked stone-cold evil."

"The guys with the guns . . . was one of them kinda fat, or overweight, and in his forties?"

"Yes, and he seemed to be their leader," said Tim.

"Carson," Braxton said, shaking his head in disgusted unbelief. "Just what we need," he added as what Tim had said earlier now registered with him. *Two monsters now. This is way outta hand, and so is Carson*, he thought to himself.

One of the cultists put his robe on Darlene, and Tim cuffed her with her arms behind her back. Then Tim assisted in getting Darlene over to his car, and into the back seat, while Braxton slowly followed. Tim got in the driver's seat and Braxton eased his way into the car. He read Darlene her rights, just to ensure a clean collar. He planned to do it again once she was awake, but at least Tim could be a witness to it now. Tim started his car and they drove off the property as other cars started and split up behind them. When they finally came to 234, Braxton said, "Take a right here."

"To Pine Hills or Waveland?"

"Pine Hills; I have deputies there. They can take Darlene into town."

"OK," said Tim and he drove them the short distance to the roadblock. Caleb Donner and Tony Larson were there this shift. Braxton got out of the vehicle and turned to Tim.

"Wait here, and don't worry," Braxton said, wincing from the pain in his shoulder. "By the way, good job taking Darlene out."

He walked over to his deputies, who had both of their vehicles blocking the road with lights ablaze. They looked as though they were having a relaxing evening.

"Sheriff, you look like a sack of manure!" said Caleb. "You do know you have a knife in your shoulder, right?"

"Caleb," Braxton said without acknowledging the knife, "has Carson been through here?"

"Nobody but the CDC came through. I think they went into Pine Hills to camp out for the night."

"I've got a prisoner in the back seat of Tim Beaver's car. Tony, ride with him to the County Jail in Crawfordsville, and when the prisoner comes to, give her the Miranda."

"Yes, sir," said Tony. "What's the charge?" He was another green Deputy, but he was eager to do his job.

"Attempted murder of a law-enforcement officer—me," said Braxton.

"OK," said Tim, and with that, he got in Tim's car, and they turned around and headed away toward Crawfordsville.

"You need to get to the hospital. I'll take you," said Caleb.

"Not yet. We're going into the park," said Braxton through the pain. "Somehow Carson slipped through the roadblock and supposedly has a Bigfoot in a cage. But that one apparently isn't the only one in the park. My guess is Carson's group is going to take the one they have and make a run for it. It's only slightly illegal what he's doing, but he's not getting away without a good explanation. And I want the CDC guys to know what's been going on behind their backs, if they don't know already."

The two mounted up in Caleb's squad car and off they went toward the park, leaving the single police car to act as barricade.

"Oh," began Braxton, "put an APB out on my vehicle. It was stolen while I was unconscious at Darlene Campbell's house."

25

BRAVO TRINITY

(From the notes of First Agent Christopher Griffin)

Respect—Just a Little Bit

There are persons who demand your respect without earning it. Send them away. There are those who insist that you endorse the sin they commit. Close the door of fellowship to them. There are men who require you to validate their ungodly lifestyle choices. Separate yourselves from them. In the postmodernist, politically correct society we live in, we stand apart. We understand that to show respect for any "thing," it is required that that "thing" must be worthy of respect. Fools beg for praise from the wise. They demand tolerance, but they will not tolerate righteousness. They cry "hate speech" when Truth is proclaimed, and they are the first to spill blood because of it, demonstrating where the "hate" actually originates. Will we continue to share the Truth with the ungodly? Yes. Will we offer a better choice to those who cannot see their error? Of course. Will we offer mercy and love to those who hate righteousness? Always. But we may never entangle our lives with, never be yoked with, never be anchored to that which will drag us down into the pit. Does this make us better than the heathen, better than the godless, better than the sinner? Never. It only keeps us as effective tools for their reclamation, by the hands of a loving God. His purposes are accomplished best when we yield to Him, not sin. And the godless will know the way to godliness by our love for our Creator, our love for each other, and, of course, our love for them.

+⸻⸻+

The dust had settled and the star-light optics helped a little, but Rock pulled a chemical lightstick from his sleeve pocket, snapped it, shook it, and tossed it behind them. It made the visibility in the first chamber a bright yellow color, and shadowy, but otherwise clear. Tick and Cheese went to each side of the first room with weapons drawn, and Rock took the center position, two M&Ps aimed at the tunnel.

"Lateral formation," Rock said, and the two other men moved to Rock's side, Tick on the left and Cheese on the right. Slowly they moved forward. Rock holstered his left weapon to grab another lightstick. They stepped over the water trap and slowly but steadily traversed up the cave's ramp leading into the second chamber. None of them knew what to expect beyond a giant with great strength and nasty teeth. These creatures were smart and Knightlight's activities around the globe had made them very cautious when it came to their lair protection. Rock was hoping that more time was spent digging and shoring up the lair rather than trapping it. They looked at the walls, the ceiling, and the ground, as well as ahead, for traps, wires, levers, and a monster.

The walls had tree limbs broken and shaped for use as pillars that were shale rock plated above and below each. They could tell that it was solidly built for long-term use, rather than a temporary hide.

"Side split," Rock said. Tick went left against the wall, Cheese went right, and Rock went behind the Big Cheese.

The center of the tunnel had footprints up and down the floor, but there were none in the center just ahead of them. It looked solid, but the creature obviously stepped over that place consistently.

"Do we spring it?" asked Tick.

"No," said Rock. "If it's a pit, then we'd be OK, but if it triggers a cave-in, or an explosive, we're hosed. Just remember where it is."

The Bravo Trinity moved up to the second chamber. Rock popped the lightstick and tossed it in. All was illuminated, but it was a little too bright since the stick was in front of them. Rock pulled his left weapon again and slowly led the three in.

The room was larger than the first, and there were many stolen items scattered about within. There were actually very few items on earth that a being ten feet tall, without electricity, needed from the much smaller humans. However, a couple of long couches could be made into a bed and a dinner table could be used like a coffee table. But the things most often found in a lair were books, matches, and hacking weapons like swords, picks, and axes, and there were plenty of each stored here. The Nephil-Adam lived simple murderous lives, much like the Amish sans the murder. But they knew their day was coming when they'd be the masters of men and their technology. Many of the older ones spent their time learning almost everything knowable that had ever been published, because they'd had time on the earth to do so. They also had patience because they *knew* their purpose, and of course, they communed with demons that had run to and fro throughout the earth ever since the fall of man.

Some of the Nephil-Adam were collectors, sometimes of art and fineries, but more often they liked human skulls to catalog their kills. They'd had time to collect whatever they desired. Some liked gold and jewels, but all of them liked sharp weapons. Some were given to creating art, to painting their lair, or to training others of their kind in the art of combat. But all were nurturers of the infants in their charge, while demons bred more of their kind. They took care of the female parents until the five-month gestation period was over. Then they would often feed the newborn first with the blood of the mother. Sometimes the mother would survive childbirth only to be killed immediately after. Sometimes the delivery itself would kill the mother. Of necessity, the monsters fed the young, taught them to read and write, and taught them to speak in other languages. They taught them the ways of stealth, murder, and duty. They had a chain of command, a hierarchy under the ancient Tammuz, but even he was under another satanic hierarchy of demons. Long ago they established a communications network to pass information to one another, and a code of honor among themselves. Yes, they were vicious, demonic, and murderous terrors who enjoyed killing mankind and consuming them. Still, there was a degree of respect that each had for the others, to varying degrees anyway, and all were under the impression that their master had some measure of respect for them. They were wrong. Though they were brilliant beings, they did not know how completely deceived they were. The fact that they had a code of honor gave them a false sense of morality, while they were, with few exceptions, utterly depraved.

The three looked around the room, and to their surprise, there was another tunnel that led to a natural cave. The Chaneys were uncanny locaters of caves that no human had ever known existed. Of course, they had assistance from demonic entities, often their parent, but Chaneys seemed to always have a more elaborate, albeit less than neat, tunnel system, which is almost invariably linked to a natural cave.

"No Chaney in here," Cheese said quietly, speaking of the second chamber. The suspense was intense because all knew that *it* was aware of their presence. It also knew the cave/tunnel system, including the traps, and would see them coming now that they'd announced themselves. Fear gnawed at each of them, but it was a familiar enemy; and though it would not incapacitate them, it did weigh them down.

"Stupid electric eye," said Tick.

"At least we know there's always a second exit and venting. We're going to get our trophy and we're all three going to walk out of here with our damsel in distress," Rock said quietly to his men, hoping to quell the fear.

Another roar erupted, loud and angry, coming from inside the cave. It wasn't just a roar, it was an *oath* in Greek. Translated, it roughly proclaimed, "I'll wear your heads like jewelry, you sons of a pig." In times past, that was exactly what some of them would do to their victims.

"Oh yeah?" replied the Cheese. He was shaken by the comment, but not so much as to make him speechless, just unimaginative in his retort. Cheese was the youngest, but his skill with the Greek language was the best in the trinity. Sometimes he regretted it.

"Quiet, Cheese," said Rock.

"We're here for the girl!" shouted Rock with boldness, knowing that the monster could speak English. "And we'll remove your head for the men you've murdered!"

It became angry, roaring anew, now that it was sure who had entered its lair. Knightlight had a reputation among the powerful creatures, and, more to their concern, it carried a record of success with it. They were not the crypto-zoologists that the beast may have been expecting to perhaps *stumble* upon the cave. They were the edge of the sword. At least, that's what Rock hoped that it believed, and belief can be the difference between life and death.

Rock was always concerned about getting these beasts too angry. He still reflected upon the first time he'd encountered one, in his home, but he had been able to keep that memory from hindering him. His real concern was that if it charged them and though they could mortally wound it, the charge itself might still take out the team, perhaps leaving all four dead in the end. It was a "bull elephant" scenario that he didn't want to provoke. But the truth was, regardless of the way you chose to confront one of these brutes, all avenues were unsafe; and it was a fearful thing to stand before any of them.

"Reverse V," Rock whispered, and the team moved out from him, Tick to his left-forward position, Cheese to his right forward.

At that moment, Tick heard a whimpering sound within the large tunneled-out room. He raised his arm, pointing toward the beaten-up set of couches off to their left, motioning that there was something in that direction.

"Tick's hailing a cab," Cheese whispered to Rock.

"Secure that, Cheese," Rock whispered back to him. He knew humor was a way to allay fear, and Rock usually participated in it, but not when you are about to be face to face with the beast. "Switch left," Rock ordered, and the formation moved as one and closed in on the source of the sound.

Beyond the first couch, the three saw Cindy Stroud, hiding behind the second, curled up, dirty, clothes torn to rags, leaf-covered, and whimpering as if she'd lost all hope in the world. She could not see them, of course, as the only light was on the opposite side of the room and illuminated very little to the unaided eye. She did hear them, but she knew that nothing could withstand the power of the monster that had killed Bill and captured her. She knew that all she could do was to wait until the horror in the cave beyond killed the men. And she knew that the monster would then likely feed her with their shredded carcasses. She placed no hope in them at all. That is why she whimpered. She was crying for them, and for the sake of hopelessness.

"Cindy," Tick whispered. "Cindy Stroud. We are with the Federal Government. We're here to rescue you."

Cindy said nothing and closed her eyes tightly, knowing they were dead men. She held her knees up to her chest and shivered, and cried weakly.

"She's not talking," Tick said to Rock.

Rock broke formation and moved to the couches. "Watch my six," he ordered the two, and they turned from Rock, facing the cavern's opening.

"Miss Stroud. I am Agent Moreau. You will be safe soon."

Rock unslung his rifle and set it down. He then removed his backpack, unzipped it and pulled out a flashlight, set it down, and removed the water bottle, placing it in Cindy's hands in an effort to give her a sip. She took it in shaking hands and drank, then set it down. Rock picked up the flashlight, and with his hand cupped over it, he clicked it on for a second and back off, placing it in her hands. He hoped to comfort her with the gift. Then he pulled out a thin Mylar thermal heat blanket, opened it, and covered her shivering body with it.

"Miss Stroud. We are federal agents. We are trained to kill *monsters*, and we are *good* at it. Just wait here and when the monster is dead, we will come back for you. We know you have been through Hell, but you've been strong and the worst of it is over. Stay down, stay quiet. We *will* come back for you," Rock whispered. He handed his rifle to her, but it was clear that she could not see it, so he moved her hands on it.

"Take my rifle. You can kill monsters with it. You have my flashlight. So sit still and the blanket will warm you," he said, trying to offer the most comfort he could to the poor woman. "We *will* be back, but if you see something, and feel the need to shoot it, use the flashlight and make sure it isn't us first."

He was unsure whether his words were understood by Cindy in her current state of mind, but seeing her, and knowing what she'd been through at the hands of the Hell-spawn creature, made him angry and more emboldened to take the head from the beast. It was always a risk to leave a weapon with a victim, as there is a great chance the poor soul would take her own life. Another risk is that the victim had become brainwashed and would fire upon the team, or would panic and shoot anything that moved. But Cindy gave no signs of confederacy with the beast, and they would definitely have been detectable. She obviously needed the strength of self-empowerment. She needed to know that she could kill the monster even if they failed.

"We will be back as soon as we kill it," Rock promised. He rose quietly, knowing he'd spent too much valuable time assisting the girl. He placed his backpack on once more, turning back to engage the Chaney.

"Flank the entrance," Rock said, "Then follow me in on my signal."

The Cheese took the right side, leaning on the wall at the opening and peering around into the darkness beyond, while Tick took the opposite side and stood in a pose identical to the Big Cheese's. Rock holstered his weapons momentarily; then he grabbed two lightsticks from his vest, popped them, and tossed one to the left inside the cavern, and the other to the right, allowing them to see into the cave, if only a forward view of it. Then he extracted two slender canisters from his hip and pulled out a neoprene slipcover. He placed only one of the canisters in the slipcover, using it as an outer cushion for it, and Velcroed it down inside, allowing only the top to be exposed. He did not alter the other one at all. Then he leaned into the cavern a little. There were a few crates against the far cave wall that were marked "Fresh Fruit," which must have been stolen for feeding the woman. There was a big shovel, an axe, and a pick leaning against the wall and other equipment that had obviously been procured from the Amish. There was some gardening equipment, pots, potting soil, and even concrete bags. It looked as if the creature might be in the process of remodeling the cave, but try as he might, Rock could not see around the corners to either to the left or the right.

"We are federal agents from Knightlight, and we come against you in the name of Jesus Christ," shouted Rock into the yellow glow of the cavern. It was a breach of separation of Church and State in the minds of some, but it had saved hundreds of lives, and would continue to do so while this form of danger walked the face of the earth. **"I don't suppose you'd like to surrender, or at least tell us where Tammuz is hiding?"**

A rage-filled roar bellowed out another curse in Greek. It translated, roughly, "Consume excrement and live no longer." The good thing about the response is that it told the team approximately *where* in the cave the creature was standing. Locating the target was critical to neutralizing it . . . and critical to their continued existence. Its voice was off to the right of the cave entrance, and back at least twenty feet.

"You will not survive the day," said Rock. **"We're your escort back to Hell."**

This was the most dangerous moment of any hunt, when the quarry knows that the enemy is upon it. The quarry is possibly cornered, but ready, prepared for this moment as well, and set to kill the first thing it sees. "Target right, twenty feet. Eyes shut. 'A and B.' Three count on 'A,' before open, then weapons free . . . . Now hold your ears," Rock whispered to them, holding the two canisters for them to see.

Rock, with his left thumb, popped the fuse on the first canister and tossed it into the cavern with a noisy metal clatter. He then popped the fuse on the second neoprene-covered canister and tossed it in afterward. The second canister made a much softer sound, hardly noticeable. Then he stepped aside next to Tick, closed his eyes, held his ears, and readied himself to run into the cave, guns a-blazing, knowing he would see the beast, just four seconds from now.

"*BANG!*" went the first canister, releasing a heavy concussive force with a brilliant and blinding light that flash-bangs were designed to produce. Three seconds until entry. Rock was sure the monster would close his eyes and ears to the first grenade the very second it saw or heard it clatter on the cavern floor. The creatures were smart and knew very well what grenades do. However, with its eyes closed, and surely its hands on its ears, the second grenade would be unseen, unheard, unnoticed. Rock also knew that it would immediately open its eyes and look to see who entered the cavern after the first grenade had detonated. Two seconds until entry.

"BOOM!" went the second flash-bang, hopefully blinding and deafening the creature that did not expect a second grenade. One second until entry. Rock drew both of his weapons.

Rock charged in and dove for cover behind a rock shelf that had resisted erosion better than the other areas of the cavern floor, turned to the right, and fired his weapon at where he presumed the creature was, without actually seeing it. Tick and the Big Cheese followed Rock in and took positions at his right and left, also firing on the assumed position of the monster. That was when they saw the big, old Marshall amplifiers across that end of the cave, now shot to pieces. Immediately, they traced the visible cables running over to several car batteries to their left connected to a simple soundboard, and another cable out of that, going around the wall extending *behind* them. The monster had tricked *them*.

"Well, this isn't good," said the Big Cheese matter-of-factly.

Immediately, they turned around and saw the beast towering over them, wielding a double-bladed axe. It **ROARED** in anger, and with a sweep of its arm sideways, the flat of the axe slammed into the Big Cheese's side, sending him across the cavern, his optics flying from his head. Cheese landed at least twenty feet away, where he skidded and tumbled on the damp shale floor, and into the far wall. Tick and Rock pushed themselves backward, but both were swiped by the monster's backhand and knocked to the ground, rolling with it and moving away from the beast. Tick's optics were also damaged in the attack, and Rock lost one of his weapons from his right hand; but both rolled away from the monster and readied to continue the fight.

The beast stood before them, massive and terrible . . . and, they realized, blind! They *were* tricked by the beast, but Rock's own ploy had also worked. Though the beast was not really injured—just deaf and blind, its fur in the front singed—its sensory incapacitation would last only a few seconds longer.

The monster staggered around in rage, swinging its powerful arms in great swipes but connecting only with air, but it was closing in on Rock and Tick's position. Both men aimed and fired at the beast, knowing it would be their only chance to do so in concert. They hit it multiple times, but not in the head, as the beast was moving erratically, and furiously. It screamed and bellowed, throwing the axe mightily toward Rock, barely missing him. But now it was clear that it was regaining its ability to see. Hearing, however, would be longer in returning. It moved to face down the guns before it, and it smacked the weapons away from the two men, knocking them down at the same time. And then it was upon them! They could not maneuver away from the creature. It grabbed both men by the legs, squeezing hard, and lifted both Rock and Tick easily into the air, upside down, as it cursed them and tried to master control over the pain inflicted by the bullets that had penetrated deep into its flesh.

Rock pulled a knife with a seven-inch blade from his boot and swung his body up toward the monster. With all the force he could manage, he plunged his blade into the creature's inner thigh where it met the groin, and then he twisted it. The monster *SCREAMED* and let both men fly from its hands in two different directions. They both hit the shale cavern floor hard, bouncing and sliding, and in short order, both were temporarily incapacitated.

The monster went *MAD*. It shouted in horrific pain, cursing, rolling on the ground cradling its groin, howling, bellowing, and thundering. The Big Cheese could hear it, and as he looked upward, he realized that he could barely see. It was dark with only two glow sticks lighting the big cave, but he turned his head and saw nobody but a huge bearlike thing rolling and screaming in front of the cave entrance, kicking up dust. He didn't have all his mental acuity at the time, because he'd had his senses knocked loose, so he just lay there looking at the giant thing scream and writhe. He knew where he was, but it didn't seem to feel that anything going on around him was important, dangerous, or of much concern to him . . . it was just there, and he was just watching it, detached from it.

Tick, bruised and beaten, slowly slid himself farther away from the beast in search of Rock. His optics didn't work, so he cast them off. His gun was around there somewhere, and he did have a sidearm on his hip, but he wanted to get farther away from the terrible creature before he drew and used it. Since the furious creature was occupied with the results of its spontaneous castration, he figured he had time to move to some semblance of safety. The rolling, screaming ball of fur on the floor was barely visible to him, so until he could identify the head, he didn't want to exacerbate the situation at the moment. Slowly, painfully, he slid away from the beast until he was at the wall where the destroyed stereo speakers were placed.

Rock was out cold for a minute, and when he came to, he wasn't as disoriented as the Cheese, but his legs were numb. He lay flat on his back, trying to make them move, knowing that if he didn't he'd be dead soon, but they weren't letting him do anything. He'd landed on his back after being tossed, and nothing below his waist was talking to him. Then he reached around his back. He found the gun that was first smacked from his hands. Pulling it out from under himself, he realized that it was the thing stabbing his back. It must have been pinching a nerve center, because as soon as he removed it from behind, his legs started to tingle painfully. He still couldn't make them move, but he could *feel* them again. While he waited for his mobility to return, he pulled his optics, which had dropped around his neck, back into position over his eyes. Only one side was functioning, and the lens had a vertical crack in it. He could see, but he had no depth perception and his sighting eye had no visibility, so he pulled them off his head. He released the magazine on his weapon, quietly set it down next to him, and pulled a fresh magazine from his belt, slapping it home as gently as possible. Then he pulled out two other glow sticks, snapped them, and tossed them near the beast for a semblance of illumination. He forced his legs to move in preparation to use them to rise.

The monster had pulled the knife free from its groin with a defining roar, and dark, thick blood was all around it from the injury. It was also having difficulty getting up because of the pain. Rock saw Tick to his left, over by the wall. He looked as if he was also shaking off his tumble. But the beast also saw Tick, and with the knife it pulled from its body, it targeted Tick. The beast deftly threw the knife, from a sitting position, very fast, very hard, and directly at Tick's chest. Tick dropped back with the impact, and Rock lost sight of him.

Rock knew that the light armor in their suits would protect the wearer from a high degree of blunt-force trauma, and deflect knife and claw slashes from any attacker, but he also knew that the armor wasn't made to stop the piercing action of a forcefully thrown knife. Rock saw how the knife hit his partner. Then he moved his attention, quickly scanning the room for Cheese, and saw him lying across the cavern, just watching the monster.

"Cheese, get to your feet, soldier!" Rock shouted to him, pulling a powerful LED flashlight from his belt as he forced himself to rise. He shined the light in the direction of the monster, illuminating the huge, hairy black mass with large, eerie, green reflective eyes and sharp teeth.

Cheese heard Rock and tried to shake some sense into his dazed mind. However, all of his instincts told him to either play dead or run away, so he attempted to bolster his courage instead. "Father, help me," he whispered.

The monster reared itself up now on both pillarlike legs, though still bleeding profusely. It looked right at Rock with fire in its eyes, ready to finish the fight, ready to feed on its enemy.

Rock, on unsteady legs, aimed and fired his weapon, striking the fierce creature in the neck, but immediately feeling that his weapon had jammed, and knowing it was out of battery.

There were several reasonably common types of jamming in semiautomatic handguns. Rock's weapon had ejected the previous shell casing, but had failed to seat the next round properly. It was "riding the slide." But Rock could not tell exactly which type of jam had occurred, because that required visibility to be sure, and that wasn't possible at the moment. Rock reflexively swiped his flashlight hand over the top of the slide to clear it, if it had stove-piped and the casing hadn't cleanly ejected. That would have cleared it, but that was not the issue. All that took two seconds.

The monster realized that Rock's weapon had jammed and it lunged at him. Rock instantly dropped his gun and moved backward, while he grabbed something from his hip that looked like a black crucifix. Rock held it up in the air and shone his light on it, and the monster stopped, unsure of what manner of weapon Rock was now brandishing, though certainly not fearing a crucifix in the least. The thought almost made it chuckle, if not for the excruciating pain in its nether regions. It knew that Knightlight was always changing their game, always trying something new, always keeping the engagement unpredictable. So it waited for Rock's move before it advanced farther. It trusted Rock as much as it knew that Rock trusted it.

Although it was a dangerous tool, Rock chose to deploy a device they called the Thread, though it had never been actually used as a *weapon*. The Thread's purpose was to be set as a trap around a deployed mobile base, but they were rushed this evening, and Rock still had several in his pack since the camp was deployed in haste. The Thread worked like this: The crosslike device had a trigger and a remote button, both on the pommel. When the trigger was pressed, both sides, or "arms" of the "cross," would shoot two anchor battery-spikes laterally, which were each connected by a triple-braided "nanotube" carbon fiber, or an invisible and nearly unbreakable "thread" between each battery-spike that anchored itself, one on each side. When the battery-spikes embedded themselves in a tree or wall, they automatically retracted the fiber to optimum tension, creating an invisible molecular thread only 600 atoms thick. These traps were usually set between trees at about an eight-foot height *only* when the mobile base was going to be vacant for a period of time, or if all team members were going to inhabit the mobile base for a while. Everyone under seven-and-a-half feet tall was safe from slicing the tops of their heads off, but as long as the traps were set around a mobile base, there was an invisible danger to "supernaturally altitudinous" intruders.

The "cross" device that deployed the thread was also a remote control. When an agent wanted to get rid of the dangerous trap, he would simply press the button on the remote. The battery anchors would then produce an electric charge strong enough to overheat the thread, and it would burn itself up like a light-bulb filament does when exposed to the air. The nanotube fiber self-destructed visibly, with incandescent proof.

Rock shouted, "Thread!" announcing the dangerous deployment to all teammates able to hear him before he pulled the trigger.

The demon-spawned colossus watched in puzzlement as it witnessed Rock holding up a religious icon. *"**What foolishness is this?**"* it wondered, still in agony from his wounds. *"**Are they truly expecting me to react to this cross as if I am some manner of Dracula?**"* It almost chuckled at the thought regardless of its anguish.

At that moment, while the beast's eyes were transfixed on the "cross" held aloft by Rock, the presumed Christian icon simply exploded without causing the monster any discomfort at all. It was as if the famed Knightlight—the Giant Killers—were nothing but clumsy, albeit brave, and had equipped themselves with party favors instead of true weapons. It believed that the Knightlight agent's device was a failure, and also that it had given its prey more time than it deserved to remain alive. It shook its head for the briefest of moments, just before it dove straight for Rock.

Rock jumped sideways to avoid the monster's lunge coming at him, and it was clear that it dove *under* the Thread. As Rock jumped to the side, and while he was still in the air, the beast's outstretched arms smacked Rock's legs, sending him spinning like as maple tree's seed, all the way to the ground, but fortunately, he was beyond the creature's immediate reach. Rock, rolling under the Thread to the other side and putting some distance between himself and the beast, rose to his feet and stood there in defiance of its arrogant prowess. The beast rose also and squared off against Rock.

"It doesn't have to be this way, Rephaim!" spoke Rock, breathing hard, but finally getting his second wind. Then he reached behind his back and pulled out a machete, challenging the legendary creature.

"You can die today, and all your wisdom and knowledge will be lost to the world," Rock said, "or you can live and spend the rest of your life reversing your course, maybe doing something of value. It's your call. But this is your last chance."

"Knightlight is finished, and you don't even know it yet," the creature growled. *"You have no idea what you are up against, gnat! We've waited long for this day!"*

"What?" Rock thought, immediately perplexed by the monster's comment. *"Finished? Waited long for what day?"* Rock felt that there was much more going on around him than he knew, but there was no time to dwell on it.

"Say hello to your wife, Moreau. You are about to see her again," the creature concluded.

Those words stabbed Moreau's heart as keenly as any knife could, but Rock made no outwardly sign of the wound.

The monster stepped forward menacingly, but then stopped. It looked at the wall to its left and saw a tiny blinking IR marker light on the Thread's battery-spike. The light was invisible to the unaided human eye, and barely visible to the aided eye, but the eyes that had just detected it were more than merely human. The creature then looked in the opposite direction and saw the other light across the cave. It looked puzzled for a moment, but then it smiled. It was a predator's smile just before the kill of its prey. It understood what the lights meant, and it bared its great white teeth and fangs.

"An invisible garrote wire . . . very clever. How sad for you that I've detected it," it boasted. *"Take your last breath, dragon-slayer."*

And that is precisely when the Big Cheese, with all the force he could muster, slammed into the humongous fiend from behind, using his full 220 pounds against the giant. The creature was forced forward just a step and a half by the impact, and Cheese recoiled to the ground behind the angry Rephaim as if he'd tried to move the Washington Monument by himself. The creature turned around and simply kicked Cheese across the room as if he were a small dog. Then it turned back to Rock, eyes almost glowing with hatred. It turned toward the Thread's marker lights again, with a puzzled look. Bending down, it started to duck under the invisible wire, but as it did, its head separated from its neck, fell off its shoulders, and thudded onto the ground. Its body followed immediately afterward. The mouth on the great beast was moving, spewing forth curses that would never reach the ear of anyone, and in a matter of moments, it ceased and the fire in its eyes went blank.

Rock flipped the remote switch, and 100,000 volts went across the Thread, vaporizing it completely. "Cheese," Rock called out, "greenlight! Are you all right?"

"I'll be all right, eventually," Cheese said weakly, lifting his battered and beaten body up off the ground. "Where's Tick?"

"He's by the stereo speakers over there. The creature hit him with my knife. I think the wind's been knocked out of him."

"I'm all right," said Tick, still flat on his back, staring skyward. "What happened?"

"The Chaney threw my knife at you. Fortunately, it hit you 'hilt first,'" explained Rock. "Must have hurt like the devil, but I knew you'd be able to walk away from it."

"Thanks," said Tick, "your confidence in me is exceeded only by your compassion for a fallen partner."

"I didn't have time to go over and hold your hand, amigo," said Rock. "Cheese, go take a few pics of your trophy before we burn it. We've got to get the girl to a hospital and find out what's going on outside. We could have company soon."

"My trophy?" asked Cheese. "You used the Thread; I just encouraged the wolf-man to walk into it."

"No arguments," said Rock, taking a flashlight from his leg strap and going back into the living area of the lair. "Cindy," he called. "We are fine and you are safe now . . . I'm coming back to you."

With his flashlight on he entered the secondary chamber where Cindy was still huddled, assuring her that it was no trick. He walked over to her and took another thermal blanket out of his pack and wrapped it around Cindy, helping her up.

Rock, like his brothers, was sore and tired, and it took conscious effort to keep moving. As their leader, he'd hide his physical discomfort to assure his men that he was ready for any other surprises that might greet them. It was his hope that the rescue was the end of their combat for the evening, but that was not always the case. And with the prospect of the cultists, he steeled himself for more, while hoping for a break.

"It's dead, ma'am," said Rock. "Would you like me to show it to you, so you know it's dead?"

"You're alive," Cindy whimpered. "That's proof enough."

"I'm going to need you to ride piggyback on Agent Ledford so that we can get you to our camp, get some warm clothes on you, and get you to a hospital. Are you OK to travel?"

"I think so," said Cindy, and then she began to cry, with great sobbing tears. Rock held her, a little uncomfortably, but warmly.

"It's OK," he said. "You've been through Hell, but the worst is over now."

"I'm pregnant," she said, and wept bitterly.

"I know, Miss Stroud," assured Rock. "But you're safe, and you're not the first to be in this condition. We'll see to all immediate needs, and then you will have counselors who will help you through this. You will be fine as long as you don't give up. What was done to you was evil, but you and the child within you are innocent victims. We will make sure you get the help you need."

Rock walked Cindy slowly toward the center of the living area to the mouth of the large cavern, and let her sit on his backpack while the team finished their jobs.

"Cheese, light the beast up," said Rock, knowing that Cheese had covered the body with a highly incendiary thermite blanket—a "T-blanket"—that, when activated, would cause a "Goldschmidt reaction," burning the creature to the ground. It was the quickest way to vaporize the corpse. Of course, the composition of the blanket was a little off-formula of most standard thermite compositions. This tool needed to work effectively on a large body composed of 80 percent water without burning too long, or causing undue harm to anyone nearby, and especially needed to *leave no trace.*

"Tick, have you made your evidence sweep?" asked Rock. Finding Tammuz was the prime goal as "he" was the physical mastermind of the enemy where these creatures were concerned. But finding evidence of other cells, covens, sleepers, and stalkers was also of import. The creatures were coordinated, contacted often by spiritual messenger, but they were known to send messages that were coded in books that they collected and passed around. Their plans, maps, strategies, and goals could sometimes be discovered and deciphered by the evidence in their lair. And this time there was absolutely an open admission of some ongoing sortie against Knightlight itself. It was very strange and definitely foreboding.

"Affirmative, but nothing to report," said Tick.

"Then find us an exit, please," said Rock. He assisted Cindy in rising again and went into the cavern.

"OMW," said Tick, since he was already *on his way* to do just that.

Tick lit a match and the smoke was his guide to a hole in the cave ceiling, a vent. Tick moved deeper into the cavern and performed the same exercise, the smoke directing him east toward a heretofore-unexplored area within the long cavern. The passage narrowed ahead of him. Rock, with Cindy clinging to him, followed Tick. All heard the loud combustion of the T-blanket, and the cavern behind them was brightly, explosively lit. Cheese caught up with them and also assisted Rock with Cindy, and then Rock let him have her to carry as he moved ahead of them to help Tick. Fortunately, it wasn't long before Tick found the exit. There were traps there too, but from this side, they were easily detected and defused, and summarily, all reached the surface, back into the open night air. The exit came out by Sugar Creek, taking them part of the way back toward their camp.

The team began their journey back to Pine Hills. They moved slowly because of the dark, and also to give the lady in tow a gentler ride, but this time they paid less attention to being silent. Still, they would use their flashlights only when truly needed because of their concern about being spotted by the cultists. Now wasn't a good time for another confrontation. As they left Shades SP and crossed back into Pine Hills, they heard several vehicles leaving the park. They were too distant to see them, but it appeared that they were leaving by following a DNR outbound trail that cut between the parks and would not be detected by the officers at the roadblocks.

As the Trinity-plus-one group finally reached their camp, it was clear that either the cultists had stolen some of the cryptos' vehicles or the cryptos themselves had come back to retrieve what belonged to them.

Bravo Team reached their mobile base and deactivated the defenses. Cheese took Cindy inside and assisted her in getting ready to travel to the hospital, while Tick checked all monitored recordings of active communications. Rock stowed his gear and the team's packs, ammo'd up, and went to Tick at the communications panel.

"We're no longer being jammed," said Tick, with a headset over his ears now that he was jacked into the system.

"Good," said Rock, who was contemplating activating the MU's defenses since they still did not know whether another attack on them was imminent.

"Well, maybe good, maybe not," said Tick. "I can't reach Spectacle or anyone at Archangel. I've got Sat-Comm. We're broadcasting, but receiving nothing from their uplink, and I can't even ping them from the terminal."

"All right, let's get to a landline ASAP," said Rock. "We can do that at the hospital when we take Miss Stroud."

"Wait," said Tick, placing a hand on his right ear to hold the headset tight. Looking at Rock with an expression of surprise, he said, "You've got to hear this!"

Tick unplugged his headset and ran the recording backward to the time-mark he desired, then directing audio output to the cabin speakers.

"This is a broadcast from the cryptos' shortwave about an hour ago," Tick said. And with that, he clicked the play arrow on the screen and allowed Rock to hear the message.

"This is Malcolm Carson," it went. "We have all strived to find the truth behind the unknown. For centuries we have heard stories of monsters and giants . . . ." It continued to the long-winded announcement that Malcolm had actually captured his Agnostopithecus.

*"**Brilliant!**"* Rock shouted sarcastically, palming his forehead. *"**There are two of them here!*** That's why the advance team couldn't nail it down to just one type." He shook his head and furrowed his brow. He couldn't believe they all had missed the possibility.

"They're changing up the rules. I've never seen a Rephaim working with an Emim. Not in modern times, anyway," Tick said, agreeing with Rock.

"So those were Carson's vehicles we heard in the park," said Rock, just realizing it. "All right, we've got to head straight to Turkey Run!"

"What about the girl?" asked Tick.

"Cheese can follow us in *this*," he said, indicating the mobile base, "and we'll get one of Sheriff Braxton's deputies to take her to the hospital. You and I'll take the Hummer. You go stock it now because we're bugging out in five."

"Roger that," said Tick. "Wait," he said, "I remember Carson saying that he was staying in Waveland at the bed-and-breakfast on Main. Since we are almost in Waveland at the turn to Turkey Run, maybe we should drop by the B&B and see if we can catch them there?"

"That's Officer thinking," said Rock, confirming the good idea. Honestly, Rock thought that Tick should be the leader of his own team, and in truth, he'd had his opportunities to do so in the past, but Tick chose to keep within his Trinity because the three of them were not just brothers-in-arms, but a very coordinated strike-force. Tick did not want the team to suffer his loss, but not for reason of arrogance, or vanity, but for reason of unity. It was an act of nobility that he'd made that choice.

Rock went back to the Big Cheese and explained the situation to him privately, noting that Cheese had dressed Cindy's abrasions and clothed her comfortably. Tick began moving equipment, mostly weapons, into the Hummer. He took a few provisions as well, and popped another fizzcap for energy and to reduce the pain he was currently experiencing after the battle. Then he began removing the camouflage from the MFB, pulling up stakes. That was when Braxton and his Deputy showed up at the site.

26

MALCOLM CARSON

(From the notes of First Agent Christopher Griffin)

Life on Mars

Is NASA really interested in Mars for a valid reason? What does the space agency need from Mars? What is on Mars that makes it immediately valuable to mankind? Now don't get me wrong, the exploration of space is a valid science. Advancements in innumerable fields have benefited from space exploration technology, but that really isn't the goal concerning Mars, now is it?

Do we need the Martian land because of global overpopulation on earth? No, populations are stabilizing and showing a declining trend, and there is no immediate way to transport men and sustain them on Mars. Is Mars needed for farming in order to feed the world? No; in fact, if we stopped giving unstable nations money and paid them with food instead, we wouldn't have to pay our farmers not to farm, and we wouldn't be giving an immediate ability for enemy nations to buy weapons to use against us. We could go back to the business of feeding the world, and stop throwing away money and lives for treaties that are worthless to begin with. Do we need more information from Mars so we can understand man-made climate change on our planet? Apologies. I realize that is the most idiotic of questions, but there are many who believe in a myriad of idiotic things these days.

Current Mars missions are more closely related to the SETI project—the Search for Extraterrestrial Intelligence. Science cannot validate the theory of evolution. None can demonstrate it or prove that it is anything more than a story. But there is another way, they believe, that they can prove it: Move our origin to another planet. It is referred to as evolution by means of panspermia. It does not offer proof, but is another story that requires "less proof." It moves the problems for the creation of life completely off this world, but it solves nothing by it. If they find liquid water—a lifeless mineral—they'll think they are onto something. But even better, if they find actual living microbes on Mars, they'll think they've solved a key riddle regarding evolution, not realizing that they simply found "life" and not its origin.

Is there life beyond this planet? Absolutely, but most likely not the kind of life NASA is interested in. When this nation is trillions of dollars in debt, and must deal with disease, hunger, poverty, famine, war, and much more, isn't it wise to use what we have to help mankind now? Isn't it time that Americans demanded value and accountability for the money they allow their government to use? Mars isn't going anywhere—not <u>that</u> soon, anyway.

Malcolm's chest hurt as if his ex-wife were dancing on it in stiletto heels, but he was determined to ignore the pain in denial of Jake's insistence that he'd undergone an acute myocardial infarction. Pride pushed him through all pain, and he wasn't going to let anything hinder him in his moment of glory. To his consternation and embarrassment, he *did* have to rebroadcast his speech so that he could secure the claim of capturing his Agnostopithecus. Afterward, he assisted Jake in setting Travis's leg, which had a broken fibula and was bleeding due to the large fingernails that pierced it. As they finished with Travis, John Cosworth and the rest were pulling their vehicles next to Malcolm, trailed by the backhoe.

John Cosworth jumped out of the truck and rapidly moved over to the cage in the ground, playing his flashlight over it and then down into it. The smell was horrible, but that only added encouragement to the hopeful Cosworth.

"Well, I'll be—WE DID IT!" said Cosworth, in somewhat frightened awe of the specimen.

"Of course we did," said Carson, feeling the pain lessen, and ignoring his own wet pants. "We are going to turn crypto-zoology into a mainstream field of study, and stand the scientific community *on its head.*"

"Is it sedated, then?" asked Cosworth.

"Yes. It was quite angry when we encountered it," said Malcolm. "It was probably as scared of us as we were of it; but we shot it up, and it should be out for a very long time since it's been triple-dosed."

"Triple-dosed? I hope it's not dead. Let's hook the cage up and pull it out of the pit," said Cosworth, stepping back and letting his crew move in to hook up the backhoe to the titanium cage so that it might begin the process of extracting the very large, very sturdy cage.

"Who has a working camera or cell phone?" Malcolm asked the others. "We need to document the capture and every step of our journey to the habitat."

"I'll do it," spoke Dr. David Williams, one of the biologists who had not been injured much during the Wiccan attack, but who, like all the others, had his share of bruises and abrasions. Quite a bit of their equipment was damaged during the attack, and everything that wasn't functioning was left behind at the camp. Williams had a working digital camera with a flash in his truck, and carrying it in hand, he came out, taking a picture with every step toward the men who were extracting the cage.

"We've got one of the office trailers in tow, and we can take that back to our campsite," said Cosworth. "At least we'll be able to set up a lab and spend the rest of the night studying the creature before we move it to the CQ facility. We can strap it down and get measurements, samples, temperature readings, and lots and lots of pictures."

As the heavy cage was drawn from the pit, the beast within could be seen by all in the flashlight beams that played upon it and engulfed it. It was big, lean, and curled up in a ball at the bottom of the cage, but it looked like a ferocious monster of legend and lore. And it looked . . . dead, just as Cosworth suspected.

"**You killed it,**" said Malcolm, speaking to Jake, though looking only at the caged beast. "**You killed my Agnostopithecus!**"

"I tranq'd it just like all of us were about to, but I had to keep it from killing Travis," Jake shouted back in his own defense. "That thing is an angry, murderous *MONSTER*, and it wanted all of us dead!"

"**You shot out its eye, and jammed a needle straight into its BRAIN, you crazy freak!**" shouted Malcolm, now being held back by Cosworth, without much effort on account of Malcolm's weak condition.

"It might not be dead," said Cosworth, keeping him from advancing on Jake. "We've got to get it back to our camp quickly and see if we can revive it."

"**Well, get it the on the flatbed, lock it down, and let's get outta here. Those agents are in the park somewhere, and if**"

they see it, *it'll definitely be dead if they have a say about it,"* spat Malcolm.

The troop managed to get the cage on the trailer securely. Cosworth, on a quick thought, took an e-tag gun and injected the beast with the pill-sized tracking device, then moved back, allowing the men to cover the cage with a thick green tarpaulin and tie that down. Then everyone mounted up, and the caravan began to roll back through the park, up and down steep inclines, without spilling any cargo. They made their way into and through the previous camp where the CDC agent's SUV was still parked, but who fortunately was not there to stop them. The backhoe was dropped off at the camp, since there was no further need for it. The truck with the office trailer in tow was waiting for them and joined the parade as it passed it by. They drove up the hill, eventually emerging from Pine Hills and crossing over into Shades, taking their previous DNR route. It was an agonizingly slow ride for Malcolm, who rode with Cosworth, while the others were divided up into the other trucks, either celebrating with the champagne that someone had uncrated from their gathered supplies and distributed among the men, or tending to injuries incurred on this insanely glorious day for the crypto-zoologists.

It took a full hour to travel the twenty miles back to Turkey Run, under the cloud-covered Indiana sky. Travis was taken to the hospital in Crawfordsville for medical attention after his encounter with the creature. But Malcolm refused to go, not knowing at the time that the ER was destined to receive him later, if not sooner.

Of the three state parks, Turkey Run was the most frequented. The volume of campers was nearly at its peak now for the summer. The camp given to the cryptos was the most secluded, but tents and RVs belonging to vacationers were visible from the site, and the Sasquatch hunters had to pass many by campsites to get to theirs. The noise created at their approach woke a few curious campers, who observed the caravan passing by.

Malcolm's party made their way to the campsite, where they parked their vehicles and began to set up the trailer, leveling it and anchoring it. They hooked up the electrical and plumbing, while those who needed to change their clothes and wash up did so. Inquiring eyes peered out their tents to the spy the newcomers, wondering about the early-morning commotion; but seeing nothing special, they tucked themselves back inside, going back to sleep, for a short while, anyway.

Then the "Crypto Team" gathered around the cage for a good look at the creature, and to make sure that each of them was in some of the many photographs that were taken with the beast, all the while celebrating. Malcolm got on the shortwave and contacted CQ, requesting an emergency pickup by helicopter. He wanted this creature gone before Knightlight got wind of it, which he was certain would inevitably happen, so alacrity was of utmost import. Malcolm was informed that a helicopter would not arrive until after a storm nearing Vermillion County had cleanly passed through Parke County. Illinois was currently being hit with a violent thunderstorm, and it was on the border of Indiana, which meant there were air restrictions and warnings above Malcolm's location.

"We're trying to detect a pulse on the creature," Cosworth said to Malcolm as he entered the trailer where Malcolm was making shortwave contact. I'm not sure it's alive, but if so, I don't want to lose the capture of the century."

"Of course we don't want to lose it. What do the doctors think we should do?"

"They want to bring it into the trailer and treat it as an emergency patient, maybe take it to a hospital . . . I said absolutely NO to the hospital suggestion," said Cosworth.

"Good," said Malcolm. "We'd lose control of the situation if it left our hands."

"So, we'll strap it down in here, and get a couple saline IVs in it, run some tests, and treat the wounds. We may even have to inject it in the heart with adrenaline, but we're just guessing until we can examine it."

"We have to be careful, John," said Malcolm. "That moron *Jake* was right about one thing: It's dangerous. But I don't want it to die by any means. So do what you need to do to keep it alive, but just make sure it's strapped down good—and whatever you do, don't let it regain consciousness until it's back in its locked cage."

Meticulously, the trailer was prepped and readied for treatment of the beast, and two men plus Jake had tranquilizer guns in hand, just in case. Malcolm wanted to prevent Jake from having one, but Cosworth told him that if the beast needed to be taken down again, he'd rather have someone around who would actually fire his weapon, rather than fall over wetting himself. He ignored the fact that Jake had done both *before* he took his first shot.

Six men secured straps around the beast and used a "come-along" to pull it out of the cage to where they could get their hands on it and move it inside the trailer. It was heavy, 300 pounds at least, and the six men struggled to move it, fairly dragging it to the steps of the trailer. There they set it down and arranged themselves to move the titanic animal through the door that was designed for a human frame. Together, they managed to get it in, sliding it into the open area of the trailer where all their equipment would encircle it, and then the six drew back and exited the trailer so that the scientists could examine it on the floor.

It was surreal. The monster on the floor looked out of place in the artificial lighting of the trailer. It was a colossal nine feet, eight inches of black, hairy, fanged horror lying in a clean, civilized environment.

"It's tied up, but it isn't strapped down to anything. We need it completely immobile," said Malcolm. "Put some anchors in the floor around it and get it secured first."

John Cosworth instructed the crew to do exactly that, but he wanted Malcolm to shut up and let his team do their job without his interference. "That'll be all the advice we need for a while, Carson. My team will handle this."

"See those fangs?" asked Malcolm, pointing to the creature on the floor. "I saw them up close, and I don't want them snapping at me again."

"We're handling it," said Cosworth firmly.

While his team worked, Cosworth tried to locate a pulse on the creature, but could find none. He looked up to Dr. Williams, also in the room, still taking pictures, and shook his head, indicating that he thought the beast dead.

"We may need to use the defibrillator," Williams said.

"Yes, I agree," approved Malcolm. "But we *need* to be careful first. Until it's tied down firmly, we shouldn't try to revive it."

"Malcolm, you may be the omnipresent overseer of the project *in toto*, but I'm the team leader here. I'll be glad to entertain any thoughts you might have, in time, but I'm the one giving the orders at this site, so don't tell me what to do," Cosworth said firmly.

John Cosworth was never a *big fan* of Malcolm Carson's. Yes, he envied him a little because in the world of crypto-zoology, his was the most famous name. But he behaved like the north end of a southbound horse toward most, and Cosworth was already tired of it. It had been a long night for everyone, a very long night, and he didn't want to overreact, but he did want Malcolm to know who was in charge, once and for all.

Malcolm acquiesced for the moment and stepped over to Cosworth, kneeling next to him. He was very tired, and his chest hurt as if he'd been caught between the hammer and the anvil. The creature scared him, and it was palpable even now. There was something about this beast that *did* seem evil, and though his mind told him that it was just a visceral "fight or flight" reaction to a possible predator, he could not shake the words Moreau said about it, try as he might. This Sasquatch looked more like a dangerous killing machine than "Harry" of the Hendersons.

The crew affixed bolts to the floor of the trailer, connecting them to the frame, and then the nylon straps that wrapped the beast were tightly anchored to the bolts. The beast was as secure as possible on such short notice, and with the equipment they had on hand. Dr. Williams gave Cosworth his camera and put an oxygen mask, connected to a small tank, over the face of the thing on the floor. He tried to secure it on the creature but found that he'd need to cut the elastic straps and use duct tape to affix it. Travis brought in an IV stand, and Dr. Williams put two saline bags on the pole, placing the largest needles he had into the infusers coming out of the bags. Cosworth continued to take digital images throughout the process.

"I'll remove the tranquilizer darts first," said Williams, who took a pair of surgical pliers and pulled the darts, with some effort, from the neck, the forehead, and then the eye socket. It took several minutes for the doctor to clean the socket—it was messy business. He removed the destroyed eye, which was nearly twice the size of a normal human's eye, and then sprayed some antibiotics into the socket, packed it with gauze, and added tape over it for a patch that turned red quickly.

"That eye patch isn't going to hold. The blood will soak the tape and loosen it," suggested Cosworth.

"It's all that's needed at the moment," said Williams as he continued his work hastily. "If it's alive, I'll wind the tape around its head. If it's dead, the patch won't fall off while it's on its back."

Williams then rubbed the beast's large, limp hand, swabbed it with alcohol, and inserted the needles into the creature's veins, taping the infuser tubes down on the hirsute hand that sported sharp, long, black nails. A chill went down Williams' spine simply on account of being in the same room with the bound titan, conscious or not. Then Dr. Williams gambled and injected one of the infuser bags with penicillin without knowing whether it was safe, or whether it would cause a possible allergic reaction, or even whether the dosage was correct. So he made an educated guess on the dose and hoped for the best. Then the doctor attempted to detect a pulse from the creature's wrist. He waited. He moved up and down the wrist. He found nothing.

Malcolm was watching everything. He did his best to keep silent and allow Cosworth's team to do their job without his intervention, regardless of the fact that he had much to criticize. Then he saw the look on Dr. Williams' face and knew there was cause for alarm.

"It's dead, isn't it," said Malcolm. "We've got to give it a jolt *now*!"

"Hang on a minute, I haven't checked the carotid for a pulse," said Williams.

Cosworth motioned to Jake and the two other men holding guns to stand on the other side of the body. He wanted them to be prepared to shoot if needed. Dr. Williams placed his hand under the thick jaw of the beast, feeling around until he was relatively certain that it was in the right place.

"Nothing," said Williams.

"Then SHOCK THAT THING NOW!" erupted Malcolm.

"Go ahead, Dr. Williams," agreed Cosworth. "I'll get an adrenaline syringe."

Williams grabbed the defibrillator box that was sitting next to him and opened it. It was a single self-contained unit with gel-patch appliances. With this type of defibrillator, you would open it up, press the charge button, and—once it turned red—place the entire opened box on the patient and press the outer case button to discharge it into the patient. While it was momentarily charging, the doctor opened a conductive gel pack and set it on the beast's chest, peeling off the back so that the gel was exposed on both sides. The charge light turned red.

"Clear," said the doctor, though nobody was touching the monster, and he placed the open pack on the beast's chest, held it in place, and discharged it.

The beast surged upward forcefully, pulling away from the floor anchors as if it'd been affixed only by masking tape, and tossing the defibrillator and Dr. Williams off its body. Then the beast fell back at rest, and Williams scrambled to get up off the floor, with a little assist from one of Jake's tranq-gun-wielding companions. As if the experience hadn't fazed him, the doctor picked up the unit and set it to charge again.

"That is one powerful animal," said Williams, feeling again for a pulse.

"Anything?" asked Malcolm.

"No," said Williams, who then placed the defibrillator back on the creature, placing his full weight on it this time. "Clear," he repeated and hit the discharge button. The beast convulsed again and tossed the doctor and the defib unit off itself again violently. Williams was dazed this time as he lifted himself off the floor. The unit was visibly broken or at least it was clearly not safe to use again. The doctor searched for a pulse once again. Nothing indicated life in the beast.

"Give me the adrenaline," instructed Williams. Cosworth handed him the syringe.

Dr. David Williams felt the chest to see whether there was a gap between the ribs where he could insert the needle directly into the heart. He found slight grooves, but no clear space. He jammed the needle into the chest where he surmised a gap existed, but the needle didn't penetrate beyond the skin. Removing the syringe, he felt the chest again, but could find no better opening. He lifted his hand and slammed the needle into the chest, but the needle broke and stuck into the bone.

"The skeletal structure on this creature is . . . abnormal," Williams said. "Its bones and cartilage are thicker than they should be, and there doesn't seem to be a gap between the ribs big enough to slide a needle through."

"I'm not a physician," said Cosworth, "but what you're saying isn't a human or an ape characteristic."

"At the moment, I'm just saying that it's a tough animal," said Williams. "But I don't think we are going to be able to revive it. Not with the equipment we have here." He rose from the corpse and stepped back, covering his nose due to the smell that he wished to endure no longer.

"It's still of great value dead," said Cosworth. "Not as much as a living specimen would have been, but it is still the find of the century."

"If it's dead," began Malcolm, "then why does it still **scare the tar outta me**?"

"I um . . . I don't know," said Williams. "But I've been scared spitless since I saw it in the cage."

"Me too. Somehow, this is different than what I'd expected. This creature *feels* like, well, a *monster*, or more than just an animal, anyway. I'm glad to know that I'm not the only one who's terrified by it," said Cosworth.

"Anyone have a problem with a suggestion . . . about . . . well . . . removing its head to be sure it . . . well . . . to be sure it **stays dead**?" Malcolm asked.

"What?" asked Cosworth. "Remove its head? Are you nuts? Why would we do that?"

"I know it sounds dumb, but it doesn't sound too far-fetched under the circumstances . . . . Actually, someone suggested it to me once, and yes, it sounded dimwitted then, but I'm not sure that it isn't the right thing to do," said Malcolm, somewhat sheepishly. "It would just prove that it's dead, that's all, and we'd be able to store the body and head separately, so if the body were taken from us, we'd still have evidence."

"*No*," said Cosworth, thinking that was the stupidest thing Malcolm had ever said. "Absolutely not! Nobody is damaging this creature, and nobody is taking it from us."

Dr. Williams pulled out a pair of pliers from a drawer next to him and removed the needle that had been left in the giant corpse's chest.

"Can we wash this thing down?" asked Williams. "The smell alone is making me nauseous."

"We'll have it taken outside and washed it up. We're gonna have to wrap it up in a tarp so it won't draw flies," said Cosworth. "Then we'll lay it on the truck and figure out how CQ is going to want to pick it up."

"Wait a second," said Malcolm, "If it's dead, wouldn't it evacuate its bladder and bowels?"

"Maybe it did it in the pit," said Williams. "It smells like it did, and then wallowed in it."

Jake put down his rifle and the other men did as well. "I'll get the other guys in here and we'll move it out," he said, and the three men exited the room, leaving Cosworth, Malcolm, and Williams alone, pondering the creature.

"I don't understand why we're still afraid of it," said Cosworth. "I'm almost petrified of it, and that doesn't make any sense."

Sounds of a siren nearing them drew their attention outside. The three men left the trailer to see what was coming. Carson pulled the door shut behind them as they watched the red strobe lights nearing their camp.

"What's this all about?" asked Malcolm.

"I told Jake to call the paramedics so they could check you out. He was sure you had experienced a heart attack, and I was sure you wouldn't leave the camp, so I had him make the call."

"Now just a stinking minute," Malcolm started, "I'm all right. Just a little chest pain, maybe a pectoral cramp. But that wasn't a heart attack."

"Let them check you out," instructed Cosworth. "They can tell you one way or another."

"They will not. I'm not leaving this site until I go with the CQ helicopter," said Malcolm.

"You will, if you want to get back in this trailer," said Cosworth, turning to the trailer's door and locking it, then pocketing the key. "I won't be responsible for the great Malcolm Carson dying on my expedition."

Malcolm gave Cosworth an angry look and decided that he'd better let them examine him if he was ever going to get his way. He had no idea that ten minutes from now, John Cosworth would be the one dying.

27

CRYSTAL

The bathroom was quiet, the tile floor, cool, and when Crystal opened her eyes she could not even remember where she was. She sat up, and her hand felt something thick and wet that had pooled next to her. She lifted her hand and saw that her index finger was dripping with what she believed was red paint. She held up her finger and watched it run the length of her finger into her palm. She'd never painted anything in this color of red. "Curious," she thought. Slowly she rose, grabbing the sink to assist her, to steady her. She looked around the small bathroom, but the walls were white and there were no paintbrushes or rollers around, and still she could not even guess where she was. She was dizzy, raising herself up too quickly, no doubt, and she held the sink to prevent herself from falling down. Then she looked in the mirror. Written upon it in crimson paint were two words. She stared wonderingly at the words: "Kill Moreau."

"Kill Moreau," Crystal giggled aloud. The words were funny to her for some reason. She didn't really understand them, but somebody had obviously painted them there, and there must have been a reason for it. She put her finger up to the mirror and saw that the paint on her finger looked to be the same color as the words. Then she saw her own face behind the words, and there was paint on her forehead as well. She blinked her eyes into focus and then she ran some water to wash off her hands and face. The cool water helped her dizziness and seemed to shake her out of a trancelike state. She wasn't completely in her right mind, but at least she could tell that she wasn't. As she raised her head and looked back at her reflection, the recollections of her ordeal flooded back to her as if a memory dam had crumbled, and a rush of images filled her mind, bringing her up to date. Fear held her spellbound as she looked at the words on the mirror again. She was the only one in the bathroom, but the words that were written there, she could tell, were not in her handwriting.

The lights, she thought, but it was more of an inward gasp than a statement. *Did the lights make me write it?*

Crystal began to shake uncontrollably. She thought she might be possessed, or that aliens had abducted her, or even, perhaps, that past lives had intruded into her mind. To her, anything was possible after what she had experienced, and she completely lacked context to understand it.

"Moreau," she said aloud, and the sound of it startled her into silence, afraid she might have been heard by the lights. She covered her mouth with her hand to be sure she spoke no more. She didn't want the lights to hear her. But the lights were nowhere to be seen in the small bathroom. Silently she continued her thought: *Moreau would know what happened. But how do I contact him? And what if I try to kill him while he's trying to help me?*

Crystal's body shivered despite the warmth of the evening. She knew that the room could not keep out what had attacked her, and she had only one clear exit. She did not know how long she'd been unconscious, but at least the room was empty. Removing the hand from her mouth, and pursing her lips, she gently grabbed the knob of the bathroom door and carefully gave it a clockwise twist until the latch was free. Then she nudged the door open a crack, and tried to see inside the bedroom. The lights were off in her room but she could tell that there was nothing directly in front of the door. And since those lights were not illuminating the room, she hoped they had left her alone. Before opening the door any further, she thought about taking the towel-rack bar to use as a weapon, but then realized that if the lights could move through a closed window, the bar would not be very effective. Her mind was clear once more, and she knew she had to face the unknown alone.

With great care, she pushed the door open, bracing herself for whatever lay beyond it. She saw mostly darkness, and that was encouraging. The lights were not inside, so she stepped to the window and peeked out to see whether perhaps they were waiting for her outside. But they were not there. On her nightstand, she grabbed her phone and pressed the speed-dial, but she had no "bars" and her phone was useless beyond giving her a moment of light, which instantly faded as if the battery were drained by her touch. She tried the light on the nightstand, but it wasn't working either, so she inched her way over to the bedroom door and tried the switch. The lights came on, to her relief. Then, as she turned around, she gasped. In the corner was a rocking chair and upon it was the landlady, moving back and forth, slowly and silently, and until now in the dark. It was the owner of the bed-and-breakfast. She was an elderly woman, but now she looked dead, except for the rocking movement. Her eyes were open, and she was looking straight ahead, unblinking, and her eyes weren't right. They were, well, dark. They looked lifeless, though she continued to rock steadily.

Maybe the lights attacked her, and she hasn't snapped out of it yet? Crystal thought to herself.

"Mrs. Haver . . . ," Crystal stammered. She couldn't remember the complete name of her landlady. She didn't want to get close to the woman who looked, she was hesitant to admit, zombielike, so she kept back from the rocking corpse.

"Are you all right?" Crystal asked, now backing toward the door to her room.

The frail old woman stopped rocking and lifted her head, but did not turn it toward Crystal, her eyes just staring forward as if they were made of dull glass—like a doll's eyes. Her mouth opened and a voice came from it, but it was not a woman's voice, and the woman's lips didn't even move.

"Kill Moreau," the guttural voice commanded, and the woman turned her head toward Crystal, seeing nothing with them. They were the eyes of death.

Crystal backed against the bedroom door and grasped the handle behind her. The door was locked. She turned around and grabbed the knob with both hands, but the brass doorknob would not open. She pulled and twisted it, but it would not give, so she turned back to the woman.

"Get out of my room!" she shouted, while moving over to her laptop. She picked it up and held it in front of her to shield herself from whatever it was—woman, ghost, or zombie—in the room with her.

"We will let you live," it said to her. *"If you kill Moreau!"*

Crystal saw that there was red on the woman's right index finger. She or "it" must have been the one who wrote the message on the bathroom mirror, and then it suddenly came to her, *in my blood.*

"I don't know what's going on here," Crystal said, "but I've had about enough of it! Now get out of my room, or, or I'll shove this laptop in your *word-hole* and take your keys myself!"

The old woman rose from the chair and clumsily pulled a revolver from her dress pocket. She did not hold it threateningly, but limply, as if she were a marionette moved by an unseen puppeteer.

"He is coming," said the voice inside the old woman. "Kill Moreau *or die*," it said, and it dropped the revolver on the bed for Crystal to pick up. Then it looked at her with dull eyes and something inside the dead woman made the corpse smile. Then the three lights came out of the body they occupied, and the body of Mrs. Haversham fell to the floor like an empty pillowcase, inanimate and unliving. Crystal screamed.

28

NICK OF TIME

(From the notes of First Agent Christopher Griffin)

Demonology 101

Chapter One: Demons Are the Sons of God of Genesis
6:2-4 (an excerpt)

If the above title did not explain it clearly, let me dispel all doubt: The Sons of God are not human children of the line of Seth. End of Chapter One.

Chapter Two: Dealing with It

There are actually only five specific Old Testament references to "the Sons of God"—two in Genesis, three in Job. The references are to beings greater than mankind. Anything else is a mistake. The many New Testament references to "the Sons of God" pertain to those who place their faith in the Jewish Messiah, Jesus. There is, hatred for the new Sons of God by the fallen one-third of the Old Testament's Sons of God.

Though they are fallen, it does not mean that demons have yet been outcast from Heaven, apart from those locked in the deep, as Satan and one-third of the Host of Heaven still have access before the face of God, and power upon the face of the earth. It also does not mean that they no longer serve His purposes. The Scriptures declaring the "fall" of Satan and his angels are both historical and prophetical. Much of Biblical prophecy, while speaking to events that are contemporary to the prophet—the near-future events—also speak to distant-future events, even those which are yet to come in our time. Dual and multiple fulfillments are not rare.

Demons are at work behind every war, every cartel, and every nation. They are manipulators of death and destruction, and are unrepentant. Satan was the instigator of it Eden's downfall, and was also there to take the title deed of this universe from man, and "authority of ownership" was imparted to him—to a degree, anyway. Now it should be noted that in ancient times, title deeds had seven seals, and this deed is specifically referenced in the book of Revelations. Satan still has authority in this universe, though he no longer holds the deed to it. Jesus took it captive from Satan just before He rose from the grave, but the seals are still unbroken. Heaven help those who are on the earth when the seals are break.

Demons are powerful. One could wipe out the entire population of the planet in a single night. What stops them? God, of course. They have certain permissions and liberties, but it is not carte blanche. Nothing happens in this universe without God permitting it, but not all things "allowed" are "God's divine will." Far from it.

Demons have different names, but those are unimportant. They have different strengths, duties, and roles, but those are also not that important. A demon tempting a human to eat too much chocolate is as much a demon as one attempting to possess a human.. The biggest difference between the two is in the human or "target" of the demon. Temptations are everybody's experience and anyone can resist temptation or fall prey to it. A Christian can not only resist, but make the enemy flee. Possession rarely happens at the drop of a hat. One usually gives himself over to dark forces repeatedly in order for a demon to take hold and get a good grip on the target. The will of a man is not easily superseded because it is a gift from God for all mankind.

God has set a choice before us—Life or death, blessing or cursing—and encourages us to choose life that we and our children may live.

Christians can be oppressed, not possessed. Greater is Christ in you than he that is in the world. Ignore the Hollywood stereotyped exorcisms. Possession is most often the choice of the possessed, either directly or indirectly. Remember, Biblically, the ratio of healings and exorcisms were about 50-50, so there are many more out there with demonic issues than most realize. Our society has covered it over with psychiatry, and medicated much of it into manageability.

The Bravo Trinity was readying to roll out when Sheriff Braxton and his Deputy pulled up beside the Hummer. Tick, still pulling up the stakes of their camouflage, looked up and waved down the Sheriff. Rather than getting out and walking down to the

MFB, Braxton had his Deputy drive down to it. From inside, Rock observed their approach on the monitor while he was writing down some information. He pocketed his notations and exited the rear of the mobile base to meet them. Then he quickly went over to the passenger window, seeing the Sheriff rolling it down stiffly.

"That's one big truck," commented Braxton through the pain of his wound.

"Sheriff, what the heck happened to you?" asked Nick, seeing the knife and blood on Braxton's shoulder. "You should get to the hospital," said Nick, with due concern.

"I will, but I needed to let you know that Malcolm Carson has made a capture of his Bigfoot, and apparently, by the account of one of the cultists, there's two of them out here."

"Thanks, Sheriff. We've just confirmed that ourselves when we played back his broadcasts," replied Rock. "It's worse than we thought, but we've still got a handle on how to proceed. We rescued Miss Stroud, and she's with us. The beast is dead. Can you transport Cindy to the hospital with you? We need to get to Carson fast."

"Of course," said Braxton. "Is she all right?"

"She's dehydrated, and she's been through a horrific ordeal, including rape . . . and she is pregnant. My organization has councilors that I'll have visit her at the hospital once she's been treated. She needs to stay there for several days, but she should be fine."

"Good," said Braxton, then added, "you look like you took a pounding yourself."

"We frankly got the *beat pooped out of us*, but that is not too unusual in our line of work," said Rock. "We're alive, and we're prepared to move to the next objective.

"Oh," said Braxton, "the *cult* members have been identified, and their leader is on her way to the County Jail."

"Excellent news, Sheriff," said Rock. "Is that how you got that souvenir in your shoulder?"

"Yes," said Braxton. "The witch's name is Darlene Campbell, and her group will be rounded up by tomorrow."

"Very good," said Rock. "On your way out of here, I need you to do something for me. I know it's out of your jurisdiction but I need you to make two calls for me."

Rock pulled out a piece of paper and handed it to the Sheriff. Braxton looked at it and understood.

"I can do that," said Braxton.

Rock pulled out his Knightlight card and gave it to the Sheriff. It had Rock's contact information on the back. "You need something in the future, partner, you just ask."

"And you know how to contact me, so the same stands," said Braxton.

"We'll bring out Miss Stroud and then you can get going," said Rock.

"Agent Moreau?" spoke Braxton.

Rock turned around and faced the Sheriff again. "Yes, Sheriff?"

"Thanks for finding the girl," he said, speaking of Cindy.

"It's been a team effort, Sheriff," replied Rock. "We just did our part, and I appreciate that you were able to do yours with success. You have our thanks as well. We're not in contact with our central office yet, but when we're able to report in, I'll make sure that my superiors take note of your assistance. The war you've found yourself in is heating up, and we're glad to make allies anywhere they can be found."

"I'm just a peace officer but I'm glad to know there are men out there like you. You know what George Orwell said," commented Braxton. Rock shook his head, unsure.

"People sleep peaceably in their beds at night only because rough men stand ready to do violence on their behalf," quoted Braxton.

"*That*'s a quote that I'll commit to memory, Sheriff Braxton," said Rock as a parting statement, as he saluted him farewell.

Rock entered the MFB and assisted the Big Cheese in guiding Cindy out of the vehicle and gingerly placing her inside the Sheriff's vehicle. She was weak and tired, but it had been of great encouragement to her when she had learned that the beast had been killed, and more so as they had helped her through the cavern and she knew they had burned its dead carcass to the ground. She was indebted to her heroes and was reluctant to leave them, but she knew that Sheriff Braxton would see her safely to the hospital.

Braxton knew that he shouldn't try to discuss Cindy's ordeal with her, and before Cheese and Rock brought her to their car, he had instructed Caleb not to mention the fact that *a second creature exists*. Then, unceremoniously, Caleb backed the vehicle away, turned it around, and he, the Sheriff, and Cindy drove up the hill and out of the park on their way to the hospital. Cindy began to offer the entire story to Braxton, which began with the hike and ended in the rescue, and she only just finished when they pulled into the hospital parking lot. The Sheriff was amazed that she had been able to keep herself sane through the trial she had emerged from, and Caleb was in awe of the tale, but not sure how much of it might be true or might be shock. He was very glad, however, that he was not part of the confrontation with whatever attacked her.

Braxton was admitted, treated, and scripted, but refused to stay at the hospital afterward. He knew he'd have a busy day with rounding up the cultists and sorting out the entire mess, so Caleb took him home just as the thunderstorm hit. It took little time for Braxton to stiffly undress himself and climb into his bed. He was out mere seconds after he closed his eyes. Even at the height of the storm, Braxton slept through it soundly.

✦

Rock drove while Tick rode shotgun in the Hummer, and the Big Cheese drove the MFB behind them all the way to Waveland.

They crossed SR-47 and onto 59, over the bridge, past the Sheriff's post, and up the hill past the diner, following 59 around the curve, and down the road to the bed-and-breakfast where Malcolm was staying. They parked their vehicles and all three met in front of the two-story house.

"I don't see Malcolm's Land Rover on the street or behind the house," said Rock.

"Then we'd best get moving to Turkey Run," offered Tick.

"Someone's awake in the second-story bedroom," commented Cheese. "It looks like they're watching late-night TV."

Then Tick felt it. He'd felt it long ago, and he felt it now. "That's not television," he said. "There are Moroni up there."

And as if on some demonic *cue*, all three men heard a muffled scream from the room. The flickering blue light was casting a female shadow on the curtains, and they knew Crystal Carson was in danger. The Cheese and Tick pulled their guns from their holsters and began to move to the front door of the home, but Rock whistled them to stop.

"*Swell*," said Rock. "This mission's got it all and we're not even getting a breather."

"What's the call?" asked Tick.

"We pray before we confront," said Rock quietly. "Not by might, nor by power, but by His Spirit. Weapons stay down here."

"Roger that," said Tick, bowing his head, and the Cheese did the same.

"Start us off, Tick," said Rock, bowing his head.

"Father," said Tick, "You have all authority in Heaven and in the earth, and we ask You to disarm the enemy we are about to face. We respectfully request that You pull down the strongholds of the enemy in the name of Jesus. We trust in Your might. We have no weapon that can hinder the enemy, save your Holy Word. We have no strength beyond Your enabling. Please pour out Your Spirit on us, and let loose Your angels to do battle against the forces of darkness before us. We ask for our protection, but more so for the Carsons'. In the name of your Son, and by His blood, we plead on their behalf. Help us stand fast before the rulers of darkness in high places. Help us send the enemy to flight. We ask You to be with us, and to move us, and that our very being be hid within You. We ask this in the name of Jesus, trusting that You hear our petitions. Amen."

"Amen," agreed Rock and the Big Cheese.

"Let's shake the gates of Hell," said Rock, and the three climbed the steps to the porch.

"Hold the line," said Tick.

"Hold the line," said Rock and the Big Cheese as Rock broke the window on the front door, reached in, and unlocked it from the inside. The three trusted that God's Spirit was with them, and so He was. They knew it.

Carefully, the three entered the home that was also a B&B, and began their ascent to the second floor, where they stopped. They knew which door to breach, so Rock gave the Big Cheese the signal to break it down. Another scream erupted from the room and Cheese slammed into the door with full force. It gave way to his powerful coercion, and the three made their egress from the hallway into the bedroom, into the dark light of the enemy. Immediately, they smelled ozone and brimstone mingled together. It was a caustic smell. They saw that Crystal was on the bed and blue-white lights darted at her and about her, trying to force her to take the gun and still commanding her to kill Moreau. They saw the dead woman on the floor by the rocking chair. If evidence told the entire story, half of Knightlight's job would be unnecessary, but the evidence never told the entire story.

"Crystal," shouted Rock, "Come to me."

"*HELP!*" Crystal shouted through her tears. "They want me to kill you!"

"I'd advise against it!" Rock shouted back, hoping the jest might calm her a bit.

As if to silence her, small jagged bolts of blue lightning stabbed at her struggling figure while she kicked and screamed against them. Then they shot out toward Rock as he entered the room, but they could not seem to hit him. Something unseen was deflecting the energy from him, and though it was not always that way, Rock was glad not to be tossed into the hallway, perhaps even down the stairs, by the powerful energy bolts. Rock knew that God was with them and His host was fighting before them.

"Leave in the name of Jesus," Rock commanded the lights, and they were pushed out of the way by the authority of the Lord Almighty. "Come here, Crystal. Get behind us."

Crystal rolled off the bed and ran to Rock, ducking behind him and holding herself to him.

"You have no authority here," spoke Tick. "Jesus is with us and His host is before us! Leave this place in the name of Jesus!"

The lights were forced against the wall and could not advance on the four no matter how they tried. Unseen to the four were angels of God in full combat against the demonic entities that were visible. But there were many more enemies than the tree lights indicated, and a battle raged before Crystal and the Knightlight agents, and the only indication of it was that the lights had no power to attack them.

"The victory is the Lord's," spoke Rock. "Jesus is the authority in this world! Flee in the name of Jesus."

"Leave this place by the power of His Resurrection!" shouted Tick.

"We bind you, chain you, and cast you out in the name of Jesus!" shouted the Big Cheese.

"Thank You, Father, for the Victory," spoke Rock. "Thank You for pulling down the enemies' strongholds."

"Thank You for Your Son, for Your grace, and Your strength! Praise Your name!" said Tick.

The lights flashed and then dove into the corpse of the old woman, bringing her seemingly to life and raising her up to her feet with horrific quickness. They made her growl and hiss and they shook the dead body violently, as if some entity were climbing inside it for a full body-suit fitting, which was nearly the truth of it. The puppet of the Moronis looked like it was readying to spring at the men.

"The girl is ours," it spoke from within the old woman without moving her lips. It was a mockery of a resurrection. The inhuman creature before them spat accusations against the Trinity of men. It shouted obscenities and shouted out the sins the agents had committed in the past and not-so-distant past. It was very accurate, and it was all very true. It stung them each, wounded their spirit, but it did no real harm to the men; for each charge had already been forgiven, and paid for in Christ. Still, it was very unpleasant to hear it and know it was true. Demons accuse with perfection and shame with a vengeance. It is an ugly thing for a man to see himself through the mirror of truth, and even worse to hear a merciless enemy spell it out to him.

"Enough!" shouted Rock, and the demonic hellish creature went silent.

"Sh . . . she's a zombie! *She told me to kill you!*" Crystal screamed and cowered, grasping Rock's arm and holding her eyes shut against the ghastly sight of the dead woman.

"The Lord rebuke you," said Rock, and the woman's body acted as if she had been slapped hard. Then the demons inside forced the corpse to advance toward the four. Their presence gave the dead woman's body supernatural strength and she raked her fingernails in the air in front of them. Black blood began to drip from the corpse's mouth as it spat vile words of cursing at them.

"Leave NOW, in the name of the King, in the name of *Jesus*," shouted the Big Cheese, and suddenly the lights shone out the back of the woman's carcass, nearly losing control of it, only to return within and advance once more upon them.

"Leave in the name of *Jesus*," commanded Rock and Tick in unison.

The lights were forced out the back of the woman, and pushed through the wall, and were not seen again. The dead body of the landlady collapsed to the floor, no longer defiled by the enemies of God and man.

All three men breathed a heavy sigh of relief, nearly stumbling as the tension left their muscles. The battle was always intense, and the rush of Godly presence was palpable. Men use drugs to feel a euphoria but that pales before the Joy of the Lord. Still, the presence of God could wear a man out fast, if it did not also sustain him. Crystal clung to Rock and her legs gave way. Immediately Rock turned, holding her arms, and knelt with her as the other men gathered around.

"It's over, Crystal," said Rock to the weeping, frightened young lady.

"They wanted me to kill you. They killed Mrs. Haver . . . something, over there," she cried, pointing to the woman on the floor. "They made her move, but she was dead. What are they?"

"They're nothing to be trifled with, Crystal. They are not from this world," said Rock.

"But they *have* been forced from this place by the power of God," said the Big Cheese.

"And to tell you the truth, that's who you need in your life," said Tick.

"I'm afraid I . . . I mean . . . do you think I might be possessed?" whimpered Crystal.

"I don't think so, Ms. Carson. They retreated into the body of the dead woman, not into you. They would have rather been in a warm body. Instead, they animated the dead woman; but she wasn't actually a zombie, they just used her like a meat-puppet. Possession is not as easy for them as you may think," said Rock. "If you resisted them, and it appears that you were doing exactly that, then you should be fine. You can resist them, but you lack the authority to make them flee."

429

"Thank you for coming," she cried as she hugged him. She felt his strength and was comforted by his arms around her. "So, God is real, then, isn't He?"

"God is more *real* than we are, Crystal. We are His creation. We don't exist without Him being real," said Rock earnestly.

"All I've ever known has been a lie then," she said, trying to stop the tears.

"Yes," said Rock. "Just like all I ever knew was a lie until God showed Himself *real* to me, years ago. Usually He's more subtle than this, but just as God is real, so is Satan."

"Fortunately, Satan is no match for God," said the Big Cheese. "Though we're in the middle of a war, and though there are casualties, *our side* wins . . . in the end."

"But there are still losses on our side until then. We need to get going," said Tick, and Rock knew he was right.

"Agent Ledford, call 911 and get an ambulance here to collect the old woman," Rock said. He then added to Crystal, attempting to gently extricate himself from the hug, and failing, "You should go to the hospital so they can make sure you're all right."

"I'm going with you," she said in a no-nonsense way.

"Very well. We need to get to your father," said Rock, lifting her up while she still clung to him like a koala to a eucalyptus tree. It reminded him of the times his wife had clung to him, back when she was part of him. It felt warm and strange and nostalgic at the same time. He shook off those thoughts quickly because that was not his life anymore. The enemy was still at hand, and there were others who needed his team's aid.

Gently, Rock moved Crystal away, making sure she could stand on her own, but putting distance between himself and her. Then, by the hand, he led her downstairs as his men followed. The three exited the B&B and Rock took Crystal to the mobile base, sat her down, and made sure she was comfortable before he exited and spoke with his team.

"An ambulance is on the way," confirmed the Big Cheese to Rock.

"Copy that. Follow me to Turkey Run," said Rock to the Big Cheese. "Tick, you can keep Ms. Carson company, and keep her calm. Get some liquids into her and make sure she's warm. She might be in shock. Keep trying to establish contact with Spectacle. When we get to the park, we need to be ready for anything, from a fight with Malcolm's crypto-zoologists, to facing another monster, so check your ammo."

29

THE TURKEY RUN MONSTER

(From the notes of First Agent Christopher Griffin: The Nature of God)

God is . . . ; that in itself says much. God is Love; again volumes have and continue to be written about that point. Here is more: God is sovereign, mighty, and eternal. God is all-wise, all-powerful, all-knowing, peerless, and flawless. God is lonely. Now that is something that few mention. God desires fellowship from those who would love Him just because He is. God desires men to trust in Him, casting their cares upon him. God is humble and lovingly condescends to mankind just for such fellowship, and He serves the least of men with compassion, with grace, and with care. God is righteous, is faithful, and rejoices when men trust in him. He is a righteous judge. He is a disciplinarian to His children, but it is a fearful thing to fall into the hands of the Living God if you are not His child. He desires peace on earth, and good will toward men, even though it cost Him the death of His own Son. He holds the complexity of this universe in the span of His hand, but He is simple in his tender mercies and love.

God generously gives authority to others even when they are undeserving to wield it. He knows exactly what He is doing even when there are others carrying out His will. When we pray, it is not to change His will, as His will is perfect. Prayer brings us in order, not the other way around. Prayer changes us, and enables us to walk according to His divine will. His will is never a "whim"; it is always calculated, righteous, and flawless. He gives and takes away with wisdom, compassion, and mercy. God loves his creation.

TURKEY RUN STATE PARK

8121 E Park Road • Marshall, Indiana 47859 • 765-597-2635
2,382 Acres   Established 1916

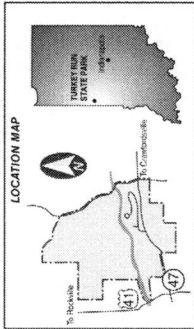

LOCATION MAP

To Rockville
To Crawfordsville
TURKEY RUN STATE PARK
Indianapolis
411
47

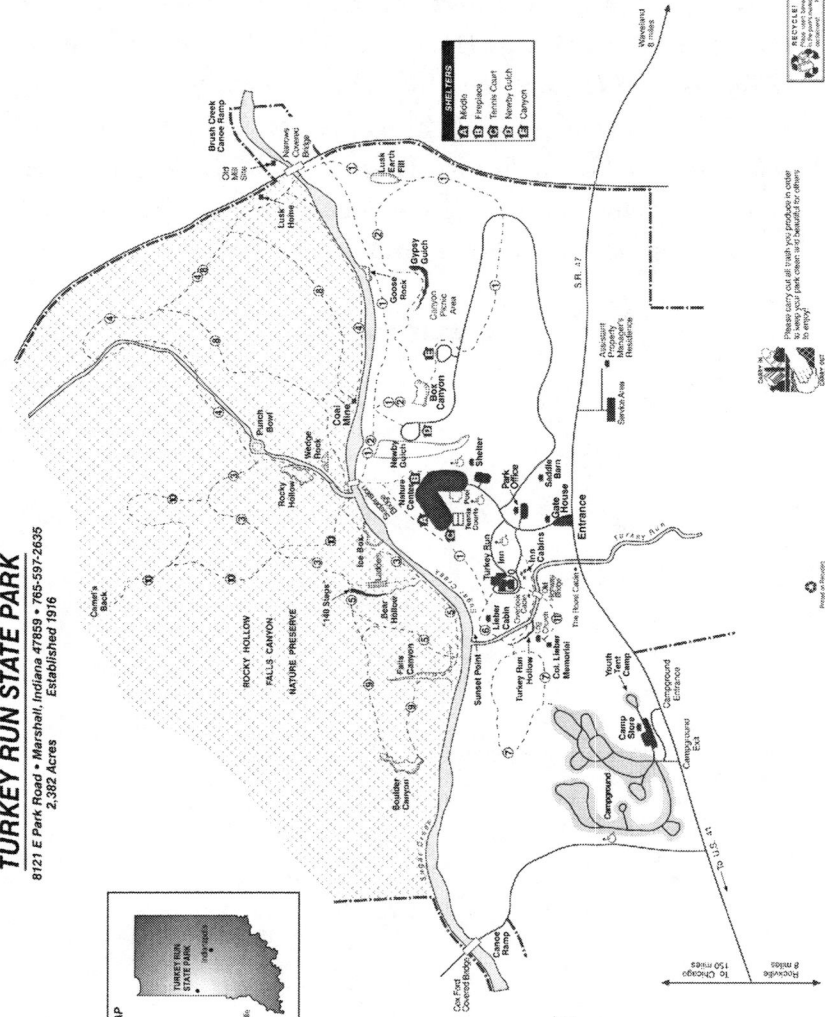

Brush Creek Canoe Ramp
Old Mill Site
Narrows Covered Bridge
Lusk Earth Fill
Lusk Home
Gypsy Gulch
Goose Rock
Canyon Picnic Area
Box Canyon
Punch Bowl
Wedge Rock
Coal Mine
Newby Gulch
Nature Center
Tennis Courts
Nature Shelter
Park Office
Saddle Barn
Gate House
Entrance
Turkey Run Inn
Ten Cabins
Lieber Cabin
Col. Lieber Memorial
Youth Tent Camp
Camp Store
Campground
Campground Entrance
Campground Exit
Canoe Ramp
Cox Ford Covered Bridge
Camel's Back
Rocky Hollow
Ice Box
'140 Steps'
Bear Hollow
Falls Canyon
Sunset Point
Turkey Run Hollow
Boulder Canyon
ROCKY HOLLOW FALLS CANYON NATURE PRESERVE

S.R. 47
To U.S. 41
To Chicago 150 miles
Rockville 8 miles
Waveland 8 miles

SHELTERS
Middle
Fireplace
Tennis Court
Newby Gulch
Canyon

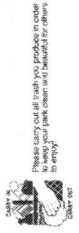

RECYCLE!

Stay on Marked Trails.
Trails Close at Dusk.
Bicycles Prohibited on
Trails and Service Roads.
Swimming and Wading
in Sugar Creek are
Prohibited within the Park.

Approximate Scale in Miles
0   1/4   1/2

TRAIL TABLE		
TRAIL	MILEAGE	TRAIL TYPE
1	.3	Moderate/Rugged
2	.7	Rugged
3	1.7	Very Rugged
4	.2	Moderate/Rugged
5	.5	Moderate
6	.7	Moderate/Rugged
7	.7	Moderate
8	1	Moderate
9	1	Very Rugged
10	1.4	Moderate
11	.5	Easy

LEGEND
Road
Hiking Trail
Boundary
Accessible
Nature Preserve

Crystal rode quietly in the mobile base, accompanied by Tick, who gave her a blanket to keep warm and a cup of coffee, which she sipped while looking around at the base's equipment. It was a smooth ride within the powerful machine. She was impressed with all the technical gear and weaponry within the vehicle. When she first saw it, she thought it interesting that the first four sets of wheels in the front, of the eight in total, could turn, making cornering amazingly tight. It was like riding in a fortress, and it comforted her. But she was so very tired, and every time she blinked, let alone closed her eyes, she saw either the lights or Mrs. Haversham, so she fought to keep them open. She knew that she had experienced true evil. She knew that she was unequipped to confront it, and but for the Grace of God, she knew she wouldn't have survived it. That knowledge nudged her, and pushed her, and she realized that she needed "more" than what she currently had. She also knew where that "more" was.

"How can I have what you have?" she asked. "How do I become a Christian?"

"You simply have to believe in Jesus Christ as your Lord and Savior. You have to receive His free gift of salvation, and then start your new life with Him. It is called being 'born again,'" Tick said. "I can lead you in your prayer of salvation, if you would like me to, but before you do, I think you should know the price of it."

"The price? I don't understand; you said it was a free gift."

"It cost Jesus His entire life down here with us, and it *is* a free gift to you, but it will turn your father against you, it will offend your colleagues, and your friends will look upon you with derision just because you believe. It puts a sword, that is, 'the Word of God,' in your hands, and all who see you wield it will challenge you, tempt you, and wound you. Most will believe they are doing something 'good' in doing so," said Tick.

"I'm not afraid, but I understand what you mean. I'll be on the other side of their fence."

"It's more of a minefield than a fence, and there is only one path through it. Are you sure?"

"Please," she said, and since she'd seen people pray before, she intuitively bowed her head. Though not required, it is a show of humility.

"Repeat after me," said Tick. "Father, thank You for Jesus." Crystal repeated after him. "Who came into this world . . . ." Tick paused each time so Crystal could keep up with him. "To pay for my sin . . . . He was sinless before God . . . . And He took my sin upon Himself at the cross . . . . So I could have His righteousness given freely . . . . And He rose from the dead *bodily* after three days . . . . Having power over death itself . . . . Which is the penalty of all sinners . . . . For the wages of sin is death . . . . But the gift of God is eternal life in Christ Jesus . . . . I believe it . . . . I receive it . . . . I ask You now, Jesus, please come into my heart . . . . Come into my life . . . . Be my Lord . . . . Pour Your grace out on me . . . . Pour Your Holy Spirit out on me . . . . Forgive me of my sin . . . . Help me to repent for my sin . . . . To turn from it . . . . I'm sorry for my sin . . . . Help me to live for You . . . . Help me to live thankfully before You . . . . Humbly before You . . . . Graciously before You . . . . In Jesus' name . . . . Amen."

"Thank you," she wept, but this time they were tears of relief and belief. She *KNEW* now, beyond any doubt, that the Lord was real and had just saved her. She was eternally grateful. "Now what do I do? I feel light . . . like . . . like Scrooge did after he was visited by the three ghosts. I feel . . . joy."

Tick smiled down at her and gave her a gentle, friendly hug. "Now the world is new to you. God and His angels are rejoicing. Now you need to dive into God's Word and see what He has to say to you personally. You need to talk to Him often and just abide in Him. Get plugged into a Bible-believing church and study the Bible and share your faith with others. Jesus also gave us instruction to be baptized as a public statement of your faith, and identifying yourself to the world as a believer, so whenever that is convenient, I encourage you to do so. It is a step of faith, a work of faith, but you are already saved, so don't think it is required for your salvation."

"Thank you, Agent . . . ," she stammered, not remembering his first name.

"Cavor . . . and it was my pleasure," he said in all honesty.

Then she remembered she had her cell phone with her.

"Agent Cavor, should I call my Dad and let him know we're on the way to his location?" she asked.

Tick looked at her for a moment, not sure why she'd even ask. It's still a free country after all, so permission wasn't a question. But then he remembered that even if she was outside, she most likely wouldn't get a signal.

"Ms. Carson, you may do whatever you think best, but we seem to be in a cell-blackout zone, and your cell phone's signal isn't going to penetrate the plating here from inside. Beyond that, our equipment will likely interfere with it, so I recommend you use our communications center. And if you don't mind, I'd like to trace it to the source so we can make sure we meet up with him," said Tick.

"I would very much like you to pinpoint his location . . . . He doesn't know what he's done. He's in danger, isn't he?" she asked.

"Yes, Ms. Carson, his entire team is in grave danger," said Tick as he led her to the comm center and showed her how to make the call. "Do you mind if I listen in, or is it private?"

"Please do," she said. "Any help you can offer is appreciated." Crystal now trusted these men with her life, completely. She knew they were the answer to the danger her father was in, and she was prepared to get her father to safety if they had to drag him away, kicking and screaming.

Crystal placed the headphones on, dialed Malcolm's phone, and heard the phone ring on his end . . . and then it rang again . . . and then again . . . on the fourth ring there was an answer.

"This is Malcolm," Carson said.

"Dad, are you all right? Where are you?" she asked.

"Crystal, I'm sorry, Princess, I was so excited, I forgot to call you . . . ," said Malcolm. "I did it! I've got my Agnostopithecus! We're taking care of some details, but we're going to bug out soon and I'll come and get you when we do. They think I've had a heart attack and some EMTs are checking me out, but don't worry, I'm fine."

"Dad, you've got to get away from it *now* . . . . It is dangerous, and it's exactly as Agent Moreau said—it's a deadly killer."

"Well . . . first of all, it's dead, so you have nothing to worry about, but where are you calling from? I don't recognize the number. Are you still at the bed-and-breakfast?" Malcolm asked.

"No, Dad, I was almost **killed there**! I was attacked by, well, **demons**, I guess. But I was rescued by the Knightlight agents and we're on our way to you," she said.

"Knightlight!" exclaimed Carson, and cursed. "That explains it. You're probably suffering from Stockholm syndrome or something. They're messing with your mind."

"Ask him if the monster still has its head attached," coached Tick.

"Dad, shut up for a minute! You said the monster is dead . . . how do you *know*?" she asked.

"There is no heartbeat, no pulse even after we tried to revive it . . . it's dead all right," said Malcolm.

"Does it still have its head attached to its body?" she asked.

"Of course it does, Honey. It's the only specimen we've got, and we're not going to disfigure it just to accommodate an old wives' tale," said Malcolm.

"Tell him to get out of there and take his men with him," instructed Tick.

"Now listen to me, Dad, get as far away from that thing as possible. *I mean it*," said Crystal.

"What's gotten into you? You mentioned demons? Being attacked? What's going on?" Malcolm demanded.

"Dad, it's all true what they said . . . what Agent Moreau said," she pleaded, knowing what stubborn ignorance she was confronting in her father . . . the same stubborn ignorance she herself had only hours ago. "Don't argue with me, just get away from that creature and go somewhere safe. Get in the Land Rover and come back toward Waveland."

"Crystal," Malcolm said, as if she were 8 years old and he were putting up with a fantastic story that would turn out to be a nightmare. "You're tired, and frightened, and we'll be there to get you soon. Just calm down and wait for me, and stay away from **Dominic Moreau!**"

"Dad, **GET OUT OF THERE!**" Crystal shouted to her father just as there was a loud explosion over the phone, and then Crystal knew that their communication had been cut off on Malcolm's end. Still she shouted out, "**DAD!**"

"We're only five minutes away, Ms. Carson," said Tick, placing his hand on her shoulder to calm her. She was distraught, scared, and tired, and now she feared for her father's life. She sank back in the chair at the comm station and wept, while Mike Cavor stood behind her and prayed for what to say to her. All three men, Mike and his teammates, had been put to the test this evening, but Crystal had not even known the nature of her test, how to face it, and how to face the next test before her. Mike asked the Lord for wisdom, and noting that Crystal was calming down, he passed her a tissue and waited for her to reach composure.

"Everything OK back there?" came the voice of Rock over the speakers, from the Hummer they were following.

"Everything's OK, with us," said Tick, "but Crystal just called Malcolm. He was suddenly cut off. He's at the Turkey Run site, just like we thought."

"We're almost there, Ms. Carson. We'll do our best to make sure your dad is safe," said Rock.

"Thank you, Agent Moreau," she said, now in better control of her emotions.

"Ms. Carson just asked Jesus into her heart," said Tick.

"That's the best news I've heard all day," said Rock. "Congratulations, Ms. Carson, and welcome to the family."

"It's Crystal," she said. "I mean, I want you to call me Crystal."

"Welcome, Crystal," said Rock, his voice betraying the unseen smile that his face wore because of the good news. He knew that Cindy Stroud's life was temporarily saved this evening, and that was something, but Crystal's eternal life had just been saved, and above all, that was what Knightlight or any Christian prized the most.

"Here's the turnoff to the park. We'll be at their campsite's turnoff in a couple of minutes," said the Big Cheese over the radio. He was driving as fast as was safe, maintaining a close tail on the lead vehicle.

"Once more unto the breach, dear friends," Rock quoted a wise fellow named Will.

"Hold the line," said the Big Cheese.

"Hold the line," replied Tick.

"What's that?" asked Crystal. "What's 'hold the line' mean?"

"Oh . . . well . . . it's a battle cry of sorts. It reminds us that we are to stand fast . . . to be unmovable, unshakable before the enemy. If we win or lose, the battle is the Lord's. Our enemy is stronger than us and it knows it. But the Lord goes before us, and regardless of how or where He leads us, we'll hold the line."

30

OF MONSTERS AND MEN

(From the notes of First Agent Christopher Griffin: The Hunt)

The best hunter is the one who keeps his quarry ignorant of being hunted. The hunt changes to a battle or a race when the hunted becomes aware of the hunt. Men of the world, believing themselves to be hunters, are in reality the hunted. Satan laughs at them, while Death waits for them. Satan does not love the hunted; he only wishes to devour his prey. It has never been Satan's desire to rule in Hell. It is not his desire to claim the souls of men that they may fight against God at his side. Satan wants to rule Heaven, and the universe, and trample over men simply because God made them in His image, breathed them to life, and loves them. Oh, he will assist men in obtaining worldly possessions, power, and wealth, but that is just bait for his prey. He's not interested in men beyond finding ways to turn their hearts from God, and then to destroy them. We are the game. But what happens when the game gets wind of the hunt? It makes it hard for the hunter, and causes the hunter to curse the hunted, and exert more effort in the hunt.

Ideally, a hunter wants to kill his prey instantly. Barring that, he wants to cripple the prey for a near-future kill. Barring that, he wants to make his prey bleed so that it will give up its life's blood over time. Barring that, it wants to prevent it from an avenue of escape, and keep it ignorant of a way for its salvation. But the hunter would rather be unknown to his prey so that the kill is made without a struggle. When that fails, and the prey is aware of the hunt, the hunter knows that the tables can be turned on the hunter, to his vexation.

Now, we who know the Lord are aware of the hunt and the hunter. We who know the Lord must become the wise prey. We must turn the tables on the hunter. We must be on the attack. We must run against the hunter, or at least show him that we will not play his game. The prey must resist the hunter and rob him of his victory, but here is the secret: The hunter has already been robbed of it from the foundation of the world. Soon he will understand that very fact. Soon he will see that his time is short. Soon he will see that his defeat is at hand. Until that day, stand fast. Until that day, hold the line.

Malcolm was lying down with the cell phone up to his ear and was speaking to Crystal while the EMTs were hooking him up to a portable EKG monitor. It was uncomfortable, but he ignored it in order to speak with his daughter. She sounded, well, crazy to him. He expected her to be elated about the news of his victory, but it seemed to make her frightened. She spoke of nearly being killed, and rescued, and none of it made any sense to him. Why on earth was she worried for him? His camp was teeming with strong men and the creature was dead. It was about the safest place he could think of being, under the circumstances. But while that last thought was still fresh in his mind, and while he was trying to relay that to his daughter, along with the fact that she needed to "stay away from **Dominic Moreau . . .**"

. . . the trailer behind him exploded.

Every head in the camp turned toward the trailer as it was ripped to shreds from within. The monster tore through it as if it were made out of popsicle sticks and papier-mâché. Debris was tossed in all directions and once-confident men were felled by the mighty roar of the creature within. It emerged from the clusters of vinyl, aluminum, and insulation that were falling back to earth. It was a dark and fierce creature. It had hate in its one good eye, and the blackness of death in the other. There were screams from campsites all around, mostly because of the monster's howl, but a few got a glimpse of the towering beast. Chaos ensued as the creature stepped toward the crypto-zoologists. John Cosworth was standing next to a tranquilizer gun, and had the presence of mind to pick it up in his shaking hands and level it at the beast. But the beast was fast and unafraid of the threat, and in an instant, Cosworth was grabbed by the throat, while sharp and pointed teeth sank deep into his shoulder, and the meat of his neck. His entire left arm and most of his neck were torn from his body and spat out on the ground. Blood dripped from the monster's mouth while it drank from Cosworth as if he were a soda can. Then the beast lowered the body and wiped its bloody lips with the back of its empty hand. The corpse that once was John Cosworth was tossed effortlessly into a nearby tree, his head hanging down behind his back on what was left of his neck. His horrific and abrupt end was to be merely the first of many.

Dr. Williams was luckier. As the monster bellowed and stomped through the camp, the doctor was backhanded and launched onto the hood of one of the trucks parked nearby. Unfortunately, his camera was thrown from his hands to parts unknown when the creature gave him the powerful smack.

Jake and his partners with the guns were hit by debris as soon as the monster erupted from the trailer and were only now regaining their feet to see the giant upon them. Their guns, however, remained on the ground, and the monster's claws gutted one of the men in an instant, grabbing the second and smacking Jake with the eviscerated body of the first. Then, lifting the second in the air, it pulled him apart and took a bite out of the upper thigh before tossing the body parts to the ground. Jake stayed on the ground, frozen in fear under the corpse of his friend. The creature looked toward the strobe lights on the ambulance, and moved on.

Malcolm Carson sat up the moment he heard the trailer erupt, but the pain in his chest immediately returned, and he clutched his chest and lay back down in agony and fear. The attending EMTs were horror-struck at the monster. In panic they fled away from Carson to the front of their emergency vehicle, locking themselves in, and leaving Carson alone on a gurney by the ambulance, with his second heart attack.

The towering beast turned toward the ambulance and advanced. It was aware of everything and everyone since it had placed *itself* within the trap that was supposed to capture an "Agnostopithecus." It knew the name they called it. It was amused by it. It knew springing the trap was a necessary step to advance the plan, and though that had cost it an eye, the wound would eventually heal. It knew that the scientists would take it into their camp and would believe it to be dead. It knew that they would not be able to keep it a secret from Knightlight, and that if Dominic Moreau survived the first trap, he would run to the second, to the third, the fourth, and so on. The creature was informed by familiar spirits that Moreau was on his way to the camp. But what it did not know was that when it had heard the name of Dominic Moreau from Malcolm's distant voice outside the trailer, Moreau was not actually present at the time. It was a miscalculation that would be soon rectified.

The creature knew that the plan was going to work, that much was certain. Even if it failed *here*, the plan would continue, and another would succeed. It had taken years to devise, a decade to set in motion, and many of the Brotherhood had to be sacrificed for the plan to move forward. Knightlight had been a thorn in Tammuz's side for seventy years, and Moreau for the past twenty-plus, but until recently, there was no way to coordinate a devastating strike against them and remain hidden from the public. Tammuz, however, was patient. Time was ever on his side, and the *Image* was nearing perfection. Around the globe this very day, the "strike" was taking place. Knightlight was the target, the quarry, the prey—but not just the strike-teams . . . *all of it*.

Knightlight had twelve teams, but the Brotherhood had readied twenty-four sites to be certain that all strike-teams were deployed, and then some. With their hierarchy intact, Knightlight would rebound within months unless their chain of command was obliterated. Yes, the strike-teams were the tip of the spear, but even disarmed, the head of their enemy must be severed. It was the Knightlight strategy turned back against them. It was just as they were trying to achieve against Tammuz. Just like that insipid Hebrew did to the hero of Gath. This night, many of the Brotherhood would give their lives for *the plan*, for Tammuz himself—traps within traps, deaths upon deaths, blood upon blood. But the plan *was* going to work, and Knightlight would fall.

The monster, *this* monster, was known within the ranks of the Brotherhood as Ka-tes-thio: the Devourer. It was 453 years old—still fairly young for its kind. It was raised in Central America, but had moved across both upper and lower continents many times during its life. It usually stayed near military bases, scouting, leaving only to find prey, and then returning or moving to the next location on its planned route. The Brotherhood consisted of clans, and Ka-tes-thio was from the clan called the Mighty Shadows. All clans were governed in the form of military hierarchies that ended with the clan's patriarch, their "Crown." The Crowns were the Brotherhood's only direct contact with Tammuz, though all in the Brotherhood communed with the fallen ones—the familiar spirits. Even though the clans hated each other, their hatred of mankind and his God was their common bond forcing them to work as one, as in the days before. Above all that, even above Tammuz, there was the Dark Master to be served. In him was the power, his will was the law, and in him was the downfall of mankind.

With no Moreau in sight, the beast prepared to turn the camping area into an abattoir until Knightlight arrived. It looked around and relished the panic it inspired. Men ran to and fro in the camp, casting wild shadows in the emergency vehicle's strobes and spreading fear outward, like the concentric rings of an impact tremor. A cacophony of screams and shouts filled the air and the power of it felt good to the monster. One day soon, it thought, most of these miserable, insipid, and weak humans would be allied slaves, and that was a point of disgust for all the Brotherhood. But until then, they were prey and a delicacy at that. Healthy flesh tasted good. Too often Ka-tes-thio would have to settle for the scraps of human debris. Drunks, drug users, prostitutes, the homeless, they all tasted foul, but tonight was a feast.

The Devourer moved toward Malcolm, growling. It, snarled and sniffed the air, and observed the prostrate Malcolm lying on the medical gurney, so helpless, so human. *Malcolm* had given it the false assumption of Moreau's presence. Though he had been a useful tool, and instructions had been given to leave him alive if possible, none of the Brotherhood would be too concerned if he became a meal. He smelled of sweet, fat flesh. It was Malcolm who had caused Ka-tes-thio to revive too soon, and now he would be harvested for that mistake. Then, from the south, the beast saw the lights of human law enforcement approaching. They were coming into the camp, and they were moving fast. The creature turned back toward the writhing body of Carson, observing his pain and fear at the proximity of the monster. It stood over him, towering mere feet in front of him, enjoying the fear that its presence inspired in the juicy meal that squirmed so helplessly before it.

Malcolm was still clutching at the pain in his chest, but also trying to scoot off the gurney and get away from the giant beast that was an incarnate nightmare. His mouth could only produce a moan of fear and pain intertwined. Malcolm was now cognizant that this thing which threatened him was no mere animal. Perhaps he had already become aware of that fact when he'd first encountered it while it was caged. He was also distinctly aware that he had only seconds to live, yet was helpless before the horror. Its frame was gigantic, its countenance evil, its smell overwhelming, and its power unstoppable. Besieged with the sensory-input overload, Malcolm closed his eyes against it, and held his breath before the beast, believing it to be his last. Now he waited for the inevitability of death.

The creature stood over the shuddering body of Malcolm Carson, observing his pain and relishing his fright. It derived enjoyment from prolonging terror; they all did. It was delicious. Malcolm, still holding his breath, eyes shut, exhaled and grabbed another deep breath, but death had not come yet. Then Malcolm opened his eyes with the next exhale, knowing that the monster had not moved, but hearing sirens coming his way. It gave him a moment of hope.

Ka-tes-thio bared his teeth, salivating at the thought of tasting more flesh, and then looked again to the lights. They were close now, and the beast knew its meal must wait. But there was more meat close at hand, and it would not leave the area until Moreau felt its teeth in his neck, while his beating heart was crushed by its grip.

The Indiana State Police cruiser pulled into the camp with lights flashing, and to the trooper's astonishment, the headlight revealed a titanic monstrosity ahead. The DNR ranger came in his SUV just behind the cruiser, parking next to it, and the trooper and the officer became firsthand witnesses of the beast. They had been contacted by Braxton, at Rock's request. Rock knew that Knightlight's communications were compromised, and also that state troopers and DNR officers could reach the site before the Trinity could, since Knightlight's first stop was going to be within the town of Waveland. Braxton told them to expect a dangerous situation, and said they needed to come into the park swiftly and forcefully. He said nothing specific about the creature because they would not have believed it. He did warn them emphatically, though, telling them that a dangerous man-killing animal was being held by the scientists in the park, and that the animal was not properly contained. That was as much as he could give away.

The beast just stared at the officers, somewhat puzzled by the abruptness of their appearance. It bared its glistening red-coated teeth again in the headlight beams, and its single eye reflected back at them. Its coarse black fur shone blue in the light. The two officers got out of their vehicles in awe, and stood behind their open doors, both completely speechless, both wondering at the sight. Then the creature howled at them, displaying its fierceness, and the officers almost went to the ground before its prowess.

Ka-tes-thio looked down at the pain-stricken, cowering Malcolm, and grabbed the gurney that he lay upon, brusquely rolling him off it to the ground. Using it to launch at the patrol vehicle, it flung the gurney through the air and smashed the hood and windshield of the ISP vehicle. The force sent the gurney careening on, behind the patrol car, and out of sight. That seemed to snap the trooper and the officer out of their astonishment. Immediately the two ducked down behind their car doors, and while the trooper attempted to call for backup, his shaky hands ended up pulling the cord out of the transmitter. At the same time the DNR officer grabbed his shotgun from the inside roof mount and hastily pumped it, to chamber a shell. Both men were as frightened as they'd ever been before, and they had been witness to many things that would terrify lesser men, but their training made them move to action.

The trooper pulled his sidearm and leveled it at the beast, not knowing whether the towering creature was a man in disguise (he doubted it) or whether it was an animal (which he doubted as well), or something supernatural—he had no idea. Regardless, he shouted "Indiana State Police! Don't move!"

It should be noted that animals do not actually laugh. They can be playful, and vocalize sounds indicating happiness, but no animal actually laughs, as that is a uniquely *human* ability. A trained chimp can make an audience believe it is laughing by mimicry, or a dolphin can chirp a familiar sound, but that is merely the audience being induced to project their own humanity onto something inhuman. It happens every day. This day, something apparently inhuman, at least from the perspective of the DNR officer and the trooper, began to laugh at them, but it was anything but funny . . . . It was disarmingly horrible—so much so that the DNR officer dropped his shotgun and wet himself without even noticing it. It was not something that could be prevented without experience, and neither man had had such an experience before. It was an intensely "spiritual" attack that law enforcement training rarely mentioned was possible, let alone covered in their manuals.

The trooper rose from his crouched position and steadied his arms by resting his wrist on the open car door, but still the .45-caliber Glock shook in his hands. The monster in their headlights slowly, threateningly advanced upon the two law enforcement officers. Quickly, the DNR officer picked up his shotgun from the ground, and heard his counterpart fire his sidearm at the beast in a burst of three rounds.

The monster barely acknowledged the impacts of the .45 slugs, but it saw the shotgun coming up and chose to turn at a right angle to the men and lunge away from them and into an adjacent campsite, evoking new screams and shouts of terror. Finally, it lumbered in an arc, away from the crypto-zoologists' camp, but planned to revisit it upon the completion of its circuit. It would do so as many times as necessary, and kill as many as it wished, until Knightlight arrived.

"What in the world was that?" asked the trooper to nobody in particular. But the DNR officer heard him and just shook his head in bewilderment. Neither of them had ever seen anything even close to what they had just witnessed, but both knew it was a danger now loosed upon the next campsite. Together they began to follow the beast, but cautiously and slowly. They knew, in their gut, that whatever it was, it wasn't something they truly wanted to catch up to. They forced themselves onward to the defense of those they'd both sworn to protect. Lesser men would have run, but lesser men were not considered for law enforcement. They moved after the beast toward the sound of a distant thunder coming from the west.

The creature was so dark, it was easily lost in the shadows. Still, the two armed men pursued it. They were afraid to fire at where it *might* be because of civilian casualties, but it left a clear trail of horror behind. For reasons unknown to the two, it made sure to never be very far ahead of them. The sky above lit up for brief moments, allowing them to see for split seconds, and then they were plunged into severe darkness immediately afterward. It was a nightmare they'd rather run from.

The Mobile Field Base pulled into the Turkey Run State Park, following Rock in the Hummer, and headed straight for Carson's campsite. Rock was working out in his head what to do, while looking at the park's map on the HUD, memorizing the trails and landmarks, and steering. A lot of it depended, though, on what was happening at the site ahead of him.

"Satellite shows that the thunderstorm is approaching from the southwest . . . it is quite close," announced Tick, breaking the silence in Rock's Hummer.

"Copy that," said Rock. The teachings of Sun Tzu took weather into account for battle strategies, and there were opportunities to use weather to one's advantage. But a storm would most likely be a hindrance to the agents in the here and now. A job needed to be done, though, fair weather or flood.

His team was beaten and weary, but again they were fully armed and would engage the situation in any necessary way. As they closed on the site, it was clear that Braxton had made the call that Rock had requested of him by the appearance of red-and-blue low-profile strobe lights ahead. He truly appreciated the Sheriff's assistance this night. Then he saw several people frantically running across his path. It was not a good sign. A little closer Rock saw both law enforcement vehicles with their doors open, and more people were running frantically all around the park, obviously because of their quarry. He knew that the situation was already critical.

"Pull up just behind the trooper's car," Rock said to the Big Cheese over the radio. Then he added, "Tell Agent Cavor to break out the heavy artillery and give Ms. Carson, I mean Crystal, the code for the door locks. I want her secure inside, but I want her to be able to let others inside at her discretion, or to be able to lock it behind her should she need to evacuate."

"Roger that," said Tick, who had communications open.

"Better light up the SLED too," added Rock. "We want to be seen this time."

"I'm on it," said Cheese. He set the LED panels to white, nearly making the MFB visible from space. Then he added a crawl—a marquee message that scrolled around the vehicle—with the simple words in dark red: "Come inside for safety." It was a common PC screensaver app available on virtually any computer.

"Are we going to pursue on foot?" asked Cheese.

"It's a big park, and our trophy's fast—dirt bike, quad, and Hummer for this one. You get my ride, Tick can have the quad, and I'll take the dirt bike," replied Rock.

"Roger that. Parking and setting level footers now," said Cheese as he shut off the engine.

The three hurriedly met in the back of the MFB to get a weapons load out and make sure Crystal was going to be OK. They all took new magazines for their dual sidearms, filled their pockets with standard-issue weapons, and even took a Thread deployment stick just because it seemed effective in the last round. But as to heavy weaponry, each had his own preferences. Rock took a silenced AR-15 with soft-point rounds and Teflon bullets alternately stacked in the magazine. The Teflon rounds were armor piercers, and the soft-points were the damage makers. His gun would fire two rounds with each trigger pull. Tick chose the SAW or M249 machine gun, which was a powerful weapon. He'd prefer a sniper rifle, but that was not a viable choice because the forest precluded a distance shot. The Big Cheese slung an AR-15 of his own, and then he grabbed the heavy MDPE-1.5, a weapon that Bravo renamed the SST, or the Substitute Science Teacher—because testing it was a confusing bugger of a challenge. On the other hand, the ordinance it launched was, frankly, hellish. The operations manual for the weapon was 412 pages thick, but 99 percent of it was unnecessary technical jargon geared for a machinist and maybe a physicist.

MDPE stood for "Mass Driver Projectile Emitter," and the weapon was developed by the Springfield Armory for military use as an antitank weapon. It was a portable rail-gun launching 1.50-caliber folded steel rounds. Although six feet long, it was Cheese's choice since he was going to be in the Hummer. The MDPE used electromagnetic energy to push solid ordinance along a vacuum-sealed rail chamber at ever-increasing speed until it was propelled beyond the magnetic influence, toward the target at burn velocity. It could be mounted to the hood or roof of the Hummer, targeted and fired from inside the vehicle, or carried with full charge and battery pack to be fired manually as a rifle, but if so, it could be fired just *once*. The weapon was their heaviest, but it could penetrate tank armor and make a kill-shot through full-grown trees. The targeting system, when mounted, was an automated multi-lock system, meaning it could target a heat signature behind a tree, or lock onto a specific vehicle engine type, or even a heartbeat. It isn't considered a stealth weapon even though the sound it makes when fired is suppressed by means of an IR laser channel to superheat the air in the ordnance's path, changing the speed of sound with that channel and therefore the sound barrier threshold. The only noise it truly makes is the extremely impressive sonic boom(s) during deceleration on impact, and, of course, the impact itself. Though it was audibly stealthy, there was a visual burn trail because of the friction the ordnance made against the atmosphere, marking the origin of the projectile clearly, though obscuring it with smoke at the same time. The only real problem with the weapon was getting the initial target lock, and the time it took to charge the weapon for a second volley. There were several experiments on the shooting range attempting to employ *smart* projectiles fired by the weapon, but no matter how well the guidance systems were shielded, the magnetic forces of the gun itself wiped all programming from the smart shells.

"What about the PA suits or the nano-drones?" asked Tick.

"Not this time," said Rock. "We'll need mobility. If it was a confined space, and we could deploy at the entrance of a lair, then I'd say yes to the PAS. And the drones won't be able to withstand a thunderstorm."

The PAS was a Physical Augmentation Suit, also known as a "smack-down suit" because with it on, an agent could match the physical strength of a Nephil-Adam. The problem was they were not quite as fast or maneuverable as either man or beast, and the power pack lasted only forty minutes. Once drained of power, the suits were a heavy burden to the wearer and would have to be discarded for later retrieval. Each man had one in his own size, and they were an impressive piece of technology, but they were good only for certain scenarios. Nano-drones were small VTOL robots that could assist in aerial observation, tracking, swarming, targeting, or even firing on a target. They were multipurpose flying robots but they became useless in high winds, or tight quarters, and often had difficulty navigating below the treetops in a forest, which is why Rock did not deploy either in the other parks.

"Roger that," said Tick, while making sure he had all his gear.

"Will you please find my father?" Crystal pleaded.

"Of course," said Tick.

"We ready then?" asked the Big Cheese.

When Rock was sure they'd finished arming themselves, Rock turned to Crystal. "Do you know how to handle a firearm?"

"Yes, Agent Moreau," she answered.

"You can call me Nick," he said. "What's your weapon preference?"

"My carry weapon is a Walther P-22, but I left it in the Land Rover and Dad probably parked it here somewhere. Under the circumstances, I'd *prefer* a 12-gauge pump shotgun with a shell extender tube, if you have one."

"Don't you just love her?" asked the Big Cheese. He knew he could fall for any woman who actually wanted to be armed with a *shottie*. Cheese pulled his own shotgun from his locker, kissed it, and then handed it to her with a box of slug loaded shells.

"Thanks," said Crystal as she took it from him. She pulled back the pump ever so slightly to make sure there was a shell loaded, then pushed it back into battery.

"Monitor the external cameras here," Rock said to Crystal as he guided her gently to the comm station. "If anyone wants in, feel free to let them in, then lock it behind them. This base is virtually impregnable, so you *will be safe*. This mic," he said as he handed it to her, "broadcasts to the external speakers so you can even call people over here to safety, and you will be able to hear outside as well."

"Got it," she said. Crystal was a quick learner, and used similar equipment in the field.

"This channel," he said while showing her, "enables you to listen in to us, but don't communicate with us unless you have an emergency. We're going to be pretty busy. And you can monitor both at the same time, like this," he showed her, and then left *that* setting enabled for her convenience.

"We've gotta move now. But, Crystal, will you please pray for us while we're out there?" Rock requested.

"I, um don't really know how," she replied.

"Not a problem. Just talk to God, tell Him what's on your heart, and ask Him to be with us. He'll love to hear from you," said Rock.

"Opening bay doors," said Tick as the back end of the MFB opened and lowered, doubling as a ramp. Rock unmoored the dirt bike and Tick did the same with the ATV. Cheese exited the rear first and moved, as best as he could with his heavy burden, to the Hummer. He mounted the rail-gun on the passenger's side hood magnetically, and then with the lockdown clamps, and connected it to power and the cabin controls of the truck. It took him only seventeen seconds.

Just before Rock put his tactical helmet on, his cheek was kissed, and it surprised him; but realizing it was Crystal, he smiled.

"We'll find your father," Rock promised.

"Thanks for saving me," she said. "I don't think those things were going to let me live."

"I'm sorry you had to experience that, Crystal, but you made it through," he said. "You are one tough gal."

"Come back in one piece," said Crystal. "Please," she added.

Rock nodded, secured his helmet, and signaled to Tick, and both started their engines.

"Move out," Rock said over his helmet's mic, and the two exited the vehicle. Just before Crystal could close the door, three people seeking refuge ran up to and inside the MFB. Crystal closed and locked the door as soon as they were in. She bid them to sit and be quiet. Then she moved to the comm station to listen to the Trinity. Immediately, she began to pray for . . . everything she could think of. It was her first time.

31

END GAME

(From the notes of First Agent Christopher Griffin)

To Serve Mankind

The enemy has many goals, but few are within their abilities. They want to depose their Creator, and that is impossible. They want to destroy the Church, but that is also not within their power. The enemy knows that the best way to destroy mankind is to serve mankind, that is, to simply give him whatever he desires, and mankind will destroy itself. However, but for the asking, God can give mankind the desires of His heart. Service to a Righteous King is not just an honor, it is the greatest blessing beyond any human desire. The best way to serve mankind is to help him find his own created purpose, and lead him to the one-on-one relationship with his humble and loving Creator.

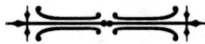

The sound of gunfire echoed in the distance, and people continued to shout and run around the campgrounds. Sunrise was an hour away and darkness still reigned, but now there was a bright glow to the south, artificial light. The night sky was intermittently, increasingly lighting up as well, indicative of the approaching storm. The smell of the beast was vague, because the air wasn't moving, but the fear of the beast was a lingering presence. There were no crickets or tree frogs or any other sounds besides the varying screams, shouts, and gunshots again. Then the sound of motorcycles erupted in the night, and as they closed, their sound drowned out the rest.

Malcolm lay behind the ambulance on the ground, still immobile, chest pounding. He looked skyward at the roiling blackness above him. Beautiful stars were there earlier in the night, but were gone now, replaced by angry clouds in the heavens. Carson hit himself in the chest hard, remembering Jake hammering on him earlier, but it was not helping much; in fact, it only added to the pain. The approach of the motorcycles was loud now, and he turned his head to see them stop beside him. It had to be Moreau. He was the last person Malcolm cared to see . . . excluding the rampaging monster.

Rock stopped his motorcycle next to Malcolm Carson, lowering his kickstand, shutting off the bike, and removing his helmet, all with rapid fluidity. Malcolm looked up at him. Anger overcame any pain he was experiencing.

"Where's my daughter, you—" Malcolm spat, searching for an appropriate swear, but he was cut off just before he launched it.

"She's safe," Rock said. Then he looked straight into Malcolm's eyes, narrowing his own, and said, "Do you have any idea what you've done? You've released a monster in a populated area. I'm going to save as many lives as I can, but **you're** gonna have to live with the consequences."

Rock spent as much time with Malcolm as he could spare. Tick pulled up next to Rock's ride, while Rock moved to the front door of the ambulance. As he approached, he noticed that two medics had locked themselves in the front of the ambulance for fear's sake. Rock pulled his sidearm and his FBI ID and tapped on the driver's-side window, holding both in plain view. The wide-eyed medic on the driver's side cautiously cracked the window so that he could hear what the armed FBI agent wanted from him.

"Get your rears out of the vehicle, and help the man behind your truck, *NOW*," Rock commanded, and immediately both doors popped open and the medics evacuated to the rear of their ambulance.

"And then help everyone else with an injury before you leave," Rock ordered as he holstered his weapon, pocketed his ID, and followed the medics to the back of the truck. He heard the crack of gunfire to the south, and then again. It was moving to the southeast of his position. Then it was lost in the sound of thunder.

Rock put his helmet back on and spoke into the mic for Crystal's benefit, "Crystal, Malcolm is being attended to by medics. There aren't any wounds on him, but I think he may have had a heart attack. It's being dealt with, so don't worry, and absolutely do not come out of the mobile base."

Crystal was relieved and worried at the same time. She almost replied to Agent Moreau, but remembered that he instructed her not to, so she restrained herself. She wanted to thank him, and get more information on her father, but she settled for what Nick had told her.

Rock mounted his bike, started it, and then heard Tick ask, "Which direction?"

Rock turned his head halfway to the right, and nodded. "That way," he said to Tick, indicating southeast. Then, to the Cheese, he said, "Go night-screen and tell me what you see to the southeast."

The Knightlight Hummer had a heads-up display in the windshield and could switch to IR or UV interpretational displays at the touch of a button. It had passive multispectral cameras and a computer and could combine all camera input into a composite on the windshield display. The headlights were also equipped with powerful IR and UV lights that could be activated at another touch of a button; on the roof of the Hummer were more lights, and it sported a driver's-side spotlight with the same lighting capabilities. Of course, he had the HUD for the rail-gun displayed as well. A bolt of lightning pierced the dark sky to the immediate west of the State Park, making a moment of static on all displays from EM sensory overload, but it would still be twenty seconds before the deep rumble could be heard. Cheese lit up the wooded park ahead of them with the complete spectrum of lights his SUV boasted, and confirmed that all sensors were operational.

"I've got a glimpse of a big signature moving ahead of, and away from, two small signatures," said the Cheese, "at 320 meters, give or take. It looks like the big one is pacing the smaller ones . . . intentionally trying not to lose them."

"Roger that," said Rock, instead of an expletive that almost came out of his mouth, but he checked himself before he'd have to apologize for it.

Cheese was watching the two men ahead of him, waiting for Rock's direction. He had the rail-gun loaded and charged and was ready to follow the two agents to the gates of Hell if necessary. It was then that it struck him: He *was* ready to follow the two agents to the gates of Hell. In fact, the only time fear had the best of him, that is, the moments when he was truly afraid, was when he didn't have his boots on the ground, figuratively speaking. When he was in the cave, he'd engaged the beast barehanded. *BAREHANDED!* Fear before the mission, yes, perhaps regrets afterward, depending on the outcome, but his determination while at the task was unshakable. Fear for his own life was absent when others needed him. He silently thanked God for that epiphany. It was a personal revelation from the Lord, one that actually brought tears to his eyes. Rock was right; his training kicked in. But the fight was in him as well, and it wasn't going to go away easily. Love hates evil, and he knew that he hated any who would slaughter innocents, and Heaven help them if they tried to harm his teammates.

"Lead the way, Boss," Cheese confidently spoke in his mic. "I've got your back," he said with assurance.

"Glad to hear that, amigo," said Rock, as he adjusted the AR-15 slung on his back. "We're heading southeast. Run silent, and dark, and try to keep up."

"Visor down, switching to star-light, IR, and UV composite," said Tick as he and Rock readied themselves. "Suppression is go," he added as his quad-runner silenced its engine.

This time they used the more expensive, and heavier, tactical bike helmets with 3-D visor displays. The low-profile cameras on each of the two vent bumps sent images to his screen in excellent

3-D detail. The helmets were form-fitted and padded to hug their heads so that a bumpy ride would not jiggle the camera around. And *this* ride was sure to give them many bumps.

Rock took off and moved out on point as he switched his own bike's engine to suppression. He could hear every leaf that was crushed under his tires—and Tick's, behind him, too—and the breeze in his helmet made the loudest of sounds at the moment. He loved to ride silent . . . when he wasn't heading straight for a monster that wanted him dead. The Moronis were targeting *him* specifically and that was a new and unsettling turn of events. He didn't let his teammates know precisely *how* unsettling the news was to him. Their enemy was obviously far more coordinated that any had guessed. In truth, they'd had plenty of time to observe the operation of Knightlight. They'd had many years to plan and coordinate a powerful counterstrike, and it appeared that's exactly what they were serving up today—a wholesale attack on the Agency. Hopefully it wouldn't be a successful one. Rock's team had been off balance and misdirected since Tick's distress code was sent out . . . . Somebody *was* selling out his team, and the enemy was striving to gain the upper hand. So far, they'd been able to compensate, but there was no guarantee how long that could last.

They passed through the forest quickly and silently, cutting across Trail 7 and heading toward Trail 6. Rock was leading the pack through the widest paths between trees to accommodate the Hummer behind them. They were closing rapidly on the target when Rock heard gunfire. This time it was clearly not very far ahead.

"All stop," said the Big Cheese, as he had the best equipment to see ahead of them. At any given time, each man had an obligation to make a command decision when warranted. Any order that kept them alive was the standing order. Tick pulled up next to Rock and both noticed that drops of rain were beginning to become visible in their light beams, and the air began moving the upper parts of the trees.

"The target has changed course and is coming to us," continued Cheese as they all halted their pursuit. Cheese pulled up beside the two. "I've got a distant shot . . . do I take it?"

"What's the proximity of the trailing signatures?" asked Rock.

"In and out of LOF. Trailing targets are roughly ten meters behind it," said the Cheese, referring to the line of fire. "It's getting closer . . . you should be seeing something within a minute or so."

"Make your shot five meters ahead of it, to the north. Enable targeting laser so it can see where you're firing, then move it and mark your target with the laser. That should put the fear of God in it," said Rock.

"Copy," said Cheese.

"One more thing," said Rock. "Get on speaker and tell the trophy that you are coming for it, and once the officers are clear, tell them to stand down and head back to the camp. Got that?"

"Copy that," said Cheese.

Firing directly at the target, at the moment, anyway, could take out the DNR officer and ISP trooper as well, so that was not an option. Rock knew that the campgrounds were behind them, and was relatively sure that nobody else would have headed north while running scared, as north of the camp was a dark, foreboding forest. Adding to that, no other heat signatures were evident. Still, a man is responsible for every shot discharged, and he was about to have Cheese let loose one very powerful shot. He knew that the Knightlight protocol was to assault the creature at an angle and move in, and he was pretty sure the creature approaching knew that as well. Tonight they seemed to know just about everything.

"Tick, follow me north; we're going to funnel the target to a kill zone," said Rock.

"What kill zone?" asked Tick.

"Anywhere away from campers that gives us a clear line of sight," said Rock.

"That's not standard procedure, Rock. It splits us up. Are you sure?" asked Tick.

"I think *standard procedure* is going to get us killed tonight. Cheese is safe in the Hummer, and we've gotta outrun it," said Rock.

"Copy that," said Tick, and the two took off to the left of the SUV. They accelerated swiftly away from the Cheese, knowing there was little time to get in place. The forest was dense, but navigable. Their multispectrum headlights bounced about the trees as if children were going wild with high-powered flashlights. Stumps and deadfalls also became evident ahead of them as past storm damage and age had left their marks on the land. After only two minutes they crossed Trail 7 and headed northeast toward the south bend in Sugar Creek, keeping themselves south of the creek.

"Target closing on me, but slowing down. It's keeping itself just ahead of the officers. I hope it doesn't turn on them," said the Cheese.

"Just wait until your trailing signatures are well clear of the SST," commanded Rock while his bike seemed to hit every possible bump in the forest. "Prepare to fire, but if you have to move in on it . . . you do whatever you need to do to keep those officers safe."

"Roger that. Preparing to fire," Cheese confirmed. He wanted to fire before it got too close, and while Rock and Tick were not downrange, and especially when the officers in pursuit were out of the line of fire. Timing and placement were critical to warn the beast that it was heading toward certain death, while keeping all others from ending up in black bags. He'd never forgive himself if he was responsible for a friendly-fire kill.

"I see it clearly now . . . ," said Cheese, "and I think it sees me too!"

"Fire at will," said Rock, moving rapidly at an angle away from the target.

"Letting it fly . . . NOW," said Cheese as he pressed the trigger.

The projectile Cheese launched was nothing short of spectacular. It was as if he'd fired a meteor that flamed brilliantly, and left a blazing smoke trail behind it. As it connected with a line of trees, it exploded them in a shockwave of supersonic mayhem, just in front of the beast. The entire wall of trees became lit up and splintered in the explosion. The BOOM it made was nothing short of awesome, shaking the ground and the air about them, and stopping the monster in its tracks. Cheese saw that the creature was looking in his direction. He turned on the halogen headlights just to be sure he was seen. It appeared to be surprised and angered by the carnage that was directed in front of it. Then it looked at the targeting laser that was now glistening on its chest. This time *it showed fear*, perhaps for the first time in its life. The officers in pursuit of the beast dove for cover when the forest ahead exploded, not knowing what had happened. Mere moments later they played their flashlights on or near the beast, and began firing at it again, having no clear shot for the trees and the brush between them, and shooting in the Cheese's direction.

When Ka-tes-thio saw the tree line in front of it explode violently, it was shocked and awed. It had not expected that level of firepower to be loosed upon it. Then it saw the bright green laser beam aimed directly at it. The brilliant dot shone clearly on its hairy chest and the ray could be seen all the way back to the truck on the hill. The monster didn't know that it would take several minutes for the rail-gun to recharge for a second shot. Choosing to survive the next barrage, and in an attempt to be missed by the trees that were now falling in front of it, it leapt northward, and ran away, believing that it was a sure thing to be fired upon a second time. It was also aware that there was more than one agent to pursue and kill. It had hoped at least one of them had been killed in the Emim's lair. Moving powerfully, the escaping creature gave chase to his other foes.

The heat signatures behind the beast also retreated from the man-made thunder, and began to move away from the creature.

"I heard the SST, Cheese," spoke Rock. "Status?"

"The Maxie is moving in your direction," replied Cheese.

"Tell the law that we've got this; then begin pursuit, northeast, toward us, and bring your A-game," said Rock. Lightning flashed behind them, making their night vision go brilliantly white, forcing Rock and Tick to slow in order to raise their visors and regather their bearings. Rock signaled to Tick to switch to visible headlights and they kept their visors raised. Droplets of rain began to increase for the storm was about to break upon them, and the wind gusts began to bend the treetops above.

"Roger that, I'm four-wheeling in the direction of your GPS," said Cheese. "The trophy is inbound, and the wind is picking up." Then he flipped the communications to external speakers and broadcast audibly to everyone and everything in the vicinity.

"This is Agent Ledford of the FBI. We are in pursuit of your target. You are instructed to stand down and return to the camping area where you parked. Follow the bright glow to the southwest, behind me, and wait for our all-clear," said Cheese for the officers formerly in pursuit of it. He knew that the officers most likely had lost their bearings during their chase, so his brief instruction should get them to safety. Cheese pursued the monster on the run, keeping the left of his windshield transparent so that he could see, but keeping the right half in night-vision mode to track the beast. The creature was fast and could dodge around trees with little effort, while the Hummer had to keep moving left and right around each, losing ground with every turn.

"I've still got the target, but it's gaining on you faster than I'm gaining on it," said Cheese. Lightning broke the darkness and all night-vision sensors went white.

"The terrain is rough ahead," said Rock. "There's a small creek running south-to-north; I think it feeds into Sugar Creek. We're crossing now and it isn't deep, so you should be able to traverse it. Herd the target in a northeasterly direction, east of our present position. The map showed several areas ahead where we might be able to get a clear shot at it, but I'm working on a plan."

"Roger on all, but I don't think I'm herding it as much as it's chasing you," said Cheese.

Rock and Tick moved through the underbrush under the dense stands of trees. It was slower than they wanted with a monster bearing down on their position, but they made progress, passing the Lieber Cabin and then connecting with Trail 1. This trail would take them past the Turkey Run Inn and the Nature Center, just to the north of them. More lightning shone round about, making daylight for the briefest of moments, then receded to a deeper darkness for another moment as their eyes adjusted. The wind howled in the trees above and blew behind the two much faster than they were traveling. Then the storm broke upon them like a tsunami. Rain, in torrents, flooded the park and visibility was further obscured. Leaves blew with the rain, and limbs and branches reached out at them as if they were alive.

The monster ran northwest from the Hummer, leaping over deadfalls and dodging standing trees with great strides and agility, while feeling the rain mat down its hair as water clung to it in a cool embrace. The strong wind blew the creature's wet fur into its good eye, and it was getting difficult for it to see. It cursed the vehicle behind it while doing its best not to be a target for the hated Knightlight. While it was leading the police on a chase, it had received word in the spirit that its counterpart in Pine Hills was dead and Moreau was alive, and now somewhere ahead of it. It wanted Moreau, but spiritual forces were in play, both with the beast and against it. More than anything, it wanted to sink its teeth into Moreau's neck. It wanted his blood dripping down its beard with sweet and ragged flesh in its mouth. Knightlight had killed its •mate years ago, and Moreau was the man who pierced her skull with a spike. It wasn't by order that Ka-tes-thio hunted Moreau, though those orders were clearly in its favor, but it wanted blood-vengeance against the man who had destroyed its clan, and ripped its beloved Hudropoteo from its life.

Nephil-Adam had all the feelings and emotions of man, and, if they identified with their demonic parentage, all the hatred toward mankind as well. Satan himself hated the fact that God loved a weak and ignorant people. He hated God for taking the glory and credit for the works of Lucifer, the Morning Star. He hated that God would place His Spirit and breath on mortals, and worse, that He would become one of *them* and die on their behalf to save them. It was beyond disgusting to Satan. But soon his chess pieces would be in place, and his enemy's "knights" would be taken off the board. Soon the Beast would rise, the Image of the Beast would be perfected, and the False Prophet would usher in the New Age, but it was not soon enough for the devil's taste. It was not easy while the "Church," the *real* "Church," still occupied this world. All within the Brotherhood agreed that the occupiers *must be removed from this world* . . . but they did not know that God Himself also had that in mind for His true believers.

Straight-line winds pummeled the Hummer as it struggled to keep up with the beast. The Big Cheese crossed the creek that his partners had traversed shortly before, and moved as best as possible onto Trail 6. But the vehicle was not as agile as the creature it pursued. Lightning intensified and the whole area lit up moment to moment, and the wind shook every living thing outside the Hummer. If not for the technical equipment onboard, Cheese would have lost the beast long ago, but he could still see the electronic signature of the monster that was running in the right direction, for the moment, anyway. Suddenly, Trail 6 merged with Trail 1 and Cheese was able to speed up, at least matching the monster's pace now, and trying to make up lost ground.

Rock and Tick were also making much better time, now that Trail 1 leveled out. The wind was still pushing them from behind, and hail was beginning to drop from the sky. There were no obstructions ahead of them so they increased their speed further. They were almost able to match the wind speed for a few moments, and now they were on a heading for one of the major features of the park. It was thankfully just ahead.

"Tick," said Rock. "We're not going to be able to coax it out in the open for a clear shot."

"I know. And this storm is reducing visibility. Ouch," said Tick as a golf-ball-sized hailstone smacked him in the middle of his back, and then another. "Ouch . . . . So what's the plan?"

"There's a suspension bridge that crosses the creek up ahead of us," said Rock.

"That's a good choke point, but only if it follows us," said Tick.

"I think I can guarantee that it will. I think I know the right bait," said Rock.

"Um, I'm afraid to ask," said Tick, trying to hear Rock over the hail hitting his helmet as lightning flashed and crashed around them, not to mention the roar of the wind.

"Remember in the cave, where the Rephaim indicated its familiarity with Knightlight?" asked Rock as hail began beating them both all over, and covering the area around them.

"How could I forget it," Tick replied, pulling his ride up next to Moreau's on the paved but icy street.

"It had intimate knowledge of my wife, and it knew *me*," said Rock. "This has all been staged . . . a trap to kill *us*, but I think even more specifically, to kill Bravo's team leader."

"I guess it *does* look that way," agreed Tick, while using his left hand to wipe ice balls from his speedometer.

"That makes *me* the best bait we have," said Rock, "and knowing that gives us a tactical advantage."

"OK . . . but not a desired one," said Tick. "I know where this is leading, and I'm not sure the risk is going to outweigh the advantage."

"I have every confidence in you and Cheese," said Rock, as they approached the Nature Center at the head of Trail 3.

"What's the setup?" asked Tick.

"I hate to interrupt, girls," said the Big Cheese over their headsets, "but you have an angry inbound closing on your six, and it is going to be on your position in less than a minute."

"Roger that," said Rock.

"We'd better move," said Tick.

"Follow me *fast* . . . and be careful navigating the trail stairs," said Rock, and the two sped down the hill and across the picnic areas to a concrete embankment that had stairs with several landings, which would ultimately take them down to the big suspension bridge. Rock was careful not to go too fast on the icy concrete, using his feet to help stabilize him. At least they'd been able to pace the storm for a few minutes or the beast would have already overtaken them. Still, the hail was intensifying and covering the stairs—covering everything in lumpy ice—and the wind threatened to knock them off balance and down the stairs. The two navigated all the way to the bottom without incident, and when they'd cleared the steps, Rock looked back up them, feeling uneasiness, and then he knew why.

At the top of the trail stairs, looking over, was a colossal, soaking-wet one-eyed vampire. It snarled at them, and the lightning lit up in horrific brilliance behind it as the storm raged, seemingly at its command.

"Move!" shouted Rock. The two sped the short distance to the bridge, where Rock drove up the concrete stairs and pulled onto the long bridge, stopping at its head. Tick pulled up immediately behind it and stopped, the ATV being too wide to access the bridge.

"Climb on," Rock ordered Tick, and he saw that the monster was at the base of the trail stairs and running at full tilt toward them. It would be on them within twenty seconds.

"I'm at the top of the stairs," said Cheese with the blazing Hummer lights shining over the edge. "What do I do now?"

"Train your weapon down here and cover the south bridgehead," said Rock. "If it comes your way, kill it regardless of our line of fire."

"Roger that," said Cheese, knowing that it could be deadly shooting in their direction with the powerful weapon.

Tick, clinging to Rock's back, felt the G's as Rock accelerated away from the ATV. They were immediately hit full-force by the wind gusts, causing them to slip on the ice-covered wood slats, and slamming the two into the wooden side panels of the bridge. Both abruptly spilled over the handlebars, landing on their backs, and sliding twenty feet past the upturned motorcycle. Both felt pain as their slung weapons dug into their backs. The wind howled at them, the hail beat on them, and lightning and thunder rattled them as they tried to rise and regain their footing. The bridge writhed beneath them. Both men, in the middle of the bridge now, in the full fury of the storm, held the side rails of the bridge with their gloved hands. Both silently hoped that they would be insulated from any lightning bolts that now threatened to crash upon the steel cables that held the bridge taut above Sugar Creek. The bridge swayed and bucked in the seventy-mile-an-hour wind gusts as the two men struggled to stand and get their weapons ready.

At the south end of the bridge, a wet, black, and angry horror faced them. Its good eye was aflame, and the empty socket of the other bled and oozed. Its teeth shone like ivory daggers, and the creature's fur gleamed blue in the lightning that seemed to be bowing to its will. Its talons grabbed the side rails and it shook the bridge mightily. The bridge oscillated, nearly reaching catastrophic resonance, straining with the tension of the support cables and threatening to yield to the powerful forces besetting it.

"GET BEHIND ME!" shouted Rock to Tick, trying to be heard over the clamor of the storm while keeping himself from falling down. "GET TO THE ROCKS ON THE NORTH SIDE OF THE BRIDGE FOR A CLEAR SHOT!"

"ROGER," shouted Tick, who backed away and tried to make his egress from the bridge to the rock face on the north side of the creek.

The monster wanted Moreau to see it coming . . . to see death coming. It wanted to shout to him vile words that would inspire fear in him and loose his bowels, but it knew that the wind would snatch its words from the air. Instead it stared at the man with a hateful glare, silently calling on the forces of Hell to cause dread in Moreau's heart, and feel the hatred that the beast had for the small and insignificant man. He summoned blow after demonic blow to batter Moreau's spirit, while the storm and its very presence pummeled his senses. The creature slowly advanced, lifting its leg to step over the ATV at the bridgehead.

"CHEESE, BE READY . . . I I'M ABOUT TO ORDER YOU TO FIRE ON MY POSITION," shouted Rock.

"Negative," said Cheese. "Can't get a lock in this hail, and I've lost LOF because of the concrete abutment. I can estimate its position if you tell me what quadrant of the bridge to fire on! Don't make me fire on *your* quadrant!"

"NO PROMISES!" shouted Rock, as he raised his rifle and shot at the ATV's gas tank. The bullet missed the ATV but hit the monster in the femur. Rock was surprised that he could hear the creature's howl of pain, but it roared in his ears, and he felt supernatural forces trying to make him fold and give up his life to the monster.

"FATHER!" Rock shouted. "YOU ARE WITH US! WHAT CAN STAND AGAINST US?" It was a rhetorical question.

At that moment, no fewer than three bolts of lightning struck the bridge. Everything suddenly went white. Jagged blue-white spider webs of electricity shot about the entire bridge structure. The bridge seemed to go incandescent. Time seemed to have stopped. Rock felt like he was being lifted to the sky on white tendrils . . . light embraced him . . . he floated toward a black sky and he noted that he seemed to be one with the light. It danced about his body . . . lifting him with a million tiny fingers . . . . He thought perhaps this was the hand of God lifting him and taking him home . . . and soon he would see his wife and daughter again. He smiled and let the light lift him . . . and he could almost see his family's faces above. Then he *did* see them. He smiled with relief and gladness . . . they smiled back at him with a brightness of their own shining about them. He felt love and a joy so deep that he knew he was at the gates of Heaven. Then he felt something in his spirit and heard the words, "It is not your time, Nick." They seemed to say this without moving their lips. "Not yet . . . ," they said in loving and tender voices, but there was nowhere else he'd rather be . . . he could remember nothing else . . . he just wanted to grab the clouds and pull himself all the way into Heaven. He was almost there. "Not yet, Beloved," said the final voice. Suddenly, the light went off, and he dropped like a cold, wet fish on the deck of the bridge, and for some reason his body still breathed. And for another reason . . . he wished his body didn't. "I was THERE . . . ," was all that was in his mind. Later, as he looked back to that moment in time, he'd wonder whether it was really a glimpse of Heaven, or just a vision of Heaven that unconsciousness and his imagination induced . . . . But he'd never dreamed of Heaven before, and at least for that one moment, somehow he *KNEW* that he was there, and his joy was indescribable.

Tick had just reached the end of the bridge before the lightning descended upon it . . . but only just. The wind threatened to throw him down, tumbling to the riverbank below, but he clung to the rock and ascended to the east as carefully as he could, where he was determined to get to a position, knowing he had only seconds to do so.

"ROCK," shouted Tick, "ARE YOU ALL RIGHT?" No answer was forthcoming. He repeated his call three times before he heard a response.

"I'm breathing," said Rock as he faced the fact that he still lived. He felt saddened by the thought. It was a tremendous effort to get his body off the deck, but he forced it.

When the lightning struck the bridge, the beast took a bolt across its chest because, while shaking the bridge, it had to grasp the steel cables firmly. It was a bad move, and the beast knew it. Unbridled electricity bridged its body, scorching its hair and skin. The beast's iron grip on the cables was intensified by the bolt, and it bent the cable with its enhanced might, only to be tossed backward into the concrete abutment behind it. It lay there for a moment, not realizing what had happened. But then the voices told it to get up and kill Moreau, and all memory of its mission flooded back into it. It rose from the man-made stone that was covered in ice, and felt the wind reinvigorate it. Dawn would be breaking soon and that would make it a better target, so it was time to end Moreau, which it was more than ready and willing to do.

"What's happening down there?" asked the Cheese. "I'm ready to take a shot, but I need to know where to aim."

If the bridge was broken down into quadrants, Rock was at the lower edge of the third quadrant away from the Cheese—almost at the second. The monster was just now entering quadrant one, and it was not going to stop this time.

"ON MY MARK, FIRE ON QUADRANT TWO!" Rock shouted as he picked up his weapon and leveled it at the beast's head, all the while the storm threatening to knock him from the bridge.

"I HAVE A SHOT!" shouted Tick, slightly in the lee of the stone cliff he'd climbed to.

"TAKE IT!" shouted Rock, who pulled his own trigger in bursts of two rounds.

Tick let the fiery blaze of his weapon stream down the length of the bridge striking and missing the monster and bridge alternately because weapon was slippery, violent, and the wind and hail continued to buffet him. The creature howled in pain and anger and strode toward Moreau with only his death in its mind. Rock fired as well, aiming for its head, not seeing clearly, but knowing that as the giant horror closed in on him it would be easier to hit.

Then the monster mustered all its strength and roared at Moreau, and advanced on him regardless of the rain of bullets, or the wind and the hail. When it was merely twenty feet away, Rock sighted the head of the terrible creature.

"MARK!" Rock shouted, and pulled his trigger, striking the vampire twice between the eyes. It was dead on its feet . . . and then it exploded as The Big Cheese pressed the fire button and the steel projectile shot forth from the Hummer like a blazing comet, striking the concrete abutment, knocking a one-foot-wide hole in it, punching through it. The shot hit the creature in the lower spine, exploding through it and penetrating the deck, splintering it just two feet in front of Rock, and embedding itself deep in the riverbed below. The water sizzled as the missile hit it.

Rock was thrown back by the force of the sonic boom, and was splattered with blood and fur from the monster—and concrete chips landed everywhere. When the creature was struck by the steel meteor, it was immediately bisected, and gravity pulled it through the hole in the deck, into the creek thirty feet below.

Rock lay there, letting the storm have its way with him . . . but the storm seemed to have given up, or moved on. The wind died down and the hail turned back to rain, and then even the rain ebbed. Rock wanted to just lie there, eyes closed to the world, but to his surprise, he was lifted, and then *ordered* to do otherwise.

"Get up NOW, Rock!" shouted Tick as he lifted Dominic Moreau to his knees and then forced him to stand.

"What?" asked Rock.

"THAT!" shouted Tick, pointing downstream.

Rock saw it. Though his eyes beheld it, it still took moments to register in his mind. As soon as it did, he got to his feet and immediately began to use the cables to traverse the deckless span, trying to get back to the south side of the bridge without dropping off it.

The roaring tornado in the distance twisted and danced perhaps half a mile away from them, and seemed to see easy prey as it moved menacingly toward them, swallowing the river water. The floating parts of the creature were rushing toward it.

"What?!" exclaimed Cheese. "I'm blind up here! Did we kill it?"

"One monster is down," said Tick, "but we have a bigger one bearing down on us. The storm has dropped a tornado!"

"No way!" exclaimed Cheese. "Now nature's giving us the boot."

"Get outta the Hummer and meet us at the base of the stairs," ordered Rock, making Cheese immediately get out of the SUV and begin a hasty descent.

Tick followed Rock across the broken bridge, reaching the other side as well. Nature's furious finger was white at the top, brown in the middle, perhaps from soil it had been sucking up—and it was surprisingly green at the bottom. It was the first multicolored tornado either man had ever seen. It pushed an awful smell in their direction, and it was getting close. It sounded as though several express trains engines were racing toward them. Tick and Rock ran down the bridge's abutment stairs, noticing that Tick's ATV must have been blown off the bridge when the rail-gun was fired. The two ran to the base of the concrete trail stairs, meeting the Cheese at the bottom of it. All three turned back to see the tornado embrace the center of the bridge, and Rock forced the other two down onto the ground off to the side of the hill in a small hollow in the earth by the nearest stand of trees. The wind howled around them and debris flew above them in a counterclockwise spiral. Trees snapped and debris scraped at the men, but the tornado seemed to have lost its desire to pursue them. It continued downstream, jumping and descending as it wished until it was out of sight.

The Trinity got themselves off the ground, checked their equipment, and slowly, very slowly, ascended the concrete stairwell to the Hummer. All three men sat in the SUV and just rested. They were beat. Their job was done, and they just didn't want to move. Rock almost dozed off, but the Cheese started to snore, which snapped Rock out of his near slumber, and he woke the Big Cheese and Tick.

"We've got to get back to camp," Rock said.

"All right, but I request to have first shift in the sack on the way home," said Cheese. Then he started the Hummer and drove to the Turkey Run State Park's gate, pulled out onto SR-47, drove down, around, and up past the Turkey Run High School, and then made his way back into the park's camping area. It was a trip that took only five minutes, but time seemed to be moving very slowly for the weary men. Cheese pulled into the campgrounds and onward to the north end, parking by the Mobile Field Base, just as dawn began to light up the sky behind the thunderhead above.

32

Loose Ends and Deadly Beginnings

The men were tired and sore and could barely move as Cheese parked the SUV by the MFB that still blazed the alert in marquee fashion. Now there were four new State Police vehicles in the campsite, and the officers had taped off the area around Malcolm's trailer and Land Rover, and most of their campsite. External cameras on the huge truck showed Crystal that the team had made it back alive. She opened the back bay and waited for it to fully extend before exiting with several scared people who had found solace within the wheeled fortress. Rock opened his door and slowly, wearily stepped out, the other two men taking it as a cue to dismount as well.

Crystal ran over to Rock. She was very relieved to see him again. She gave him a big, tight hug, kissing him on his cheek. He was too weak to defend himself.

"I was so afraid for you," she said. Then she stepped back from him at an arm's distance. "Did you roll in a pile of manure?"

"Miss Carson," Tick intercepted the conversation, trying to manage a smile, "Agent Moreau just survived the biggest manure storm I think we've ever faced."

"Is it safe now?" she asked Rock.

"Yes, Crystal, now it is," Rock said. "How's your father?"

"The paramedics said that he *did* have a heart attack, but that he was in fair condition, and they took him and a few others to the hospital in Crawfordsville just a couple of minutes ago. I said I'd follow them into town once I was sure these people were safe."

Rock smiled. "Glad to hear that. Well . . . we need to clean up and check a few things. There have been some activities tonight that we can't explain yet. We need to check with our home base of operations, maybe with other agents."

"How big is your organization?" she asked.

"Not big enough, it seems, but don't you worry about it. This area is 'in hand' now. Apart from our own internal issues, I'm now concerned about some of your father's other sites."

"I can give you a list of their locations and who is manning them, I mean, if you want me to. Dad may not like it but he's not thinking clearly and doesn't really know what he's been up against. Even after all of this," she said, not wanting to betray her father, but knowing, *believing* much more than *he* was able to.

"We have information on those sites already, and we're fully deployed at any that have a high probability of contact. The problem is a lack of communication at this time," said Rock. "Are there any others in the MFB that need medical attention?"

"No, but John Cosworth was killed. It was horrible. I think two other men who were his are dead, but I'm not sure. John's body is still lying over there where the police are," she offered.

"I'll have to talk to them in a few minutes," said Rock.

"Good. They wanted me to come out and talk to them, but I told them that I wasn't opening the door unless they needed shelter," she said.

"Thanks, Crystal. You've been a great help to us in keeping these people safe. It was something that we couldn't do while we were in pursuit," Rock said. "You may feel free to take the Hummer to the hospital while we clean up and get our bearings. Your Range

Rover may need to stay here until the State Police conclude their investigation."

"I'm not sure I want to be alone just yet. Do you mind if I wait for you and catch a lift?"

"Not at all," said Rock. "Sit in the Hummer and relax while we get ready."

The Big Cheese and Tick were talking to the men and women gathered around them, some from the safety of the MFB and some coming from campsites to get an explanation. They were told that a dangerous animal escaped from Malcolm's trailer and attacked the scientists. They were told that the animal was put down and that there were no other animals released. Some objected to the idea that it was "just an animal," while others accepted the story and moved on. To quell the objectors, the two agents directed them to the troopers at Malcolm's camp for a better explanation; it was also an effort to buy them some time before they had to speak to them. It wasn't quite a fair thing to do to the troopers, but the agents needed to get into the MFB and take care of other unfinished business.

The Trinity entered the MFB and closed the ramp behind them. First thing was to check themselves for wounds and dress them. Most were in the form of bruises, but there were scratches, abrasions, and some second-degree burn marks, but those were easily taken care of. Next, they changed clothes and washed up. The MFB was a self-sustaining campsite so it had no external requirements for sewer, water, or electrical hookups, though they could be used if available.

"Tick, see who we can contact. We aren't jammed so see what's preventing satellite comms, and then try everything to get Spectacle or Archangel or any other field agent. If you can't get through, we'll make a call from the gas station on the other side of the campground, the one with the colored palm trees.

"Copy that," said Tick, who was the best communications tech on the team. If he couldn't get through, nobody on the team could.

"Cheese," said Rock, "dismount the Substitute Science Teacher from the Hummer, then get our weapons in order and rearm this station so we can go right back into combat."

"Roger that," said the Big Cheese. "Are we expecting to go back into combat before we head home?"

"Actually, I think there may be something worse to consider," said Rock. "But I don't have any confirmation regarding that yet, so let's just be prepared for anything."

"Good enough for me," said Cheese. He moved with the speed of an old woman who had just tumbled from ten flights of stairs, and at the moment, he was the fastest of the team.

Rock exited the MFB and walked over to the Hummer, where Crystal opened the door and met him before he crossed the front of the vehicle. It was clear that she wanted to be near him, and Rock was truly conflicted knowing that. Again she hugged him and kissed his cheek.

"You smell much better this time," she said almost gleefully.

"Crystal," Rock began, and then realized he had no idea what he wanted to say. In battle he was Rock, but sometimes he just needed to be Nick. It wasn't schizophrenia, but it was a way to keep his emotions in check depending on the situation. Rock would not let anyone into his heart, especially the enemy, but Nick might at least be able to admit that there was a heart that could be accessed beyond friendship.

"Yes?" she asked, still hugging him tightly.

"I . . . I think you are a beautiful and sweet young woman," he said, not knowing whether that was what he really wanted to say.

"Thanks," she said, still clinging to him. "You are uncomfortable that I am attracted to you, aren't you?"

"Um . . . yes," he admitted, realizing that he was beginning to blush.

"That's all right," she assured him, letting him go and taking only one step backward, in respect for his comfort. "I am much younger than you, and you are a man whose life is built around your mission. But I *believe in that mission*, and I think that you shouldn't be afraid of being close to someone. I know you are, but you shouldn't be."

Unbelievable! How can you read my mind when I don't even know what I'm thinking? he thought. What she'd said was true, though, Nick had to admit. She somehow was able to cut through the turmoil in his heart and mind, and hit the nail on the head. That in itself scared the tar out of him.

"I have a job to help people, Crystal. It places me in grave danger regularly. It isn't fair for me to become attached to anyone. I don't give my heart away easily and I can't afford to give any hostages to fortune. I've lost a wife and a child to these monsters, and I don't want to lose anyone else," he said in all honesty, and opened himself up to her in a way he'd not done in a long, long time.

"You can't control that, though. You do *know* that, don't you?" she asked. Nick could tell that she was wise beyond her years, and beyond her limited *life in the Lord*. "The world has changed drastically for me in the past few hours. I *know* what you believe is *Truth*, now. I know that God *is*, and He is my Savior. I know there are angels and demons, and most of all, that the Bible is right and true in every way . . . . That one step of faith I took was one that changed me forever. But it's *because* they *are real* and *true* that proves that there is hope for love, and hope for victory, and hope that God will use men and women to fight on His side. I want to fight for something true and real. I realize that I may not be ready for it yet, but I will be sometime. I would like to fight by your side, but if not, I'll find a way to do it on my own, and then maybe you will see what I now see. Hope is alive in Christ, and it is alive in me because of Christ."

"Dang," Nick said. "I've never seen such a transformation. I'll tell you what. Let's go slow and see what the Lord has in mind for you, for me, and perhaps for us. I've got to get back to base, but

482

I'll keep in touch with you. Please promise me that you'll read the Bible daily, pray often, and focus yourself on your relationship with Him, before any thoughts of a relationship with me. We've both had a head-spinning night, and we both need time for clarity and discernment. Agreed?" he said, extending his hand.

"Agreed, Nick," she said, and took his hand, pulled herself to him, and kissed him full on the lips. His knees nearly buckled, but he allowed the kiss, and returned it, and then gently ended it, releasing himself from her in a way that would not show any signs of rejection.

"I . . . um," Nick began, and tried to focus back on his job. "I've got to talk to those troopers, and then we'll be on our way to Crawfordsville."

"OK," she said with a hopeful smile, and allowed him to part company.

Nick walked away from Crystal, and then, while looking at the troopers ahead, Rock took over Nick's stride and met with the law enforcement officers as their equal. He showed his credentials, FBI this time, and explained that Carson's group had lost control of a wild animal that attacked and killed Cosworth and the others. Also that Crystal Carson was instrumental in leading the FBI to Carson's camp, and that chase was given until the animal was cornered, killed, and then, to the surprise of all agents, sucked up in a tornado, not to be seen again. It was all true—mostly anyway—except for the lie of omission, which Rock acknowledged to himself was still a lie.

After that explanation, and after fielding a few questions and giving them some contact information, Rock excused himself, letting them know he had to return to his home office. He looked over to the Hummer and saw Crystal giving curious looks at the dashboard GPS. She seemed to be taking notes. Then the back of the MFB opened up and Tick exited with the Big Cheese following. Rock walked over to the men.

"I've checked our equipment and it is in perfect working order, but still I can't reach anyone. It's as if nobody but us is broadcasting. I've even tried shortwave, but nothing. Something's wrong, and it isn't just the satellites. Apart from a semaphore, or an Aldus lamp, I've tried everything."

Crystal exited the Hummer, catching the last part of Tick's conversation.

"Have you tried your GPS?" asked Crystal.

"What do you mean?" Cheese replied.

"The GPS in the SUV dashboard just received this message. It was on the LCD screen, so I copied it. Here," she said and handed the paper to Rock.

"You can have *his* job," said Rock to Crystal, while pointing at the Cheese. He took the note from her and read it aloud to his men, "Alert—All Agents: Archangel Emergency Distress. Lockdown condition. Comms down. Recall code Zulu-Grumbugs."

"That's was all of it, and then the screen cleared and the message repeated, twice more, and then stopped in midsentence," Crystal said.

"Oh my," breathed Rock, understanding the gravity of the message.

"Grumbugs must have hacked the Global Positioning Satellite and sent the message. Even if all communications are down, the GPS would still be active. It's not a communications relay, but it does transmit data. Wow, Grumbugs is more brilliant than I've given him credit for," said Tick.

"We've got to move out *now*," said Rock to his men. "Follow me in the MFB to Crawfordsville's hospital. Then we're heading out to Archangel."

"We're not driving all the way back there, are we?" asked Cheese. "That would take twenty hours at best possible speed."

"No. We're going northeast, to Grissom Air Force Base. We're going to commandeer a C-130 and get to the bunker as fast as possible," said Rock. "Mike, call ahead; I want it fueled and on the tarmac when we pull up."

"Roger that," said Tick, and both he and the Big Cheese mounted up in the MFB and prepared to roll out.

"What does it mean?" asked Crystal.

"It means that our main base is under attack," said Rock.

And the danger is ever before them . . . but Knightlight holds the line.

END OF BOOK ONE.

Next: Knightlight—Building a Better Beast

CPSIA information can be obtained at www.ICGtesting.com
Printed in the USA
LVOW080321180613

338814LV00002B/4/P